LOVE BLEEDS RED

ALSO BY LAUREN GREENE

<u>VENGEFUL HEARTS</u>

Dark Romance Series

Book 1 - I'm Not in Love (I Promise)

Book 2 - Bulletproof Love

Book 3 - Love Bleeds Red

<u>PALM COVE</u>

Small Town Interconnected Standalones

Book 1 - Fight For It

Book 2 - Fight For Her

Book 3 - Fight For Us

<u>GREYRIDGE</u>

Small Town Holiday Themed Novellas

Book 1 - Holiday Heartstrings

Book 2 - Holiday Hook-Up

AUTHOR'S NOTE

Hey loves! Before you dive into Bailey and Leon's story, I want to be upfront with you about the content. This book is definitely intended for mature readers (18+) only, and I want you to be able to make an informed decision about whether it's right for you.

This story contains themes of:

VIOLENCE & CRIME
- Organized crime and criminal activities
- Gun violence and weapons
- Murder and attempted murder
- Death scenes
- Human/sex trafficking (depicted)
- Physical assault and violence
- Blood and injury
- Kidnapping and captivity
- Strangulation and choking (non-consensual)
- Fire and arson

- Police interactions
- Stalking behavior
- Abuse of power
- Blackmail
- Corruption

PSYCHOLOGICAL & EMOTIONAL

- Sexual assault/rape (depicted on page)
- Sexual abuse and sexual harassment
- Drugging and forced intoxication
- Captivity and imprisonment
- Severe trauma and PTSD
- Physical and psychological torture
- Emotional abuse and manipulation
- Behavioral conditioning and grooming
- Starvation and food control
- Mentions of pedophilia (not depicted)
- Suicidal ideation and intrusive thoughts
- Panic attacks and anxiety
- Depression and dissociation
- Grief and mental distress
- Substance abuse and addiction
- Forced addiction and withdrawal symptoms
- Victim advocacy and legal proceedings
- Medical treatment and recovery
- Therapy
- Parental neglect (mentioned)
- Claustrophobia
- Classism, elitism, prejudice, and racism
- Poverty (mentioned)

SEXUAL CONTENT

- Explicit sexual content including oral sex, fingering, and

penetrative sex
- BDSM themes including dominance/submission
- Rough sex and spanking
- Consensual non-consent
- Praise kink and degradation
- Dirty talk and begging
- Mirror sex and mirror play
- Mutual and guided masturbation
- Barebacking/unprotected sex
- Marking and biting
- Aftercare

A Note on Trafficking:

I want to acknowledge that Bailey's trafficking experience in this story doesn't reflect the most common patterns of human trafficking in real life. According to my research, the vast majority of trafficking cases involve someone the victim knows —a family member, romantic partner, or trusted acquaintance. Stranger abduction scenarios, while they do occur, are far less common. This is a work of *fiction*, and I've taken creative liberties with the narrative.

If you or someone you know needs help, please contact the National Human Trafficking Hotline at 1-888-373-7888.

This list of content warnings isn't complete, I'm human and may have missed something, but I wanted to give you a good idea of what to expect. Your comfort and safety while reading means everything to me, so please make sure to check in with yourself and practice self-care while reading.

If you have specific concerns or triggers you're worried about, please don't hesitate to reach out to me on social media – I'm always happy to provide more detailed content information.

Take care of yourselves!

Lauren

For the survivors and fighters who prove that even when your heart bleeds, it still beats.

PROLOGUE

My heart bleeds in the dark.
One step closer, but so far to go.
Every breath torture.
Every beat, another cut.

I'm hollow.
Unraveled.
Without you, there's nothing but
The void you left behind.

Blood on my hands.
Your name on my lips.
This hunt won't stop
Until you're back at my side.

Burn it all to ash.
Set the world alight.
I'll destroy anyone
Who dares stand in my way.

Love bleeds red, darling—
And I'm drowning in it.

PART 1

BAILEY - MAY 23RD

Jasper's friend keeps looking at me. Not like staring in the same creepy way Doug from third period does. More like glances when he thinks I'm not paying atten-tion. I know it's not scientifically possible but I swear I can feel his eyes on me.

Like yesterday, I was laying out by the pool before work. It was so nice out, not humid and gross like it has been. The pool's been freaking freezing, so I haven't really taken advantage of it much. Mom keeps nagging Dad to call someone to trim the tree in the backyard, it's blocking the sun from warming the water. Anyway... I was laying there, some random summertime Spotify playlist on in my AirPods, eyes closed, when there was a tickle on my skin. For a second, I swore there was a spider crawling on my arm.

When I opened my eyes, I spotted him turning to walk back inside from the deck.

Leon. That's his name. We've met before, but not much more than saying hi or sitting across long dining tables when we've gone out for birthday dinners and stuff for Jasper and Damon. He's British. That accent is OMG. But he's been here since classes ended, staying downstairs in Jasper's stupid bro-tel. At least Leon's quiet compared to the other two big idiots. They're lucky I love them. Mom's been running herself ragged, making sure they have enough food and clean towels while still working overtime. I've been trying to help without her noticing... like restocking the downstairs mini fridge and doing extra loads of laundry when she's at work. With Leon too, just like offering him drinks and stuff so he feels comfortable. Of course, Jasper and Damon never do stuff like that. They probably expect everyone to feel cool with rummaging the fridge of someone they barely know.

I know you're literally paper and not a person but what should I do? I guess I'll just wait and see... I mean, he's probably too old for me. And he's Jasper's best friend. Plus, why would someone like him even notice me? Jasper's boring little sister. It would never work.

Right?

CHAPTER ONE

BAILEY - BEFORE

I'M PRETTY SURE THERE'S A SCIENTIFIC LIMIT TO HOW many times you can listen to your roommate fight with her boyfriend before you snap. Like, *literally* snap—the kind that lands you on those *I don't know what happened, I was fine and then suddenly I was standing over her with a bloody knife* shows where they interview your neighbors about how *quiet and normal* you seemed.

I think I'm approaching that breaking point.

"You're sorry? You weren't sorry when she sent you those nudes, were you?" Layne paces our tiny dorm room, her side a wreck of everything she's abandoned mid-crisis. A mixture of half-eaten meals, inside out clothes, and textbooks she's ignored for weeks, while I try my hardest to tune her out. "Don't you dare," she continues into her screen. Full volume speakerphone, of course. "No! You want to play like that? I'll show up at her job and make her wish she wasn't born!"

Our episode of *Snapped* might be a double feature if I don't intervene.

I toss my phone to the side and get up from my bed, closing

the distance between us. She barely notices I'm beside her until I lay a gentle palm on her shoulder. "Hey," I say in my most soothing whisper. "Just hang up. He's an asshole."

"Who's that?" Clay asks, even though, to my dismay, he's seen me every day this month.

Layne scoffs and points the phone in my direction. "It's Bailey, dumbass. Who else would it be?"

"How am I supposed to know? I'm not there."

I rub my temple, willing the forming headache to go away. I ran out of Advil and it just started raining. It would take a migraine of epic proportions to get me to leave my room and walk to the pharmacy tonight.

I don't bother whispering this time. "Hang up. He's not worth it."

"Bailey says I should hang up on your sorry ass," she repeats, her face getting progressively more red.

"Baby, please. I promise nothing happened. Let me come over there."

I shake my head, mouthing the word no, and make the universal slashing my neck signal with my hand. It's like one of those TV moments where the dog has to choose which owner he likes best. Will it be me or Clay?

Layne looks at me with wide eyes. Then she looks back at Clay, her expression softening as he begs and pleads. Then up at me again. I hold my breath, waiting on her to say something... anything.

Choose me. Hang up.

I'm practically chanting the words in my head.

"Bye, Clay," Layne finally says before she hits the end call button. I sag in relief and blow out a stream of air.

"Yes, girl," I say, squeezing her shoulder. "You don't need him. Let him stay home tonight and stew."

Silently, I'm thanking the universe for throwing me a bone.

No Clay means maybe I can get Layne to relax, eat junk food, and watch a movie... without having to hear the two of them making out or *more* on her side of the room.

"You're right. It's just so hard. Why am I, like, programmed to accept his lying bullshit? Do you think it's from childhood? My dad was kind of a dick to my mom." She shoves a box out of the way with her bare foot and flops onto her unmade bed.

I haven't started my psych classes yet and even if I did, she'd need someone much more experienced than me to analyze her.

"Maybe," I say with a shrug. "I'm proud of you though. I know it's hard to say no to him."

She groans and grabs her pillow, clutching it to her chest. "Why does he have to be so hot? He looks at me with that stupid face and I want to forgive everything he's ever done."

Clay? Hot? He's not my type.

"Let's watch a movie and order some pizza," I say, hoping to distract her. She rolls over and grabs her phone, tapping it to life. Her eyes gleam with that guilty look she gets when I catch her eating my last cheese stick. "No!"

I jump up and grab her phone. "Bitch, give it back. I wasn't going to call him."

"Layne Hailey Parks, you're such a liar!" She reaches for it, but I straddle her and hold my hand up high.

"Get off," she squeals, trying to buck me off. "I promise I won't call him."

I narrow my eyes. "Swear on something important." She wiggles under me again. "You know I have an older brother who I wrestled all the time, right? I can do this all day."

Finally, she goes limp. "Fine, I swear on my dead grandma that I won't call him back."

I lower the phone a few inches. "And..."

"And what? God, you're like a fucking koala. How are your thighs this strong?" She grabs for the phone.

"And you won't text him either," I say.

With a huff, she agrees, so I drop her phone into her waiting hand before rolling off her, careful to avoid her sheets. She hasn't washed those things since we moved in... there's way too much Clay DNA on there.

"Good girl," I say in a deep playful tone.

She snorts a laugh. "Oh my God, stop or you're gonna make me fall in love with you."

"Listen," I say, plopping back onto my bed, and playing with a loose thread in my comforter. "You deserve to be called a good girl everyday. Just... not from me."

We laugh for a good minute, my chest feeling lighter than it has all day. "What about you?" Layne asks.

"What?"

"Who's calling Miss Bailey Shea a good girl?" Layne waggles her brows.

"No one," I answer too quickly.

"Right," she says with a snort. "That's why you've checked your phone a hundred times in the last hour."

I roll my eyes and drop my phone which I instinctively picked up as soon as I sat back on my bed. "It's nobody."

She sits up and levels me with a devious smirk. "Well, if that's true, then you won't mind going out tonight."

I glance down at my baggy sweatpants and Ghostface T-shirt I've had since 1oth grade. "Does it look like I want to go out? Plus, it's raining."

"Please," she begs. "I need something to distract me. Or I can call Cla—"

"You promised. Swore on Grandma Parks. I can hear her now, rolling in her grave. She'll haunt you to a life of stale desserts and decaffeinated coffee."

"How could you bring up Grandma's love of coffee and desserts in a time like this?"

"I hate Clay that much, that's how," I say, keeping my tone playful.

"Come on, Bails. It's Friday night. You have the whole weekend to study and I know for a fact that they're not checking ID's tonight at Heat."

"Yeah, 'cause the creep who owns it is always *in* heat. The dude's worse than a feral dog." I laugh at my joke, but sadly, Layne does not. In fact, she stares at me with the most pathetic wide eyes.

"One drink and we can leave," she pleads. "I promise I'll stay with you all night."

"Layne," I groan. She hops off her bed and climbs onto mine, messing up the blanket.

"Please, I won't bug you for the rest of the month. Just give me tonight. And I'll do your hair and makeup."

"Fine. One drink. And we're stopping for Advil first. And you're paying for the Uber."

I'm such a freaking pushover.

"Anything else, your highness?" she asks in a terrible British accent, making my mind flash to the guy with the actual British accent that hasn't texted me back all day. The guy I can't stop thinking about.

I make a show out of pretending to think, until she whacks me with my pillow and shuffles to the closet, pulling out her shortest black dress. "Let's make Clay and whoever the hell you won't tell me about wish they weren't assholes."

"He's not an—"

"AH-HA!," she yells. "I knew there was a guy. That's it, you're telling me everything. Get over here and let me straighten your hair."

"This is abuse. I'm going to find the RA. What was her name again?"

Layne's too busy fiddling with her hair supplies to do anything but snort. I know when to relent, and right now, if I want any peace tonight I need to give her a tidbit. She pats the edge of her bed and I sit, pulling the scrunchie from my hair.

"Damn girl, your hair got long." She runs the brush through my tangles, not as gently as I'd like. "Okay, you know I have no patience. Who's the guy? It's gotta be someone from back home."

She snags a particularly bad knot and I wince. "I can do the brushing." I try to grab the brush from her but she pulls it away. "This reminds me of being in kindergarten when my mom would do tight French braids because she was terrified of me coming home with lice."

"Sounds traumatic," Layne deadpans. "I had a bowl cut for kindergarten, so I win."

"Oof." I wince. "Yeah, that's pretty bad."

"Stop stalling," she says. "The guy?"

With an exaggerated eye-roll, I grab my phone and swipe open my photo app. I have one picture of us from the summer. It's not the best, but Leon's smiling. A real smile that reaches his hazel eyes.

"This is him." I show her my screen and she lets her hand drop, taking my hair with it. "Ow! Okay, I'm taking over the brushing."

She grabs the phone, and zooms in on the photo. "This is the guy? This hot man right here?" Her voice could set a world record for highest octave.

"Yeah, that's Leon." I shake my head, holding back a laugh from how flabbergasted she looks. "What?"

"Bails, this is the hottest man I've ever seen. Holy fuck how could you have kept him from me?"

"Take a breath," I say.

"I literally cannot. Tell me everything. Who is he? How? Why? What? Did you bang? Of course you banged. Was it good? Girl, I need details."

What can I say without giving away too much? But really, she's just Layne. It's not like she knows Jasper or anyone from back home. And it'll feel good to talk about him. It's been kind of lonely holding in the fact that I fell in love this summer.

I tilt my head and pretend I'm thinking for an extra minute. Seeing her squirm is too much fun. When she threatens death by straightening iron, I finally give in and tell her the shortened version of my summer with Leon.

The best summer of my life.

WE'RE HUDDLED under my umbrella, narrowly avoiding puddles until we reach the pharmacy. Layne bolts over to the makeup section, while I read the signs to find the over the counter meds. My headaches has only gotten worse in the hour it took us to get ready. Layne's screeching about Leon probably didn't help.

The place is crowded, considering the weather. Not just other students lingering around the snack aisles, but locals as well. Couples and families, and a few people still in work clothes. I guess everyone's looking for a wild time. Nothing says Friday night excitement like moderately priced laundry detergent and tampons.

I adjust my too short dress, one of Layne's, and forge ahead, ignoring the stares from a group of guys I've seen on campus.

When I reach the med aisle, I scan the shelves for the cheapest ibuprofen they have. A notification sound from my purse distracts me. My stomach does a little flip of anticipation before I even look at the screen.

> Leon: I'm so sorry I didn't text you earlier… stuck in a study group all day. How's my gorgeous firefly doing tonight?

I'm grinning like a fool in the middle of the aisle but I couldn't care less. God, I miss him.

> Me: Oh you know, taking full advantage of the college experience.

I snap a selfie and hit send.

> Leon: Are those constipation medicines? I don't know if we've reached that level of honesty yet, love.

Oh my God. I look up and yup, I'm standing right in front of a big bottle that says Bowel Buddy. Kill me now.

> Leon: I'm joking. I think after the hot wing incident, we've surpassed all levels of intimacy. Also, you look stunning. Did the pharmacy require formal attire?

I'm about to type a response when someone bumps into my shoulder and I drop my phone.

"Shoot, I'm so clumsy," the man says in a slightly accented voice. He has slicked back light hair and stinks of overpowering cologne.

I wave him off and carefully bend to pick up my phone so my entire ass isn't on display, but he beats me to it. "Here, let me."

He hands me my phone with a grin. Something about it

makes my skin crawl, but I've been taught to be well-mannered. "Thanks."

I turn back to the shelf, searching for the meds I need so I can get out of here. A few seconds later, his friend appears— tall, dark-haired, not bad looking but way older than me, and dressed in a suit. "You find the Benadryl yet?"

The light-haired man with the accent says something under his breath, but I can't hear thanks to the PA system's static-filled announcement about a sale in aisle three. Thankfully, they move to the other end of the aisle. I take a breath, and grab the ibuprofen.

Time to find Layne and get out of here.

As I pass by the two men, a security mirror mounted near the ceiling shows my reflection and theirs, watching me from the end of the aisle.

Why are men so damn creepy?

"Have a good night," the first man says.

I offer a polite smile and nod before upping my pace toward the check out counter.

"What do you think of these lip colors?" Layne sticks out her forearm where lines of different lipstick shades paint her arm like stripes. "I can't decide on dusty rose or mauve dreams. They say your perfect shade should match your nipples. I should check my phone, there's definitely pics."

"Uh huh," I say, glancing over my shoulder at the two men who just joined the line.

"I guess I'll buy both. Might as well. I have Clay's card on my Apple Pay." Layne chats away beside me while I grab a water from the check out fridge and pay. I barely take in what she says, between the pounding behind my eyes, the whoosh of the automatic doors bringing in cool damp air against my bare legs, and the leering gaze of the light-haired man. I'm too distracted. I'd give anything to be back in my cozy bed.

A black SUV idles outside in the parking lot while we wait for our Uber. Its windshield wipers are squealing louder than Layne's chatter. Through the tinted windows, I swear I can make out a pair of dark eyes watching us. I've never been happier to get into an Uber by the time ours arrives ten minutes later.

Even so, the entire drive to Heat, I can't shake that sketched out feeling. Before the night gets away from me, I text Leon back. He always makes me feel better.

> Me: Grabbing a drink with Layne… wish me luck!

CHAPTER TWO

LEON - PRESENT DAY

Being back in London feels exactly how I thought it would—like a heaviness settled on top of my chest and won't let up. My body felt the shift before I stepped foot off the plane. I guess it's true what they say about muscle memory. The irony of this being where Bailey is, isn't lost on me. My personal hell becoming hers. It'll only fuel me to find her as fast as possible.

My feet pound against the gleaming tiles of Heathrow as I search for a restroom before picking up my luggage and hailing a cab to Mum's. Travelers weave through the crowd. Business people dressed in smart suits clutching briefcases, exhausted families pushing trolleys piled with luggage, tourists meandering around shops selling overpriced shirts and tacky souvenirs. The familiar London bustle, indifferent and relentless. Someone knocks into my shoulder, almost pulling my carry-on backpack off, without an apology or even a backward glance.

That's when I notice a man pulling a young woman along, his fingers wrapped around her arm like a vise. I keep my eyes on them. There's something about her gait that seems off. He proceeds to knock into a tourist in his hurry, yanking the poor thing's arm hard enough for me to notice from several feet away. Is she... pulling back? Resisting?

I don't think on it for another second before I follow them.

My jaw clenches as the details around me seem to blur into blackness, a one-way tunnel leading me straight to them. The noisy airport fading to no more than a hum in my ears.

They stop in front of the restrooms and I linger around the corner, straining to listen.

"You have two minutes to do your business," he says, grasping her shoulders with enough pressure to make her recoil. "Do you understand me?"

She speaks so low, I can't hear her words, but I can tell by the pleading look in her eyes that she's scared. She can't be more than twenty—pale and thin with hollow eyes, wearing loose clothes.

My fists clench and it takes every ounce of resolve I possess to not intervene immediately. Instead, I watch as she walks into the women's restroom, and the man, who looks to be older than me, dressed in jeans and a jacket, carrying only a small overnight bag, positions himself against the wall, checking his phone with jerky fingers.

Beside me, an older woman stops to fiddle in her purse and I see my opportunity. I tap her on the shoulder. Her kind eyes greet me as she asks, "Can I help you, dear?"

"I'm sorry to bother you," I whisper, leaning close to her, "but I'm concerned about a young woman who just went into the ladies room. She seems to be in trouble. Would you mind checking on her?" I give her a description of the girl, adding, "If she seems frightened, could you ask if she needs help?"

The woman's expression shifts from confusion to understanding and her eyes dart briefly to the man by the restroom door. She nods firmly. "No problem at all, love. I was heading in there anyway."

As she walks away, I sigh in relief.

Now to take care of him.

With my head lowered, I purposely bump into him, knocking his phone from his grasp. "Watch it," he growls, bending to pick it up, but I'm faster. I snatch it while keeping my flustered appearance, and catch a glimpse of an open message thread where he shared photos of that young woman.

I steal a glance at him as I head toward the nearest maintenance corridor, opening the settings to disable Face ID. "Hey!" he yells. "Get back here!"

Come on. Take the bait.

With an agitated look at the women's loo, he huffs and takes off after me.

That's right, follow me.

In any other situation, I'd have been able to disable security cameras and unlock doors, but they've increased security measures ten-fold since I started learning the tricks of my trade.

This leaves me with few choices.

I spot a security officer ahead, and make my way toward him, my breath coming in quick pants. I slip the phone into my pocket so I can analyze it better later. Could be a lead... imagine the coincidence.

"Sir," I manage, before the guy catches up, forcing fear into my tone. "That man right there." I gesture toward him. "He left a bag near the restroom. I thought I heard it buzzing, and he seems off. He was dragging a young woman around. I think she might be in trouble."

The officer's eyes widen, and he calls for backup, barely giving me a nod before he takes off after him. Within seconds, two more officers appear from different directions.

I duck into a crowded souvenir shop, and watch the man's

takedown unfold from a distance. Three officers surround him, one with his hand on his holster. The man glowers as they escort him away from the public area, most likely to an interrogation room.

My plan may not pan out, but hopefully it gives the woman enough time to get help. And I've got his phone. Who knows what kind of nuggets I'll find in it.

For now, I blend into the crowd as I head to baggage claim. Just another traveler in a sea of people. The heaviness in my chest feels slightly lighter as I picture that man's face the moment he knew he was caught. And if I'm wrong about him, so be it. But I have a strong feeling my instinct is spot on.

———

ONCE I PICK up my luggage, I find a spot outside and lean against the wall, waiting for my rideshare to arrive. I'd love to start digging into that guy's phone, but there's not much I can do right now without my equipment set up. It'll have to wait.

Instead, I finally switch my phone off airplane mode and smile as I'm greeted by a long line of messages in the group chat.

> Jasper: Miss you buddy. Don't worry, I'll take good care of your bike.

I shake my head and scroll down.

> Damon: Should I hide the keys? Text when you land.

> Jasper: I'm hurt... also can't hide what you can't find.

> Falin: I have the keys and no, I'm not giving them to either of you. Lee, Havoc and Mayhem say hi xoxo

> Blake: Be safe… miss you already!

I laugh under my breath. I miss those hellions too. All of them.

> Me: I landed safely, am heading to my mum's now.

Notifications light up my screen but I swipe them away. After the long flight and the time change, not to mention the anxiety of being back, I don't have it in me to yammer on. Instead, I pull up the thread I've looked at everyday for the past year and a half. My insides twist when I read the last message Bailey sent.

If only I'd answered her. Met her there. Done *something*.

> Firefly: Grabbing a drink with Layne… wish me luck!

I've texted her everyday since. Multiple times on most days. Until the number no longer worked and then I moved the messages into a notes file.

Her last tracked location was a nightclub called Heat. We did everything but strip the place to the studs after she was taken. The police interviewed every possible witness, and of course we followed up with the same people too. Her roommate, her friends, random strangers that mentioned seeing her.

Nothing but dead ends.

Eighteen months of them, day after day, knowing she's out there somewhere suffering, and I was the last person she contacted. *Me.* And I couldn't even tell my best friends. That secret eats me up inside.

I switch my phone off before I chuck the thing out the window.

FAMILIAR BUILDINGS and sights blur past as we head into Mum's neighborhood, toward the same home I grew up in, the home I haven't been back to in over three years.

I can still remember the day I decided to leave like it was yesterday. I'd just gotten back from the weekend away with my father. The weekend that changed it all. I grip the strap of my carry-on so tightly my knuckles turn white before grabbing my sketchbook and pencil to give myself something to channel the rage.

The charcoal glides its familiar path—the curve of her eyes, the slope of her nose, the arch of her lips. I'm in awe every time I draw Bailey from memory. My mind remembers her features perfectly, even after all this time.

Of course I would. She's the most beautiful girl I've ever seen.

Before I know it, we've reached the house. I grab my belongings, tip the driver—something I've grown accustomed to from living in the US—and slowly make my way past parked cars and the small patch of grass where a few daffodil bulbs push their way through the moist earth. The narrow brick row house stands shoulder to shoulder with the others along the street like dominoes, all in exactly the same state of disrepair. It's sad to see how the red brick has faded and chipped from years of rain and neglect.

My luggage wheel catches on the concrete step leading to the front door. Once I dislodge it, I stand there for a moment, staring at the tarnished brass knocker.

As I lift my hand to knock, the door swings open with a creak from the same old rusty hinge. "My baby is home!"

Mum launches herself at me, not paying any mind to the many bags in my hands. I laugh and gently drop what I can, wrapping my arms around her small frame. Her hug is warm, her scent exactly like I remember. Floral mixed with something menthol from the cream she rubs on her arthritic joints. I close my eyes and let myself get lost for a moment, forgetting the real reason why I'm home.

Mum pulls back and stands on her tiptoes to hold my face between her palms like I'm still a child. "Let me look at you! America's been good to you—you've filled out. Grew a few inches?" Her honey brown eyes search my face and she tsks. "You look tired, love. The flight was terrible, wasn't it? All the ladies at work talk about how much air travel's changed nowadays. So expensive, so dull."

"It's not too bad," I say, gently pulling myself from her embrace and picking up my bags. She's still staring at me, her eyes filled with emotion. Guilt hits me like a sack of bricks. I've been a shit son. "It's good to see you, Mum."

I close the door and step past her into the narrow hallway. From what I can see, the house hasn't changed. It's still meticulously clean with mismatched furniture that belonged to my grandparents, the dusty rose carpet pilling in the high traffic area, and Mum's collection of porcelain figurines lining the mantel. The clutter somehow works, but the space seems so much smaller than I remember.

"Your room's all ready," she says, fussing with a spot on the staircase railing. "I've kept it just as you left it. Washed the linens and aired it out a bit. I did move some of my sewing things in there. Hope you don't mind."

"Thank you," I say as I follow her up the narrow staircase. All our faded family photos still line the walls. Mum and me at the beach. Nana and Pops holding me as a baby. Me in my secondary school uniform. All smiles and hugs as if there wasn't a gaping hole in our lives.

"How long will you be staying?" She can't hide the real question from her tone. *Are you finally coming home for good?*

"Not sure yet," I answer. "Got some business to sort out."

She stops at the top of the stairs and turns to face me. "Your father's business?"

"No," I say firmly. "My own."

I almost slip up and ask what she knows about my father's business, but thankfully, I catch myself. Her face falls slightly. She's always pushed me toward him, treated him like he deserved our love and respect. I could never figure out why. I've spent years resenting her for that. For accepting Alfred's money, for the lonely childhood I had while she worked multiple jobs, for the secrets she kept about my father until I was old enough to find out myself.

"Well, you're welcome as long as you need. I've missed you, son."

And here comes the guilt again. At least she's getting it all out of the way from the start. Despite it all, I know she did her best. And who am I to think negatively about taking his money? I'm doing the very same thing.

"I've missed you too," I say, reaching to give her hand a squeeze.

My old bedroom is exactly as I left it. The twin bed in the corner covered with my navy blue quilt, my small wooden desk pushed up against the wall with the window that overlooks the street. There's even a few of my drawings from art class hung up, the paper faded and curved at the edges. The only addition is Mum's sewing machine and neat piles of fabric scraps and pattern pieces.

"I'll let you get settled," she says, hovering in the doorway. "Dinner in an hour? Unless you want to rest."

"Dinner sounds great," I tell her. "I need to set up some equipment first though. Work stuff." I start to unpack my gear from the first bag.

"Still with your computers, not much has changed there. Well, I'm making your favorite, shepherd's pie. Thought you might be missing proper English food after all that American rubbish."

If she only knew how delicious that American rubbish is.

"Want a cuppa? Or something to eat now?" She picks up a cable and fiddles with the end.

"I'm okay. Thanks, Mum." She puts the cable down and sighs, hopefully taking my hint.

"Call if you change your mind."

She leaves me to it, and I shut and lock the door behind her. Time to figure out how I'm going to fit everything on this small desk. Three laptops, external drives, various cables, and the specialized equipment I'll need. This isn't everything, most of it is still in New York, but I'll make do.

Within twenty minutes, my childhood desk has transformed into a command center that young Leon would marvel at. At least Alfred's money has gone to a good cause.

I power everything up and connect to a secure network, routing my connection through multiple layers of protection. The last thing I need is someone tracking my activities back here. The phone I snagged off that creep sits heavy in my pocket.

I pull it out and tap it open, finding nothing useful in his messages, just photos of that girl. Most likely, his business was done over the phone. Smart, I guess, but disappointing for me.

No names. No mention of who he works for. Certainly nothing about Bailey.

I connect it to my laptop and check it for anything hidden, but come up empty. Fucking wonderful. Even so, I copy everything to my secured drive before wiping it and removing the SIM card and battery. I'll dispose of each part separately later.

A moment goes by where I wonder if I've genuinely gone mad. Was I seeing things that weren't truly there earlier? Did I want that man to be a criminal, trafficking that woman? Or is that all I can see anymore after everything?

A knock at my door pulls me from my thoughts. "Dinner's nearly ready, love."

"Okay, be down in a minute," I say, pocketing the pieces of the man's phone and grabbing my burner phone I'd been charging. With a hopeful sigh, I message my old friend.

> Me: Cruz, it's Leon. I'm back in London. Need to meet. Urgent.

He responds within seconds.

> Cruz: Holy shit Colter... I thought you'd never set foot on this soil again. Usual spot? 11?

I glance at the time. That gives me a few hours to have dinner with Mum and get prepared.

> Me: I'll be there. Bring whatever you've got on trafficking activity. Paying well.

> Cruz: Fuck, do I want to ask?

I think of Ray and his guys and that heaviness settles in my gut again.

> Me: The least you know the better.

I slip the phone into my pocket and roll my lip ring between my teeth. Time to get through dinner with Mum. Make small talk, tell her just enough to satisfy her curiosity, then see what I've missed the past three years.

BAILEY - MAY 30TH

I don't know if Leon sleeps. I woke up last night around two. There was a thunderstorm, it literally shook the house. I tossed and turned for like an hour, until I finally decided to get up and bake some banana bread for everyone to have for breakfast.

I don't know if it's stress or this restless energy that I can't quite tamp down, even though I've been going to the gym more than normal. Reading used to calm me down too, but lately even rereading all my favs isn't helping. But, I guess I'm worried about starting classes in the fall. How Mom and Dad will take care of themselves without me here. Don't get me wrong, they're amazing and I know I'm lucky to have them. So many of my friends growing up had parents who were a hot mess. They're just kind of like too nice, maybe? Or they work too hard? I don't know, I'm just worried they won't remember to turn off the burner, or change the batteries in the smoke alarms, or even simple things like taking their vitamins.

I'm rambling now. Back to the banana bread. So I got up, went to the kitchen and Leon was there sitting at the table in the dark, besides the light from his laptop. He scared the shit out of me. I think I scared him too because he jumped when I gasped and we both ended up awkwardly laughing and staring at each other. I was in my cat pajama shorts, so that was fun. It's whatever. He's been here for a few days now so I'm sure he's spotted me looking way worse.

Okay, so the staring got intense! I think butterflies were literally doing circus moves in my stomach. I asked what he was doing up so late and he shrugged, saying he was programming something. I told him I was going to bake and he said he didn't want to bother me, to which I was like no, you're fine! But he got up, because of course, he didn't want to hang out with me at 2 AM. BUT, I was wrong!

He opened up the pantry door and started to grab ingredients!

I mean, he probably just felt bad leaving me alone in the kitchen, but still...

We baked together and I don't know... it was really nice. Talking to him feels natural, even though I'm nervous and awkward. He kind of is too, which is so funny to me. But by the time we took the loaf out of the oven, he was joking with me more and he's funny in a quirky way.

I need to get ready for work, I'm closing tonight. Lucky me.

But I told Leon he should come by and I'll snag him some free food. Whatever he wants, as long as he doesn't share that info with my brothers because I think I'd get fired if they asked for freebies. Jasper eats more than three grown men.

CHAPTER THREE

BAILEY - BEFORE

HEAT IS THE PERFECT NAME FOR THIS PLACE. I'M ALREADY sweating. Techno pounds from the DJ booth matching the pulsing in my head, as we snake our way through swaying bodies toward the bar. The lights are dim, apart from colored spotlights pointed at the booth, but I still narrow my eyes to help the pain.

Come on, Advil, do your thing.

One glance at Layne practically bouncing in front of me helps to cheer me up a bit, but I'd still pay every dollar I have to be anywhere else. "Come on!" she yells over the music. "Drinks!"

A couple holding hands walks directly in front of me, cutting me off from Layne as I tell her, "I shouldn't."

She either doesn't hear me, or doesn't pay attention. I'm betting on the latter. We spot a few girls from our floor at the bar, and Layne waves them over. "Here, it'll help you feel better." She shoves what I think is a lemon drop at me with pleading eyes.

"Just one," I say, annoyed with myself for how fast I give in.

I tilt my head back and swallow. *Shit, it's sour.* My eyes water but the burn feels good going down. Warmth spreads through my chest, giving me a small reprieve from my headache.

Layne grins as she sways to the music. "See? Told you it would help."

"What makes you think it helped?" I ask, wiping my palm across my lips.

Caitlyn and Ashley, both wearing matching silver dresses, squeeze in next to us. Caitlyn's hair is twisted up in space buns with glitter dusting her shoulders. They hug Layne, grabbing shots from the bar and downing them.

"Bailey! You actually came out!" Ashley shouts over the music, pulling me into a hug. I'm hit with a whiff of vodka and vanilla body spray. "I feel like I never see you here."

Caitlyn leans across the bar, waving a twenty at the bartender while three guys hover nearby, staring way too long at the way her dress rides up.

"I had to beg her," Layne says. "Clay pissed me off again, so she couldn't say no."

"Wow," I say under my breath. "Glad to know how easily manipulated I can be." No one is listening to me, as Layne shoves a beer in my face.

She knows I hate beer.

"Oh my God!" Ashley says, pointing toward the entrance. We all turn to see what she's pointing at. "It's Josh and his roommate."

"Josh?" Layne asks, eyeing them with a raised brow.

"From Waller's class. English. You seriously don't remember him?" Ashley asks, craning her neck for a better view.

"Wait," Caitlyn says. "Is that Kyle with him?"

"Kyle can choke on his drink." Ashley rolls her eyes. "After what he pulled at the party last weekend, I'm so done."

While they debate about whether or not Kyle should be allowed to live, I pull out my phone and check for notifications. Nothing but a few new junk emails and an Instagram notification that my aunt in Colorado liked the story I shared about the decline of literacy among children. Leon hasn't texted me back. I try to ignore the sinking feeling in my chest, but it sticks around like the stubborn bitch it is. We're an hour away from each other. He's... him and it's Friday night and... *No.* I'm not spiraling. I already feel shitty, and stressing over Leon won't help. He's probably working or studying or out with my brother and Damon, doing whatever it is those three do.

"More shots!" Layne yells, passing me a sticky, half-spilled cup. "Oh, your phone is out." She grabs it, slings her arm around me, and snaps a picture of us together—me looking bewildered while she sticks her tongue out, head tilted toward mine. "One more shot and then let's dance!"

She pushes my phone back into my hand and turns toward the bar. There's no way I'm taking another shot. I'm already wobbly and my head still hurts. The photo she took lights up the screen. It's cute and definitely captures our personalities. Something in the background catches my eye though. I turn my brightness all the way up and zoom in. Is that the light-haired guy from the pharmacy? My stomach drops as I whip my head around, scanning the crowded space. I can't spot him now, but looking back at the photo, I know without a doubt it's him. And he's staring right at us.

I hug my chest and move closer to Layne. She takes it as a cue to start dancing on me, so I sway with no real rhythm while I search the crowd for those cold blue eyes.

"To getting Bailey out on a Friday night!" Layne says, holding up her shot to cheers with Ashley and Caitlyn. "Bails, here."

She holds the drink out to me but I shake my head. "You guys can have it."

"More for me," Ashley says, double-fisting the cups. I'm so going to be holding someone's hair back tonight.

"Let's go dance!" Layne says, pulling me out onto the packed dance floor. It's a sea of writhing bodies moving as one. The bass rumbles through the floor and up my legs, making my bones vibrate. My stomach lurches from the overwhelming smell of sweat, alcohol, and perfume.

Layne starts swaying her hips. She's totally in her element, loving life. She screams, "I love this song! Come on!" and grabs my hands, raising them above her head. I try to match her energy. *Really, I do.* Maybe like thirty percent effort. But it's not happening tonight. My movements must look stiff and unnatural compared to everyone around me.

We *dance* like that for three songs. I get groped, bumped into from behind, and pushed against Layne which she takes as me dancing up on her.

"Isn't this great?" she shouts into my ear, her words slightly slurred.

I force a smile and nod.

Telling her about my claustrophobia would be pointless as the crowd swells around us. As the next song begins the dance floor seems to shrink, too many bodies move closer and closer, pressing against me until I can barely breathe.

"Water!" I shout into her ear and gesture toward the bar. She nods and lets me pull her away from the crowd. The relief is almost instantaneous. I suck in a breath. It still doesn't smell the best, but at least I can get it down into my chest.

"Can you order me a beer? I'll be right back, gonna go fight my way to the bathroom." Layne passes me some cash but I shake my head.

"I got it. Just be quick." She squeezes my hand and leaves.

Each step she takes from me has my pulse drumming in my ears. It's the worst feeling, like I'm somewhere else. Lights blur, sounds drown out. The space around me thins like I'm looking through a paper tube.

I get bumped and knock into the woman in front of me. She wobbles on her platform heels, spewing a few choice insults my way, but I barely hear her.

"Sorry!" I yell, or maybe I whisper. I don't know anymore. I spot a clear space at the end of the bar and move toward it, step by step, like I'm lost at sea and that small vacant spot is a lone island among the endless blue.

I get my cup of water, although I don't remember asking for it. The cold liquid feels incredible sliding down my throat. I close my eyes and try to block out the chaos around me. It's not until Layne wraps her arm around my shoulder that I open them.

"Where's my beer?" she hollers.

"Shit. I forgot. I can—"

"Oh my God, Bailey!" She grabs my arm, digging her nails into my skin. "He's here!"

"What? Who?" I dart my eyes around the room and don't see anyone recognizable.

"Clay!" She points at the far end of the bar and adjusts her dress so her tits are barely covered. "That bastard. We fight, and he thinks he can just come out and find someone else to hook up with."

"Maybe he's looking for you."

"You think?" she asks, her expression softening.

"Go on," I say, waving her off. It's inevitable, she's going to confront him. It's just a matter of me telling her to leave me be or not. I'd rather sit here alone than have to listen to her go off about Clay until he notices her. Or maybe I'm right, and there's a slim possibility that he's here for her... Anything's possible.

I sip my water and try not to stare as Layne and Clay go from fighting to making out within two minutes. I figured that would happen. He pulls her onto the dance floor and they get swallowed up into the crowd.

There's no reason for me to stay here any longer. I'm sure Layne will understand... Hell, she probably won't even notice I'm gone until her and Clay wind up back in our room to pass out.

I feel so loved.

I pull my phone from my purse and open Uber. At least a fifteen minute wait. Not too bad considering it's Friday night. Hitting order, I push my half-full water onto the bar and make my way toward the door. I'd much rather wait outside, even if it's still drizzling.

Blissfully cool air hits my face once I'm out the door. I don't even care that I have to walk through a cloud of cigarette smoke to get to the corner. It's still better than being inside.

I double check the street sign and send a message to the driver letting him know where to pick me up. I'll text Layne too. It's the right thing to do, even if she ditched me first.

> Me: Hey, heading home. Head's still killing me. Be safe... love you

The smokers head back inside as the drizzle gets heavier, leaving me alone under a dim streetlight. It's quiet except for the muffled thump of bass from inside the club. I watch the app, waiting for the little car icon to stop at my location. Twelve minutes until my ride arrives. I'll probably be soaked, but there's no way I'm waiting inside.

I swipe my text thread with Leon open again. Still nothing. I don't want to admit to myself that it hurts... I'm more mature than that. These things happen. People get busy. It happens to me all the time.

But not with him.

I lean back against the wet brick building and scroll up through our messages from earlier this week, pausing on one from Tuesday night. *Sweet dreams, Firefly. Can't wait to see you soon.* My chest tightens. He started calling me that after—

The squeak of wet brakes startles me. A black SUV idles against the curb. I glance at my phone, but the little car icon is still a few blocks away. A car door slams and footsteps echo in the quiet.

Before I can process what's happening, someone grabs me from behind and clamps a strong hand over my mouth. I can't run or call out for help, they're too strong. The scent of cologne is familiar and suffocating.

"Hello again."

That voice, the accent.

My phone slips from my palm as I'm dragged into the open car door. I kick uselessly but my feet barely touch the ground. The last thing I see before I'm plunged into blackness is the dark-haired man holding a syringe.

CHAPTER FOUR

BAILEY - BEFORE

Unrecognizable voices pull me from unconsciousness. Deep and grating against my throbbing skull. I crack my eyes open but can't see a thing. There's nothing but pitch-black. Something's covering my nose, my mouth. It's a thick fabric blocking out any trace of light. I know I can breathe but can't seem to pull the air into my lungs.

I try to move my arms but they're heavy and tightly bound. Some kind of restraints bite into my wrists.

Oh God.

Reality slams into me, the memories coming back like light beams through fog. The club, waiting alone on the curb, the black car, the stranger's face before everything went dark.

"Help!" I attempt to cry out, but my throat is raw. My voice is no louder than a whisper. "Help me."

The words are barely audible even to my own ears, but I have to try, have to make someone hear me before—

The voices are closer, and I freeze, holding my breath as footsteps approach. Panic tightens my chest, my already heavy limbs shake, but I steel myself. I'll hold it together, figure out where I am, who has taken me.

"We're moving her tonight. I don't care what he said." Whoever it is sounds tired, like his last nerve is frayed.

"But—"

He lets out a long breath. "I'm not in the mood, Yuri. We don't answer to him, despite what he believes. Get the van ready and call Ace. You'll pick up the others on the way."

The others?

I don't have time to think, to move, to scream before heavy footsteps reach the space around me. I can almost hear his bones creak as he bends, his breath close enough that I smell the alcohol escaping his lips as he sighs. "You're awake." Not a question, but an observation. I stiffen, keeping my mouth closed tightly. "Would you like some water?"

I don't want anything from him, I just want to go home.

The air shifts around me as he stands, stepping far enough away that I release the breath I'd been holding. If I could see. Move my arms. Then maybe I could figure out how to get out of this. I test moving my legs. They feel weighted down and tingly but I think I could walk.

A sound—maybe a twist of a water bottle, a cap being flung against the hard floor. Then he's there, lifting the rough fabric away from my mouth. I suck in a breath, not caring that I'm swallowing his scent too. He brings the water bottle to my lips and tips it back. "Drink."

I don't have a choice. The second the cool liquid hits my lips, I gulp it down greedily. I shiver as it spills onto my chin and drips down my chest. It's only now that I realize I'm freezing. My damp dress clings to my skin and my legs are bare against the cold floor.

"That's good, Bailey. Drink more," he orders. And I do. My throat feels less raw with each sip.

He knows my name. Do I know him? Someone from campus, maybe? Could this be a terrible prank gone wrong?

Or is this an act of kindness before brutality? Some kind of penance from a monster? He must need to keep me alive and well for whatever he has planned next.

He takes the water away and pulls the cloth back down. My claustrophobia makes me feel like I'm dying.

"Please," I rasp. My voice comes out less gravelly, but my throat is still sore. Not as painful as my head though. "What—what do you want?"

No answer, just a slow emptying of his lungs. "Do you need to use the bathroom?"

I haven't even fully assessed my body, but this could be a chance to escape. I nod, and the movement sends a pulse of pain behind my eyes that has me biting back a whimper.

Without another word, he lifts me by the waist, hauling me onto my wobbly feet. Positioning himself behind me with his hands on my shoulders, not tight, almost gently, like the time my dad had me close my eyes as he led me into the garage to show me my new bicycle.

"Walk, and don't try anything."

The first step I take is painful, like pins and needles. I stumble but his grip tightens, holding me upright. Our footsteps echo against what must be concrete, bouncing through the space around us. I focus on the sounds, trying to piece together where I am. Each noise travels too far, like we're in some giant empty room. A warehouse, maybe.

My pulse pounds as he guides me forward. There's a change in the ground, the sounds, even the air smells different here. Thicker, like sweat and metal.

"Three steps up," he says flatly. I lift my feet carefully, testing each step before moving up.

He holds me still, and I hear the squeal of hinges.

"It's a bucket," he says. "I'll loosen your hands, but the hood stays on."

A bucket? He pulls on my restraints, slicing through them until my hands drop apart. I stretch and test the strength in my fingers which tingle as blood rushes back to them. After a moment, I don't hear his retreating steps.

"I can't... not with you standing there," I whisper, clinging to whatever shred of dignity I have left.

He sighs, that same tired sound. "Get used to it, Bailey. Privacy isn't something you'll have anymore."

"But I—"

"You have thirty seconds," he says, voice more on edge than before.

Shame creeps over me, stronger than fear, as I fumble with my dress, trying to position myself over what feels like a plastic bucket. He's watching me, probably getting off on this. His words play on loop while I manage to go. *Get used to it, Bailey.* I'm truly fucked. No one knows where I am. What will they do to me? I'll probably die here.

When I'm done, he ties my wrists again, looser than before, but still secure. As we walk back, I pick up other sounds. The whir of machinery in the distance, far away voices, metal clanging against something hollow.

"Almost time to move," he mutters, sounding like he's talking to himself more than me. He pushes me back to the floor. It's colder now, the concrete feels like ice. "Stay here, and stay quiet so I won't have to drug you again. Nod if you understand."

I nod as his phone rings, echoing through the space like an alarm bell. But it's the man's next words that have my body shaking.

"I'll bring her out back."

HIS NAME IS SWEEPER. That's what the other guy, Yuri, calls him before he closes the van door. I have a feeling I'll wish it was Sweeper here with his exhausted sighs and gentle grip soon enough.

The van door only opens once in the long drive, letting in crisp autumn air that feels like a blessing in the stifling space. I count four women, five including me. Four different cries and pleas with gravelly voices echoing my own fear. One of them whispers a prayer that has tears leaking onto the fabric of my mask. Wherever they were before now, at least they were together. I want to talk to them—the others. Ask names and offer what little comfort I can, but fear holds my voice captive. Fear that the man seated back here with us will do what he threatened, and it's not killing us, not in the literal sense. What he threatened was much worse.

After hours of driving, we've stopped. Yuri and the other man climb out of the van, speaking loudly in Russian. Their voices fade as they move away. Now's my chance.

"Hello," I whisper. "Are you all okay?"

A few hopeless seconds go by before someone answers. "Not really."

She sounds young, barely out of her teens like me. Those two words shake yet they have this inkling of defiance to them. Something I can admire.

Then another, small and meek. "I'm scared."

I want to reach toward her voice, offer some comfort in this darkness, but my bound hands and frozen limbs hold me back. Instead, I use my voice. "I'm scared too. What's your name?"

"Don't tell her," the first voice says sharply. "She can't be trusted."

I should feel hurt, but she's right. If they're also masked, they have no idea I'm in the same position they are. I stay quiet to save my strength.

"Listen to her voice, Cat. You really think she's one of them?" another woman to my left says, her voice nasally.

"What the fuck, Lydia? Why did you tell her my name?" Cat seethes.

Lydia—I think she's the one who was praying earlier. I file their names away in hope that we'll be alive long enough to use them later.

We're cut short by the van door sliding open again. "Time to go," one of the men barks.

All at once we're grabbed and pulled out. Some of them fight, probably Cat, but I keep quiet. I don't think I'd have the strength to fight if I wanted to.

I hear a hard smack, and someone yells, "Move your fucking feet!"

There's crying. So much crying that it takes everything in me not to join them.

"We should have drugged the bitches," the other man says.

I'm shoved hard in the back and stumble forward, knocking into one of the others. We both go down hard, but with my hands restrained I can't break my fall, so I land awkwardly on my side, scraping my covered face and bare shoulders against the rough ground. I cry out, but before I can fully register the pain, I'm hauled back to my feet with a punishing grip. "Walk!"

Tears stream down my cheeks, making it harder to breathe in the hood. The fabric clings to my nostrils as I try to inhale. Cold air hits my skin through my thin dress. I may as well be wearing nothing at all. My brain struggles to make sense of anything without the ability to see, but I force myself to focus. Count steps. Memorize turns, note sounds and smells. Anything that might help later.

Leon would be calm in this situation. He'd tell me to be

patient, to observe. The thought of him centers me momentarily. Does he know I'm gone yet? Has anyone realized? I imagine my phone, abandoned outside the club, lighting up with messages from him. From Layne. From my parents.

My mom's voice plays in my head. That final talk we had on move in day. "Always be aware of your surroundings, Bailey."

But how can I when everything is shrouded in darkness? Still, I try.

The man digs his fingers into my upper arm as the ground changes beneath my feet. Uneven concrete to what feels like threadbare carpeting. We're indoors now. It's warm but somehow I know I'd be safer back outside. The air reeks of cigarette smoke and body odor.

"Bring them in the main room. He'll be here soon," Yuri says.

The man's grip eases slightly on my arm, and I store this information away. Maybe they relax when they think we're secure. That might be useful knowledge later. I'm not going to scream or fight like Cat—not yet. I'll find a moment, an opportunity, and I need to be ready for when it comes.

We're herded into a room and told to sit on the floor and not move. At least it's covered in musty smelling carpeting and not more cold concrete. My whole body aches, and the reprieve from being on my feet is welcome, even as my mind races through scenarios, possibilities, escape routes I can't even see.

Heavy footsteps pace the floor and one of the others trembles close enough that I feel her against my shoulder. "It'll be okay," I whisper, not believing it myself but needing to say something. She trembles harder. I shift over so our bodies are touching, seeking comfort for us both, but something hard presses against the side of my head.

"I told you not to move, bitch. Maybe I should teach you a

lesson? You'd like that wouldn't you? Asking for it in that dress."

My stomach drops. "No, please. I'm sorry," I manage to say through chattering teeth. "I won't move."

The sound of his belt unbuckling has me curling into a tight ball. The object against my head—a gun, most likely—slips down. Time slows as I calculate my options, none of them good.

"Don't touch her!" Cat yells. More of the girls cry. But me, I'm frozen, mind racing as my body refuses to move.

"Shut the fuck up or you're next!"

His zipper sounds so loud. It's the only thing I hear.

Until another voice, cold with an accent slighter than Yuri's, pulls me to the present. "Anton."

One word and Anton stops moving. The authority in those two syllables is unmistakable.

"King—I wasn't. It's not—"

A single shot fires and something heavy crashes down in front of me. *Anton.* Hot liquid sprays my legs. The warm wetness soaks through my dress instantly.

Oh my God. Holy shit. I'm going to die.

I bite my lips so hard I taste blood, swallowing down the scream that threatens to escape.

Footsteps come closer and I smell it, even through the metallic scent of blood. Cologne, so strong my eyes sting. I've smelled it before.

"Don't worry, girls. I took care of him."

As a large palm glides along my shoulder and toward my hood, I know in my gut that this man is so much worse, and as the fabric lifts away, revealing his face, my suspicion is confirmed.

CHAPTER FIVE

LEON - PRESENT DAY

I GET OFF THE TUBE AND DUCK DOWN A DIMLY LIT cobbled side street covered with years worth of graffiti. The smell of spilled beer mixes with the industrial scent of the railway above me. There it is. The Arch. Just looking at its run down sign brings me back in time. We'd head here to get pissed since it stays open past midnight and they never minded a few kids taking up a table in the back so long as we kept quiet.

We learned a lot here. Me, Cruz, Abel, and a few others. Had our first pints. Played our first poker matches. Got into our first fist fight. Same night, coincidentally. It was at The Arch that I landed my first paid hacking gig. Where Cruz mixed up with a dodgy crew. Where I know I'll find some answers about Bailcy.

Bailey.

Just thinking her name makes my chest ache. It's hard to stay focused, keep my emotions in check, when every spare moment, my thoughts drift to her. Her smile. The gleam in her blue eyes when she'd say something embarrassing about Jasper. Those lips that would bring me to my knees.

She's not just some missing person to me. She never was.

As I step inside, the whole place vibrates from a train passing overhead. Dust unavoidably lands in drinks and sprinkles people's hair. Through the haze of particles in the air, I spot Cruz hunched in our old corner booth, wearing the same faded backwards ball cap he's worn for years. He's ganglier than when I last saw him—lost some weight maybe? Either that or I never really noticed how long his limbs were, but from here, his legs barely fit under the booth.

He spots me and nods, holding up a pint. "The prodigal son returns."

I clap a hand on his shoulder and offer a small smile. "Cruz. Alright? You still getting into trouble?"

"Got myself a wife. Last year. She's a real firecracker, would rip my balls off if I got into trouble," Cruz says with a chuckle as I slide into the booth across from him. "Nearly took my head off last time I stumbled in at three in the morning."

"Is that right?" I ask, picturing the Cruz I know as a proper family man.

His phone vibrates against the table and he holds it up, laughing. "Like we summoned the devil herself."

"You better get that," I say.

"Ah, she can wait." He leans forward, looking me over. "America's done you well, hasn't it? You've filled out. Got that expensive haircut. Teeth look suspiciously white. Look a bit tired though, around the eyes."

Tired doesn't begin to cover it. Can he tell that I haven't slept properly in a year? That my life has been endless nights spent at my computer, drinking too much caffeine, searching for any trace of her. And God, the nightmares. Bailey's cries in the dark, her hand reaching for mine before she's yanked away, just out of my grasp.

"Just order me a pint, will you?" I laugh under my breath. "I'll need one if this is how the night's heading."

"Next one's on you," he says before sliding out and heading to the bar. I take a moment to check my phone, reading over a few unopened messages in the group chat. Mostly pics of the cats being cute... which I hate to admit make me smile.

I miss them all more than I expected. Jasper with his incessant jokes, Damon's quiet strength, Blake's kindness, Falin's fierce intelligence. They're my family. And Bailey is the missing piece.

When I look up, blinking back the wave of emotion, Cruz is right there, full pint in hand. "Bottoms up."

I take a long swig, feeling my shoulders loosen already. "Thanks. Needed that."

Cruz stretches his legs so they're sticking out from under the table. "So, what brings you back? Last I heard, you were finishing up uni in New York?"

"Gathering some information," I say. Cruz raises his brows and gestures for me to go on. I lower my voice. "On a missing person. Trafficking victim. All my intel points to her being here in London."

"Trafficking victim, eh?" Cruz leans back, resting his arm on the booth. His jaw clenches as he fusses with his cap. "That's some heavy stuff."

"Keep your voice down." I take another sip of my beer, watching his face carefully. Cruz may be a few years older and married, but I can tell that he hasn't changed much. "It's important."

"Right, sorry." He scans the area around us before adding, "What's this got to do with me? I'm just a bloke with a mortgage and a wife who thinks I work in IT support."

"Come off it. You still know people. You've always had your ear to the ground."

Cruz scratches his chin, taps the side of his glass. I'm reeling him in. "Look, I don't mess with that sort of thing. Never have. And especially not now."

"I'm not suggesting you do," I say quietly. "I know you better than that." His face softens, and I know just how to get him to talk. "It's for someone I know well. Someone I care for."

He sighs, looks over his shoulder again, and finishes his beer in one swig. "What do you need?"

"Information about a business called Mech Express. Anything connecting them to London operations."

And just like that, Cruz turns white as a sheet. "You come back here and want to poke the hornet's nest day one? I've heard of them. Bad news. Not something you want to get mixed up in."

I'm getting impatient, but bite back the harsh words that are bursting to come out. "I know, trust me on that. I need something, Cruz. Anything."

Another train rumbles overhead, and dust falls from the ceiling, landing on the sticky table. "I haven't heard much but I know they're not what they say. The company has some bad dealings. The owner, Orlov, has ties in East London. Might've had a client not too long ago that got stiffed and asked me to do a little digging. Problem is, he keeps it air tight."

"I know," I say with a sigh. "Bastard's been hard to crack."

"There's his charity organization. Office is in some posh building in Canary Wharf. I'd start there. I've heard they host parties. I bet your father—"

I put my hand up to stop him. "I'm not involving my father."

He shrugs. "Just a suggestion. Anyway, last I heard, he's got this group of rich blokes from all over the world involved in this charity. All of them squeaky clean when I dug in, but there must be more to it."

My fist clenches around my glass. *The Brotherhood.* That must be what he's talking about. "What kind of charity?"

"Tell me more about this missing girl," he asks. "She's American?" I ignore his question.

"Any names of people who might be more directly involved? Someone who would know more details?" He rubs his chin, like he's thinking of a measured response.

"Like I said, there's the charity office. Might try there." Cruz leans forward, lowering his voice again. "I don't know what you've gotten yourself into, but whatever it is, be careful. These trafficking networks have connections everywhere. Police, government, you name it."

You have no idea.

"I can handle myself," I say instead.

Cruz laughs. "Yeah, I bet America's made you hard, hasn't it? I remember when you were just a skinny hacker afraid of your own shadow. Now look at you. I bet you could win some real money at The Irons."

I shake my head. "Haven't heard that name for a long time."

"I can get you in. I know a guy." His eyes gleam and he looks exactly like the teenage mischief maker I've known for years. He gestures to the bartender for another round.

"You mean Tank? Pretty sure she remembers me." I scratch my chin, giving him a hard time before adding, "I'll think about it." Fighting at The Irons didn't work out too well for me last time, but Cruz is right. I have gotten stronger. Plus, I've got a good deal of pent up rage to release being back here. Physical pain to overpower the guilt of failing her may be what I need.

The bartender puts two fresh pints on the table and Cruz immediately grabs his. "I know who I've got my money on." He sips, wiping his mouth with the back of his hand. "You. I see that look in your eyes... Scary, man. Like a killer."

He laughs at his joke, not knowing how true his words are.

"I need to go," I say, placing my full beer on the table and standing up.

"I mean it, Colter. Be careful. And if you need backup—"

I grab a few bills out of my wallet and drop them on the table. "I've got backup, but thanks for the offer."

He nods, and drops his gaze to the bills. "Still a vault, huh? Some things never change."

"Take care of your wife," I say, giving his shoulder a squeeze. "I'll be in touch."

I can feel his eyes on my back as I walk out of the pub. I feel bad for being an ass, but I refuse to get Cruz tangled up in this mess. At least I got something out of him. Less than I'd hoped for, but it's a start.

A light drizzle falls from the sky as I make my way back to the tube. I pull the collar of my leather jacket up to ward off the chill in the air. My mind is already working on a plan. Check out this charity, see where it leads me. It's not much, but anything helps. In the meantime, I'll continue to monitor everything on Mech Express. If Ivan Orlov is here, I'll find out, and emptying his accounts will be the least of his worries.

Tilting my face to the dark sky, I make a silent promise to her. *Soon, Firefly. I'm coming for you.*

BAILEY - JUNE 1ST

I'm so exhausted but I have to get this down before I pass out.

Leon came in to work tonight. I was halfway embarrassed because working at Burger Palace isn't exactly glamorous, thank you grease-stained apron, but also it's a job and I make decent tips so can't complain. It was right in the middle of the dinner rush. I looked up and there he was, sitting at the corner booth with his laptop like he'd owned the place. My heart literally skipped but I don't think it showed on my face. I hope.

He waited for the line to slow, then ordered a burger and a milkshake... and refused to let me give him free stuff. I swear, if he could have jumped over the counter to help me he would have. He went back to his booth and I got super busy again, but it was really nice knowing he was there. Every time I glanced over between taking orders, he'd catch my eye and smile.

Not in a weird way, just... I don't know. Like he was happy to see me? Which is probably me reading too much into it but whatever.

Then around seven, these two guys came in, college-aged, clearly drunk, probably pre-gaming before going out to the bars. They were dicks from the start. Complaining about the line loudly, being so obnoxious. Then they finally got in front of me and said stuff like "make sure it's cooked this time" or "no soggy fucking fries." I felt my body tensing up, but I was like it's okay, they'll leave soon. Then I told them it was going to be twenty-three dollars and the one guy got so loud. "Twenty-three bucks for this shit? That's fucking robbery! You'd have to show your tits and ass for me to pay that for a fucking burger."

My face got so hot but I just forced a bigger smile and told them I could grab a manager. I hate confrontation, especially at work where I have to smile and nod and can't even attempt to stick up for myself.

But then Leon was just... there. I didn't even see him coming. He didn't make a big scene or anything. He just put his hand on the counter, and in this calm but kind of scary voice said something like, "I think you gentlemen owe the lady an apology. And perhaps a more generous tip for her excellent service during what's clearly a busy evening."

The way he said it... God. It wasn't loud or aggressive, but his voice was like "you better not try anything with me." They actually apologized and left a fifteen dollar tip on their order.

After they left, I just stared at him, like I short-circuited. Maybe I mumbled something like "You didn't have to do that," but he just shrugged and said "Yes, I did." Then he went back to his booth like nothing happened.

I kept thinking about it for the rest of my shift. How he didn't hesitate for a second to come to my side. How he made those guys actually feel bad about being jerks instead of just telling them to leave.

I've never had someone do that for me before. Jasper would have probably started a fight, and Damon would have given them a death stare until they left on their own or maybe fought them too. I never know what mood he'll be in. But Leon... he handled it like an adult. Like someone who actually cared about...

CHAPTER SIX

BAILEY - BEFORE

Traces of Anton's blood still fleck my skin. Under my nails, along my arms, up my legs. I memorize the burgundy stains as King finally comes, focusing on them instead of the brutal way he uses me from behind. It's not the first time, but I'll never get used to this.

King. That's what he tells us to call him. The narcissist bastard thinks he wears a crown. It's nothing but self-importance and violence that keeps his little band of assholes in line.

Maybe it's been days since they dragged us from the van. Maybe weeks. Time becomes a blurred haze from the drugs they force on us and the deprivation of the outside world. Blackout curtains on every window hide any sense of day or night. All I know is the way he uses me feels never-ending.

If I keep my eyes on my nails, on Anton's blood, I'll remember not to scream, not to run, because next time it won't be his blood—it will be mine pooling beneath me. That doesn't stop the tears from streaming down my face, soaking into the rough wooden desk. It doesn't end the whispered pleas from escaping my lips—calling for my mom, my dad, Jasper, Leon. Names that already feel like they're from another life.

The house, I've come to learn, is a temporary space while King makes permanent arrangements for each of us. Information circulates among us girls like contraband, passed in hushed tones during bathroom trips or when the men guarding us pass out drunk.

"He said one week."

"I heard two."

"He found a buyer."

"There's a party soon."

"I think he has my sister somewhere."

Each time I hear something new, I can't help but let hope slip further and further away.

He's just finished with me again. His cologne cloys at my nose and clings to my skin, mixed with the sour, thick musk of sweat. There's pain radiating throughout my body, but more than that, shame burns deep. I feel hollow, dirty, raw. With every brutal thrust, he cleaves pieces of my soul. Every slap, every cruel bite of thick fingers into my flesh drains my dignity, leaving me as empty as a discarded husk.

He yanks my hair to pull me upright and my body follows his commands by muscle memory alone. My scalp screams from all the times he's ripped me across the room by my hair. I bite back the hurt, but I have to brace my arms against the wooden desk he has me pinned against, wetting my hands in my own sweat and tears.

"That's my good pet," he says, smoothing his palm over my knotted hair with all the tenderness of a rabid animal. "You've earned a meal today."

My hollow stomach groans as if on cue. I can't remember the last time I had a real meal, something more than the packaged granola bars and packs of crackers they've thrown at us. Even after licking the packaging clean, my hunger pangs are so visceral, they're one of the only things reminding me I'm alive.

He finishes buckling his leather belt, the same one he used to bind my hands the first time. Then he grabs my chin, forcing my face upward until I'm looking directly into his eyes. They're the darkest blue, so cold and devoid of emotion, I wonder if he's even human. "I just told you you're getting a reward, pet. What do you say?"

For a moment, I think about spitting in his face. It would feel so good to defy him, even with just a small act. Consequences be damned. Instead, my tongue darts over my cracked lips, tasting blood, and I give him the response that'll keep me alive another day. "Thank you."

His hand moves lower, caressing the front of my neck, fingers splayed across my throat while he coos something in Russian—the language has become a trigger for my fight or flight response. Then his grip tightens, cutting off my air as he brings his face no more than an inch from mine. The stubble on his jaw scrapes my skin as he speaks. "Remember who owns you, girl, and be grateful it's me in here and not my men downstairs. They're dying for a taste." As the final word leaves his lips, he cups my pussy roughly with his free hand, making a sickly groan that vibrates his chest.

I struggle for breath, my hands instinctively clawing at his cracked knuckles. Black creeps into the corners of my vision and I know this is it. This is where I die. Half naked in some monster's crumbling mansion, miles from everyone I love.

He must see that I'm on the edge of consciousness, because he finally releases me, letting me slump against the desk.

His retreating footsteps echo against the wooden floor, each one giving me the slightest sense of relief. He opens the door and lingers at the threshold while I suck in deep breaths of stale air. "Yuri! Get in here."

I'm trembling now, clinging to the oversized white T-shirt they gave me so they could dispose of my bloody dress. Yuri hasn't hurt me... yet. But his stare follows me every time King isn't looking, calculating eyes that give me no hint of what he's thinking. If King were to leave the house for good, I'm sure he'd jump at the chance to hurt me.

Heavy footsteps pound up the stairs, and Yuri appears, huffing from the exertion. "King?" he asks stiffly, craning his neck past King into the bedroom where I haven't moved a muscle.

"Bring her a meal and then let her get cleaned up for later." King's voice is casual, friendly even, but I repeat his words in my mind.

For later?

Yuri nods, and King pushes past him into the shadowy hallway. "Who else is ready for tonight? We need three."

Yuri pulls a hand through his dark greasy hair, leaning against the doorframe. "Any of them would do, but maybe you should pay a visit to the mouthy one."

Oh God, I know they're talking about Cat—fierce, defiant Cat who still fights back despite being in this situation for far longer than me. Cat, who whispers to us about escaping. Panic squeezes my lungs.

King laughs low and plants a hand on Yuri's shoulder. "You're right. If tonight goes well, I think you're due for a reward too." He glances back at me. "Something for your hard work."

Acid churns in my empty gut as Yuri's gaze meets mine. I can't read the expression in them, it's too dark, but I know there's nothing kind in his eyes. "You're too generous, boss."

King pulls out a money clip, thick with bills, from his

pocket and shoves it at Yuri. "Make sure they have the necessary clothing for tonight."

Then he walks away, toward another one of the bedrooms, looking like an evil spirit. His shadow stretches long and narrow against the dull gold wallpaper. As his footsteps fade, I curl into myself, making my body as small as possible, trying to disappear even though I know there's nowhere to hide.

"Follow me," Yuri commands, emotionless.

I want to cover myself. Pull the tattered blanket off the bed and wrap my shoulders in its warmth. But Yuri starts walking and I know if I don't follow, I won't eat today.

He leads me downstairs into the kitchen. I've only been in here once, and briefly enough that I didn't take in the sterile cleanliness of it, completely opposite of how I'd imagine a kitchen in this situation would be. There's two guys sitting at the table, one typing on his phone and the other eyeing Yuri carefully.

"Out," Yuri tells them. No explanation. No hint of his mood. They obey immediately, glancing at me with wide eyes before heading into the back of the house.

He gestures to a chair and wordlessly walks to the fridge, taking out a loaf of bread and some plastic-wrapped cold cuts. I sit but feel unnerved from his silence. With King, there's no guesswork. No reading his mood. I know what I'm getting when he steps into the room. But not with Yuri. He's never outright hurt me. Never raised his voice. It's the stoic way he stares... the way he makes me want to know what he's thinking.

He drops the sandwich in front of me on a paper plate and my stomach groans. For a moment, I just look at it, afraid to move. Until he mutters something under his breath in Russian, and says, "Eat." I take a bite and swallow so quickly, I nearly choke.

The whole time I eat, I feel his eyes on me. Eventually, he

turns, filling a glass with water from the tap and pushing it in front of me. I gulp it down, and he refills it. Drips slide down my chin.

His phone rings, so I take the opportunity of him being distracted to search around the room. Old windows with thick drapes close off the outside world. There must be another exit besides the front door. Maybe if I can get Yuri on my side, get him to sympathize with me, I can find a way out.

I take another sip of water as he finishes his call. "Done?" he asks.

I nod slowly. "Thank you."

He scoffs and turns toward the hallway. "Upstairs now."

"Really," I say, forcing cheeriness into my tone. "That was the best sandwich I've ever had." Starvation will make anything taste incredible. He stays quiet, so I chance a question. "Where are we going tonight?"

The only sound is his booted footsteps on the hardwood floor and the long sigh escaping his lips.

I take slow measured steps behind him, hoping to stretch time. As we reach the staircase, cries from one of the other women echo against the walls. Maybe I'm imagining it, but I swear I see Yuri flinch.

Adrenaline pounds through my blood, and that urge to run, to hide, pulls at me with ferocity. Out of instinct, I step closer to Yuri—just for a moment before I realize he's one of them and recoil.

"Let's go," he mumbles, barely glancing back at me.

"Sorry." I sweeten my tone. "I'm just so afraid."

It's not a lie. My legs are barely holding me up, and after hearing that soul wrenching wail, the sandwich churns in my gut.

He leads me to the bathroom where we're normally supervised and allowed to use a few times a day. Riffling through the cabinet, he pulls out various bottles and a bar of soap, arranging them on the edge of the tub. A hot shower will be a small blessing in this cruel place. But is he going to watch me with those emotionless eyes?

He twists the knob and the pipes groan from inside the wall. Steam envelops the small space quickly as he tinkers with the temperature. "You have five minutes."

"Please... where are we going tonight?" I ask again, more desperate to know the answer.

He ignores me, but something flickers in his eye and he bends to reach into the cabinet again. A razor in hand, he says, "Ten minutes." His eyes stray to my legs and slowly back up to my face. "Shave everything."

He doesn't have to say what's going to happen tonight. That one command tells me enough.

As he hands me the razor and steps into the doorframe, I glance at it, weighing every possibility. Could I somehow hide it, use it as a weapon? Terrible thoughts swirl through my mind. How I could end it all. Make it quick. Die by my own terms.

He must notice because he stops and narrows his eyes on the razor too. "Undress. Now I will stay."

My heart sinks, but a part of me expected no less. As my filthy shirt hits the damp bathroom floor, and Yuri's eyes stay fixated on the razor still in my clutched hand, I realize I've lost that chance. I don't know if I'm relieved or disappointed. Probably numb.

Yuri doesn't touch. He barely looks at me as I shower away caked-on grime from my skin. I wish I could say I feel clean. I still feel just as dirty. No amount of scrubbing will take away what King's done.

I drip dry for a few moments until Yuri hands me a fresh white T-shirt from under the cabinet and leads me back to my room.

He hesitates in the doorway as I stand there, shaking from the cold with water dripping down my back.

"I will bring clothes." He sighs, then adds, "You will entertain tonight."

I nod, but he's already left.

CHAPTER SEVEN

BAILEY - BEFORE

Cat, Jasmine, and I get loaded into a van by a few of the men that work for King while Yuri watches with a sharp eye. Goosebumps cover my limbs and I can barely control the full body shakes that began the moment I finished showering. None of what I'm going through compares to how Jasmine is looking. She's inconsolable. They slapped her, drugged her, and now she's barely coherent other than small sobs that escape her lips every few seconds. She huddles close to Cat, who stares ahead with a blank expression.

While the two men in the front seat talk animatedly, I lean closer to Cat and whisper, "Where do you think they're taking us?" A blink and sniff are the only signs she heard me. "Are you okay?"

Her bloodshot eyes find mine, and even in the darkness, I can make out the shadow of a bruise around one eye, poorly concealed under caked foundation.

"Do I look okay?" she says through gritted teeth.

My first instinct is to feel hurt, but words don't sting like they used to. "It was a dumb question, I guess."

Jasmine shudders, and Cat pulls her closer, whispering something in her ear. I can't help but feel jealous of their obvious closeness. I'd give anything for an ounce of comfort in this nightmare.

"She's lucky to have you," I say. "Did you know each other? I mean, before."

The van drives over a pothole and I lurch to the side. Through the windshield, I catch blurred highway signs.

"Lucky?" Cat says with a sarcastic tone.

"I just meant—"

"I know what you meant." She moves a piece of hair from her eyes and checks that our captors aren't paying attention before speaking again. "She's my cousin. My baby cousin. I promised my aunt I'd look out for her when she moved to the city."

"How old?" I ask, straining to see her features in the darkness.

"Fifteen," Cat says, disgusted.

"Oh God."

"Yeah. Except her new 'boyfriend' got to her before I knew what the fuck was going on. She left a note. *Be back in a couple days.*" Her voice lowers. "I looked for her... Three months later, I end up here too."

This poor girl has already gone through so much. Thought she'd found love, only to be dragged into the biggest hell imaginable. I feel sick.

Shaking my head, I try to come up with a response, but nothing I can think of carries the weight of what I want to say.

Cat nods. "I know."

"What about you?" I ask tentatively.

Cat scoffs. "Don't worry about me, new girl. They won't break me."

Her words say one thing but her tone tells another story. I

turn, giving her space, and stare out the window at the green overpass signs flashing by.

One reads fifteen miles to Manhattan. We're still in New York. Somehow I thought we had to be much farther from my school. I feel worlds away from that life.

Mile by mile, the scenery changes from shadowy trees lining the highway to towering buildings and glowing lights. Traffic slows to a crawl as we hit the city. Stop and go hell that has the driver cursing and banging the steering wheel.

Through the windows of passing cars, I catch glimpses of passengers singing along to their music, couples talking, people simply existing without fear. Just normal life that I took for granted. Help is so close, I could reach out and touch it. People surround us on all sides, but I'd be dead before I could even grab the door handle.

"Even if we were right in front of them, they wouldn't see us, you know," Cat says. She releases a long breath and continues. "We're the invisible ones. The ones they send thoughts and prayers to online so they can feel better about their own privileged lives. One look at us and they'd turn up their noses, cross the street, pretend we don't exist. We're dirty now. Broken. The kind of problem that makes them uncomfortable because helping us would mean admitting this shit actually happens in their perfect little world."

I scrunch my brows and start to retort, but she cuts me off.

"Trust me on that, new girl. I've seen it firsthand... more than once." She nods toward the men arguing in Russian. "That's how they keep us. They know we're beyond help. They make sure we look like the kind of people society has already given up on."

"Shut the fuck up back there!" the passenger spits, then immediately starts back with his argument.

My entire body clenches but Cat just holds Jasmine closer.

"Have you ever tried to get out?" I ask after a few minutes pass.

Cat scoffs and turns to stare out the window. "Can't."

"Why?" I ask so quietly I barely hear myself.

"Because they'll kill her if I do," she says, looking down at Jasmine. "And probably make me watch first. That's their favorite game... making us choose between saving ourselves or protecting someone weaker. They know exactly which choice we'll make every time. Fucking bastards."

There's so many more questions I want to ask her, but now's not the time, especially as our captors quiet down and Jasmine stirs. So instead, I count cars, silently wondering if Cat's words are true. Would my call for help be ignored?

FINALLY, we park around the back of a building. I have no idea what it is or where we are, but nausea rolls in my gut and anxiety grips my chest, making it impossible to take a full breath. They haul us out of the van. Jasmine can barely hold herself up on the stilettos they forced us to wear. She cries out as she's yanked from Cat's grip and dragged ahead by the driver. I hold back the cry that tries to escape, while Cat's body goes rigid. She'd kill them if she could.

It's a brisk night and standing out here half naked in nothing but sheer lingerie doesn't help. If I didn't already feel raw and exposed from everything done to me at the house, this would do it. But there's no time to dwell on that, not as the passenger pulls something from the glove box.

His oily dark hair shines in the dim streetlight, and pock-marked skin stretches across gaunt cheekbones. When he smiles at Cat and I, he reminds me of a skeleton. "Back up against the van," he says. "Fight and I'll make it hurt."

My heart pounds but Cat holds her head high and obeys. She's done this before. Been in this exact situation. So I follow her lead. That's when I see what he's grabbed. A syringe.

No, no, no.

"Please," I whimper as I watch in what feels like slow motion.

His eyes narrow and he moves in front of me first. "What did I say? Bitch and moan and I'll make it hurt."

Then he jabs me in the upper arm—hard. In a matter of seconds, my cry of horror warps and my eyelids droop. The world tilts sideways and shadows bleed together like dripping black paint. My knees buckle and darkness creeps in from the edges of my vision, pulling me under.

I fight it, desperate to stay conscious, but I know the drugs will win.

I blink, and suddenly I'm staring at a popcorn ceiling, water-stained and gray. The musty smell of mold and cigarettes fills my nostrils as I try to focus on my surroundings.

It looks like some kind of run-down motel room. I'm alone... or I think I am. The bed beneath me, firm with coils digging into my back, feels like it's swallowing me whole.

My eyes keep trying to drift shut.

I wake to a noise—a door shutting. My eyelids are heavy but I use every ounce of strength to pry them open.

"What a pretty young thing you are." A man's voice. Footsteps against thin carpeting. My head is too heavy to lift, my limbs like lead pipes.

"No," I cry. "Please, help me."

Do the words come out? I can't tell.

"Shh," he says. "It's okay. I'll take good care of you. Give you exactly what you want."

A zipper that sounds louder than a bullhorn and then his hands are on me. Fingers moist with sweat. Breath stale and reeking of onion. I cry out. I try to kick, to punch, but his weight pins me down as he shushes me again and again.

I close my eyes and wait for it to be over as he uses me. I can barely make out the details of his face—his age, his race. But the way he grunts as he pumps inside me—that I'll never forget.

It's over quick... or at least I think it is. Moisture collects between my legs and on my lips where he kisses me as he walks away. Maybe it's my tears, maybe it's his saliva... I don't know. The hinge squeaks and the door thuds shut.

I shudder and shake, scrambling up the bed, trying to wake the fuck up from this nightmare. What was in that needle? I can barely hold my head up.

"Help!" I yell as loudly as I can through the sobs. It's barely audible. "Please!"

Where is Cat? Jasmine? I hope they're okay.

The door opens again and I try to curl into a ball, but my heavy legs will barely move. I smell him this time. A nausea-inducing mix of cigar smoke and body odor.

"Help me," I whimper, even though I know it's in vain.

His laugh echoes in the stark room as he hovers above me. I blink up at him, taking in his skin, leathery and lined, his dark hair with salt and peppered temples, his pressed suit and tie. He runs a hand through his hair and his gold watch glints in the dim lamp light. For a fleeting moment, I wonder if he's here to help me. "You're new. I can see why you cost extra."

My heart sinks as I fight to roll toward the other side of the bed. "Please, I need—"

He grabs me by the ankles and pulls me toward him. "Uh, uh. Stay put if you know what's good for you."

I continue to pull away, my legs gaining a bit more strength. "No, no, no..." The words leave my lips in a stream of pleas until he slaps me, hard and without warning across the mouth. It's so quick that I taste the blood before I feel the stinging ache.

"You will stay put while I undress," he booms, harsher and louder than I've ever been spoken to. "You understand me?"

I don't know what to do... *I can't do this.* When I don't answer right away, he slaps me again. My lip splits open. "Answer me, bitch."

My hands automatically move to cover my face as I cry. "Yes."

"Good... you're learning already."

His potbelly sags low, and his chest is full of thick graying hair. I don't look at his shriveled dick as he rolls a condom on. "Can't be too careful," he says. "Don't know where you've come from."

He pulls me by the wrists and maneuvers me so I'm on my stomach, legs hanging off the bed. He's rough... so rough. Fingers squeezing around the back of my neck as he yanks my head off the mattress.

I want him to just get it over with already. What does it matter anymore? But instead, he uses his thick fingers inside me. He pinches and slaps me. He pries my legs open and groans into my exposed flesh... dragging this out and making me feel dirty. I wish I could have more drugs. Sleep through this inevitable hell.

When he finally pushes inside me, hissing out curses like prayers, he finishes in three pumps. *Thank God.*

I lay there, waiting for him to move. For him to get up, get dressed and leave. But he doesn't. I'm too scared to open my mouth. Too afraid to know what else is waiting for me. Then the door opens. And I chance a glance in that direction.

It's the driver—over six feet tall, probably two hundred and fifty pounds of muscle. But it's not him that has tears streaming down my face. He has Jasmine in front of him, shaking and crying.

The driver barely looks at me as he shoves Jasmine in the room. "Twenty minutes."

The man, his limp dick still out, condom full and sagging at the tip, just nods. "Close the door."

Jasmine leans against the wall, her curls wet and plastered against her cheeks. Her lingerie torn, breasts barely covered.

The monster who used me walks toward her. "You look so pretty with tears running down your face. Come, join your friend."

CHAPTER EIGHT

BAILEY - BEFORE

"No!" I cry. "Don't touch her. Take me." The words come out automatically.

I lift my body as much as I can and grab him around the middle, digging my nails in hard.

"Bitch," he grunts, and backhands me across the face. Jasmine's wails combine with my own, but I won't stop fighting.

For her, I have to try.

I scramble, using every ounce of strength I have to lift my heavy limbs. "Hide!" I yell to Jasmine, but she's already slumped against the wall.

The man's face turns beet red, his breath coming in angry huffs. Before I know what's happening, he yanks me by the hair, tossing me off the bed. My head cracks against the nightstand and everything goes black.

"... what happened to her?"

"Told you she was a fighter... They all fight at first."

My skull throbs with each word. I know one of those voices. *King.*

There's no crying... Why isn't there any crying?

I cup the side of my head, where an egg-sized knot has formed. It's so fucking sore, I could vomit. Then the images come back to me... How he threw me off the bed. Jasmine slumped on the floor.

A warm hand touches my arm and I cower, forcing my eyes open.

"Bailey," he says. "I'm going to help you up now. It's time to go."

His voice is familiar. Even without seeing his face, I know who he is. He was there that night at the pharmacy. *Him.* The one who gave me water when I came to, took me to the bathroom, sent me away. *Sweeper.* "Where is she?" I rasp.

He ignores my question and grabs underneath my arms. I don't struggle... I can't. But I ask again, "Where's Jasmine?"

King's cellphone rings and he glances at the screen before sighing. "I need to take this. Bring her to the van, and I'll meet you up front."

Sweeper nods, and as he drags me to my unsteady feet, I notice a crimson stain on the carpet next to the bed. My pulse kicks up and every terrible thought I tried to keep hidden floods my mind.

Jasmine is hurt. Or worse. Where did they take her?

Sweeper leads me to the bathroom, standing over me as I use the toilet and clean myself up with shaking hands. I'll never be clean though. Not really. Sweeper's quiet and calm, like this is a mundane task for him. Somehow, I almost wish he were angry and rough and mean. I hate him more for offering quiet indifference.

He wraps a threadbare towel over my shoulders and guides me outside. The cool air assaults my skin, waking my tired eyes, but I immediately start shivering and clutching the towel tighter.

He doesn't say another word until we reach the idling van

where Cat already sits waiting, looking just as worn out and broken as I feel. Her eyes dart past me, brows furrowed. I shake my head subtly. *She's not here.*

Her eyes widen in response.

"Get in," Sweeper says to me. His phone rings, so he drops my arm and I have to grip the doorframe to keep steady. He checks the screen and says to the driver, "Take them back... and feed them first. Whatever they want." He reaches into his pocket and shoves a stack of bills at the driver like we're groceries he's paying for.

"Got it, Boss."

Sweeper turns away to answer his phone, but Cat's voice rips through the quiet, sounding raw and desperate. "No, we can't leave. Where is she? Where's Jasmine?"

The driver turns to face us and smiles. If I had the strength to wipe that look from his face, I would. "She's not coming."

Cat summons whatever strength she has left and lunges for him. She screams as her nails dig into his face. "You bastard! What did you do to her?"

"Get off me, you crazy bitch!"

Cat's lost her mind, clawing and scratching, screaming for Jasmine. The driver slams his hand on the horn and a long blast echoes through the empty lot.

Sweeper appears at the van door within seconds, phone still pressed to his ear. Without missing a beat in his conversation, he reaches into his jacket and pulls out a syringe. Cat sees it coming and fights harder, but the driver has her pinned now.

I'm frozen... watching this unfold like it's a movie. It's not real. None of this could be real. I want to help her, but what can I do?

"No, no, please—" she gasps, but Sweeper jabs the needle into her neck. There's not a hint of emotion coming off him as he caps the syringe and fixes his gaze on me. I shake my head, my eyes widening. He must see that I'm done fighting, that I have nothing left to give, so he turns and closes the door.

Within moments, Cat's wild thrashing slows and she sags back against the seat. Her eyes lock onto mine as the drug takes hold. They're dark pools filled with grief and rage and a desperate plea that I can't answer. It kills me.

"Don't you fucking try anything," the driver seethes as he glances at me through the rear view mirror. He shifts the van into reverse and cranks up the music—a pop song that played at Heat the night I was taken. My body trembles and I close my eyes, trying to block it out.

I scoot closer to Cat and take her hand in mine as her eyes gently close and her head comes to rest on my shoulder. "It'll be okay," I whisper, knowing it's a lie. "I've got you."

Jasmine—wherever you are, I hope you're safe. And I'm sorry. I'm so fucking sorry I couldn't help you.

IT'S a rare quiet day in the house. We haven't had one of those in the weeks since Jasmine was taken from us. Cat, Lydia, Elise, and I are sitting together on the floor of the main room watching comedy reruns on the huge flat screen. The one nice piece of "furniture" they have in this house. Yuri keeps pacing in and out of the room, keeping an eye on us, but there's been no sign of King today, or any of the other brutes that usually hang around being loud and obnoxious and leering at us all day.

We were able to shower this morning, and were given pizza this afternoon. If I didn't know better, it's almost like a normal weekend hangout with friends. But I do know better. My stomach's been in knots all day waiting for the other shoe to drop.

I pick at my dried bottom lip until it stings and I taste

blood. With Yuri on a call, pacing the hallway, Lydia nudges me. "How's your head?"

I shared whatever details of the night with the girls as soon as I could when we were dropped back off at the house that night. Lydia, who I learned is the oldest of us at thirty and a mom of two, has been keeping her eye on me and Cat since.

"It's doing okay today, but it hurt like a bitch to wash my hair."

She reaches out a gentle hand and pushes my hair away from my ear to check on the slowly healing lump. If only she saw all the bruises on my body, I'm sure she'd freak out. I know I did when I looked in the mirror the next day.

"Let's still keep an eye on it," she says.

There's so much I want to ask her. All of them, really. We only get short spurts of time together like this and more often than not, someone, if not all of us, are given sedatives. But not today.

"I don't trust him," Cat seethes. "He's being too nice today. They've gotta be planning something for tonight. I fucking know it."

She's probably right, but I don't want to say that out loud.

Elise—who's normally quiet, whether from her natural personality or from being overly sedated, I don't know—drums her fingers on her thigh and suddenly speaks up. "I don't think they are." I turn to her and notice that there's sweat beading on her pale brows even though the room is chilly. It's making her light hair stick to her forehead in damp strands. She wipes it away with a jerky hand. "I overheard Yuri on the phone. Something about laying low for a few days."

Both Cat and Lydia stare at her for an extra beat, until Cat asks, "You feeling alright?"

Elise takes a second to answer, once again pushing her hair off her face. "I'm fine."

Cat narrows her eyes. "When was your last dose? You're fucking shaking."

Lydia, takes her hand and squeezes it. "What can I do to help?"

Elise releases a shuddered breath. "Fuck, I don't know." She pulls from Lydia's grip and cradles her face with her hands. "It's been two days. I need something."

I look to Cat and Lydia and we're all sporting the same expression of helpless concern. Cat, being Cat, gets to her feet. "I'll go say something to Yuri. What's the worst he can do to me?"

Her unspoken words hang in the air. She's already gone through hell. What else is there?

"No," I say, standing up from the floor. "I'll go."

I don't know what propels me to step in. Maybe it's that I've seen how Cat gets under Yuri's skin. Or that I've seen him show the smallest modicum of kindness my way. Whatever it is, I'd rather be the one putting myself out there than see Cat get hurt.

She raises a brow. "You sure? After everything that happened, you're not in the best shape either." Her expression drops, and I know she's thinking about Jasmine just like I am. I straighten my spine.

"I'm sure. Just keep an eye on her." I gesture to a quickly fading Elise.

My feet carry me into the hallway before my brain catches up. The pizza churns in my gut, but that feeling has been almost constant anyway. Yuri's voice carries from the kitchen. He's speaking in Russian, but whoever he's talking to, it doesn't seem like a heated conversation. It's... softer. More familiar.

You've got this. It's just a question. Like Cat said, what's the worst that can happen?

The floor squeaks, alerting him to my presence, and he

spins around, looking me up and down with narrow eyes. He speaks low to whoever he's talking to on the phone before ending the call, slipping his phone into his back pocket and crossing his arms around his chest.

"What are you doing in here?"

My mind goes blank for a moment under his sharp gaze, but I quickly remember Elise and her shaking hands. "It's Elise. She's not feeling well." He lifts his chin to look past me. "She's in the living room. I'm the only one who came to tell you."

He nods slowly. "What would you like me to do about this?"

"She needs a dose... Whatever drugs you all got her hooked on." My voice comes out sharper than I intended it to. "And water... Ice cold water."

Yuri pulls a hand through his thinning hair and laughs low. "*We* got her hooked on?"

I nod. "What else would it be?"

"She brought that problem with her," he says, turning to the sink. He fills a cup with water and starts to hand it to me, then pauses and adds ice from the freezer.

I take the cup, forcing my cold, shaking fingers around the chilled glass. "And the drugs?"

A slow smile spreads across his face. "You've got balls on you. I'll see what I can do. Anything else, *lvitsa?*"

"That's all," I say, having no idea what he just called me. I'm not pressing my luck by asking for anything else.

"Well then, I suggest you get back where you belong before I lose my patience." All hint of amusement is gone from his voice. I nod and hurry back down the hallway to give Elise the water and when Yuri comes in ten minutes later with a full syringe for her, I can't help but smile through the fucked up situation. Whether Elise was an addict before she got here or they got her hooked, I don't care. No one deserves to suffer that way. Plus, I'm sure the drugs are one of the ways King keeps her. That and the armed fucking brutes that watch over us night and day.

"Get your rest," Yuri says, monotone. "You all have a busy night tonight."

My face falls and the words slip out. "But I thought—"

"You thought what, *lvitsa?*" I scramble back from the sharpness of his tone. "At least you won't have to travel." He bends and tilts Elise's flopped over head up. "This one's in no state to go anywhere."

I open my mouth to speak, but Cat reaches for my arm and shakes her head. Yuri clears his throat and leaves again, not bothering to look over his shoulder.

"It's not worth it," Cat says. I'm taken aback by how much she's changed since Jasmine's disappearance. That fight, that spark of life, it's dimmed.

Lydia wipes at her eyes. "I can't fight it. Fuckers have my kids."

My mouth drops open. "They have your kids? Where are they?"

"They don't actually have them, thank God. No. But my sister has them, I think. Still, they'll kill them all if I toe an inch out of line. I'd never risk their lives."

Cat clears her throat. "My abuela and baby brother... they'll kill them too. And Jasmine..."

Her voice catches as she says Jasmine's name. Lydia and I reach for her at the same time, offering whatever comfort we can. With both women in my arms, the thought hits me. What do they know about my family? About Layne... Leon? What if they're watching them too?

CHAPTER NINE

LEON - PRESENT DAY

After giving my old bike a well-needed tune up, I fly down the street, the hum of the engine and wind whipping against my skin temporarily drowning out my exhaustion. I couldn't have rested even if I wanted to, not with Mum badgering me to eat and to get a bit of sun. I'd get more rest on a bench at the tube station than being at home with her. And then there's the message I woke up to from my father's assistant.

> Alfred Colter requests the pleasure of his son's company for dinner. The Savoy, Saturday, 8 PM. Business opportunities to discuss.

No greeting, no asking how I've been—just summoning me like I'm another underling at his beck and call. I should have known it wouldn't take long for him to sniff me out once I landed in London. He has eyes everywhere.

Seated on my bike, riding through these familiar neighborhoods, reminds me how much has changed in the time I've been away. How much I've changed. The last time I rode these streets, I'd just gotten back from holiday with my father. His attempt at bringing me into his world. I wish I could rewind time, and ask myself why. Why did I want his approval? His love? The same love he'd withheld throughout my childhood suddenly dangled before me like bait. After what I saw there, glimpses of the real person he hides from the public eye, I knew he was no father to me. Not even a person I wanted to be acquainted with.

The guys and I have done some depraved shit, but there's a difference. We've never hurt an innocent person. Never gotten off on holding power over another, leveraging lives and trading in human suffering with a smile on our faces.

What I saw that weekend, hidden by a veil of glittery chandeliers, leather sofas, and crystal whiskey glasses, were men who toasted to destroying lives. Rich powerful men with women draped over their laps like throw blankets, their smiles ugly and insides rotten. I watched my father grip the shoulder of a younger business man, whispering something in his ear that made his face drop. Then saw that same man on the news not even three days later. He killed himself. And that's only one instance, not including the pressure put on me those three days.

Alfred Colter may be a foreign secretary who could secure me a life of wealth and power, but if that life would turn me into a man like him, then I'd rather die. Mum and I had next to nothing most of my life. I watched her work two jobs to keep me fed and clothed while he flaunted his wealth across London. I wasn't good enough for him then, so why should I let him in now?

I hit reply to his message, stared at the blank screen, and after ten minutes, left it unanswered. I need to think on it. When Falin uttered the word London last month, I had a feeling I'd need to go to him for help, but it's tearing me up inside. On one hand, perhaps there's value in making a deal with the devil, especially when I'm hunting for answers about Bailey. If there's even a chance he knows something, I need to find out.

I park a short distance away from the address Cruz gave me this morning. He was right about this charity being in a posh area. I should have thought harder about dressing the part before coming here. Smoothing out my pants, and pulling my hand over my hair to combat the dent my old helmet surely gave me on the ride over, I open up the message on my phone again. Before I can over think it, I respond that I'll be there.

It's odd to have that be the only message in my texting app. The group chat is surprisingly quiet. Maybe they started a different chat without me in it? Why would I need to read about Jasper playing his guitar too loudly, or Damon using all the milk? Still, my chest aches slightly at the thought that they're going on without me, even if it was my choice to come here alone.

It's no matter. Right now, I have other things to worry about. Squaring my shoulders, I make my way to the building, and find the office in question on the fourth floor. *Legacy Global Outreach.* There's very little information about the organization online, but that won't stop me from digging in more later. If it has connections to Orlov or The Brotherhood, I'll find out.

The space looks expensive with its minimalistic furniture in muted tones, floor to ceiling windows overlooking the Thames, and reception desk that looks more like a piece of art.

The receptionist, a young woman about my age, openly gawks at my appearance before blinking up at me. "Do you have an appointment?"

"Hello." I smile, and step closer to the desk. Color tints her ears. "I do, but forgive me, I seem to have forgotten the name of the associate I'm meeting with. My assistant scheduled this meeting months ago, and I'm afraid I'm terribly absent-minded."

She laughs and that flush creeps along her cheeks. "It's no problem. What's your name?"

I stumble, but only for a moment as the alias I'd recently used slips out. "Randy. Randy McAllister."

Her mouth sets into a straight line while she types. I try to keep my eyes from darting around the room. Lying is always difficult for me.

"I'm sorry, Randy, I'm not seeing your name on Ms. Bowman's schedule. Perhaps there's a mistake?"

"I hate to be a bother, but before I open my wallet, I like to have a face to face sit down. Especially when it comes to the large amount I'm planning on contributing. Would you mind seeing if she's available to meet with me?"

At the mention of money, her demeanor shifts. Her back straightens and her voice drops to a more professional tone.

"One moment, please." She picks up her phone to make a call while I pretend to admire a painting and the river view. I'm actually checking for cameras in the obvious places. After a few moments, she hits the end button. "She must be on another call. I'll just slip back there and check."

"Thank you," I say, forcing a wide smile.

The moment she's out of range, I dash behind her desk and snap photos of everything I can see. Notes jotted on Post-its, open windows on her computer, email lists. There's not enough time to do much more than this. As the clacking of her heels on the polished marble floor get closer, I take one last photo of Ms. Bowman's digital calendar. A name stands out to me as if it's written in bold, twenty-five point font.

Ivan.

It could be a coincidence. There must be hundreds of thousands of Ivan's in the world. But my gut is telling me that *this* Ivan is the one I'm after.

I tuck my phone in my pocket and hurry back to where I stood before just in time for the receptionist to get back. She smiles at me, but this time it doesn't reach her eyes and there's nothing but forced cheer in her tone. "I'm sorry, Mr. McAllister, but Ms. Bowman is unavailable today. Shall I make you an appointment for another day?"

"Yes, please. Her soonest available," I reply, looking her over. "I'm sorry if this is forward, but are you okay? It's just that you seem upset now and I'll never forgive myself if I'm the cause of your bad day."

Her eyes briefly leave the screen and meet mine, and for a flash I see genuine hurt in them. "I'm fine, thank you for asking."

The receptionist turns back to her computer, smoothing her features into a practiced version of herself. It doesn't take much to see that she's being treated unwell here. "Ms. Bowman has an opening next Thursday at 2 PM."

"Perfect," I say, leaning casually against her desk. *Think.* What would Damon or Jasper do in this situation? I notice the tension in her shoulders, and the way her eyes narrow as she inputs my name into the schedule. I need to learn more. "I didn't catch your name."

"Emma," she answers, keeping her eyes on the screen.

"Emma," I repeat, softening my voice. "I hope I haven't caused any trouble. You seemed quite cheerful before you went to check on your boss." She glances up at me as I add, "I know you said you were fine, but you don't seem so."

She turns her head toward the hallway where she came from, then back to me. "It's nothing. Just a busy day."

I take a calculated risk and layer on some Jasper charm.

"Did you get reprimanded for trying to help me? That hardly seems fair."

Her eyes widen slightly, like we're in on a secret, before she catches herself. "I—No, it's not like that."

I give her a kind smile, the one that most people don't expect from me. Not how Jasper smiles and makes women drop their knickers, but my own version—honest, with just a hint of vulnerability. "Look, I'm sorry if I got you in trouble. Maybe I can make it up to you? Coffee sometime? I promise not to talk about charitable donations."

I can tell I've snagged her as a genuine smile brightens her face. "Ms. Bowman can be... intense."

"Intense sounds like a polite way of putting it," I say, lowering my voice.

Emma glances around before leaning closer. "She's not always like this. I don't want this to sway you from donating. It's just—She's under a lot of pressure herself. Especially when they come in."

"They?" I keep my tone casual, all the while the name Ivan flashes through my mind like a neon light.

"Her bosses," Emma says quietly. "I make sure to take my lunch hour when they're scheduled for meetings. The way they look at me... it's like I'm not even human."

My body reacts like I'm seconds away from cracking into a protected system. Pulse quickening, muscles tensing. I keep my tone friendly. "Sounds like proper arseholes."

"They are," she agrees. "Last time they were here, one of them—the older one with the accent—he undressed me with his eyes and asked Ms. Bowman if I was available after hours. Luckily, she had my back, but she reprimanded me after they left. Said I was dressed too provocatively."

I force myself to breathe normally. In through my nose, out

through my mouth. "Do these charming gentlemen have names? Just so I know who to avoid if I become a donor."

Emma hesitates. I can almost see her mind battling with itself. "I probably shouldn't..."

"Of course, I understand," I say, stepping back from the desk. "Professional discretion and all that. It's important."

She seems to appreciate that I'm not pushing, and continues. "The main one is Russian, I think. Mr. Orlov. He practically owns this place, even though his name isn't on any of the paperwork. And then there's that diplomat who comes with him sometimes. Very posh, very cold."

My mouth goes dry. "Diplomat?"

"I think so. Colter, I believe. They had me book dinner reservations for them once. Some Michelin-rated place. Like I said, very posh."

My stomach drops to the ground floor. My father. My fucking father is working with Orlov. The room seems to tilt, and I grip the edge of her desk to steady myself.

"Are you alright?" Emma asks.

"Fine," I manage. "Just remembered I'm late for another appointment." I straighten, forcing myself to keep it together. "Thank you for your help, Emma. I'll see you next Thursday."

I back away, nearly colliding with a potted plant. My mind races as I try to make sense of this new information. The dinner Saturday, is it a trap? Does my father know why I'm in London? Does he know about Bailey? How involved is he in all this?

I grab my phone with trembling hands as the lift arrives. I should update the group chat, but my mind is jumbled. Instead, I slide it back in my pocket. I need to take a ride and decide if I want to change my RSVP.

Saturday will be here before I know it. Do I want to face

down the devil I know? Or stay far fucking away from Alfred
Colter?

BAILEY - JUNE 5TH

 Shit, I fell asleep with my pen in hand last time I wrote in here.

 Whoops.

 Must be a theme since I fell asleep on the couch last night. Maybe I was waiting up to catch a glimpse of Leon when the guys got home... Okay, I definitely was.

 Putting on Scream for the hundredth time wasn't a good idea though. I was knocked out seconds after Ghostface tells Casey he wants to play a game. Next thing I know, I woke up this morning, covered in Mom's throw blanket which was in the storage ottoman, the TV turned off, and curtains drawn.

 It could have been anyone in the house. But Mom and Dad were already in bed watching Law and Order when I started my movie and I know Jasper and

Damon aren't usually that considerate. Nothing bad but they're in their own world.

It had to have been Leon.

I'm thinking about saying something to him. Except, I have no idea how to bring it up. He's not like any of the guys I've talked to and that scares me more than I'd ever admit to anyone.

I wish I had someone to go to for advice, but all my friends are busy doing amazing things this summer. Chloe is backpacking through Europe with her family. Rachel is road-tripping across the country to go to her cousin's wedding in California. And anyone else is either happily coupled or we're not close enough to talk guy stuff with. They don't need me to bother them.

Which is probably why I've been using this journal like a lovesick eleven-year-old with a crush. It's helping though... getting my thoughts on paper.

I guess I'll write again if I ever get up the nerve to really talk to him.

CHAPTER TEN

BAILEY - BEFORE

SHRIVELED LEAVES CRUNCH BENEATH MY FEET AS I RUN faster than I'd thought possible. Arms pumping, I sprint, weaving through tree trunks, and for the first time in forever, I feel alive. My chest heaves but I manage to suck in enough air to keep going—clean air, forest air, free air. I'm so close. The road is right there... if only I can run faster.

My limbs feel lighter than ever before, like I could float away from all this. Or maybe that's just the knowledge that I've finally escaped. Only a few more feet and I'll be free. I can hug Mom and Dad... Jasper. Damon. Leon. If he'll still have me once he finds out what they did to me. How they used me.

Dawn creeps through the canopy, painting everything golden. Almost there.

Almost—

"Bailey!"

My name slices through the morning air like a blade. I whip my head around, stumbling. No. No. No. I'm so close. That voice—it follows me even into sleep. King's voice.

"You can't get away from me, pet! I own you!"

When I turn back, the trees have moved. Impossibly and silently, they've shifted closer, their branches reaching for me like twisted fingers. The golden dawn light dies, swallowed by shadows that seem to breathe.

"Bailey, I'm here. Run to me!"

It's Leon's voice that drifts through the darkness now, so close I could almost touch him.

Two voices... one of my dreams and one of my nightmares.

I reach toward his familiar cadence, trying to show him where I am. That I'm so close. But bark bites into my palms. The trees have become a cage, the branches weaving tighter as I desperately push against them. I writhe free, the sound of his voice giving me strength even with needle-sharp limbs piercing my skin, and warm blood dripping down my arms.

"Leon!" I scream from deep within my chest, but it's no more than a whisper. "I'm right here. Can't you see me?"

He's calling my name, over and over, but I can't reach him. I can never reach him. I can't help the hot tears that stream down my cheeks.

The branches wrap around me like coarse, skin-tearing rope, like gnarled hands, squeezing and choking until there's nothing left but King's laughter echoing against my lifeless, blood-streaked body.

"I own you. I will always own you."

My eyes snap open to darkness. Real darkness. Familiar darkness. I hold my hands up, checking for scratches, but of course, there's nothing there but my dry, chafing knuckles. Just another dream. But it felt so real... and Leon, his voice was so close.

Could it mean he's searching for me? It's silly to hope at this point. It's been so long now. But imagining that they've given up on me—my family, my friends... him. It's too painful to bear.

Cat snores softly in the bed beside me, anchoring me back to the present. We've been allowed to share a room. A small comfort since they brought us to this new house.

Hours go by while I toss and turn, picturing that dark wood. When the morning sun shines through the dirty glass, I finally get up, and pad to the window as quietly as I can.

The trees must span miles. Bare like dark spines crowding the vast landscape. I'm grateful for the view anyway. It's something external to focus on in this nightmare.

We've been in this house for a few months now. Or at least I think. I haven't been able to keep track of time as much as I'd like. After the last party, Yuri and a few of his guys moved us here. Cat heard whispers about a suspicious neighbor tipping off the cops, but that could have been wishful thinking. Though I swear I saw the same dark sedan parked across the street three times the week before we were moved. The windows were tinted, but there had to be a person sitting inside—watching, waiting.

I knew from the start that first house was somewhere to keep us short-term. I guess I never thought about what would happen next beyond my small hope that I'd be able to escape... or be rescued.

Besides being allowed to share a room with Cat, it's been quieter here. We haven't had any visitors since we moved. And King hasn't shown up. A reprieve I don't trust. My stomach churns, remembering his cruel voice in my dream. His body hovering over me. His vicious touch. I keep waiting for the moment he'll walk through the door. His heavy footsteps announcing his arrival before that suffocating cloud of expensive cologne fills the room.

I'm always listening for those footsteps, always dreading the moment his scent invades my nostrils again, sharp and nauseating and wrong. I know Cat feels it too... We all do.

The dread of what's to come. The sliver of hope that still remains.

The mattress creaks and Cat groans. "Jesus, B, it's barely dawn."

"Sorry! I couldn't sleep." I cross the room and flop back on the bed beside her. "Don't be mad at me."

"Mad? Nah." She rolls to her side and stretches her legs. Her dark tangled hair partially covers her face. "I thought I heard you talking in your sleep earlier. Whimpering, maybe." Her voice gets softer. "Was it about him?"

"I don't want to talk about it."

She doesn't push, only nods. That's something I've grown to like about Cat and the others. They don't pry.

I slip out to use the bathroom down the hall, and when I get back, she's crouched by the bed, one hand shoved under the mattress. The door hinge gives me away with its jarring creak, and she yanks her hand back like it was bit.

"Checking your stash of crushed crackers and granola bars again?"

"And cash," she says, standing and brushing off her knees. "Don't forget that little detail." She heads for the door, probably to take her turn in the bathroom. "And keep your damn voice down about it. They find my shit and I'll have to kill you." She pauses at the doorway, glancing back with a smile. "And I'm starting to like your annoying ass."

I smirk and mime zipping my lips as she closes the door. She hasn't shared exactly how much cash she has stashed under the mattress, just that she ramped up her scavenging after Jasmine was taken. Dropped coins "forgotten" on the kitchen floor, a few bills slipped from "visitors" wallets while they were distracted—she even managed to snag a twenty from one of Yuri's new guys, Erik. What she had to do to get that twenty, she wouldn't tell me, but I'm assuming it didn't come easy.

The floorboards in the hallway groan under someone's footsteps, so I crouch on the side of the bed, holding my breath. There's a small knock before the door swings open, revealing a half asleep Lydia and Elise. I release a breath.

"Erik came in our room a few minutes ago, requesting a pancake breakfast. What the hell are we? His personal housewives?" Lydia yawns as she perches on the edge of the bed. "Why are you on the floor?"

Elise does a sideways flop next to her and scoots up to the head of the bed, wrapping herself in the blanket Cat and I share. She rubs her eyes and adds, "Could be worse."

"You're right. He could have asked for eggs Benedict or some shit." I can't help but snort. She picks at her nails, the three of us quiet for a few minutes. "Imagine us on some reality show—the real housewives of Shitville. Pancake breakfasts by day, tied up and fucked by night. We'd be celebrities."

Elise lets out a dry laugh. "What are you smoking this morning?"

"Nothing. That's the problem." She huffs and lays on her back. "Where's Cat?"

"Bathroom," I say. "She should be right back."

But if Erik is awake, who knows how quickly that could change.

Lydia seems to be reading my mind. "Speaking of Erik, he seems to really like Cat."

"And I think she knows it too," Elise adds.

I join them on the bed, careful to avoid Cat's snack stash. I've picked up on the way Erik seems to favor her, but I'm curious what the others have seen. "Why do you say that?"

Lydia raises a thin brow and holds up her palm. "One, he's always staring at her, and not like the others stare, like they're thinking of all the nasty shit they want to do. He's got those obsessed heart eyes. Of course the moment she glances his way, he's back to the swaggering tough guy act. Two—" She holds up another finger. "—he brings her little things. Extra food, cigarettes, even gave her that hair tie she's always wearing. And three—" A third finger joins the count. "—yesterday I saw him slip her something when he thought no one was looking. Money, maybe? Or a note?" She shrugs. "Either way, it's dangerous. For both of them."

She's notices so much more than me, but that's not surprising. Lydia still has the eagle eyes of a mom, even though she's been away from her kids for almost a year. That kind of superpower never leaves. I remember my own mom being the same way.

Elise blinks at her, and says through a yawn, "Shit."

"What?" Lydia asks.

"I never noticed all that."

Lydia gives her arm a caring squeeze. "That's why you have me."

"Maybe we should get dressed, see about this pancake situation," I say. "Cat can't still be in the bathroom. I bet she's already downstairs."

Lydia smirks. "See? Told you."

"You don't think she actually likes him, do you?" Elise asks on her way out the door. "He still works for *them*."

I shrug, genuinely unsure. I never would have thought Layne would stay with her cheating bastard of a boyfriend, and I've witnessed so many other friends make questionable choices in partners. "She hasn't said anything to me, but I'll ask her when lwe're alone."

"Good," is all Lydia says as she heads out into the hallway to get dressed. She's not the only one who's had a keen eye on Cat these last few weeks. I've noticed the changes in her too. I'll find out what's going on tonight... Hopefully she'll be in the mood to talk.

I dress in a pair of sweatpants and a T-shirt, both hand-me-downs with someone else's scratched out name in Sharpie on the tag. The elastic waistband is stretched and threads fraying, but I'm grateful for the warmth. Other than a few secondhand pieces, all we've been given is cheap lingerie that grates against my skin.

I pad barefoot down the stairs, stopping when I hear murmured voices coming from the kitchen.

"When?"

It's Cat's voice. There's no mistaking the plea in her tone.

"I told you, be patient," a male voice answers. Erik, most likely.

I listen for the others—Yuri's accented inflection, the abrasive chatter of his lackeys, and of course, I listen for King. I'd rather expect him to be there and prepare for the worst, than the alternative. There's only the two quiet voices though, so I roll my lip between my teeth and try to make myself heard as I cross the threshold into the kitchen.

"B." Cat quickly steps away from Erik. "I didn't hear you coming downstairs."

Erik nods at me, messing with the baseball cap on his head.

"I heard something about pancakes?" I ask tentatively and Cat raises a brow. "Lydia said."

I start to explain as Erik crosses the kitchen and pulls a box of mix out of the cabinet. "Just add water," he says.

I'm struck by how fucking bizarre this whole morning has been, but pancakes are pancakes. I'll take them while I can.

Lydia and Elise join us a few minutes later, the former taking over my batter mixing and tutting at the too thin concoction, whispering that her granny would roll over in her grave if she saw her using a premade mix.

Soon the smell of sizzling pancakes fills the space. Erik stays quiet at the table, watching us work in the kitchen, directing me where to find the artificial syrup, another thing that makes Lydia clutch her chest. I spy him sneaking glances at Cat every few seconds though, and I'd bet money if I had any that she knows exactly what he's doing.

At the first bite of warm, syrup-drenched pancake, I close my eyes and chew, savoring the flavor. Even made with lumpy box mix, they taste better than anything I've eaten in weeks.

I can almost imagine mom in the kitchen on Sunday mornings, her huge electric griddle spitting as she pours homemade pancake batter onto it, perfectly circular. Bacon sizzling in a frying pan on the stove, getting extra crispy, how we all like it. She chugs coffee with French vanilla creamer out of her Snoopy mug, grumbling that she can't wait until Mother's Day, when she can be the one getting served breakfast.

I'd serve her a million pancakes in bed if it meant I'd get to see her again.

Before I know it, I've cleared my plate and chugged my entire glass of water. When I look up, I notice Erik staring at me. He rubs his stubbled chin and asks, "What's your deal?"

I glance side to side where Cat, Lydia, and Elise have gone quiet before responding. "What do you mean?"

He leans his forearms on the table, tilting his head as if it'll help him get a better look at me. He points to Lydia. "She's the mom." Then Elise. "Junkie." And finally to Cat. "And what is it that he calls you? The mouthy one?" He smirks as Cat glares at him. "What's your whole thing?"

"She's the newbie," Cat says through a mouthful of pancake.

"Nah," Erik says. "Not anymore, from what I've been told."

"What have you been told?" I ask, although I'm not sure I want to know.

He shrugs and scrapes his fork along the edge of his plate. "Enough."

When he doesn't elaborate, I tuck a piece of hair behind my ear and shrug. "I'm nothing special. Just a girl... A girl who wants to go home."

My words seem to break whatever happy illusion bubble we were momentarily visiting. Erik's eyes narrow as he says, "Well, 'just a girl,' I hate to be the one to tell you, but you're never going home. Not after what I found out this morning."

The pancakes sit heavy in my gut.

"The fuck does that mean?" Cat asks, her voice sharp. She looks taken aback, betrayed.

"I shouldn't have opened my big fucking mouth." He shoves back from the table and knocks his fist against it... Not hard, but enough to get our attention. "If Yuri asks, you didn't fucking hear anything from me. Got it?"

His eyes are locked onto Cat's, but it's me who nods, barely whispering, "Got it."

Erik hurries from the room like his ass is on fire, leaving the four of us staring at each other in stunned silence. The warm, syrupy comfort of moments before has evaporated, replaced by the cold reality that whatever temporary reprieve we'd found in pancakes and morning chatter was just that—temporary.

Cat's fork clatters against her plate. "What the hell was that about?"

But I already know. Deep in my bones, I know. Whatever Erik found out this morning, whatever made him look at me like I'm already a ghost, it's bad. Really bad.

Lydia clears her throat. "I'll do the dishes."

CHAPTER ELEVEN

LEON - PRESENT DAY

THE RIDE BACK TO MUM'S THAT EVENING FEELS SURREAL. While I weave through traffic, my mind whirls with this new information. I knew my father was a grade-A bastard, but working closely with Orlov?

What the fuck?

As I pass by familiar landmarks, memories spring up like corpses that won't stay buried, their skeletal hands reaching for me. There's the park where Mum would push me on the swings while we waited for him to show. My fragile heart full of hope as she pushed me higher and higher, chattering on about clouds in the shape of animals, or what new movie was playing at the cinema. I'd barely listen, too busy checking the gate every few minutes, certain this time would be different. This time he'd show, and I'd tell him all about my high marks in school. He'd smile down at me, finally proud.

Years of rejection became nothing but a hollow ache in my chest. He never showed and I finally stopped waiting.

I idle at a light in front of the corner shop where Mum used to buy me sweets after we waited long enough. We could never afford it, but she couldn't bear to see me upset. She'd skip meals if it meant spending that extra money brought a smile to my face.

I'd get to pick whatever I wanted, even the sticky taffy that would rot my teeth or the fancy chocolate bars in the foil wrapping, and we'd sit on the bench outside sharing them while she told me that some people just didn't know how to love properly, but that didn't mean I wasn't worth loving. She'd pull me into her side and stroke my hair while I let myself cry over a man who was never worth a single tear.

I was lucky to have Mum, and Nana, and Pops. They were my rocks in a childhood marked by disappointment and broken promises. They picked up the pieces, assuring that his absence had nothing to do with me, even when I was convinced otherwise. What kind of father looks at his son and decides he's not worth the effort?

Now I know the answer to that question. The kind who associates himself with someone like Orlov.

I park the bike with shaking hands. Without the hum of the engine, my thoughts grow louder, more demanding, and my jaw clenches to the point of pain. The receptionist's words replay on loop. *"Mr. Orlov... and that diplomat who comes with him sometimes. Very posh, very cold... Colter."*

Mum greets me at the door before I can reach for my keys. Her face lights up when she sees me, but as I step inside, her smile drops.

"What's wrong, love? You don't look well."

I want to unload, to tell her everything. About Bailey, about what Alfred's involved in, about the hell I've been living in for the past year and a half. Instead, I let her wrap me in one of her fierce hugs. I can't put my burdens on her, she's gone through enough, and for reasons I can't understand, she still holds Alfred on a pedestal, even after all this time.

"I'm fine. Just a long day, is all," I murmur into her shoulder, breathing the familiar scent of her rose hair oil.

She pulls back to study my face. Mine is a mirror of hers, full lips, down-turned like a reverse bow, identical noses, straight with a subtle upturn at the tip, dark expressive brows, prominent cheekbones. The only exception are my eyes. Those I inherited from *him*. "Tea?"

"Please," I say.

I put my helmet away, grab my sketchpad and pencil from the small black backpack I carry on me at all times, and follow Mum into the kitchen. She goes about her ritual, filling the kettle, setting tea bags into mugs, arranging biscuits on the handprint plate I painted in primary. The normalcy of it warms my chest. This is the sort of thing I've missed. The same type of thing Bailey had with her family before she was ripped away.

"So," Mum says, settling across from me at the small table, "tell me about this business that brought you home."

I can't help but chuckle despite my dark mood. "You're almost as nosey as Nana and Pops."

"Well, I learned from the best," she muses.

I flip to a blank page in my sketchbook, and without a conscious thought, start sketching Bailey's eyes. Mum bites into a biscuit, keeping her gaze trained on my downcast face. I don't want to drag her into this, but I know I need to give her something or I won't hear the end of it.

"There's someone," I say quietly, focusing on the curve of Bailey's cheekbone coming to life. "Someone important to me who's... missing."

Through my periphery, I see her hand pause halfway to her mouth before she calmly places her half-eaten biscuit back on the plate. I force myself to look up from the sketch, needing to gauge her reaction.

Her face has gone still, her lips pressed into a tight crescent.

I remember that expression from childhood, the same one she'd wear when I'd get home late without calling, a split lip and bruises adorning my face.

"Missing? What happened?" she finally asks.

"She was taken. I've been trying to find her for over a year now." I avoid the harsh reality—words like trafficked, kidnapped, sold. Even letting them float around my mind has me clenching my pencil.

I add more details to my sketch, the scattering of freckles along the bridge of her nose, the hint of a scar on her chin from where she tripped on a rock when she was seven, the way her eyes narrow slightly when she's deep in thought. Mum watches me draw, until her touch stops my hand in motion.

"You love her."

Not a question. She knows me better. I swallow hard.

"More than anything."

Admitting my feelings aloud to someone important feels like releasing myself from a cage. Like busting free into a full blown sprint and running and running until my limbs explode. I've been holding it in for so long, I almost forgot I was in a cage of my own making.

"Oh, son," Mum croons.

I force myself to focus on my drawing, because I know if I were to look into her eyes, I'd see sadness there, and I can't let myself break. I add shading to Bailey's hair, remembering how soft it felt between my fingers.

Now that I've thrown open those cage doors, I can't stop the words from spilling out. "She's Jasper's sister, Mum. My best mate's little sister, and I failed her. She texted me the night she was taken, and I didn't answer. I was in some stupid study group when I could have—"

"Leon," she cuts in. "Stop. Look at me."

I drop my pencil and hide my face in my hands. She pries

them free, one finger at a time, giving me no choice but to meet her gaze.

"It's not your fault."

I shake my head. She doesn't know. Doesn't understand. "How can you say that? If I'd answered her text, if I'd gone to meet her—"

"You don't know that. Whoever took her could have hurt you or worse. You cannot carry this burden."

She pushes the steaming cup of tea in front of me. Instead of arguing, I sip and go back to my drawing. I want to believe her, but I can't. I won't. I know I could have prevented her from being taken. There's no guesswork to it.

"What's her name?" Mum asks gently.

"Bailey." Saying it aloud makes my skin tingle, my stomach flip. "Bailey Shea."

"She's beautiful."

I take in the nearly finished sketch. Even in pencil, even from memory, Bailey's warmth comes through. "She is. Inside and out. She was studying to be a teacher, wanted to help kids learn how to read. She bakes when she's stressed and loves to joke around, especially with her brother. She's fierce, but not afraid to be vulnerable, kind and unselfish, and so damn brilliant, and she's been trapped in hell for eighteen months because I wasn't there when she needed me."

Mum is quiet, studying both me and the drawing. "And this business in London? It's about finding her?"

"The trail led here. To people with connections..." I hesitate, then decide she can handle a version of the truth. I've told her this much already. "To powerful people," I continue. "People who can make others disappear."

"Dangerous people?"

"Yes."

She sips her tea, her hand shaking slightly. I hope she's

putting the pieces together, because I don't want to outright tell her much more. She's wise, knows how to read the spaces between my words more than most. I never told her why I suddenly transferred universities and left home. Why I haven't come back since. But I'm sure she has an idea.

"You can't do this alone," she says finally.

"I know." I close the sketchbook and reach for my phone. "That's why I need to make some calls."

I hug Mum again, thank her for the tea and the chat, and head up the staircase to my bedroom. I want to analyze all the information I gathered at the global outreach office. It's not much, but maybe it'll offer another important detail, preferably about Orlov's connection to my father. But first, I flop onto the bed and call Damon. It's time I update him and the others on everything I found today.

He answers on the first ring.

"What'd you find out?"

I laugh and shake my head. Just like Damon to get straight to the point. "What if I was just calling to say hi?"

"Then I'd have to fly there tonight and take you to get your head examined."

"Ouch," I say. "You act as if I don't like a friendly chat now and again."

"I call bullshit. What's going on? Should I get everyone? Put it on speaker?"

I think on it. This is going to be a difficult conversation—telling them what I've discovered about my father, possibly revealing pieces of my past I should have shared with them long ago. I draw in a deep breath and release it in one long, steadying stream.

"Yeah, if they're available they should hear this." I owe it to them to open up. After letting Mum in and feeling that weight off my back, I'm surprised how ready I am to unburden myself with more. Not everything, some ghosts aren't ready to fly free. I only hope they don't hate me for holding on.

"Jas and Falin just got home. Blake's here with me." The phone switches to speaker and I hear Blake's cheerful voice say hi. She asks me how I'm doing, making idle small talk until I hear the rest of their voices come through.

"Lee!" Jasper booms. "How's tea land? Eat any beans on toast today? Ow—"

"I just smacked him," Falin deadpans. "We miss you. Tell us what's going on."

"Wait," Jasper says. "Do I need to be holding a kitten for this conversation? You know... for emotional support."

"Ignore him," Damon says. I can picture the exact exasperated look he has on his face.

"Alright, so long story... well, actually... not really." I sigh and run a hand down my face, twisting my lip ring. "Let me start over. In short, I found out that Orlov's working with someone important here in London. A diplomat."

"That can't be good," Blake says softly.

"A diplomat?" Falin asks. "Isn't your father—"

Leave it to her to immediately pick up on that correlation.

"Yes," I admit. "Orlov is somehow connected to my father." There's only silence on the other end of the phone. I inhale a cleansing breath, and go on. "I had no idea, of course."

"Obviously," Damon says.

"But... I should have known."

"How is that?" Falin drops her tone. "I mean, you've known your father is a pretentious dickhead who treats you like shit... but how the hell does that equate to him being involved in illegal activities?"

"Before I transferred universities and moved to America, he was taking more of an interest in me. In my life, in my education. He'd heard about my tech skills, and was particularly interested in learning more. At first a small part of me was... I don't know... happy to finally be getting attention from the man that refused to acknowledge me for my entire life. It was almost like the moment I turned eighteen, he decided it was time to be a father figure. He wanted to parade me around to his colleagues. Still does."

I take a breath, gearing up for the difficult part of the story.

"I agreed to a weekend away. Networking, he called it. There was a part of me that considered seeing what his influence could do for my career, my future. The entire week prior to leaving, my gut was screaming at me to cancel. But I forced myself to go. Mum was ecstatic... I was finally connecting with the man she once loved. The man that tossed her aside like yesterday's rubbish."

"Jesus, Lee, that's some heavy shit," Damon says when I stop to loose a breath.

"Yeah, with Mum, that's a whole other story," I tell them.

"Go on," Falin says. "Tell us what happened."

I close my eyes and remember details. "He brought me to some mansion in London. It was fucking massive. Alfred even chose the suits I wore... bought and tailored them for me. Dozens of men showed up. All these old money types—politicians, diplomats, businessmen. At first it seemed normal enough. Expensive booze, cigars, talking about deals and shit. But something felt off with each passing hour."

I pause, running my hand through my hair. "The women serving drinks... they were young, barely my age. They seemed almost afraid to speak. Alfred told me they were paid escorts, which I thought was scummy enough of those old bastards, but who am I to shame sex workers."

"By the second night, the men started getting more direct with me. This guy, I don't even remember his name, kept cornering me. Pushing drinks on me, going on about how boys become men and I need to embrace my birthright. Real creepy shit."

"Sounds fucking weird," Jasper's voice cuts through, all traces of his goofy side gone.

"They all kept telling me how lucky I was to be his son. How I had potential but needed to broaden my horizons. Stop being so naive about how the world works. Accept Alfred's guidance. They were frothing at the mouth to learn more about my hacking skills too."

I shift on the bed, bouncing my restless leg. "One of them, some politician with a ridiculous title, kept going on about how young men today are too soft. That my generation doesn't understand what real power looks like. He said Alfred was trying to educate me properly and I should be grateful."

"Fucking dicks," Damon mutters.

"Yeah. And Alfred just sat there nodding and smiling along like they were giving me some kind of gift. The whole weekend felt like an initiation I never asked for. Like they were all waiting for me to prove I belonged in their little club by doing something that would fuck me up forever."

I pause, remembering the look of disappointment on Alfred's face when I kept refusing their offers. "They made it clear that refusal meant walking away from everything. My father's support, his connections, any future in their world. And honestly? It was the easiest decision I ever made. I just wish I would have realized their connection to Bailey. I've tried to block that weekend from my mind."

"Don't do that to yourself," Blake says. "All of that went on in a completely different country, years ago. How would you know it was anything more than a creepy networking weekend?"

I try to let her words seep into my skin but there's a barrier shoving the words back into the open air, my entire being yelling that she's wrong. I was naive. "But the signs—"

"Which could mean a dozen different things to rich assholes," Falin interrupts. "You were young and being manipulated by your own father. Don't blame yourself for not seeing through something that twisted."

Jasper's voice chimes in, quieter than usual. "It sounds like they were grooming you. Trying to get you involved so you'd be complicit. So they could use you."

"Yeah," I agree. "And when I refused, Alfred went cold. He never gave up entirely, but he saw me leaving as a personal affront." I hesitate, but then add, "He knows I'm here. I got an invitation to have dinner with him this weekend."

"Fuck that," Damon says. "Don't go anywhere near him."

"Actually... I think I might have to."

"What if he has Orlov with him? What if they've caught on to your involvement in his massive loss of money... or of his nephew's death? It's too risky," Blake says.

"Yeah, from what you just told us, it sounds like he's involved with those Brotherhood pieces of shit," Jasper adds.

"I hear you... but he may know something about Bailey. If there's any chance, I have to go. I'll feel him out, play into exactly what he wants from me."

"Jasper's right, it's too dangerous," Falin argues. "What if he's trying to trap you?"

"It's at a fancy restaurant. There'll be people everywhere. I won't give him the chance."

"But—" Falin continues.

"Everything we do is dangerous," I point out. "But this... looking him in the eye and feeling him out... it might be our best shot at getting in. I know how to handle Alfred. I've been doing it my whole life."

There's a long pause where I hear shuffling and murmured

whispers, then Jasper speaks up. "We're not letting you do this alone."

Do I want them to come here already? Drag them into this mess when it could be a false alarm?

"I'm not—"

"Brother, you're not winning this fight," Damon says frankly. "We're coming there."

I fuck around with my lip ring, half of me relieved they want to come, the other half terrified to put them in danger. "Fine, but I need time to prepare first. Get my head right, reconnect with some old contacts."

"What kind of contacts?" Falin asks.

"The kind that can supply me with certain *things* I couldn't pack in my luggage. But also..." I pause, thinking about The Irons, about the rage I feel bursting at the seams. "I need to get myself ready mentally. Work through some shit."

"How long?" Jasper asks.

"A few days. I'll check into other leads, deal with some personal shit... Fly out Friday?" I ask. "The dinner's not until Saturday."

"That'll work," Damon says. "Gives us time to book flights and get organized."

"Promise you'll be safe until we get there," Blake says.

"Uhh," Damon cuts in. "You and Falin should stay here. Take care of the cats, do more research on the shit Leon's found so far."

I hold back a chuckle because I can just picture the death glares he's receiving. And three... two... one... an argument breaks out. I can barely hear who's saying what.

"Hey." I try to make myself heard to no avail. "Hello!"

"How dare you?"

"Why wouldn't we go?"

"It's not safe."

"Oh my fucking God, that shit again!"

"You're the one who's gotten shot twice!"

"Hey, I didn't say anything!"

I groan, and try one more time. "FUCK'S SAKE!"

Quiet, finally.

"I'm hanging up now. Whatever you decide, just let me know. As much as Mum would love to have you all, we'd be like a tin of sardines in here. I'd need to find somewhere else for us to stay."

"Don't worry," Blake seethes. "When Fal and I get our way, we'll book a place big enough. You have enough on your plate."

"And pet friendly," Falin says.

"Text us regular updates," Damon demands. "And if anything feels off—"

"Yeah, don't worry, I'll be fine."

We say our goodbyes, but they go back to bickering before I can hit end. Some things I do not miss.

I open up my text thread with Bailey, reading it over until my eyes droop. I've got a few days to prepare, and I need to make them count.

Poor Leon. He's officially been initiated into the family. Mom made her famous buffalo wings for Dad's birthday dinner tonight. Leon was being so polite, kept thanking her and taking these huge bites while Jasper and Damon (who know better) were loading up on milk and bread.

Mom's wings are basically weapons of mass destruction. I can only get through one or two before I know I'll pay for it all night. She adds ghost peppers, habaneros, the works. Dad's the only one who can actually handle them.

Leon made it through about three wings before he was taking weird breaths and sweat started pouring down his forehead. He excused himself to the bathroom, and we all knew... those wings hit him hard and fast.

Jasper and Damon were laughing like a bunch of

jerks and Mom was all, "Poor thing, I should have warned him." Dad smirked and said, "He's fully initiated now."

After ten minutes, I got up to ask if he was okay through the bathroom door.

"Leon? You alright in there?"

He groaned. "Please pretend this never happened."

"That bad, huh?"

"Your mum's trying to kill me, isn't she? This is some kind of test."

I couldn't help but laugh. "Welcome to the family. We've all been there."

"Even you?"

"Oh yeah. The first time I ate three of those wings, I stayed home sick from school the next day. I've grown a tolerance to them though."

Another groan. "Why didn't anyone warn me?"

"Because watching people discover Mom's wings is like a family sport. Jasper threw up in the yard when he was fifteen."

"That... actually makes me feel better."

"Just stay hydrated. And maybe avoid heavy food for a while."

"Noted. God, this is so embarrassing."

"Could be worse. At least you made it to the bathroom. One time, Damon—"

"Please don't finish that sentence."

When Leon finally came out, he looked like he'd been through war. Pale, sweaty, completely mortified. He kept apologizing and trying to leave, but Mom insisted on making him toast and giving him vanilla ice cream.

He avoided my eyes the rest of the night... which I totally understand. But that night, after we had cake and everyone went their separate ways, he texted me. I guess he got my number from Jasper.

Leon: I think your mum's wings taught me the true meaning of humility. Thank you for not letting me die alone in there. And maybe one day when I can look you all in the eye again you can tell me the rest of the Damon story. I need some blackmail... He's being a proper ass.

My face lit all the way up.

Me: You're welcome. And I'm always happy to provide blackmail material... just say when.

Leon: Perfect. Well, goodnight, Bailey. May I live to see another day.

Me: I believe in you. Although, I may have to save your number under Wing Survivor. Goodnight, Leon.

Leon: Honestly, your mum could use those wings to torture military secrets from enemies of the state. She has a future in... what is it called? The CIA?

I was laughing out loud.

Me: I'll let her know she has some new career options.

Leon: I'm officially scared of your dad now. How many did he eat? 12?

Me: Try 15. He's not human. We've all accepted it.

Leon: Christ. I'm never eating at your house again without a gallon of milk and a priest on standby.

Me: Don't be dramatic, you survived. The toilet might not have... but you're still standing.

Leon: Your mum was trying to kill me.

Me: Nah... we just weed out the weak ones. Congrats, you've passed.

Leon: Thanks? Should I feel proud?

Me: Oh totally. I'm extremely proud.

Leon: Well, in that case, I'll put up with Damon's ridicule. At least you're proud of me.

Me: Tell him "Fourth of July" and he'll stop.

Leon: The blackmail?

Me: Yup... and it's a good one.

Leon: You're the best, Bailey. Thank you.

Me: Goodnight, Leon.

I was grinning so hard my cheeks hurt. How does texting with Leon feel so easy and natural? Like we've been doing this forever instead of him just getting my number tonight.

I'm going to make him cookies tomorrow. He deserves it.

CHAPTER TWELVE

BAILEY - BEFORE

WE'RE ON EDGE ALL DAY, EVEN MORE SO WHEN YURI GETS back with two others in tow, new men I've never seen before. The moment his eyes meet mine, empty and cold, he barks for us to go upstairs and stay there until someone tells us otherwise. That's fine with me. I'm already trembling all over, my thoughts spinning around and around like some nightmarish carousel.

Not again. Please.

"Come sit," Cat says, pulling me by the hand onto the bed. I know she's looking closely at me, taking in my shaking limbs, my wide eyes, and raw lips, bloody from picking at them.

"How are you okay right now?" I manage to ask. "Knowing they're planning something. Knowing someone will use us again. Hurt us."

A joyless laugh leaves her lips. "I'm not okay, B. I haven't been okay for so fucking long, I don't even know what okay means." She meets my gaze, her warm brown eyes shining with fire I haven't seen in weeks. "You know what? Fuck keeping secrets." She stops mid-thought and crouches by the mattress. "I'm getting us the hell out of here. All four of us."

I lean closer, watching her. "What do you mean?"

She digs around in her stash and drops a pile of random bills and coins onto the bed. With a satisfied smile she says, "I've been planning this for a while. Erik coming here, fixating on me. I've been using it."

I eye the money, mentally calculating how much she's collected. Maybe a hundred dollars, no more than that.

"What have you been doing with him?"

She rolls her eyes. "Reading Shakespeare. God, B... I've been doing what I need to. And at least he pays me directly. Lord knows, he could have tried to take what he wants, plenty of others have." She starts to gather the money into a neat pile and stuffs it back under the mattress.

I nod, absorbing what she said. "So he's going to help you escape?"

"Us," she corrects. "And no. He doesn't know shit."

"Good, I don't think we can trust him. We can't trust any of them."

She slides onto the bed beside me. "I know. But we *can* use him."

I realize my trembling has subsided a bit, but the looming thoughts remain. Whatever Cat has planned, it'll be dangerous, reckless. Who knows what will happen? But I can't let them touch me again. I just can't.

"I have to find out what happened to my cousin." When I look over at her, she's staring out the window into the darkening sky. "Even if it might put my other family at risk. I just... need to know."

That crimson stain on the motel carpet flashes in my mind, and I nod in agreement. "What's the plan?"

TWO DAYS GO BY. Two days where we're only allowed to leave the room to use the bathroom and nothing more. We haven't been able to check in with Lydia or Elise, but I hear their footsteps pacing in the bedroom next to ours.

This waiting for what's to come is almost as bad as the act itself. I've barely eaten the hastily thrown together sandwiches they've given us, and what I've managed to choke down sits in my stomach like a weight.

"He should have come," Cat says as she paces the length of the small bedroom for what feels like the hundredth time. "He left me a note in the bathroom. *See you later.* When the fuck is *later?* I need something, B. Some kind of info. What the fuck is going on down there?"

There's a light knock at the door before it swings open. Erik appears in the doorway, his gangly frame taking up the space. It's like Cat's words conjured him into existence. She starts to speak but he raises a finger to his lips. Her jaw clenches but she obeys. I don't know how to feel, what to think as I watch their exchange.

"Come on," he whispers, stepping back to give her room.

A look passes between Cat and me as she closes the space between them. Relief tinged with fear. My pulse kicks up as I watch her disappear into the hallway, suddenly aware of how much I've grown to depend on her presence for comfort. The quiet is suffocating. The walls feel like they're closing in.

My chest tightens because this is how it always started. Alone in the room, waiting. That's when King came to me. When he beat me until bruises formed in delicate areas and blood dripped from open wounds. When he raped me, again and again... using me like I was nothing more than a doll. I start to shake and before I realize I've moved, I find myself crouched in the corner of the room, my knees folded against my chest as tight as they can go.

I wish I was as brave at Cat, as strong. Whatever she's doing out there with Erik, it's for us. The planning and stealing and acting, it's all been to get us out, to find Jasmine. She's out there letting him do unspeakable things to her while I sit here cowering in fear. Do I even deserve to be saved?

Cat slips back through the door minutes later, her pants sagging low, and her brow glistening with sweat. I straighten my body, looking her over for injuries, and wait for her to say something. When she doesn't, I ask, "Are you okay?"

She ignores my question and hurries to her spot under the mattress. "We're doing this tonight, B. You need to get ready."

I push up on my hands to stand. "What did he tell you?"

"Yuri and the others are leaving soon. Erik said they'll be gone for two hours—just two hours. I don't know where they're going, just that Erik will be here alone with us. He—he told me all the things he's going to do to me, now that he can take his time."

Her voice shakes in a way I've never heard before. She's frantic as she rips through the clothes in our small closet, finding a long-sleeve shirt from the pile on the floor. She pulls it over her head.

"Shit," I say. "What did he say? Did he hurt you?"

"No. But I won't let him try." The words tumble out in a rush of breath. "This might be our only chance to run."

"We need to tell Lydia and Elise. We can't leave them here."

She tosses a clean pair of underwear at me. "Layer these on."

I hold them, crumbled, in my hand. "You keep getting ready. I'll go tell them."

I can see her wanting to argue with me, her emotions are

always plain as day on her face, but she waves me off. When I turn for the door, she grabs my wrist, digging her fingers in hard. "Don't let them see you. And B? Two hours. That's all we have once they leave. Hurry."

Two hours.

The words echo in my head as I move toward our bedroom door, keeping my bare feet silent against the worn carpet. My hand hovers over the doorknob. I know it'll squeak when I open it. What if someone's out there?

I press my ear to the wood first, straining to hear anything but my own racing pulse. Muffled voices drift up from downstairs, but they sound distant. Relaxed, even. A burst of laughter makes me flinch.

I use the backdrop of their conversation to turn the doorknob and ease the door open inch by agonizing inch, waiting for the hinges to whine. Cat watches me, a wrinkled shirt clutched to her chest. It squeals, but less aggressively, maybe from how slow I opened it. I'll take that as a small win.

The hallway stretches before me. There's maybe twelve feet to Lydia and Elise's door, but it might as well be a mile.

Every step feels like walking on cracked ice. Like I'm seconds away from the end. I don't know how I'm staying upright.

The floorboard under my left foot groans slightly and I freeze, counting my heartbeats.

One.

Two.

Three.

Nothing. I force myself to breathe and keep moving.

Halfway there, someone slams a door below and I pause, flattening myself against the wall, my whole body trembling. Heavy footsteps cross what sounds like the kitchen, followed by the scrape of a chair.

Just someone moving around. Probably Erik. It's fine.

Two hours. I need to keep going.

Lydia and Elise's door is identical to ours with the same peeling white paint, the same old brass doorknob. I press my ear against it and listen to their murmuring voices. Good. They're both awake.

I tap so softly, I'm not sure they'll even hear me. Tap-tap. Pause. Tap-tap.

Their voices stop.

"It's Bailey," I whisper, my lips practically touching the wood.

The knob turns and the door opens just enough for Elise's wide, terrified eyes to peer out. She looks past me down the hallway before pulling me inside and quickly closing the door behind me.

"What's wrong?" Lydia sits up from where she was curled on the bed, her dark hair matted against her head. Both of them look like they haven't slept in days, based on the dark shadows under their eyes.

"We're getting out," I whisper, my words spilling over each other in my rush to release them. "Tonight. Cat has a plan and—"

A car engine roars to life outside the window. All three of us freeze, listening as it grows fainter, then disappears.

"Who just left?" Lydia asks.

The sound of footsteps on the stairs makes me freeze. Hurried, heavy steps. And they're coming closer.

"No time. Get ready," I mouth to them, backing toward the door. "Whatever you can wear, put it on. Now."

The footsteps pause at the top of the stairs. A floorboard creaks.

"I need to go," I whisper, my shaky hand already on their doorknob.

But as I turn it, the footsteps start moving again. Not back toward the stairs, not away from us.

Coming this way.

Lydia grabs my arm, holding tightly. We all stare at the door as a shadow passes underneath it, blocking out the dim hallway light.

The footsteps stop right outside our door.

CHAPTER THIRTEEN

BAILEY - BEFORE

I HOLD A FINGER TO MY LIPS AND THEY NOD. THE ONLY sound is the wind against a loose shutter, rattling outside with each gust. We stand frozen, barely breathing, waiting.

One breath.

Then two.

His shadow shifts, followed by heavy footsteps leading away from us.

Only one thought rushes into my mind. Cat.

"What do we do?" Lydia asks, her voice low. She's dropped my arm, but hasn't left my side. I roll my cracked lip between my teeth, channeling confidence I don't feel.

"First, we help Cat. Then we figure out the rest," I whisper back. "She's got a plan to get us all out."

Elise shakes her head immediately. "I can't. I'm not—I need my meds, Bailey. Without them, I'll be sick. I'll slow you down."

"And my kids," Lydia adds, her voice cracking. "If something goes wrong, if we get caught... what happens to them?"

I bite my lip so hard that I hiss. What am I supposed to say to that?

Before I can respond, a dull *thump* comes through the wall. Then another, louder this time.

"Shit," I breathe. "We have to help her."

I yank the door open and run to the other bedroom. Cat's voice is muffled in the hallway, but I hear the strain in it, the plea. Whatever game she was playing with Erik, it's over now. She needs me.

I reach the door, breathing hard and feeling dizzy. I don't hear footsteps behind me, but part of me hopes Lydia and Elise will follow. It doesn't matter. Drawing in a deep breath, I swing the door open.

Erik has her pinned against the wall, her clothes disheveled, and her hair a mess. Her eyes find mine, wide with fear. At the same moment, he notices he has company. Erik's hand drops from Cat's throat and she coughs.

"Fucking bastard," she says, rubbing her throat and scrambling back a step.

"Didn't know you wanted to join the party." He steps toward me, his eyes narrowing. "I knew you weren't just some newbie. Time to find out what you're really about."

"No." My voice shakes, but only at first. "No," I repeat louder. And then I turn and sprint out the door.

"Bitch," he spits under his breath as Cat yells for me to run. I pass Lydia and Elise, frozen in their doorway, watching.

"Come on," I plead, urging them to follow, but I can't spare a second to stop and wait. He's right behind me.

His voice is at my back. Too calm, like he's practiced it before.

"I'm not gonna hurt you. Ask Catalina. We've been having fun together." He grabs me by the hair as I reach the top of the stairs. Stinging pain explodes across my scalp and I scream, reaching up to grab his wrist on instinct.

"Please," I cry. "Let me go, I won't run."

"You're making me hurt you, newbie. He put me in charge... *Me*. I can't let anything go wrong."

He starts dragging me back toward our bedroom, my feet scrambling for traction against the smooth floor. I pry at his fist but he only tightens his grip, twisting his fingers in my hair. Each step sends fresh waves of agony through my scalp.

"Stop, please!" Tears blur my vision as I claw uselessly at his hand. "I'm sorry, I'm sorry!"

Through my sobs, I make out Lydia's voice begging him to stop, to let me go.

"Should've thought about that before you tried to run." His grip tightens, pulling harder. "Now I have to—"

His words are cut off by a choked gasp.

What the—

His hand goes slack in my hair and I stumble forward, falling to my knees as he releases me. When I turn around, Cat is standing behind him, her chest heaving, and a kitchen knife buried deep between his shoulder blades. His eyes are wide with shock as one hand waves through air, desperately trying to grab the handle.

"That's for all the *fun* we had," Cat says in a voice cold as ice.

Erik staggers toward me, but I slide back, narrowly avoiding his body as he collapses face first onto the hardwood.

"Oh my holy fuck," Lydia says as she hurries into the hallway.

I ignore her though, focusing on the pool of blood soaking through Erik's T-shirt and dripping onto the floor.

"What did you do? Shit, shit, shit!" The words pour out of

me. I crawl toward him, my hands landing in his warm blood, and check for a pulse. It's there but it's weak.

"Is he dead?" Lydia asks.

I shake my head. "He's still alive."

Elise makes her way into the hallway, quietly sobbing. "We're so fucked."

"He was gonna kill Bailey," Cat says. "I had no choice."

My eyes fix on the knife sticking out of his back. "Where did you get the knife?"

"At breakfast, but that doesn't matter. We gotta get the fuck out of here." She rushes back into the bedroom and I want to follow her. I know I should. But my legs won't move.

"We can't let him die," Lydia says quietly. "They'll kill us."

She's right. Letting him bleed out on the floor in front of me is wrong. But what he did to Cat was wrong too, what he did to me. His phone sticks out of his back pocket, it would only take a second to call 911. I could leave an anonymous tip, considering I have no clue where we are. The paramedics will come, the cops... We can tell them what happened to us. We'll be saved.

Lydia spots the phone at the same time and grabs it. "I'm calling my kids."

"Wait," I say. "Shouldn't we call 911?"

War rages in her eyes. She's reluctant, just like me. "They'll arrest Cat for attempted murder. It's too risky."

Cat storms into the hallway, dressed in layers. "What's going on? Why aren't you getting up?"

Maybe it's the resolve on her face that snaps me into action. Or maybe it's that I don't want to be an accomplice to murder. Either way, I find the strength to stand and run for my shoes.

"You're staying?" she calls to Elise. "I can't protect you if you do."

She slides down the wall, crying into her hands. "Just go."

When I get back with my shoes on, Lydia's turned away

from me, speaking quietly into the phone. I glance once more at Erik's still form before stepping around him and following Cat down the stairs.

She heads straight for the front door, but I put a hand on her shoulder to stop her. "Should we grab anything else? Maybe go get the phone from Lydia or raid the kitchen?"

"They can track us on that thing. No, let's go. We'll find the nearest house or store or something and ask to use a phone."

"To call the cops?" I ask, panting.

Her face falls. "I don't know, B."

Her way of saying no... She won't talk to the cops. I guess I can't blame her. She just stabbed a guy.

Cat twists the deadbolt and darts out the door. At the first touch of cool air against my cheeks, I shiver. It's been so long since I've been outside. It smells like smoke and pine, so crisp compared to the staleness inside the house. I suck in a mouthful of cold air, willing it to reach my chest. Cat calls my name. Tells me to follow.

But I can't move.

My feet are frozen at the threshold, and I realize one of my hands is gripping the doorframe hard enough to hurt. The yard stretches out in front of me, so vast after weeks of cramped rooms and narrow hallways. All that open space should feel like freedom, but instead it feels exposed, dangerous. My chest tightens as my breathing becomes shallow and quick. Too much sky. Too much space to run, too many places to hide, too many ways this could go wrong.

Where will we go? What if they find us?

I'm hyperventilating. What the hell is wrong with me? Cat's voice sounds like it's reaching me through miles of water.

Then she's there, grabbing my hand and pulling me forward. "B, it's okay... I've got you."

"Yeah, okay," I mumble.

It must be dusk, judging from the setting sun peeking through the muted gray clouds. I force myself to focus on the solidness of Cat's hand in mine and the way our footsteps scrape against the long gravel driveway.

"Where?" I ask as we get closer to the end. There's nothing but heavily wooded forest surrounding a dirt road—pine trees and bare oaks. We're in the middle of nowhere.

"Road's too risky," she pants. I follow her pointed finger toward the trees. "Through there. We can follow the road from the woods until we reach help."

I nod, too out of breath and shocked to vocalize anymore thoughts, but they swim through my head in waves.

We actually got out.

But we might have killed a man.

I can see my family.

Just a little further, then we'll be safe.

I'm a killer. Or may as well be.

No. I shake the image of Erik's blood out of my mind. It's not the first body I've seen here, but now we'll be safe. It's over. I can move on. I just hope Elise and Lydia are okay.

We're only a few yards from the tree line when I hear it. The roar of an engine growing louder. "Cat?" I can barely get the word out with fear choking me.

Her grip on my hand tightens as we both turn to see headlights breaking through the darkening sky and getting closer by the second.

"Run!" Cat screams, pulling me forward.

I slip on the icy gravel as we sprint up the rest of the driveway. The safety of the woods is only feet ahead. I don't know if we'll make it.

Brakes squeal as tires skid to a stop on the dirt road.

Car doors slam.

I keep looking ahead. Keep running.

We crash into the tree line, scraping against branches and scrambling over rocks. Cat stumbles over a pile of frost-covered snow and falls to her knees, but I keep my grip on her sweaty hand, pulling her up. "Come on!"

Behind us, heavy footsteps pound against the forest floor, getting closer. I can't make out the figures, but my legs start to shake.

"Fuck! My ankle," Cat cries, as she struggles to stand. I pull her again, holding her up. "B, you should go... run and find help."

"No, no fucking way. Come on, just keep going. I've got you."

But as I say it, I hear them gaining on us. Cat's limping so badly now, each step has me carrying more of her weight. I can barely stay upright myself with the panic setting in. There's no time for that though. I push through, between trees that scratch my skin, over a snowy rotted log.

But the voices behind us are getting clearer. They're angry, spitting foreign words I don't understand but recognize.

"There's nowhere to go!" one of the men yells.

"Bailey, please," Cat gasps, tears streaming down her face. "You can still make it."

"Don't make me shoot!"

Crunching footsteps and snapping branches are so close. I make a desperate sprint, barely holding onto Cat, ignoring her pleas. But as I round a bend, a hand grabs my shoulder and one of the men spins me around. Then another grabs Cat, yanking her away from me. Her fingers slip from mine, the weight of her ripped from my side.

"No!" Cat screams.

I push and pull, trying to get free, but his grip on my shoulder tightens. He seethes against my ear, his warm breath stinking of booze. "Don't fucking move."

Then I feel him cram his gun against my back.

"Let her go! Please, just take me!" Cat thrashes against Yuri, but he tosses her over his shoulder, spewing angry words in Russian. Coins spill from her pockets onto the forest floor. She pounds his back, fights with everything she has left.

I should fight too. I should try something, anything. But watching Cat's plan shatter, seeing the terror in her eyes, something inside me just... breaks. Any amount of fight I have left drains out of me like the blood flowing from Erik's wound.

I don't resist when he jabs the gun against my spine, telling me to move. I don't scream when he pushes me into the backseat of the car. It would be pointless. After the planning, the hope, the taste of freedom—it's over.

Some part of me always knew it would end this way.

THEY SHOVE us back into our room, my body already limp from the tranquilizer. I hear them talking as they drag something heavy down the hallway. Erik's body, probably. Cat hasn't said a word since they drugged her. She's curled up on the bed, staring at nothing, her eyes glassy and unfocused.

I don't know what to say, but I kneel at the side of the bed, taking her injured ankle in my hand. My movements are slow and sloppy, and vision blurred but it's easy enough to see that it's already swelled up to double its size. Without speaking, I grab a thin undershirt from the pile, pull her shoe off, and wrap the injury tight, tucking the fabric into itself.

"Is that okay?" I ask softly, not really expecting an answer.

I climb up onto the bed, not caring about my bloody palms or my dirty scratched up face. Not caring about anything, because caring means feeling, and I've had enough of that today. Whatever they do to us, it won't be worse than the sinking pit I've fallen into.

As I get settled in, ready to let sleep pull me under, Yuri's distinct voice sounds through the closed door. "Yes. Uh, huh. The blonde one. Yes, the junkie."

He must be on the phone, judging from the one-sided conversation. I tiptoe across the room and put my ear to the door, my heart hammering.

"She was so desperate for her next fix, she would have sold out her own mother. Called the moment they made their move."

No. I can't be hearing what I think I'm hearing.

"If you'd like. Yes, I can do that. No, she's useful here... a good informant."

Informant? I turn back toward Cat to see if she's hearing this, but she hasn't moved.

"Erik is dead. Yes. I'll take care of it."

I wait for more, some kind of explanation that negates what I think I heard, but his footsteps move away.

Elise. She called Yuri.

I'm frozen at the door, replaying that moment. Her staying put while we ran, quietly crying into her hands, and suddenly it all makes sense. She wasn't scared, she was waiting. Waiting for us to leave so she could make her call. If Cat finds out, she'll kill her, and I don't think I'd stop her.

CHAPTER FOURTEEN

LEON - PRESENT DAY

Between completing long overdue house chores for Mum, running searches on my father, which I haven't done in years, and messaging a few contacts, day somehow turned to night. I order takeaway curry from the place around the corner, a special treat for Mum.

She tries to hide it behind oversized cardigans and loose-fitted pants, but I see how thin she's gotten. The divot in her collarbones is deep enough to cup water. Since Nana and Pop died, and I left, who has she got to cook for? I can't let that chip away at me along with everything else though. While I'm here, I'll make sure she eats well and often.

As we eat, I give her the news that Damon and Jasper are coming in a few days, leaving out the possibility of Blake, Falin, and two unruly kittens. Of course, she declares that they must stay with us, that we'd be terrible people if we allowed them to pay for accommodations. When I remind her that the house isn't much bigger than a shoebox, she tuts, saying, "We'll manage." I'll leave that to her to figure out.

My phone beeps with a message as Mum clears away our containers.

Cruz: *Call me*

"Mum, I'm going to get some air. Be back a bit later."

She turns from the sink, hands on her hips. "Pick up some milk while you're out."

I wave her off, grab my helmet, and head outside. Once I'm through the garden and onto the sidewalk, I lean on my bike and dial Cruz.

"Colter," Cruz answers in one ring.

"Alright?" I ask, while I keep an eye on my surroundings for nosey neighbors.

"About your inquiry." His voice drops to a whisper. "You know... the hardware?"

I sigh and tilt my head up to look at the darkening sky. "Yes, I understand what you mean. You found someone?"

"Maybe."

Cursing under my breath, I ask, "Why are you asking me to call you if it's a maybe, Cruz? I need a positive."

"It's just... this isn't like popping into the supermarket for a loaf of bread. What you're looking for takes a bit of finesse."

"Alright, go on. Tell me what you know."

I can picture him fidgeting with that bloody cap of his as he takes his time to reply. "He'll be at The Irons tonight. Big bloke named Knapp. He's new to the game. Usually has a few buddies surrounding him."

"Alright, so we go to The Irons, show him how much I'm willing to spend," I say, already working through a plan.

"It's not that easy," Cruz says with a nervous laugh. "He doesn't just sell to anyone with cash."

"Get on with it," I groan, ready to kick something.

"You'll have to prove yourself. Show him you're not some wannabe who'll get himself nicked five minutes after walking away with his merchandise." He sucks in air, probably a cigarette. "You want guns, you'll have to work for it."

"He wants me to fight?" I don't know why I didn't realize what he was saying sooner.

Another drag on his cigarette. "Exactly. Not only fight, but you've gotta win."

I close my eyes, remembering the last time I was in that basement. The bitter scent of sweat and blood, the ferocity of the crowd, sometimes more violent than the fighters, how my knuckles and jaw ached for days, and that was only after I came to. "It's been years, Cruz."

He chuckles. "You've got this. It's like riding a bike. A massive bike that fights back."

"Thanks for that image."

"Listen, I saw you. You've filled out. You're not the same kid that got his ass kicked week after week trying to earn an extra buck. You can do this."

A part of me has been considering going back to blow off steam anyway. I think I've been talking myself out of it, trying to keep my composure, but now, with this new development... it's the perfect opportunity to get what I need, maybe some intel too, and work out some anger in the process.

I think about Bailey, somewhere out there in the darkness. About how I'll stop at nothing to find her. "I'll do it."

"Alright then. I'll let them know. Starts at eleven. Side entrance on Magnolia Street, same as always. And Leon?"

"Yeah?"

"Be smart. You've got nothing to prove to these blokes. Talk to Knapp, get your opponent, and win. Wife's going to rip my balls off... but I'll be there. I've got your back."

"Thanks, Cruz. I mean it."

"Don't thank me yet. Save that for after you've still got all your teeth." He blows out a stream of smoke, and when he speaks again, his voice is quieter. "Leon... whatever mess you've gotten yourself into, just promise me you'll come back in one piece, yeah? I don't want to be the one explaining to your mum why her boy didn't make it home."

My throat tightens, but I manage to thank him.

"I'll see you tonight," he says. "And don't forget to wear something you don't mind getting bloodied up."

The line goes dead, leaving me leaning against my bike on the quiet street, already feeling the familiar pang of anticipation mixed with dread. I pocket the phone and look up at the full moon, peeking out behind a cloud. Maybe Bailey's looking out at the same moon nearby. I silently send a message. *I'm coming for you.*

Mum's silhouette crosses the window as she tidies the living room, no doubt in anticipation of our soon to be guests. I should go get that milk she asked for, and maybe pick up some ice while I'm at it. I'm going to need it tomorrow morning.

<hr>

THE SIDE ENTRANCE on Magnolia Street hasn't changed in the three years since I've been. Still just a nondescript black door situated between a run down newsagent and a gyro shop that's seen better days. No sign, no hint of what lies beneath except the slight vibration of bass coming from underground.

I park my bike around the corner, attaching my helmet to the lock on my handlebars before checking that everything's secure. It gives me a moment to find my center, to push down the nerves that are trying to force their way to the surface.

A heavy mix of nervous excitement and fear has every step toward the entrance feeling like an out of body experience. It's a familiar feeling from my teenage years. Back then, I'd been driven by anger and the desperate need to prove myself, to release the rage and the hurt and the abandonment. Tonight, it's different. Tonight, I have purpose.

The bouncer is new, a beast of a man with arms like tree trunks and a callous, scarred face. His eyes rake over me, taking in my leather jacket, the way I carry myself. I'm not the scrawny, desperate kid who used to stumble down these steps anymore.

"Knapp sent me," I say, meeting his stare.

He nods once and steps aside, revealing the dimly lit staircase that descends into the belly of the beast. The air grows thicker with each step, the scent of sweat and smoke heavy in the air. I've never liked this part. The before. It's not that I'm usually an anxious person. I haven't felt this way while working with the guys, but here... waiting for my name to be called, for the violence and pain that follows, it's like holding your breath underwater.

The door at the end of the stairs opens up into a massive space lit by rows of fluorescent lights, some of them flickering, in need of a new bulb. Concrete pillars covered in graffiti tags and stickers support the low ceiling, and old metal bleachers rise in tiers around a central ring marked out in yellow tape on the concrete floor. Rusted iron beams stretch across the ceiling like skeletal remains of the old ironworks this place used to be, back when honest men earned honest wages forging steel instead of spilling blood for entertainment.

One look at the crowd and I can see what Cruz meant. The place looks exactly the same, yet completely different. There's still the mix of desperate kids looking to earn a few pounds, but now they're surrounded by men in gang colors, businessmen in expensive suits, and a handful of average looking blokes. They have one thing in common, money riding on the fights in one way or another.

I spot Cruz near the back wall, cap pulled low, clutching a

pint close to his chest. He's the picture of uncomfortable. Our eyes meet and he gestures with his chin toward the betting table where a small group of men have their wallets out and eyes sharp.

For Bailey.

I straighten my spine and walk right up to the biggest one. From Cruz's description, this must be Knapp. Middle-aged, six-foot-five easily, solid muscle, with slicked back hair and a bushy mustache. He narrows his gaze.

"You the American?" he asks, staring me up and down.

I can't help but smirk. "Hardly," I reply, raising my voice to be heard over the bellowing in the room. "You Knapp?"

The rest of his crew steps closer. Three guys almost as big as him with equally harsh faces. I'm surprised they don't fight in the ring... they'd be shoe-ins. Knapp nods. "Heard you're looking for some specialized equipment."

"Depends on what you've got."

His laugh is cold, and makes my insides twist. "And that depends on what you show me tonight." He gestures toward the ring where two men are already circling each other, trading jabs that sound wet and meaty. "I don't sell to just anyone. Too many rats out there. Prove yourself and we'll talk."

Voices roar as the current fight ends. One man's flat on his back, barely conscious and the other's standing over him, knuckles split and wearing a grin. The crowd is a frenzy of cheers and curses as money changes hands.

This is it. Can't back out now.

I nod, and make my way toward the booking table where Tank still runs the show. She's built exactly like her nickname with broad shoulders, thick arms, and muscles that rival most body builders. Her dark hair is buzzed short, and she's wearing the same scowl she had last time I saw her.

"Well, fuck me sideways," she mutters, pounding her fist on

the rickety table. "Leon Colter. Thought you'd left this shithole and moved to America."

I reach out and shake her hand, noticing some new ink snaking up her arms. "Tank, nice to see you."

"Almost didn't recognize yeh," she says. "All that ink, and fuck me, are those muscles under there?"

I laugh, probably for the first time tonight. "I've grown quite a bit."

"I see that." Someone knocks into the table, causing Tank to holler some choice words. "Sorry, it's getting unruly already. Something's in the air tonight... gotta be the fucking full moon."

"You're probably right." Even if she wasn't I'd never say otherwise. Everyone knows not to disagree with Tank if you want to keep all your fingers intact. I shrug out of my jacket, and her eyes widen.

"Don't tell me... you wanna fight tonight?"

"I do."

"Wasn't last time bad enough? You nearly died that night."

Another fight starts and with the sound of flesh hitting flesh, that unpleasant memory surfaces. I force myself to look away.

"Guess you can say I'm my own worst enemy." She pulls out an iPad, sliding her finger over the screen. "Look who's gotten high tech in my time away."

She waves me off. "This way it's random. Can't have a repeat of New Years Eve '22. What a clusterfuck."

"Sorry to have missed it."

"Cheeky bastard," she says, tapping away on the screen. "I take it you remember the Iron Code?"

I nod. How could I forget? "Iron doesn't bend. Iron doesn't break."

Meaning, you step foot in that ring and you don't walk

away until one of you can't get back up. And whatever happens here never sees daylight.

"Alright, you're up next. You better take out that lip ring... don't need to see that get yanked out."

"Thanks, Tank. Nice to see you." I knock my fist on the table, and head back to Cruz.

"All set?" he asks, still looking around nervously. I nod, and he passes me his pint. "You'll need this... for the nerves."

He's not wrong. I take a long swig. "Wish it was stronger."

He pats my shoulder. "Tell ya what, shots on me when you win this thing."

"Get your money ready, then."

I flash a grin that's mostly bravado and start preparing—removing my lip and eyebrow rings and stripping down to just my gym shorts. I stretch out my tight shoulders and do a few jumping jacks to get my heart pumping.

By the time Tank calls my name, I'm ready. Damon and Jasper never take it easy on me during fight club, and Falin's landed more hits than I care to admit. I haven't been idle these past few years. I can win this.

I step toward the ring with Cruz close behind. My eyes find Knapp in the crowd. He gives me a slight nod, a silent command to get the job done. I blow out a breath and let my mind clear.

"You've got this, Colter!" Cruz shouts behind me. A few voices join in, though I can't tell if they're cheering for me or just hungry for blood. I shake hands with the ref, a grizzled ex-boxer whose job is to make sure we don't actually kill each other.

Tank's voice booms again. "Place your bets! You've got two minutes!"

Money changes hands, people crowd the betting table, everyone buzzing with anticipation. I bounce on the balls of my feet, keeping loose, trying not to think about who might be betting against me.

"Bring out the challenger!" Tank calls.

The crowd cleaves in two, creating a path from the opposite side of the basement. That's when I catch the first glimpse of my opponent as he strides forward, his steps almost cocky.

He's about my height, lean but muscled. Not the kind you get from real work. These muscles scream personal trainers and country clubs. His dark hair is perfectly styled despite being in a humid basement. The way he smirks, chest puffed out, swaggering like he owns the place. Privileged prick.

And I know this for a fact.

He gets closer and with one look at his eyes—the same eyes I see in the mirror everyday. The same shape. The same shade of hazel with flecks of gold and green. *Alfred's eyes*.

James Colter. My *half* brother.

What the fuck is he doing here?

BAILEY - JUNE 20TH

The most amazing thing happened and I can't get my body to calm down. My heart rate is going a hundred mph, my stomach is doing backflips, and I'm definitely in need of a change of underwear (not from pee).

Let me start from the beginning.

I didn't get much sleep last night... and I know exactly why. I can't stop thinking about Leon. Ever since the wing incident and our texting afterward, something's shifted between us. I keep replaying his messages, the way he joked around with me, and wondering if maybe I'm not just Jasper's little sister to him anymore.

My room—which is normally my comfort, my sanctuary—felt too warm, too closed in. So I figured I'd make some tea and chill in the living room with a book. Well, my parents had other plans. They came in bickering and Mom started stress vacuuming while Dad put on some golf game on the TV at the highest possible volume.

Okay, I thought. I'll go outside.

Killer bees.

That is all.

Maybe not killer bees, but these bees had it out for me. I ended up running inside screeching like a wild creature, grabbing my purse, and driving straight to the library. I needed some nice, air-conditioned, quiet time.

And I did get that... for a little while. Peace and quiet to help me out of the cranky, confusing mood I'd been in all morning. It was just me, my marriage of convenience smut, and a corner table near the mythology section.

Until I felt a warm breath against my ear and jumped out of my skin.

"What are you reading?" Leon asked. No, more like crooned. Or murmured. Or purred. How does he do that with his voice?

I'm getting off track. Let me make this easier and write this in a professional way... like my own romance novel because... Well, you'll see.

"You scared the shit out of me!" I whisper-yelled.

He just stood back to his full height, hands crossed, and smirked. "Looks like a pretty racy scene?"

My face got red hot.

"No! It's—it's not racy. It's tasteful."

He leaned down again and read over my shoulder.

"In all her years of fucking, she never knew a man could feel this good. His coc—"

"Oh my God, stop right now!"

He chuckled but listened. Thankfully, because I almost died. And not of embarrassment, but from hearing him say the word fucking.

"There's nothing to be ashamed of. Everyone loves a good romance novel... especially ones with fu—"

"Okay," I said as I closed my book with more force than necessary. "I'm going to leave now."

I pushed up from my chair and slung my purse over my shoulder.

"No, don't leave," Leon said quickly. "I won't bother you. I was just teasing, trying to get you to blush."

I turned away from him, walking toward the exit.

"Right, because it's so fun to tease the annoying little sister. The virgin who refused to settle for the assholes in this town. The one who's too scared to open her mouth and ask for what she wants."

His hand circled my wrist, gently but strong enough to stop me from moving. He pulled me into the dark mythology aisle, crowding me with his body until I was pressed against the shelves.

His lips an inch from mine, and his eyes blazing, he asked, "And what is it that you want?"

I was on fire. Every spot where our bodies connected sent sparks dancing toward my core. I licked my lips, and he watched with a hunger I'd never seen before.

"I don't know—I haven't..."

He tilted my chin up so the slightest movement would have our mouths touching. "I think you know."

"Why are you following me?" My voice trembled.

"You know why," he said. His lips quirked up at one corner with that smirk that always gives me butterflies.

"I don't."

"Because I like you. I want you." He pressed his forehead against mine. "Do you have any idea how hard it's been? Living in your house, seeing you every day, pretending I don't notice every little thing you do?"

Honestly, I've never known someone to be that candid.

I think I whimpered. I can't be sure. But the next thing I knew, he closed the space between us, wrapped his palm in my hair, and kissed me like I'd never been kissed before.

I dropped the book and my purse and fisted his T-shirt, pulling him closer. Oh God, his lips were every-thing. His tongue gently slid into my mouth, exploring, tasting. I didn't know what to do so I let him lead.

My hand drifted lower like it was magnetized, pulled toward the straining bulge in his pants. "Bailey," he breathed, grabbing my hands and raising them above my head. "You touch me and I might come in my pants, love."

"I'm sorry," I whispered, feeling that blush spread down my neck.

He slid his fingertips down my arms, over my collarbones, up my neck, until he cupped my cheek.

"Never apologize for how you make me feel. You can touch me all you want... just not here."

He brushed another soft kiss against my lips and brought my hands down, wrapping his palm around mine.

"Want to get out of here?" I asked.

Those eyes, so intense, yet so warm, studied me for a moment. Dragging across my face then down to take in my body.

"I'd love nothing more."

Do you see why I'm going to combust? That was so hot, I can't stop replaying every second. Shit, Dad's calling me to help him get the burgers off the grill.

CHAPTER FIFTEEN

BAILEY - BEFORE

I DON'T KNOW WHAT'LL HAPPEN TONIGHT. THERE'S BEEN murmurs between Yuri's men... Mentions of King showing up. Hearing his name has me on edge.

Rain streaks down the window of the high-rise hotel suite where they've put us, the summer storm turning the city below into a blur of neon and headlights. Me, Cat, Lydia, and the new girl, Katie. They moved her in shortly after Cat tried to kill Elise in her sleep. She still won't talk to Lydia for stopping her. I wonder if she ever will again. I can't say that I miss Elise, I'll always hold a grudge for what she did, even though I know it was her sickness and fear that poisoned her... that she regretted making the call the moment she did it. It's better that they moved her. Hopefully, she's okay wherever she is.

"I refuse to play nice," Cat says as she shoves expensive cocktail nuts from the minibar into her mouth by the handful. "Honestly, I'm surprised they haven't fucking drugged me yet. When Yuri comes back in, I'm gonna ask for extra."

"You don't mean that," I say, coming to her side.

"The fuck I don't. Why would I want to be aware of what

these fucks will do to us tonight. There's no way out... We're stuck here, monsters are coming, and I'm just so fucking done."

"Maybe it won't be that bad," I say, knowing I'm full of shit the moment the words leave my lips.

Cat scoffs. "Don't be naive. If I were you, I wouldn't put up a fight with the needle. There's no point."

Katie, who's been sitting on the edge of the bed watching our exchange, folds her legs against her chest. Her expression of shock, of fear, reminds me of how I must have looked that first time we "entertained" for King.

Lydia's busy downing mini bottles of booze before someone comes in and catches her. I guess numb is the theme of the night.

"Maybe some of the staff noticed us," I offer. "I tried to signal to that housekeeper in the hallway. Gave her a look. Maybe—"

"A look?" Cat shakes her head. "Maybe I should do Morse code against the walls too? Or what about smoke signals from the bathroom? Fuck, B, no one's coming. No one cares enough to look past the money these fuckers are throwing around."

Her words hit like a slap to the face, but I can't be angry. Cat's just saying what we're all thinking. What I've been trying not to think for months. With each passing day that Cat gets more desperate, more despondent, I've had to find tiny kernels of hope. One of us has to keep pushing, or we'll both give up. "I don't know," I say.

"I do. They care about keeping us quiet and compliant," Cat continues, her tone clipped. "That's it. That housekeeper? She's probably seen dozens of girls like us. You think you're the first one to give her a 'look?'"

Katie makes a small sound from the bed—something between a whimper and a sob. I want to go to her. To comfort her. But really, what's the point?

"Jesus, Cat," Lydia slurs from her spot by the minibar. She tosses another lipstick-stained empty bottle, adding it to the pile scattered around the black marble counter. "You don't have to be so fucking brutal about it."

"Brutal?" Cat paces in front of us. "You want to know what brutal is? Brutal is pretending we have any control here. Brutal is giving Bailey false hope when I know—"

The door clicks. We all freeze.

It's Sweeper that steps in. He hasn't shown his face in months, not since that night with Jasmine. My heart thuds faster. He inspects the area, from the oversized sitting room to the open bedroom, checking us over. Behind him stands a man who towers over him, built like a brick wall with a large scar down his cheek, and a woman, not as tall but equally built with black hair twisted into a tight bun on her head. They're both dressed like they're waiting to break up a fight at any moment.

"Ladies," Sweeper says, sounding bored. "Time to get ready. You have important guests arriving soon."

He tilts his head, speaking low to the two people behind him, and they position themselves in the corners of the open space. They must be some kind of guards.

"Where's the meds, asshole?" Cat blurts out, hands folded at her chest.

Sweeper steps into the bedroom. There's no hint of amusement on his face. "I had hoped it wouldn't come to that."

"Well, you hoped wrong," Cat snaps back.

He sighs and brings his face inches from hers. "You do not want to play with me tonight, Catalina. One call and you know what will happen to your family."

I don't realize I've moved closer to Katie until her hand wraps around mine. We watch their standoff, Cat's defiant seething, Sweeper's exasperated authority, until he finally gives in and pulls a syringe from his inner pocket.

I close my eyes for the rest of their exchange, having seen enough needles for a lifetime.

"Anyone else?" Sweeper asks, his eyes darting between the rest of us.

I shake my head and so does Katie, but Lydia steps forward, offering him her bicep. Maybe it means something about the situation that the two newbies refuse the drugs... Maybe Cat's right, I am naive.

It hits Lydia right away, and she staggers to the bed. Sweeper curses under his breath and calls the female guard over. "Watch this one carefully. Check her vitals every so often."

"On it," she says. Now that she's closer, I can see the way her shirt barely contains her biceps. "And the clients?"

They step away from us, but I hear Sweeper reply, "Let them do what they want to her. I don't care."

She nods and takes up her place at the side of the room again. I want to vomit right here on the expensive carpeting. How could these people not react? Is everyone in the world a monster?

Sweeper walks to the door and as his palm reaches the handle, he stops. "I'm going to warn you again. You step out of line and I've given the guards permission to deal with you. These guests will get what they've paid for. I'll be back shortly. And Catalina, freshen up. You look like hell."

He's out the door as Cat lunges for the nearest object, the jar of nuts. She tries to throw it but her drugged limbs don't obey. It drops out of her hand, scattering nuts all over the floor. "Fuck," she slurs. "You freshen up, you piece of shit."

I'm at her side before the nuts stop rolling, guiding her toward the couch. "It's okay. Just rest."

"Fuck him! Fuck them all!" She gives the guards watching us the finger and then slumps back against the cushion. "Give you what I paid for," she mimics, her voice barely audible.

I smooth my hand over her hair, telling her it'll be okay all while bile rises in my throat from Sweeper's threat. Maybe I should have taken the drugs.

———

THERE'S six of them in total. Six pairs of leering eyes. Six raucous voices. Six reasons my hands won't stop shaking. Six reminders that this night will be endless.

But so far, no one has touched me. I've served drinks, listened to long-winded stories about people I don't know, flinching every time one of them shifts in their seat. Right now, I'm perched on the edge of the sofa where one of the men told me to sit after asking if I'd turn around so he could "get a proper look at me."

I keep waiting for the other shoe to drop. For the moment when they decide to abandon their pretense of civility and become the monsters I know they are. At least the other girls seem okay for now. Lydia's still passed out on the bed and Cat's halfway there on the couch next to a man who looks so ancient, I'd bet he has grandchildren older than me.

The man next to me, the one who looks like he's too sophisticated to be involved with this kind of thing, places his hand gently on my thigh. I go rigid. He notices immediately and gives me what seems like a genuinely concerned look. "Hey, it's alright," he says softly. "What's your name, darling?"

I know he's not a nice man. Logically, he's a monster like the rest of them. But his voice is kind, his smile friendly. And when I look closely into his eyes, there's something familiar about them.

"Bailey." I drop my gaze down to the floor and hope that

he'll get sucked back into conversation. His hand reaches out to cup my chin, tilting it so I have no choice but to meet his gaze. Here it is, the moment his fingers will slide down to my neck, squeezing, as harsh words leave his lips. I brace myself for it as best as I can.

One heartbeat passes, then two, and he releases a hum from low in his throat. A sound that makes me cringe. I knew it, he's no different.

His thumb brushes against my trembling lip, once, twice, before he drops his hand. "Perfect, absolutely perfect." He stands from the couch and finishes the last sip of whiskey in his glass. I notice how tall he is, how strong looking. His eyes meet mine again. "Do be a good girl until I see you again, yeah?"

I don't know how to respond. He doesn't wait for one anyway. He adjusts his cuffs and buttons his jacket before walking over to the huge male guard. They glance at me and go back to their hushed conversation. What are they saying? I know it's about me, it must be.

In my periphery I notice one of the men, tall and rail-thin, leave his chair and go into the bedroom, shutting the double doors behind him. *Lydia.*

I bring my attention back to the corner where the man pats the scarred guard on the shoulder, then turns and walks out. That can't be it. His attention was on me all night. He must be planning something. He'll come back, drag me out of here into another room, separate me from Cat and the others.

Before the door fully closes, I feel the couch dip beside me. I don't want to look him in the eye, but I catch a glimpse of his meaty hands with gold rings on every finger. Maybe if I keep my head down, he'll lose interest. "How old are you, pretty girl?"

My stomach lurches.

When I don't respond immediately he asks me again, this time dropping the sickly sweet tone. "I asked you a question."

"Nineteen," I whisper.

He snickers and reaches for his glass. Those rings clink as he wraps his fist around it. "And your friends?"

"I don't know," I lie.

The scarred guard crosses the room and places a hand on the man's shoulder. "Not her."

The man slams his glass down, sloshing amber liquid across the table. "She's too old anyway."

It takes everything in me not to lunge for him, to spit in his bloated face. Whatever made that guard intervene, I'm grateful. Until he points across the room to Katie, who's sitting uncomfortably in the lap of a middle-aged man in an expensive suit.

"That's the one you want," the guard says.

He huffs. "I'll have to settle for Fairfax's sloppy seconds then."

I flash the guard a pleading look, silently begging him to help us, but his gaze slides past me like I'm a ghost.

The next hour crawls by in a haze of careful movements and averted eyes. I serve more drinks, dodge wandering hands from the two unoccupied men, and try not to think about the closed bedroom door or Katie's terrified eyes. Cat fell asleep hours ago, and blessedly, they've left her alone. For now.

Finally, when their laughter grows louder and their words more aggressive, the scarred guard appears at my side.

"Time to go," he says quietly.

"Where?"

He ignores my question and grabs my wrist to pull me up. My eyes meet Katie's and try to convey a silent message. It'll be okay. I'm still here.

The last thing I see before he shoves me into the hallway, is the man with the rings stumbling toward Katie. Tears stream down my face. *Please let her come out of this in one piece.*

He leads me down the dim hotel hallway to another room. It's standard size, just a bed, a bathroom, a chair in the corner, and heavy curtains drawn tight. I wipe my eyes with the back of my hand, but I can't stop the tears from sliding down my cheeks.

"Wait here," he says, then locks the door behind him.

I could try to run. Try to get help. But there's no chance in hell he left me unguarded. Instead, I search the room for a phone, and only find a cord hanging from the bedside table. There's nothing useful in here. They made sure of that.

The soft bed pulls me in. I'm so exhausted, so done with this life. I curl up on top of the comforter and wrap the edge around my exposed legs. My puffy eyelids droop and in seconds sleep pulls under.

I wake to the sound of the door closing. It could have been hours later, or minutes. I'm too disorientated to tell. Sweeper walks across the room and drags the curtains open, letting soft light into the room. I squint against it, rubbing my swollen eyes.

"You're one of the lucky ones," he says without turning around. "Time to go."

Sneaking around is harder than I thought it would be. It would be easy if we were only avoiding Jasper, but we're avoiding Damon, Mom, and Dad too. Leon is fine with everyone knowing. He said so in that easy, no-nonsense way of his. It's me that's holding back. I don't even really know why. The guys might be pissed for a while... might try and kick Leon's ass, but what can they do to stop us? We're both adults. I don't know... Everyone's happy right now. I don't want to mess up the peace.

But God, the sneaking around is kind of thrilling too? Like yesterday, I was downstairs helping Mom with laundry and Leon came up behind me in the laundry room. Just pressed himself against my back and kissed my neck while I was pouring detergent in the slot. I almost dropped the full bottle. "Someone could see," I whispered. The laundry room is right next to the bro-tel, but honestly I didn't want him to stop. Not that he did. He just hummed against my skin and said, "Let them."

And being at dinner together... it's so hard to act like a normal person! Last night, Dad was asking Leon about his programming project and I'm sitting there trying not to stare at his mouth, that lip ring. At his hands as he gripped his glass of iced tea. Remembering how they felt tangled in my hair. Jasper kept looking between us like he knew something was up, which made me panic and start babbling about work until Mom told me to slow down and actually chew my chicken.

Then there was this morning. I got up early to make pancakes for everyone (okay, fine, I was hoping Leon would come up and we'd have a repeat of the banana bread date). He didn't disappoint. I heard his footsteps behind me at six, while I was whisking batter. We had maybe ten minutes alone before Damon came up for his run.

But it was such an amazing ten minutes.

Ten minutes of Leon pressing me against the counter, whispering things in my ear that made it hard for me to breathe normally. Ten minutes of him kissing up my neck, along my jaw line, until he finally claimed my lips.

When we heard Damon walking in, Leon stepped back so fast and started pouring coffee like nothing happened. I probably looked guilty as hell, but Damon just grunted a good morning and grabbed his water bottle.

I keep catching myself smiling at random times.

Mom asked me yesterday if I was feeling okay because I was "glowing." GLOWING. I wanted to die. But also... maybe I am glowing? Is that what being happy feels like? I've been missing out.

I know we can't keep this up much longer. Someone's going to figure it out. Part of me wants them to, just so we can stop pretending. So we can touch and kiss and talk the way we want to all the time.

But the other part of me loves having him all to myself, even if it's just quick moments in empty hallways and text messages late at night.

Maybe tomorrow I'll tell him I'm ready. Or maybe I'll just see how long we can keep getting away with it. This bubble is too amazing to pop.

CHAPTER SIXTEEN

BAILEY - BEFORE

I CHANGE IN THE BACK OF AN EXPENSIVE SUV—CLEAN leggings and a long-sleeved henley. He even provided a stick of deodorant and hairbrush in the bag. At this point, I'm happy for the small comforts. He's having a quiet conversation with someone on the other end of his Bluetooth earbuds—friendly, almost normal sounding conversation. That doesn't last long though. The moment he ends the call, he's back to scowling.

It's a long drive, weaving through city traffic. I must be making a face that shows how nauseated I feel, because he speaks up. "Don't vomit in my car."

"Where are we going?"

"You'll see soon enough." He stops short and I lurch forward, smacking my head into the seat. The movement doesn't help the nausea. His eyes meet mine in the rearview, and he rolls the back window down a crack.

"Thank you," I say quietly.

It's a humid summer day and the fresh air barely helps. I need food. I can't remember when I ate last. Ten minutes go by, then twenty, when he slows to pull into a gas station. "I need a cup of coffee."

There's people everywhere—commuters on their way to work, parents hauling children into car seats, busy workers in commercial vehicles filling up their vans for the day. I can't help but stare.

Sweeper's eyes narrow and he holds up his phone. "You'll stay by my side and I'll let you get something to eat. If you try anything, I'll make one call and your friends are dead. Understand?"

My friends. He must mean Cat and the others... unless he means Layne and my friends back home. God, I haven't thought about them in too long. I let my gaze linger on the bustle out the window for another second before nodding.

"Good. Let's go."

He leads me through the convenience store until we reach the busy coffee counter. "Other assholes pay eight bucks for this," he says, holding up the steaming Styrofoam. "It's all the same shit."

"I wouldn't know," I say.

"You're not a coffee girl? Let me guess, college age... You must love those energy drinks?" He adds a splash of milk and pushes a lid on.

I shake my head. "Don't like the way they make me feel."

He gestures for me to lead the way. "Go ahead, pick something to eat and drink." The coffee seems to perk him up. It's been so long since I've had any agency. The choices are almost too broad. I reach for a pack of chocolate donuts, and he nods. "What else?"

"I can get more?"

"Yes, just hurry up."

I grab a bag of salt and vinegar chips, my mouth already watering. Near the counter, I grab a water, too overwhelmed by the decisions, and at the last moment he picks up a pack of gum. The cashier, a guy who looks about my age, checks us out without even looking in our eyes. I couldn't have signaled him for help even if I wanted to.

Sweeper shoves the bag at me to hold, and leads me back to the car with his free hand on my shoulder. It moves to the back of my neck when my gaze strays toward a woman pumping gas and staring right at us. *Help me*, I silently scream. She looks away quickly anyway.

Back in the car, I tear into the donuts immediately, not caring that chocolate crumbs fall onto my clean shirt. The sweetness hits my empty stomach like a shock, but I force myself to keep chewing. Sweeper pulls back onto the highway, merging into traffic with aggressive lane changes that kill my already queasy stomach.

"Easy," he says, glancing at me in the rearview mirror. "You eat too fast and you'll just puke it back up."

I slow down, taking smaller bites, needing to finish every last crumb. The chips are next. The sharp tang of vinegar makes my mouth water and my eyes tear up. It tastes so good I could cry. I never thought I'd be so grateful for gas station junk food.

Outside my window the view changes from city buildings to suburbs, then to what looks like the middle of nowhere. We're definitely not going back to the house, and I'm not even sure that we're staying in New York. My chest tightens with each mile that takes me further from everything I know. From any chance someone might be looking for me.

The clock on the car shows that another hour has gone by when Sweeper's phone buzzes. He answers it through his Bluetooth, his voice changing to that same friendly tone from earlier. "Yeah, we're about thirty minutes out... No issues... She's been compliant."

Fire runs through my veins. *She's been compliant.* Like I'm cargo being delivered. I guess I am... but to hear him say it that way disgusts me.

"Copy that. See you soon." He ends the call and catches my eye in the mirror again. "We're almost there."

"Where's there?"

My question goes unanswered.

Twenty minutes later, we turn off the main road onto a smaller one, then through an unmanned gate. A sign reads *Private Airfield - Authorized Personnel Only.* My heart starts pounding so hard I can feel it in my throat.

"No," I whisper, not believing what I'm seeing. He's taking me on a plane. Flying me God knows where.

The airfield comes into view, where a sleek white jet stands waiting, engines running. It might as well be a casket.

"I can't get on that plane." I reach for the door handle, desperate to get out of the car. It's child-locked. "Please, don't do this."

Three men in dark suits stand near the aircraft staircase, watching as Sweeper parks the car. He turns in his seat to face me fully for the first time during the ride. His face shows something that might be sympathy or maybe just exhaustion, but it's gone so quickly I might have imagined it.

"You can walk onto that plane, or I can drag you. Your choice." He opens his door. "But either way, you're getting on."

The men in suits approach the SUV, like a dark cloud closing in. One opens my door while the other flanks the vehicle. I keep my eyes locked on Sweeper's, shaking my head again and again. What can I do? There's nowhere to run. Even if I could somehow get away, I'm surrounded by empty fields with nowhere to hide. I'm utterly alone.

"Bailey." The voice that calls my name makes me freeze. I know that accent. I know his voice.

King steps out from behind the stairs, straightening his jacket. He has that smile on his face. It reminds me of twisted barbed wire, razor sharp. And the cologne—he's not even close enough for me to smell it but it's somehow already there, suffocating me. I gag, almost losing my breakfast. I can't breathe. I can't—

"Don't make this harder than it needs to be," Sweeper says, as he pulls open my door and clamps a hand around my wrist.

"No," I cry, scrambling backwards. "Please, no. You said—you said—I was lucky," I choke out through the tears already streaming down my face. "You said—"

He sighs and tugs on my wrist. "I said you were one of the lucky ones who got picked. That's a different kind of luck than what you're thinking."

King's voice booms across the tarmac as he yells something in Russian to the men. One of them laughs. They're all evil, pure fucking evil.

"Where?" I sob one more time, even though I know he won't tell me.

Sweeper's grip tightens as he pulls me from the car. My legs are jelly, and I stumble forward before he catches me around the middle. "You'll find out when you land."

He passes me off to one of the men and the next thing I know, I'm being carried toward the stairs. It's a funeral march. Even if I make it through whatever this is, I know I won't be the same.

The engine drowns out my sobs as we stop at the bottom of the stairs where King is waiting. The man puts me down in front of him, and he looks me over with that same hungry look that haunts my dreams. Like he's getting his favorite toy back after lending it to a friend.

"Welcome back, pet. Did you miss me?"

I can't speak, can't do anything but let them guide me up

those metal stairs into the belly of the plane. As it takes off into the clear afternoon sky, I know it's carrying me away from any hope of home.

THE PLANE slowly descends through thick, gray clouds. I'm equally terrified to see where they've taken me and anxious to get off this plane. I've spent the entire flight pressed as closely against the small window as I could, avoiding King's snarky words and lingering gaze. He's been oddly tame—not by normal human standards, but from what I've come to expect from him. I'm still expecting the worst though.

Now, as we break through the clouds, darkness greets me from below. Scattered lights twinkle from inside homes that are widely spread. It must be some kind of rural area.

"Almost home, my pet. I'll be so sad to lose you, but don't worry... your friend Cat will take good care of me." King puffs out his chest and smirks as I seethe.

"Go to hell." There's so much more I want to say, but I'm not free of him yet. He can do a lot between now and landing.

King just laughs until Sweeper cuts in. "You should make the call."

"Isn't that what I pay you for?" he says.

I turn away to look back out the window, but I don't need to see Sweeper's face to know he'd love to punch King in the face as much as I would. "*You* don't pay me. Your uncle does."

They argue semantics as the landing gear comes out. I hold my breath in those final moments, but thankfully, it's only a matter of minutes we're on the ground smoothly.

Through the window all I can make out are runway lights cutting through the darkness. It must be another private airfield. This one looks even more isolated than the last. Rolling hills stretch in every direction beyond the landing strip. I squint to get a better view, but it's hard to see anything in the shadows.

When the plane finally stops, Sweeper stands and gestures for me to do the same. "Time to go."

I follow him on unsteady legs, too exhausted to fight. Humid air hits my face as I step onto the aircraft stairs. It smells like fresh rain and something floral. I'm definitely not in New York City anymore.

Two shiny black Bentleys wait on the tarmac, their lights blazing. I notice their license plates right away. White with black letters and numbers, unlike any I've seen in the US. Two people get out of one of the cars and stand beside it. Their silhouette seems to stiffen the closer we get. A man and a woman, both middle-aged with graying hair and weathered faces, wearing immaculate uniforms. They almost look like they could have been our flight attendants, although the plane I just left didn't have those.

"Ms. Harrington," Sweeper greets the woman as we reach the car. He gives me a small push forward. "As discussed."

She gives a sharp nod, and trails her gaze over me like she's assessing and finds me lacking. I fold my arms across my chest. "Indeed. We've been expecting her."

King, who must be finished with his phone call, jogs over to us. I wrap my arms around myself tighter, noticing that the woman clocks my movement. "Take good care of our guest," he tells them.

Guest? I hold back a scoff. *Bastard.* How dare he act like I have any say in this. Like I'm more than a piece of inventory in their fucked up business.

"Of course, sir." Ms. Harrington smiles but it doesn't reach her eyes. "We'll ensure she's properly settled."

The uniformed man opens the back door and gestures for me to get in. As hesitant as I am, I'd rather be with these strangers than spend another second near King. I slide in, grateful for the warmth, and look ahead out the Bentley's windshield at the long road disappearing into darkness.

As my two new captors take their places in the front seats, I watch King wave his fingers before turning toward the second parked car and disappearing into the shadows.

Good. I hope he drives off the road into a ditch somewhere.

It's one of the most awkward car rides of my life. I'm too nervous to speak first, and neither of them seem inclined to break the silence. They just drive and drive down long, winding roads, all of them dark, giving me no hints of where we are. My stomach growls loudly and the woman, Ms. Harrington, sniffs. Sorry, lady. I've been denied food all day. Can't help my bodily functions.

Finally, I spot a pair of lights in the distance, illuminating a huge set of iron gates. My pulse starts beating erratically, my breaths coming in short pants. Whatever's beyond those gates, I'm terrified to find out.

A massive sigil sits in the center, splitting open as the driver enters a code. One ornate letter C surrounded by flourishes. They close behind us with a loud clang that causes me to flinch.

Something in my gut tells me that I won't ever see the world beyond those gates again.

CHAPTER SEVENTEEN

LEON - PRESENT DAY

The ref yells, "Fight!" and James and I start circling each other. I'm caught off guard, trying to read his facial expressions, see if he recognizes me too. Fuck, I can't tell, and I can't afford to lose this fight. I need those guns.

The crowd roars for us to get going, but I block them out. We circle and circle, hands up in guard position, neither making the first move. He's got maybe an inch or two on me, but his stance tells me everything I need to know. Yeah, he's trained, but he's never had to fight for his life. That's the difference.

"So you're daddy's favorite bastard," James sneers.

I guess he does know who I am, then.

I duck under his first jab, a clean shot that would have fucked me up if it connected. "Favorite?" I laugh bitterly, throwing a quick combination that he blocks. "He pretends I don't exist."

"Bullshit." James lands a solid hit to my ribs that has me gasping. The crowd erupts. "Never stops talking about you.

Leon this, Leon that. So bloody smart, so successful at university."

I stagger back, more from the shock of his words than the hit. "He talks about me?"

He takes advantage of my distraction, catching me with an uppercut that snaps my head back. Bloody hell. Stars explode behind my eyes and I taste blood.

Spitting it onto the floor, I shake my head clear. Enough. Time to turn this around.

"'Course he does," James seethes. He throws another punch, then an elbow combination. "His perfect son who doesn't embarrass the family name."

I block just in time and drive my fist into his diaphragm. I've had enough of his bullshit talking. James doubles over, gasping for air, his styled hair now matted with sweat. I don't give him a chance to recover.

"Perfect son?" I spit, circling him as he struggles to breathe. "He ignored me my entire life. I'm nothing to him."

James straightens slowly, wiping bloody saliva from his lips. "Nothing? He never shuts up about you. Meanwhile, I'm the disappointment that can't do anything right."

He comes at me again, less aggressive now. We end up on the ground, grappling, both trying to make sense of what we're hearing. He's straddling me with one hand pressed against my throat, choking off my air supply, while the other draws back for a punch. The look in his eyes is pure hatred.

I grab his wrist and buck my hips, throwing him off-balance. We roll to the left, scraping against the rough concrete. I suck in a breath, shoving my knee between us to create space, but he's right there, sweeping away my supporting leg. We crash, my head thudding against the floor this time. He tries to mount me again, but I twist my hips and slip out from under him. We both scramble to our feet at the same time, breathing hard, circling each other again with our guards up.

I wipe sweat from my brow and smirk. "That all you got, *brother*? Afraid to get your manicured nails dirty?"

His nostrils flare and his footsteps grow heavier. I'm getting to him. Time to finish this.

"Least I know where I come from. What are you, half of *what* exactly?"

I see red.

"Racist piece of shit," I spit. He moves and there it is. My opening.

I feint left, then drive my right fist straight into his temple.

His eyes roll back and he goes down with a thud, out cold. The ref comes to check his pulse but I'm barely aware, doubled over, sucking in air to calm the spike of adrenaline rushing through me. I want to kick him while he's down... something I'd never do. And fuck, I hate to admit that his words got to me, but it was a low blow. Same shit I heard from kids at school my entire life.

"What are you?"

As if I'm some fucking alternate species of human.

I've heard it all. Ignorant questions they'd say in passing... like it was no big deal.

"You adopted or something?"

"So, like... what are you exactly? Like, what do we call you?"

And then there were the cruel ones that came as I got older. Comments I don't even want to replay in my mind. It was hard enough having a father who didn't give a shit that I was alive without bringing our racial differences into it. What James said was fucking disgusting and I'm glad he's knocked on his ass.

Tank's voice booms that I'm the winner before calling the names of the next two fighters. Cruz rushes to my side, patting me on the shoulder.

"Fucking brilliant! I don't think I've ever seen you look that angry, and that's counting the time Abel dribbled piss on your bike."

He hands me my shirt, which I use to wipe my face before shrugging it on. I don't look behind me, if James doesn't get back up, I don't give a shit. I'm headed for one person—Knapp.

"Lee?" Cruz asks. "Did ya hear me?"

"Huh?" I ask, finally registering that he's been asking me a question.

He steps in front of me, and peers into my eyes. "Maybe we should get you to a doc. Get checked out."

"No, I'm fine." I step around him. "Just need to finish up here and get home."

I'm sure he thinks I have a concussion, but really, I'm just processing. Maybe there's a *slight* concussion too, but I'll live.

"If you're sure?" I nod again. "Alright, well, I'm gonna go collect. Meet you out front?"

"You can head home," I tell him. As much as I like Cruz, I don't have it in me to carry a conversation at this point. I clap him on the shoulder, thanking him for setting this up, and head straight to a smirking Knapp.

"Have to say, I wasn't sure about you, but you won me a lot of money tonight. Had my doubts when I saw who you were fighting, but you proved me wrong."

I wipe a drip of blood from my nose with the back of my hand and square my shoulders. "Great. I need hardware, you need payment. Let's do business."

His eyes narrow and my stomach drops for a second, but then he chuckles, gesturing to the guy next to him. "I like this one."

I force a laugh. It sounds unnatural but anything to get this over with.

Knapp leans in, speaking low. "Tomorrow. 10:00 PM.

Clancy's Garage, 23 Millwall Road. Park around back, knock three times on the rear door."

"I'll be there," I say. As I pull away, his hand grasps my shoulder, holding me in place.

"Bring cash. And come alone." His thick hand releases me and he's already onto betting on the next round.

With our agreement settled, I stop by Tank to say goodbye, collecting my meager winnings. She tries to strike up a conversation, judging from the rare look of concern on her face, probably about James, but I cut her off.

I need air. I need a stiff drink. And most of all, I need to ice my head.

I WAKE to the sound of voices drifting upstairs from the kitchen. Either someone's trying to split my head with an ax or I'm paying for my choices last night. Uppercuts and copious amounts of whiskey don't mix.

I groan and sit up slowly, cataloguing the damage—split lip, bruised ribs, and what feels like a mild concussion. It'll be worth it after I get what I need tonight.

Sunlight streams in through a crack in the drapes, somehow aiming directly at my eyes like laser beams. I groan, shielding my eyes with my hand. "Bloody fuckin—"

Mum stops laughing and I hear a male voice responding. A familiar male voice—posh accent, entitled drawl.

James.

What the fuck is he doing in my mother's kitchen?

Ignoring the pain and nausea, I jump out of bed, and storm down the stairs. There he is, the sodding prick, sitting at mum's table, a cup of tea in front of him and biscuits from my childhood plate. James sees me coming and scrambles out of his seat. Mum quickly jumps between us.

"Leon, don't be angry. He's not here to make trouble," Mum says calmly but firm. "Let's sit down and talk. I'll make some more tea."

"Mum," I seethe. "Step aside."

"Please," James says, his hands up. "I don't want trouble. I came to apologize for what I said last night. How I acted."

I scoff. "Fuck right off."

"Language!" Mum scolds.

I'm too angry to acknowledge her.

"Five minutes," I growl, pointing toward the front door. "Outside. Then you fuck off and never come back."

Mum opens her mouth to protest, but I'm already stalking toward the garden, naked except for my boxers. I don't give a shit if the neighbors see, my only concern is getting this piece of shit out of here.

James follows, looking somewhat stunned.

Once we're outside, I cross my arms and glare at him. "Start talking."

James runs a hand through his dark hair which is perfectly coiffed again despite the rest of him looking like absolute shit. "Look, what I said last night... about you being mixed. That was out of line."

"Out of line?" I let out a bitter laugh. "You fucking think?"

"It was racist. And wrong." He casts his gaze downward. "I was angry and I wanted to hit you where it hurts. But that's no excuse."

I stay quiet, refusing to make this easy for him.

"The thing is," James continues, "if it makes you feel any better, our prick of a dad's never home anymore anyway. My parents refuse to get divorced because of money and status, but Mum's fucking her therapist, basically living with a new family, and God knows what he's doing up at the country estate. He's there all the time now... I can barely get a meeting with him."

Cry me a river, I want to say. But I stay quiet, shifting on my bare feet, which are getting cold in the damp grass.

"He's cut me off completely," James says, his voice turning bitter like it was last night. "Why do you think I fight in that piece of shit basement? The controlling bastard's even cutting off Mum's spending too. Keeping us both on a leash. And then to hear him go on and on about you... how you're everything I'm not, well..."

"And I'm supposed to feel sorry for you?"

He drags his hand through his hair again and meets my gaze. "No... that's not why I came. I'm just—I don't know. I'm sorry, alright?"

A noise comes from the entrance—Mum being nosey. I wonder briefly if she knew who James was before letting him into her home. I turn back to him—my brother. The word feels all wrong to describe him. Damon and Jasper—they're my brothers. In everything but blood. This piece of rubbish can crawl back to whatever Mayfair penthouse he came from.

"Your time is up." I gesture to the street where his shiny BMW sits parked along the curb, my gaze cold and unforgiving.

He walks toward his car then pauses at the gate. "For what it's worth, I'm glad I got to meet you. It's him we should hate, not each other."

I have enough hate for both of you.

When I look up he's already pulling away.

I head inside, where Mum's standing by the stove, pretending she's been there the whole time. Without a word, I grab a bag of peas from the freezer, and sit at the table with a groan. Mum places a hot cuppa in front of me without me having to ask.

"Thanks."

"Extra strong. You look like you need it."

I sip, letting the hot liquid slide down my throat, waking me up, while holding the peas on my head with my free hand. She drops two paracetamol next to my mug and takes a seat across from me.

"Do you know who that was?" I ask. She mulls it over for a moment, sipping her tea, avoiding my gaze. "Mum?"

"Yes," she admits. "I've never met the young man, but of course I knew who he was. Alfred's shown me plenty of photographs over the years."

I struggle to keep my jaw closed. "What is this relationship you have with the man that abandoned us? That barely helped support me until I turned eighteen?"

"Leon, I—"

"Nevermind, Mum. I have work to do," I say, getting up from the table. "Thanks for the tea and the meds."

She scrambles up, wrapping her hand around my wrist. "Son, wait."

I sigh, not in the mood for this shit right now, but face her anyway. "What is it?"

"James—he came here to warn you. Last night—whatever it was that had both you boys looking like you'd been through hell, well... he overheard something."

I set the bag of peas down and give her my full attention. "What kind of something?"

"After the fight, he was getting patched up when he overheard a few associates of your father. They were talking about you. I don't know what they said, but James wanted to tell you to be careful."

I shrug and pick up the peas again, pressing them against my temple. "I can handle myself, Mum."

"Leon—"

"I'm fine. Really." I turn, taking my tea with me. "I'm going to get some work done upstairs."

Once I'm behind my closed door, the guilt hits me. I feel like shit for treating Mum badly, but what does she expect? I can't deal with that right now. Especially not while my head is still pounding.

I pull out my phone and read through my texts with Bailey. They help me feel better, more centered. I stop before the messages from that night. Reading those right now would only make things worse.

Before I can go back to sleep for a few hours, something that James said bugs me. I pull up my search engines and type in his name, along with all the other details I know offhand about him.

There's the usual hits. Private school photos where he's posing with rowing teams and debate clubs. University announcements about academic achievements. A few society page mentions at charity galas, always photographed next to Alfred, looking like the perfect father-son duo.

But then I find the more interesting stuff.

An article from two years ago about a gambling ring bust at his university. I have to scan a few paragraphs to find his name. He's listed as a student who was questioned but not charged. Then further down, another article about him being asked to leave Cambridge after an undisclosed incident.

Wonder what that could have been?

The most recent hit is from six months ago. I open it, blinking against the brightness on my screen. There's a brief mention in a financial gossip column about young Colter and his mounting gambling debts at several London clubs. Looks like they've been enjoying speculating about whether Alfred would continue bailing him out.

I shut my computer down and flop into bed.

I'm not surprised Alfred cut him off. And no wonder James looked so desperate last night when he was talking about fighting for money. The bigger they are, the harder they fall and all that.

At least now I finally understand why my half brother ended up in that basement. We're both trying to escape Alfred's shadow. I just chose a different way to do it.

We went on our first real-ish date last night. I'm going to romanticize it by writing it like a scene in a book again because... well, I figure when I look back at this diary years from now, I'll have all the details right. Or as best as an amateur-ish writer who frequents fanfic sites could do it. And I want all the details. It was too good to skip anything.

Leon wouldn't tell me where we were going, just said he wanted somewhere quiet. Somewhere we could be truly alone. My pulse skipped erratically all day knowing I'd have him all to myself. I even fumbled some orders at work during the lunch rush, which I never do.

Finally, around five, Mom and Dad announced that someone left a gift card to their favorite restaurant on the table for them but it expired that night. That they were sorry but we were fending for ourselves, before they practically ran out the door.

Jasper was kind of hanging around all day, saying his old football injury was acting up... just being generally grumpy. Damon wasn't around, so he was probably just bored.

I don't know what kind of miracle worker Leon is, but about two minutes after Mom and Dad left, Jasper got a call that one of his hookups got her shift covered and she could actually come over after all, and that she was on her way.

I've never seen my brother bolt downstairs so fast, not sparing a glance at me or Leon.

"You're a wizard," I told him, as he watched his handiwork unfold from the kitchen table, arms crossed over his chest, showing off his perfect inked forearms.

"If it takes a bit of magic to get you all to myself, then I'll abracadabra all day."

He gestured for me to come to him without speaking, just slowly crooking his finger. When I got to him, he pulled me onto his lap, my chest pressed against his, my arms wrapped around his neck. "Are you ready for our date, beautiful?"

I nodded, probably looking like an idiot with how big I was smiling. His fingers traced a path along my back and God, that small touch felt so good. "Ready to tell me where we're going yet?"

"You'll see soon enough." He stood up, lifting me with him like I weighed nothing, before setting me back on my feet. He grabbed a sweatshirt from the hook by the door. His favorite sweatshirt. "Here, put this on for me."

It smelled so good, like a hint of his cologne. Warm

and cedar-like mixed with something that I could only describe as Leon smell, safe and masculine and comfort all at once.

Then we slipped out, hand in hand.

His motorcycle was waiting in the driveway, and my stomach flipped when he handed me a helmet.

"You trust me?" he asked with that mischievous smile, the one where only a corner of his lip quirks up.

My heart banged against my ribs—part nerves, part pure excitement. "Always."

The minute I climbed on behind him and wrapped my arms around his waist, I understood why people became addicted to this. There's something so intimate about it. Something I couldn't explain. He started the bike, and I felt the vibrations through my entire body.

I took a deep breath, clutching him closer as he pulled out onto the street.

"You okay?" he called loud enough for me to hear.

I couldn't find words, so I just squeezed him tighter. I was more than okay. Riding with him was incredible. The wind whipped against my face even through the helmet, and there was something wild and intoxicating about racing down those back roads with nothing but Leon's solid warmth anchoring me. Every curve had my pulse spiking, not from fear but from this incredible rush of freedom.

After about fifteen minutes, he turned down a narrow dirt road I'd never seen before. I had to squeeze my thighs around Leon and tighten my grip from the steady upward climb. When we finally crested the hill and he cut the engine, I could see why he'd brought me here.

The clearing was perfection. A little oasis tucked away from everything and everyone, overlooking the valley below. He'd already been here. There was a blanket spread under a beautiful oak tree, weighed down with a picnic basket and two battery-powered lanterns we'd used for camping as kids.

"Leon," I breathed, pulling off my helmet. "When did you do all this?"

"Today, while you were at work." He cast his gaze toward the ground, running his hand through his hair. "Is it too much? I know it's not exactly a proper restaurant, and you deserve that, but—"

I silenced him by standing on my tiptoes, wrapping my arms around his neck, and kissing him softly. "It's perfect. I love it."

We got comfortable on the blanket, Leon with his back against the tree and me settled between his legs, my head resting on his chest. He was so freaking sweet and thoughtful with what he'd packed. My favorite sandwich—turkey and swiss on wheat bread with mayo and just a dab of dijon. Exactly how I like it. Cookies from the bakery in town, and a bottle of wine. He'd brought sodas too, but figured he'd give me the option. I chose the wine. My nerves needed it.

The funny thing was, he seemed nervous too, like he wanted to make everything perfect. But just being here with him was all I needed.

We talked about everything and nothing as the sky darkened. His childhood in London with his mom and grandparents, my dreams of teaching kids how to read and why it meant so much to me. Lighter stuff too, like stupid stories about Jasper and Damon and the crazy shit they pulled at school. I felt like I could tell him anything, which was completely new for me. Usually I'm the one listening, making sure everyone else feels heard, but Leon actually wanted to know me—asked questions, seemed genuinely interested. Sounds pathetic that those little things were such a shock, but I guess I've always been okay with staying in the background.

After we finished eating, we laid back on the blanket, my head nestled in the crook of his arm as we watched the first stars appear. I traced patterns on his chest while his arm tightened around my waist. Even though every inch of me ached for him, I also felt this deep sense of peace. I didn't feel rushed to take things further, like I'd lose his attention if I didn't immediately put my hand down his pants. Again, something totally new for me.

That's when I noticed the first tiny flicker of light dancing near the edge of the clearing.

"Look," I whispered, sitting up slightly. "Fireflies."

More lights began blinking in and out between blades of tall grass, like someone scattered a handful of twinkle lights that moved on their own. Leon shifted beneath me to take a better look.

"We don't have these in England," he murmured, watching as more and more appeared. "Just glowworms, and they're pretty rare."

"Glowworms?" I asked. "I'd like to see those one day."

He kissed the top of my head. "I bet I can make that happen. Wizard, remember?"

"I should come up with a better list of requests if it's that easy," I said with a laugh.

He pushed a piece of hair behind my ear. "Anything you want, it's yours."

Almost like he summoned it with his words, a firefly fluttered close enough for him to catch in his cupped hands. We watched it glow between the cracks of his fingers, but when I looked up, Leon's gaze was fixed on me.

"What is it?" I asked, rubbing my hand across my forehead. "Do I have something on my face?"

He opened his palm and released the firefly into the night, keeping his eyes on me. "You're like them, you know. Beautiful and peaceful, lighting up everything around you without even trying. Except I'd never want to catch you or put you in a jar. That would take away how amazing it is to watch you dance around, bringing your glow to the rest of the world. Not because you feel obligated to, but because it's who you are. I'm happy to sit back and be awed by your presence. So fucking lucky."

"Leon... I don't even know what to say to that. I..." Tears sprang at the corner of my eye, as he pulled me in for a kiss. I didn't need words, the way my lips met his, my tongue sliding between his teeth, carefully tasting him, said everything I was thinking. I sucked his bottom lip, until he moaned against my mouth. And God, my body was electric.

His hands roamed over my back, gliding up into my

hair so he could angle my face and deepen the kiss. I touched him greedily, losing the timidness I usually felt. Under his shirt, smoothing along the ridges of his abs. He was so hot, I felt like I was dreaming.

"Bailey," he groaned as I slid my fingers over his nipple. I did it again, this time pinching gently. "Fuck."

He rolled us, so I was flat on my back and he hovered over me, taking in my flushed cheeks and the quick rise and fall of my chest. I watched as he caught his breath, loving the effect I had on him. It made me bold enough to raise my hips, seeking out the friction I needed.

"Please," I whispered.

His eyes seemed to darken as he took me in. Full of as much want and need as I was. His jaw clenched tight like he was trying to fight some internal battle and failing.

"Christ," he said, his voice rough. "You have no idea what you do to me. How fucking beautiful you are right now."

His thumb slowly traced along my bottom lip. I swear his hand trembled slightly, like touching me was almost too much, like he was overwhelmed by whatever he was feeling.

"I want to memorize every inch of you," he whispered, leaning down to press a soft kiss to my lips, then my jaw. "Is that okay?"

I nodded, not trusting myself to speak coherent words.

He took his time, kissing along my neck, pausing to suck gently until I gasped. He moved lower, pressing kisses to my collarbone through the fabric of his sweatshirt. When his hands found the hem, he looked up at me questioningly.

"Yes," I breathed, and all traces of nervousness evaporated.

He lifted the sweatshirt over my head, and for a moment he just stared, like he was trying to burn the image of me like this into his memory. Then his mouth was on my skin, kissing and tasting his way down my body in a way that was nothing short of worship.

"So perfect," he murmured against me. "So fucking perfect."

My entire body was on fire, pulsing, thrumming with need. And when he reached the top of my jeans, I didn't wait for him to ask. My hands were there, unbuttoning, tugging them as far down as I could. "Leon, please..."

I don't even know what I was asking for, just something to quell the aching need. One touch and I'd be over the edge.

He pulled my pants all the way off, taking his time as his hands glided along my thighs, planting a slow path of kisses along my hip bones. I was about to start begging when he finally drifted a finger over my center, so light I barely felt the touch.

"You soaked these panties for me, Firefly. Do you want to know what I'm thinking?"

Another slow pass of his finger, barely lingering over my clit. I moaned, not giving a shit if I sounded as desperate as I felt. My heart hammered against my ribs, every nerve ending screaming for release.

"I'm thinking about how sweet you'll taste when you come for me."

"Please," I begged again. His expression looked raw, almost pained, as he rolled his lip ring between his teeth and slipped his index finger into the seam of my panties. I gasped again, trying to hold still, but failing miserably. He took his time, watching my face as he decided exactly how he wanted to unravel me.

Then, without breaking eye contact, he slowly pulled the fabric to the side. "Fuck," he whispered, and swallowed hard as he drunk me in. "I've been dreaming about this, about you. You have no idea how long I've wanted this."

Finally, he slid a finger between my soaked folds, and stroked my clit gently. "Oh God, Leon, please."

He brought his finger to his lips and slid it into his mouth, like he was savoring the taste while torturing us both with anticipation. "So fucking sweet."

He lowered himself until his face was just inches from my center. I'd never felt so desired before, so completely needed.

"Tell me if you want me to stop, yeah? I want this to be perfect for you."

"Yes—Ooh my God. Oh fuck—"

My words dissolved into a stream of moans as his tongue found my clit, pressing and swirling exactly where I needed him most. It didn't take long before every one of my muscles began to tighten, that climb of pleasure building and building.

Then he added a finger, slipping it inside me, and stroking in rhythm with his tongue.

"So close... don't stop."

He lapped faster, his finger matching the same relentless pace.

Within seconds, total euphoria washed over me. My body shook as the most intense orgasm of my life slammed into me, my scream of pleasure echoing through the clearing. I didn't care—it felt too good. He felt too good.

He kept going, sucking gently at my clit, drawing every last second of bliss out of me until I couldn't take anymore. Then he adjusted my underwear and kissed his way back up my body, eyes glassy, lips glistening.

Staring down at me with the most reverent smile, he said, "That was worth every second of waiting. You're incredible."

I drifted my hands down to his belt, fumbling with the buckle as I tried to catch my breath. "Your turn," I whispered, as I worked to undo his button.

He caught my hands gently, bringing them up to his lips and pressing a kiss to my knuckles. "Let's slow down, love."

"But I want to—You made me feel so good, I should—"

"Tonight was about you." He traced his thumb over my bottom lip while he looked at me with the most tender expression. "About showing you how incredible you are. I don't need anything else right now."

"Are you sure? I mean, you must be—"

He silenced me with a soft kiss. "I'm more than sure. Watching you fall apart for me was fucking perfect. There's no rush, love. We have all the time in the world."

The way he said it, so genuinely, made my throat tight with emotion. I'd never been with someone who didn't expect something in return, who seemed more concerned with my pleasure than his own.

"Okay," I whispered, settling back against his chest as he pulled me close.

We laid there for what felt like hours afterward, just holding each other and watching the fireflies dance around us. I felt like I was glowing just as bright as they were. I never want this summer to end.

CHAPTER EIGHTEEN

BAILEY - BEFORE

THE NEXT MORNING, I WAKE IN A STRANGE BED, IN A strange room, with crisp clean air and the patter of rain hitting the window. It was so late by the time Ms. Harrington showed me to my "quarters" as she called them, that I took one look at the comfortable bed and passed out. It was a dreamless sleep, like I'd sunk into a dark pit and crawled out someone new. Someone refreshed. But now, as my eyes adjust to my surroundings, I remember that I'm not on vacation, that I have no clue where in the world I am, or what these people want from me.

The space reminds me of a summer cottage we rented when I was a kid. One main room and a bathroom with a large tub, with more bath products than I can count. To the side sits a small kitchenette with a sink, a mini refrigerator, and counter. That's the only thing in the space that looks updated. The decor, the furniture, is antique-looking.

As soon as I step to the window, I pull back the drapes and notice thick lattice covering the glass like decorative bars. Then I hear a click from outside. What do I do? There's nowhere to hide, other than the bathroom, but even that doesn't have a door.

Standing there frozen, I watch the door slowly swing open and Ms. Harrington enter. She looks exactly the same as she did last night. Immaculate uniform, hair in a tight bun, no jewelry or accents that give me any inclination of her personality. It's just her and the severe scowl that seems to be a permanent fixture on her face.

She looks me over with a raised brow. "I take it you slept well."

"I—"

She waves a hand to cut me off. "You will bathe and dress. Sir wants you at breakfast in twenty minutes."

"But—"

"There will be no arguing, no questions, and no exceptions," she snaps. "Now get."

There's a hundred things I'd like to ask, but I know she'd bite my head off. I settle on the one that's most important at the moment. "What will I wear?"

She walks to the closet, a door I didn't notice until just now, and pulls it open. It's filled with clothing of all colors. "And over here," she gestures to a small chest of drawers, "you'll find the undergarments that Sir finds most suitable."

He's chosen my underwear. The thought fills me with dread.

I meander toward the bathroom until Ms. Harrington makes another sharp remark that has me hustling inside.

In any other situation, I'd love to soak in this tub. I haven't taken a long bath since before school started. All I had were communal dorm showers with spotty hot water, and then of course everything *after*. Maybe I'll get the chance while I'm here. I wonder if I can smuggle in a toaster?

The morbid thought has me cracking a smile and then

shaking my head that I'm smiling right now. I'm fucking losing my mind. Whatever bits and pieces I have left.

I figure out the knobs and fill the tub, scrubbing my skin with the loofah until it's pink. A shower would be quicker and easier, but that isn't an option.

"I'll lay out some clothing options," Ms. Harrington calls over the running water.

Not like it matters. I haven't had a choice in any aspect of my life for months. I don't give a shit what I wear. But then as I rinse shampoo out of my hair, I remember the lingerie Yuri used to force us to put on. Maybe I *do* care.

I step out onto the heated floor and wrap myself in a fluffy towel. Ms. Harrington is standing with her back to me, rifling through the hanging garments. When she hears me approach, she turns, holding out two dresses. "Which would you prefer? Blush or heather gray?"

Her tone is no less sharp than it was earlier, but I'm still taken aback that she's giving me choices. I'd never wear either dress normally, they're too formal, too frilly. I prefer jeans and T-shirts. I answer, "The gray one." At least it's a color I'd wear on my own.

She bustles around gathering bras and underwear, tights, and formal heeled pumps. I feel like I'm dressing up for a theater performance. Within five minutes, I'm dressed in an outfit I swear my mom has worn to PTA meetings.

Ms. Harrington points at the small vanity in the bathroom and retrieves a hairbrush from a drawer. "Oh, I can—"

Apparently not.

She yanks the brush through my wet tangles until I mutter multiple obscenities through gritted teeth.

She stops suddenly and within seconds the brush handle cracks against the back of my head. "You will refrain from using such language here," she says sharply. "No arguing, no questions, and no foul language. *No exceptions.*"

My head throbs as I bite back some other choice words I'd like to give her. Instead, I incline my head in understanding. How many more rules will be added to her mantra before we leave this cottage?

She weaves my hair into a tight French braid and nudges me in the shoulder. "Time to go. Punctuality is most important."

Right, yet another rule.

She looks directly into an ornate painting that hangs near the entrance and nods once. A low beep sounds and then she twists the knob to open the door. In case there was any doubt in my mind that I'm a prisoner here, she just confirmed it.

Sometime in the last twenty minutes, the rain has lightened to a gentle drizzle that tickles my skin with each droplet. Tall oak and beech trees surround the cottage, their canopy shrouding it from the rest of the world. I note every step we take, quietly searching my surroundings for something I can use later.

She leads me along a winding stone pathway bordered by neatly trimmed hedges. The soft babble of a nearby brook muffles our footsteps. Despite everything, I feel like I've stepped into a completely different world—one that might be beautiful if I weren't being held here against my will.

When we turn a corner, I see the main house. It's a massive Tudor-style mansion built from warm red brick with black wood framing that creates patterns across the facade. At least five chimneys rise from the slate roof, giving off hazy smoke that climbs into the gray sky. My favorite part of the whole place is the climbing purple wisteria that clings to the stone archway and surrounds every bay window.

Beyond the perfectly manicured gardens, all I see for miles

and miles is nothing but sprawling green grass dotted by trees. The isolation hits me like a punch to the gut. I'm truly in the middle of nowhere. I've never felt so utterly alone.

Questions sit on the tip of my tongue, but clearly Ms. Harrington isn't much of a talker. Maybe whoever this Sir asshole is will give me some answers.

We enter a foyer, decorated exactly how I imagined it would be. Old world meets certain modern upgrades.

It's so quiet. I'd think in a house this large there would be people moving from room to room, appliances whirring... just the sounds of normal living. There's only the click of our heels against the polished marble. My already tight chest squeezes, and I have to focus on taking in slow deliberate breaths.

She leads me through a sitting room into a large formal dining room. A spread of pastries and fruit sit in the center of the table, so bright and delicious looking that my mouth waters.

"Sit," Ms. Harrington taps on the closest chair. "I'll inform him of your arrival."

And just like that, my stomach sinks.

She leaves the room without another word. I take in the empty space, listening for any other signs of movement. There's nothing... not even the tick of a clock, or the whir of air coming from ceiling vents.

Should I run? Could I make it anywhere? That's a simple answer—no. At least not yet. I need to be smart, figure out where I am and what they want from me.

I eye the butter knife on the table. Its curved silver handle polished to a shine. It wouldn't do much in the way of protection, but it's better than nothing. I slide it in the only place I can think of, the elastic of my bra.

Muffled voices make their way across the room, followed by footsteps. I sit frozen, too afraid to turn my head toward the sound. My hands curl around the fabric of my dress, wringing it into a ball, something to calm myself.

"There she is," a deep voice croons. It's somewhat familiar, but I can't place it. The accent though—English. Just like Ms. Harrington. Similar to Leon's but not the same.

I force myself to turn toward the voice, ignoring the pain of my chest constricting. The man who meets my gaze is tall and distinguished, probably in his fifties, with salt-and-pepper hair perfectly styled and wearing an expensive-looking navy suit. It's his smile that I recognize first, and then his eyes. The same eyes that peered into mine a few nights ago.

"You," I whisper. His last words come back to me. *"Do be a good girl until I see you again, yeah?"*

"Lovely to see you again, Bailey." He moves to the head of the table with fluid grace, pulling out his chair. "I do hope you slept well. Ms. Harrington tells me you were quite tired when you arrived."

Arrived. Like I came here willingly.

I don't know what to say. I guess it didn't matter whether my new captor was a complete stranger, or someone I've encountered before. Nothing changes. It's still a shock though.

"Sir has spoken to you," Ms. Harrington seethes. "You will respond."

He laughs, it's warm and friendly, but I already know better. "It's fine, Greta. Please, go enjoy breakfast in the garden. I see the sun peeking through the clouds."

Her face softens, and she nods, immediately obeying.

"I'm sorry for Ms. Harrington. She's a bit of a stickler for the rules, but my most trusted employee," he says, reaching for the kettle. "Did you sleep well?"

"I—uh—yes, I did." The words feel strange on my tongue. After months of King's unpredictable violence, this man's calm politeness is somehow more terrifying.

Something shifts in the practiced smile, but he continues making his cup of tea. "Sir," he says.

"I'm sorry?" I ask.

"You'll refer to me as Sir. I'm sure Ms. Harrington already briefed you?"

Here comes the shift. Exactly what I've been waiting for. Harsh words, or even violence.

"Yes, she did. I'm sorry," I say. He pauses, teacup halfway to his lips so I add, "Sir. I'm sorry, Sir."

He laughs again, as if I'd just told him a silly joke. "Excellent. Now, Bailey, please help yourself." He gestures to the decadent spread on the table. "My cook, Mr. Turner, really outdid himself today. I told him it was a special occasion."

I stare at the pastries and fresh fruit, my stomach growling despite my nerves. When was the last time I saw food this beautiful? This... normal?

My hand shakes as I reach for a croissant in front of me. Sir sucks air through his teeth and I jerk my hand back to my side. "I'm not one to give nutrition advice, but do you think a croissant is appropriate for maintaining your figure? It's your choice, of course." His eyes stray to the fruit bowl.

"Yes, you're right." I quickly add, "Sir."

I reach for a small cluster of grapes instead, keeping my movements slow and careful. He makes a pleased humming sound and picks up the very croissant I'd been reaching for, tearing off a buttery, flaky piece with a satisfied grin.

"Wise choice," he says, chewing slowly. "Though I must say, you're missing out. Mr. Turner's croissants are truly exceptional." He takes another bite, and I watch the golden crumbs fall onto his pristine white plate. My stomach clenches with hunger, but also something darker. A simmering rage threatening to bubble to the surface.

I push it down deep, and pop a grape into my mouth. Slowly chewing while looking down at my empty plate.

"Tell me," he continues while spreading softened butter on another piece of croissant, "what do you think of your accommodations? The cottage has been used by my family for generations. Whenever we needed to shut out the world, a sanctuary of sorts. I haven't found a place in the world more quiet."

His knife clinks as he rests it on the edge of his plate, and he stares at me, waiting for a response.

"It's very nice, Sir."

"I'm pleased you approve. Comfort is quite important for what I hope to accomplish." He takes a small bite and studies me again. "You see, Bailey, you're going to find that things operate quite differently under my care than what you've previously experienced."

The grape in my mouth turns sour. What does he know? It must be everything, or at least enough.

"There are rules here, naturally. But they're civilized rules. Reasonable ones. Nothing like what you're accustomed to." He sounds like he's discussing the weather with a friend. It's unnerving. "Ms. Harrington has mentioned a few already, I believe? No arguing, no questions without permission, no foul language."

I nod, unsure of what to say.

"Good. To those I would add, punctuality, as she mentioned, is essential. You will speak when spoken to. You will maintain your appearance to my standards at all times." He pauses to sip his tea while my vision tinges red. "And most importantly, you will be grateful for the opportunities I provide you."

Opportunities? This man is absolutely batshit crazy.

"In return," he continues, "you'll find life here quite pleasant. Regular meals, comfortable lodging, books to read, even television in the evenings if you've been particularly well-behaved. Quite a step up from your previous accommodations."

The casual way he references what I've endured has me clenching my jaw. I can't let my temper out though. I have to be careful. This man may seem civilized, but I know a monster when I see one.

"Do you have any questions?" he asks, then holds up a hand before I can respond. "Actually, let me rephrase that. Do you have any *appropriate* questions about your daily routine here?"

I swallow down the lump in my throat. If there's any time to ask, now is it. "What is it that you want from me, Sir?"

His smile doesn't reach his eyes. "Patience, my dear. All will become clear in time. For now, simply focus on settling in and learning our ways." He dabs his mouth with his napkin. "Ms. Harrington will show you to the library after breakfast. You may select three books to take back to your cottage. Consider it your first reward for good behavior."

I open my mouth to ask another question. Where are we? But he cuts me off.

"And Bailey?" His tone lowers. It's a voice I can picture speaking in front of a crowd, or holding boardroom meetings. "I do hope you understand that the freedoms I'm offering you are contingent on your cooperation. I would hate for you to lose them due to poor judgment."

A threat wrapped in niceties. I still hear it for what it is though. *Do as I say, or you won't like the consequences.*

"Yes, Sir."

"Wonderful." His smile returns, friendly and full of teeth. "I believe you and I are going to get along perfectly well."

Ms. Harrington appears in the doorway. "Sir? Shall I escort Miss Bailey to the library now?"

"Yes, thank you, Greta. And do show her the gardens afterward. Fresh air is so important for one's well-being." He turns back to me. "Enjoy your morning, my dear. We'll speak again soon."

As Ms. Harrington leads me from the room, I catch one last glimpse of him calmly returning to his lavish breakfast, as if our conversation was nothing more than pleasant small talk.

My situation may be different from where I was before, but I know better. King threw me into boiling water—brutal, immediate, impossible to ignore the skin peeling, soul-cracking death. This man? He's placed me in a pot of cool, comfortable water, and turned the heat on low, letting me simmer so gradually that I won't know I'm cooked until it's too late.

A pretty cage with plenty of room is still a cage.

As I step into the library, I force myself to remember that.

BAILEY - JULY 14TH

Okay, so... let me take a deep breath. I need to write this down while it's still fresh, even though my hands are literally shaking just thinking about it. Last night changed everything.

I'm not a virgin anymore.

God, it sounds so clinical and weird when I write it like that. What happened between Leon and me wasn't clinical in the least. It was so much better and more meaningful than anything I could have imagined. Nothing like Chloe told me it would be... which I guess I should have realized since she lost hers to Max, who's absolutely NOTHING like Leon.

Ever since our firefly date (and the most incredible orgasm of my life), there's been this palpable tension between us. It's been so hard to hide how I feel from everyone else in the house, but we both agreed that we wanted to wait to tell Jasper and Damon. To just enjoy each other without them butting into our lives for as long as we can.

And maybe it makes me messed up, but I still love the sneaking around. Knowing someone could find us making out by the pool or pressed up against the hallway wall. Leon even snuck into my bedroom the other night after Jas and Damon fell asleep.

All of this tension has been driving me insane. Not that we haven't enjoyed each other, but I wanted him. All of him. I was done waiting.

Last night, the universe finally threw me a bone. But I didn't realize it would turn out that way at first.

Mom and Dad went into the city for their anniversary. He surprised her with tickets to see a play and reservations at a fancy restaurant. It was so sweet to see her excitement, especially since work's been kicking her ass all summer.

Damon and Jasper roped Leon into going to some party. I could tell he really didn't want to go, but I told him it was fine, that if he stayed they'd think it was weird. Then he tried to get me to come with them, but there was no way. Parties like the ones my brothers go to aren't my scene. Too loud, too crowded with obnoxious drunk people, and too much pressure to pretend I'm having fun when I'd rather be literally anywhere else. Maybe if Leon and I were being honest about our relationship and we could hang out all night... but even then, I'd still be uncomfortable.

Leon finally followed them out to Damon's car, looking like a sad puppy, and I told myself I wasn't going to mope around. That it was my choice to stay home, so I'd make the best of it.

I made a bowl of popcorn, found some cheesy romantic comedy on Netflix, and got comfy in bed. My mind kept straying to thoughts of Leon though. To how he visited me at work the other day, and we made out in the bathroom stall. Or the way he touched me in the pool yesterday as the sun beat down on us. My brothers were right in the front yard working on Damon's car, and they could have come back there at any moment. But that didn't stop Leon from finger-fucking me until I bit down on his shoulder to keep from moaning.

I was getting myself too worked up. But I guess that was expected with the way my mind was wandering. I closed my eyes, not caring that my bedroom door was wide open since I had the house to myself, and slid my hand down the front of my shorts. God, I was already wet. It wouldn't take long.

I thought of Leon's voice. "Come for me, Firefly." His nickname for me is so sweet, and the way he says it... I'll never get enough.

His fingers are magic. He knows exactly how to touch me. I drew circles over my sensitive clit, my muscles tensing more and more with each pass. But I was too warm, too clothed. I needed so much more than just my own fingers.

I pulled the blanket down and let the cool air conditioning tickle my skin. Dipping my finger lower, I pictured what it would feel like to have Leon inside me. Stretching me. Filling me up.

I was so close. But then I heard a sound, like the

floorboard creaking, and I yanked my hand away, snapping my legs closed.

"Don't you dare stop, Firefly."

"Leon," I gasped. "What are you doing here?"

He walked into the room, the corner of his mouth turned up that smirk I'm obsessed with. "I thought you'd be happy to see me."

I grabbed a pillow and tossed it at him. "Of course I am. I'm just surprised. What about the party? My brothers?"

He sat on the edge of my bed, running his hand along my thigh until goosebumps appeared. "They didn't even notice when I left. I told them I had a headache." His fingers traced higher. "I wanted to surprise you... and it looks like I interrupted something interesting."

My face flamed. "I was thinking about you."

"Good," he said. "Because I've been thinking about you every second of the day." His eyes traveled down from my flushed face to where my hand had been moments before. "I have an idea. Give me one second."

He stood up to close the door, then stopped in front of my full length mirror that hung on the back of it. "What are you doing?"

"Trust me?"

"Always," I answered.

He lifted it off the door and angled it at the foot of my bed. "Now you can show me," he said softly. When I looked confused, he smiled. "Show me what you were doing before I walked in."

"I-I don't know," I stammered. "I'm embarrassed."

He crooked his finger and I scooted to the edge of

the bed. "You have nothing to be embarrassed about, Firefly. You're beautiful and sexy and you drive me wild. But I'll never ask you to do something you're not comfortable with."

Then he pressed a kiss to my lips, soft and gentle. I exhaled, forcing myself to stop being such a chicken shit. This is Leon—he'd never hurt me or make me feel like anything other than a goddess.

"I want to," I said.

He took his time undressing me, gliding his thumb over my nipples, kissing down the slope of my neck. By the time I was bare for him, I was so hot and wet, I didn't care if the entire room was a mirror.

"Every single time I see you like this I'm in awe. I can't believe you're mine."

He started to climb back on the bed, but I put a hand on his chest to stop him. "You too. This time, I want to see all of you."

He swallowed hard, but lifted his hands up so I could take off his shirt. It never got old— seeing his muscled chest covered in ink, tight abs, that perfect V that disappeared into his jeans.

I traced along the lines of his tattoos, following the intricate patterns across his skin. He watched me with hooded eyes as I undid his belt buckle, my hands steadier than they'd been a few seconds before.

"You're shaking," he said. "Let me."

I let out a nervous laugh. "It's good shaking though. Excited shaking."

"Oh yeah? I bet I can make you shake better than that."

I lightly smacked his arm. "I know you can."

He helped me with the rest of his clothes, and when he was finally as bare as I was, we just looked at each other, taking in every detail. Every hidden glance, every hurried touch, every minute of waiting and now I finally had him completely and openly.

I'd felt him through his pants before and knew he was large, but I don't think I was fully prepared for just how big he actually was. Then I noticed the glints of metal along the underside of his shaft.

"Is that..." I started, my eyes widening.

"Piercings," he said, his voice rougher now. "Do they bother you?"

I reached out tentatively, running my finger along one of them. He hissed in a breath from my touch. "No," I whispered. "They're... God, Leon."

He climbed onto my bed and positioned himself against the headboard. "Come here, love."

I crawled over to him and he lifted me easily, settling me between his legs with my back pressed against his chest, his hard cock pushing into the small of my back.

In the mirror, I could see both of us, so exposed and vulnerable, and immediately wanted to look away. "I look so..."

"Beautiful," he finished, as his arms tightened around me. "You look absolutely beautiful." He kissed the sensitive spot behind my ear. "I want you to see what I see. Don't look away."

His warm hands skimmed along my sides and up my ribcage until I gasped. I watched our reflection as he caressed the curve of my breast, teased my nipples with gentle circles. It was strange and intimate and over-whelming all at once, but so damn good.

"Touch yourself," he murmured against my neck. "Just like you were doing before I got here."

My breathing turned ragged. "Leon..."

"I'll help you," he said softly, taking my hand in his. "Guide me. Show me what feels good."

He already knew how to make me feel good, but this wasn't about his knowledge of my body. This was about exploration. About showing me how much I affect him.

Slowly, he brought my hand down to rest between my legs, his fingers covering mine. "Like this?" he whispered, pressing my fingers against my clit through his touch.

I nodded, unable to speak clearly as I watched us in the mirror, his larger hand covering mine, both of us touching me together. It was so hot, I could barely breathe.

His voice dropped to a low growl as I dipped our fingers lower, spreading my wetness where I needed it. "That's it, love. You like your fingers in your cunt?"

Oh God, his filthy mouth had me biting back a moan. "Yes..."

His eyes were focused on my face, watching every expression in the mirror, memorizing every gasp. He gripped my thigh with his free hand while our joined fingers worked between my legs. The way we looked, me spread wide, him focused on helping me come, it was too good. I felt myself spiraling closer and closer.

"Look at how perfect you are," he murmured. I felt his cock jerk along my back, and oh God, I wanted him inside me. "Keep going. Don't stop until you're shaking."

Our fingers moved faster, and it's like he could sense I was close, could feel the way my muscles tensed. In the mirror, I watched my expression as I grew closer to the edge, saw the desperation on my face. And Leon, he looked ready to combust, but he clenched his jaw, fighting for control.

I reached my free hand behind my back, gripping his cock, and working up and down his shaft. "Fuck, Bailey... Love, I'm going to come if you keep at that."

"Please," I gasped, my head falling back against his shoulder. "Leon, I want you. I want all of you."

His breath hitched. "You sure? We don't have to—"

"I'm sure," I interrupted, turning my head to meet his eyes directly instead of through the reflection. "So fucking sure."

He stilled our joined hands, his other arm wrapping around my waist to hold me close. "After you come," he said, barely holding it together. "I want to feel you fall apart first. Then I'll give you everything."

Our lips crashed together, tongues tangling with passionate, frenzied kisses. His fingers slid back along my clit, rubbing small tight circles. I exhaled into his mouth, stifling a moan.

"Watch yourself come, Firefly. See how fucking perfect you are," he said as he cupped my chin, turning my face forward.

My hips rocked into his hand as he rubbed faster and harder and soon he matched my rhythm, grinding against my back. It was all so hot, so filthy, that I couldn't think straight.

"That's it," he growled against my ear. "Let go for me."

The pressure built and built until finally it snapped. My body went rigid in his arms as waves of pleasure crashed over me, my vision blurring as I watched myself fall apart in the mirror. I threw my head back against his chest and cried out his name, my whole body shaking as he dragged every pulse, every last aftershock out of me.

"So beautiful." He pressed soft kisses along my neck as I came down from the high. "Absolutely perfect."

I was breathless, boneless against his chest, but I needed more. Needed him. I turned in his arms, cupping his cheeks.

"Now," I whispered, my voice still shaky. "I need you inside me."

I wasn't afraid. Nothing Leon could ever do to me would ever be bad or wrong. He'd never hurt me.

He lifted me gently, repositioning us so I was lying back against the pillows with him hovering over me.

"If it hurts, if you need me to stop—"

"I trust you," I said, and the moment those words slipped from my lips his expression turned hungry.

He reached over to his discarded jeans and pulled out a condom. "I came prepared," he said with a soft smile. "I hoped... but I didn't want to assume."

"Thank God," I said.

He laughed softly, tearing open the packet. I watched as he rolled it on, my breaths still coming in pants from a mix of my climax and anticipation.

He kissed me gently as he settled between my legs. He braced himself on his forearms, his face inches from mine. "Look at me. Stay with me."

I nodded, bringing my hands to his shoulders as he positioned his cock at my entrance. He looked so focused, so determined to make this perfect for me, and it made my heart feel like it could burst.

The first gentle press made me gasp, and he stilled immediately.

"Okay?" he whispered.

"Yes," I breathed. "Don't stop."

He pushed forward slowly, so carefully, his eyes never leaving mine. There was pressure, a stretching sensation that was intense but not painful. The piercings added a feeling I couldn't even explain, but I guess I didn't have anything to compare it to. I arched against him.

"Fuck, Bailey," he groaned. "You feel incredible."

When he was fully seated inside me, we both went still, breathing hard. I felt so full, so complete, like this was exactly what I was missing. Us, joined as one, as close as we could possibly be.

"How do you feel?" he asked, brushing my hair back from my face, his voice full of barely held restraint.

"Perfect," I whispered. "Please... You feel so good."

I could see his control slipping, and I wanted that. I wanted him as out of control for me as I was for him. I rolled my hips slightly, testing the sensation. It felt... Oh God, I felt so full.

"Bailey," he warned, his voice all rough edges. "If

you keep doing that—"

"What?" I did it again, loving the way his jaw clenched. "This?"

A low growl rumbled from deep in his chest. "You're going to make me lose control."

"Maybe I want you to," I whispered, wrapping my legs around his waist and pressing him deeper.

"Fuck, you better tell me if I need to—"

I dug my nails into his back and rolled my hips again, making his words cut off in a groan. He pulled back slowly before thrusting in again, deeper this time. I gasped, biting his shoulder. "Yes, more."

That broke his restraint completely. He set a rhythm that had me crying out with each thrust, his hips snapping forward, pumping in and out. His cock hitting spots inside me I never knew I had. The friction of our bodies against my clit had me coming closer and closer to another orgasm.

"Such a good girl, taking me so well," he growled against my ear. "You like feeling me stretch your tight little cunt open?"

"Yes," I moaned, lifting my hips to meet each thrust. "Don't stop, Leon. Please don't stop."

"Never." He upped his pace, pumping into me. "You're mine, Firefly. All fucking mine."

I caught a glimpse of us moving together in the mirror. Leon's corded back muscles flexing as he drove into me, my back arching to meet him thrust for thrust. I loved being able to see us... it sent me closer and closer.

"Are you watching us?" he panted, glancing over

his shoulder at our reflection. "Look how perfect we fit together."

I could barely focus on anything but the building pressure inside me. "Leon, I'm so close..."

"I know, love. I can feel you tightening around me. You feel so fucking good." He shifted my legs higher around his waist, hitting a spot that made me scream. "Right there?"

"Oh God, yes!"

He kissed me desperately, our tongues tangling as his thrusts became erratic. "Come with me," he breathed against my mouth.

I shattered beneath him, crying his name into our kiss. He followed seconds later, his whole body going rigid as he buried himself balls deep, groaning my name like a prayer.

We stayed like that, wrapped in each other, breathing hard, foreheads pressed together as we came down from the high. I never wanted this night to end.

"I love you," I whispered without thinking, instantly wondering if I made a mistake.

But then his eyes softened and he exhaled in relief. "I love you too. So damn much."

I've never felt so cherished in my life.

CHAPTER NINETEEN

BAILEY - BEFORE

I've been in this beautiful cage for three
months now.

Three months.

It's hard to believe.

Through the barred lattice windows of my cottage, I've
watched nature work its wonders. Lush green leaves slowly
turning amber and gold. The gorgeous wildflowers of summer
giving way to russet hued mums of fall. Trees shedding their
colorful leaves, and the wind scattering them in all directions.

So much change out my window. But inside these walls, it's
been three months of careful conditioning. Three months of
him slowly reshaping me into something he finds acceptable.
Three months of learning to bite my tongue and speak only
when spoken to. In that time, I've learned that Sir keeps his
estate running like a well-oiled machine. He thrives on preci-
sion, control, and above all else, obedience.

Every day I wake up wondering if my family has stopped
looking for me—if they think I'm dead. I try to remember the
sound of my mom's voice, the way my dad pushes his glasses up

his nose when he's reading. Leon's features are fading too, like a photograph behind smudged glass. But the way he made me feel is still there. A kernel buried deep inside me that I'll keep hidden, something they can never take away.

My days follow the same pattern. Wake up at seven to bathe and dress. Breakfast at eight sharp. Usually a boiled egg and some tea, or a bit of fruit and yogurt. There's always cakes and pastries, but I'm never permitted to eat those, just salivate and watch *him* enjoy them when he's there. Then, after breakfast, I go to the study for lessons with Ms. Harrington until noon. Etiquette, mainly. Then lunch, a salad or some broiled fish or chicken. Supervised time in the library or gardens, a light dinner alone, then back to my cottage by nine.

It's a routine he designed to lull me into compliance, and I hate how well it's working. Still, I have the solitary moments in the cottage to think, and wish, and dream. That's kept me going. Kept me strong. And as much as I hate the man, he hasn't so much as laid a finger on me... Not yet.

Something feels different this morning though. Slight changes that in a normal world I wouldn't notice, but here, they might as well be a neon sign. There's music playing in the dining room, a lively classical tune. On the table sits covered trays, but I catch a hint of bacon and sausages in the air. When Sir joins me for breakfast, he's wearing a gray suit instead of his usual navy, with a different patterned tie. He has a spring in his step that makes me want to crawl under the table.

"Good morning, my dear." He pats me on the shoulder and sits in his normal place at the head of the table. "Such a beautiful morning, isn't it?" he says, gesturing toward the tall windows where sunlight streams through. "Autumn has always been my favorite season. The changing of leaves, the harvest... there's something so satisfying about the transformation."

I nod and plaster a smile on my face. "Yes, it's lovely, Sir."

Lovely, splendid, superb. Acceptable adjectives according to Ms. Harrington. Because apparently the control freak bastard in front of me despises American slang. Not that *awesome, great,* or *cool* are actually slang words, but according to her they're equivalent to saying fuck, shit, and ass.

My eyes stray to the covered dishes, and of course he notices. "Ah, it's quite the spread, isn't it? I thought today called for something special." He lifts one of the silver lids with a flourish, revealing what looks like eggs Benedict. Then two more—browned sausages and crispy bacon, buttered toast. My mouth waters even though I doubt any of this is for me. As if the pastries weren't difficult enough to watch him devour all the time, I might lose it if I have to sit here eating fruit while he eats all of that.

I swallow down my pooling saliva. "What's the occasion, Sir?"

"Patience, Bailey. All will be revealed." He serves himself a generous portion, then pauses, observing me in that way of his. I wish I could hide my face behind my hands. "Please, help yourself. Mr. Turner would be heartbroken to see this go to waste."

It feels like a trap, like I'm supposed to politely refuse, but my arms betray me as they reach for the first platter. He watches my every move, gently nodding, as I tentatively serve myself small portions from each platter. After months of eating like a bird, this feels so indulgent. I know my stomach will hurt, but it'll be worth it.

"Go on," he says once I finish serving myself. I sit up straight, and grab a bite of egg with my fork. He's going to stop me, I just know it. But as I slide the bite into my mouth, he smiles. "There you are. You've earned this."

The food turns bland as I swallow it down. *Earned this.* What will this *reward* cost me?

"Thank you, Sir," I say, holding back my questions.

"You're welcome." He cuts into his eggs with precise movements, continuing, "I've been thinking quite a lot about you lately. About how remarkably well you've adapted to life here."

I take a small bite of bacon, letting the salty goodness sit on my tongue. It's so good, I could moan. I finish chewing and dab my lips with my white cloth napkin. "I try to follow the rules, Sir."

"It's much more than rule following," he says. I wait for him to continue but he takes his time, sipping from his cup and patting his lips dry. "Ms. Harrington tells me your lessons are going well. Your conversation skills and vocabulary have improved quite dramatically, and even your reading selections have shown me that you're mature for your age."

I have no idea where he's going with this, so I incline my head. "Thank you, Sir."

He lets out a pleased hum that reminds me of the first night I met him back at that hotel suite. "You're special, Bailey. Such a good, obedient girl."

I've never wished I could be someone else so badly. Someone more like Cat. I don't want to be his obedient girl. His good girl. Knowing that's how he thinks of me makes my stomach churn.

He spears a sausage with his fork and brings it to his lips. As he bites into it, his eye contact grows even more intense, more unsettling. "This is where I expect a response, Bailey."

I clear my throat. "I apologize, Sir. Thank you for the compliment."

He inclines his head then gestures to my plate. "Now, finish up. I'm sorry to say that I'll be away for some time. I have business to take care of. Ms. Harrington and the others will see that you're well taken care of and when I return, I hope to have a surprise for you."

"What kind of surprise?"

His head snaps up and I immediately realize my mistake. With my heart pounding, I add, "I meant to say, if you would be so kind as to give me a hint, Sir."

His fingers tighten around the handle of his teacup and he sucks air through his teeth. "I won't let you sully this wonderful breakfast, my dear." He sets down his teacup, and taps his fingers on the edge of the table. "But since I'm in a good mood... let's just say I've been in correspondence with a very important young man. Someone quite close to me who's been away far too long."

My mind whirls. What does this man have to do with me? My thoughts must be clear on my face as he goes on.

"No need to be frightened. He's brilliant and quite handsome, though he's rather stubborn. What he needs is the right motivation to see things from a more mature perspective." Sir's eyes gleam with pride. "A refined young woman who understands her place. Someone who can help him appreciate what he's been missing by being so resistant to the opportunities presented to him."

He finishes the rest of his tea while I listen closely. "Three months of careful preparation, and you're almost ready to serve your purpose. To help guide him toward accepting his destiny."

My hand shakes as I reach for my glass of water. "And what is that destiny, Sir?"

He chuckles and drums his fingers on the table. "I must be going. Be a good girl while I'm away."

I should be happy that he's leaving, but that conversation left me with more questions than answers.

He leaves the table, and Ms. Harrington immediately enters the room like she has some kind of sensor that tells her when he moves more than a foot, but she's not alone. Another woman trails along behind her. She's tall and thin, maybe only a few years older than me with light brown hair pulled back tight, wearing the same blue uniform that Ms. Harrington wears.

Sir speaks to them both in a low commanding tone before he walks out of the room without so much as a last glance my way.

Where did she come from? In all the time I've been here, I've only seen glimpses of other workers coming and going like shadows. There's Mr. Turner, the cook who prepares meals early in the morning and is usually gone by the time I sit down for breakfast. Then there's a gardener or two. I don't know their names and I've barely gotten a look at their faces. She must be new. Either that, or she's been kept in a different area of the estate.

Ms. Harrington clears her throat. "This is Polly, she'll be assisting me for the present. Polly has been with me for some time and knows the expectations she must adhere to."

So in other words, don't try anything. Got it.

"Hello," I say, hoping for some kind of recognition in return. Anything that tells me she could be a potential ally. Or even that she's not like Sir or Ms. Harrington.

Polly's eyes dart quickly to mine, then away. "Miss," she murmurs.

Ms. Harrington's sharp gaze moves between us, clocking every micro-movement or unspoken gesture. We both stay silent and still she clicks her tongue. "Polly will escort you to your cottage today after her cleaning duties. I have other matters to attend to." She turns on her heel and leaves us alone.

For a moment, neither of us say a word. I still don't know what to think of her, and I'm sure she's sizing me up as well. Then she asks, "Are you finished?"

"Yes, I've had enough." Although a part of me wants to stuff bacon and toast down my bra for later.

"If you'll wait in the sitting room, I can escort you once I finish clearing the table," Polly says.

"I can help, if you'd like?" If anything it would save me from extra time sitting in my cottage alone and possibly give me some time to feel Polly out.

She shakes her head, her eyes wide. "I couldn't ask that. Please, I've got it." She reaches for my water glass and our fingers brush for just a moment. The contact is so quick but in that brief touch she managed to pass me a tiny folded up note. I keep my expression neutral, while I casually move my hand to my lap. "Follow me," she says. Her face shows no change in expression, her tone completely dull. If I didn't have this piece of paper in my hand, I'd think I was imagining things.

I follow her into the sitting room and she gestures to the striped upholstered chair by the window. "Take a seat, I'll only be a few minutes."

As soon as she disappears back into the dining room, I turn and pretend to look out the window into the bright morning sun while my fingers work to unfold the tiny piece of paper. I need to be careful, there's cameras everywhere. I haven't seen them, but in the months here, I've picked up enough to learn that.

I'll have to read it discreetly, with small glances.

The handwriting is small and cramped, like she wrote in a hurry.

You're not alone.

I read the words again, trying to control my racing heart. Three simple words, but they mean more than she could ever know. I'm not alone, not as isolated as I thought. We're in this nightmare together.

The sound of dishes clinking carries from the dining room. I fold the note, and discreetly stuff it in my bra.

"Ready?" she asks in that same neutral tone.

I nod and follow her outside, unable to hide the spring in my step. When I know for certain that we're alone on the stone path, I whisper, "Thank you."

Polly's blank expression doesn't change, but her step slows slightly. "Keep your head down," she murmurs, so quietly I almost miss it. "Do what they say. But keep watching."

"Watching for what?"

Her eyes dart toward the main house before she settles on me. "Opportunities."

"But—"

She continues down the path ahead, speaking low. "I've been here a long time, watching, learning."

"How long?" I ask, taking in the dark circles under her eyes and her hunched posture.

"Long enough." She stops once we reach the cottage, opening the unlocked door. It's always unlocked, unless I'm inside.

"Will you be here later? Tomorrow?" I have so many questions... but more than that I just want someone to talk to.

"Be patient." She glances around again, before leaning in. "We'll find a way out of our cages."

Then she's gone, making her way back up the path. I'm left feeling oddly hopeful for the first time in months.

CHAPTER TWENTY

LEON - PRESENT DAY

THE WEIGHT OF THREE HANDGUNS AND AMMUNITION IN my backpack presses against my spine with each turn. The price Knapp demanded was steep, but facing my father and anyone else in my way unarmed isn't an option. At least Knapp kept his word, which is more than I can say for most men in his line of work.

I coast down the street toward Mum's, my engine barely above an idle to avoid waking the neighbors. It's past one in the morning and every house sits dark and silent. With the weapons secured, I'm finally one step closer to finding Bailey. That thought dulls the ache in my bruised ribs and the sting of my split lip.

Only one light illuminates the front door as I park along the street. The rest of the house is dark, but I know Mum's probably lying awake, waiting to hear me come in. She always worried when I stayed out late as a teenager, and a few years away hasn't changed that.

I open the door slowly, trying to avoid noise from the hinges that need oiling, and make my way up the stairs. As expected, the moment my boot touches the first stair, Mum's groggy voice drifts down.

"Leon?"

I take the stairs two at a time and peek my head in her room, inhaling her comforting scent. Some space from her has helped me clear my head. "You didn't have to wait up."

"I know," she says, shifting under the worn patchwork quilt that belonged to Nana. "Turn off the porch light before you go to bed."

"Alright. Love you."

She murmurs something back in reply, but I'm already heading downstairs, my hand trailing down the worn wooden banister. As I reach for the porch light switch movement from outside catches my eye. I move the lace curtain aside and press my face closer to the window to get a better look. There's a black car idling near the curb. Headlights off, only the dim glow from the dashboard showing any hint of light.

I yank the door open, my pulse racing, and sprint outside. My boots crunch against the path with loud thuds. But I'm too late. The engine comes alive and in a matter of seconds I'm left staring after red tail lights as it speeds down the dark, narrow street.

I catch my breath, waiting to see if they turn around and come back. My hand reaches for the zipper of my backpack, still slung over my shoulders, and I pull out the gun I loaded before riding home.

The hair on the back of my neck's standing on end, there's no way that wasn't someone waiting and watching. But who? And what reason? Did they follow me here from Knapp's? Or was it someone to do with my father?

I wait a few more minutes, my fingers curled around the grip, safety off, before the adrenaline finally starts to ebb. The street stays empty. No engine sounds cutting through the quiet.

No headlights flaring in the dark. Just the sound of my shallow breathing, and the light of the moon.

Slowly, I back toward the front door, keeping my eyes on the street until I'm inside with the deadbolt twisted tight and the porch light off. Somehow, I felt safer outside, on high alert. This house feels fragile now, its familiar comfort tainted from the knowledge that someone's watching it... watching *me*. The walls feel less solid, like they're made of paper that could tear with the smallest effort, letting anyone or anything inside.

I lean against the door, weapon still in hand, letting my heart rate decrease slowly. Logically, I have a strong idea of who that was. The timing can't be coincidence. It had to be Knapp's guys. But why? I did as he asked... paid him more than enough. Does he need collateral on me? If I put Mum in danger, I swear to God.

Unless?

James had warned me to watch my back. Something about our father.

Once I'm fairly certain whoever it was isn't returning, I head upstairs and secure my backpack under my bed. I shower and brush my teeth as quietly as possible and by the time I come back, there's a new email notification on my phone.

My stomach drops.

From: Alfred Colter

Subject: Dinner

Leon,

I trust this message finds you well. Our dinner reservation at The Savoy remains for Saturday evening at 8 PM sharp. Punctuality has always been important in our family, as I'm sure you recall from your childhood.

We have much to discuss regarding your future and new opportunities. Some that I'm eager to share.

Do dress appropriately. Let Ms. Harrington know if you need money for a new suit.

—Father

I read it twice, my jaw clenching harder each time. *Our family.* You mean the one you weren't a part of? *My childhood.* Again, where were you in that time? It takes everything in me not to hit reply and tell him exactly how I feel. But I can't... not when he could have information I need.

The black car outside makes more sense now. I'd bet money it wasn't Knapp watching me. It's my father, or more likely someone working for him. But why?

I climb under my sheets and lie on my back, staring at the discoloration of old paint on my ceiling. Only a few more days until I find out for certain what he's up to. But there's no reason to wait around until then. Tomorrow, I'm following up on the charity, and any other property my father's involved in. If Alfred thinks he can play games with me, he's about to learn that I've picked up a few new skills.

I MANAGE MAYBE two hours of sleep. My mind keeps cycling between the black car, the email, and the warning from James. Add in the aches, pains, and the split lip I can't stop biting, and I'm a miserable son of a bitch. Jumpy too. Every creak of the old house has me reaching for the gun under my bed.

By six, I give up on sleep entirely, make some tea and toast, and position myself by the front window, watching the street through a gap in Mum's lace curtains. The morning is gray and drizzly, typical London weather that doesn't help my shit mood. I hope the rain holds out before I have to check out the addresses I pulled on my father.

I'm about to get up to make another cup of tea when I hear car doors slamming outside… then a familiar raucous voice.

"Bloody hell… this place is small."

Jasper.

"Oh my God Jas, you need to stop with the terrible British accent. You're going to offend someone."

Falin.

My chest tightens in a mix of relief and panic. What are they doing here? I push the curtain aside and see a red SUV parked along the curb behind my bike, luggage pressed up against the back windows.

Jasper stands on the pavement, his clothes crumpled and light hair messed from travel. He stretches his arms overhead and looks around the cramped residential street, grinning like an idiot. Then Damon climbs out from the driver's side with his usual composure, immediately scanning the area with those eagle eyes of his.

Blake emerges from the back, her dark hair catching what little morning light filters through the clouds, illuminating her almost purple highlights. Her hair's pulled up into two buns, and she's wearing pants that hug every curve and a cropped band shirt. Beautiful as always.

Then Falin comes from the other side of the car, clutching two cat carriers that shake like they contain unearthly demons, which isn't too far from the truth. She's done something to her hair. One side is the normal platinum but the other half is black. It makes her look even tougher, but still stunning in her own way. She's wearing all black, ripped jeans, combat boots, and one of Jasper's oversized hoodies.

"Fucksake," I breathe. "They brought the cats."

I'm at the front door before they can make it up the garden path, yanking it open with perhaps more force than necessary. "What the hell are you all doing here? I said Friday. It's Wednesday."

Jasper's grin widens as he approaches, a duffel bag slung over each shoulder. "Look who's happy to see us! We couldn't wait, mate. Had to hop across the pond."

That accent. I fight the urge to palm myself in the face.

"You're looking like hell, brother," Damon says in lieu of a greeting.

"Happy to see you too," I say in a blank tone.

Blake drops her bags and runs at me, wrapping me in a fierce hug. I hold her close, fighting back tears. "We're here," she whispers. "And we're not leaving until we find her."

She pulls back and takes a closer look at my face, touching my split lip and the bruises on my cheek. "What happened here? I better look you over."

Falin joins her side, cupping my chin to take a closer look, air hissing from her teeth. "Ouch. Hope the other guy looks worse."

"It's a long story—"

"Leon? What's all the noise out—oh my word!"

Mum appears behind me in her frayed dressing gown, hair still wrapped in a silk scarf, and freezes when she takes in the four attractive and imposing Americans standing on her doorstep. Her eyes turn the size of dinner plates.

"Mum, these are my friends. They arrived early," I explain before she drops dead from shock. I go through introducing her to each person.

"Son, you didn't tell me your friends were so..." She trails off, her cheeks turning pink as she takes in Damon's sharp jawline and Jasper's carefree grin.

"Handsome," Blake finishes for her, barely holding back her laughter.

"I was going to say tall," Mum says quickly. She may as well start fanning herself. "Please, come in, come in. I'll put the kettle on. Though I'm not sure how we'll all fit in the sitting room. It's not exactly built for... for people of your... stature."

An otherworldly yowl comes from one of the cat carriers. *Ah, Havoc, I have missed you.*

Mum's eyes widen even further. "And what in God's name was that? It sounds like a banshee being murdered."

"Close enough," I say under my breath.

Jasper beams like the proud cat father he is. "That's Havoc. She's traveled across the sea and land to see her favorite uncle Leon."

"A cat—there's two," I reassure Mum, rolling my eyes. "I think I mentioned them on one of our phone calls."

Mum nods robotically, clearly struggling to take in our current situation. "Well, come on in. Let's get you settled."

Everyone squeezes into the sitting room, dropping bags and the cat carriers into whatever free floor space they can find. The girls take the couch, Damon flops into the armchair, and Jasper and I hover near the hallway. The space feels so much smaller and warmer than before already. Jasper has to duck his head under a low beam and his arm almost knocks over Nana's lamp.

"Cozy," Falin says as she eyes Mum's porcelain figures on the mantel.

"Aww, is that baby Leon?" Blake coos, pointing at a framed photo of me. "Look at those chubby cheeks."

Mum rushes over to pick it up, her smile wide. "That's my baby boy. Such a handsome lad, wasn't he?"

"So handsome," Damon says, smirking at me. "What happened?"

I narrow my eyes at him which makes him bust out a laugh. "Dick."

"So I'll just..." Mum starts, gesturing to the kitchen. "Tea. Yes, I'll make tea. Lots of tea. Do you all drink tea? Of course you don't, you're American. Coffee? I think I have some instant somewhere..."

"Mum," I say gently. "Tea's fine. Whatever you have."

"Yeah, Mrs. Colter—" Blake starts, but I cut her off.

"Actually, it's Ms. Parsons."

Blake's cheeks flush. "So sorry! I knew that... Must be the jet lag."

"No problem, love," Mum says. "Make yourselves at home." I catch her muttering under her breath, something about not having enough proper cups.

I fold my arms across my chest. "She may as well be serving the Queen. I haven't seen her this flustered in years."

"She's adorable," Blake says. "I just want to sit with her and drink tea and knit."

Falin laughs. "Is this some new alter ego you're exploring?"

"You know I love to be cozy! This is English me... I'm embracing the culture!"

"Cheerio," Jasper says but it ends in an "oof" as I elbow him in the ribs.

That's when one of the cat carriers starts rattling violently. The entire thing slides across the hardwood floor with an ear bleeding, scraping sound. "How?" I ask.

"Should we..." Blake starts.

"Let them out," Jasper says, already reaching for the latches. "They've been cooped up for hours."

"Maybe we should—" I begin, but it's too late.

Havoc explodes from her carrier like a furry missile, ears back, tail puffed, immediately launching herself onto the mantel. Three porcelain angels crash to the floor in a wreckage of ceramic shards.

From the kitchen comes the unmistakable sound of Mum dropping something heavy.

"Fuck," I breathe.

Mayhem trots out of her carrier with dignity and grace, meowing, and taking one look at the chaos before hiding under the couch.

"Havoc, you get over here!" Jasper scolds but it sounds more like he's holding back laughter.

"I'm so sorry," Blake says, jumping up to pick up the scattered pieces. "We should have warned you about the cats."

"Or about showing up early," I tease. Despite the shock, I can't help but smile, even if it makes my lip hurt like a bitch.

Mum appears in the doorway, her scarf slipped halfway down her hair. "Well, that's jus—that's fine. They're just things."

Yeah, things I was forbidden from laying a finger on as a kid. But Mum's taking it better than I thought.

After more proper introductions where she practically falls over when Damon calls her ma'am and Jasper thanks her in that flirtatious tone he can't help but use and several cups of tea, we manage to corral both cats upstairs to my bedroom with their carriers, food, and their travel litter box. I hope I'll still have a room to come back to later and not a disaster zone.

"Right," I say, closing my bedroom door firmly behind me. "We should get out of here for a bit. Lunch?"

And a pint... It's not too early.

Mum overhears us making plans and protests that she'll make sandwiches, but Blake intervenes with that sweet tone of hers. "We'd love to explore the neighborhood, it's our first time here! Maybe find a proper English pub?"

Thank you, Blake.

"The Rose and Crown is lovely," Mum says after a thought, clearly pleased they want to experience local culture. "Just down the road. Tell Cindy that Ada sent you. And Leon, bring an umbrella. I don't trust those clouds."

Twenty minutes later, we're squeezed into a corner booth, pints and fish and chips spread across the polished wooden table. Blake has a glass of wine and an allergy-friendly lunch... Damon made sure of that.

The crowd is light this time of day, mostly retired locals nursing their ales and reading newspapers. The perfect environment to catch up without anyone caring to listen in.

"So," Damon says quietly, leaning forward, "your father's working with Orlov. Tell us more."

"All sources point to that," I say, keeping my voice low. "Not sure if Alfred's using his influence for false passports, or keeping their transport of victims undercover or any other number of fucked up things. My father's position gives him a lot of power and influence, especially when it comes to international matters. There must be loads of money in this for him." I take a long drink of ale, thinking. "I'm wondering though, since Orlov is technically in financial ruin, if my father's still involved."

"Your finest work," Jasper says, with a grin.

Blake frowns, picking at her baked potato. "If they're working together maybe your father's helping him recover his finances?"

Falin finishes chewing and adds, "Whatever it is, I haven't been able to find any traces of the two of their names together. No records, nothing in the media."

"Which makes me so much more suspicious," I say.

"Exactly. What are they hiding?" Falin says, stuffing another chip in her mouth. "These are so good for bar food. We may need another order." She slides out to go tell the bartender.

I lean back against the booth, processing everything we've discussed. "I've been running searches on all of Alfred's properties since I left that charity office. It's not something I ever had the need to do before but now... There's a few properties, including his main London home, but I found the address to a countryside estate. My half brother mentioned Alfred's been spending most of his time there lately." I pause, that familiar gut feeling taking hold. "I think that's where we need to look."

Damon nods, and I can see him shifting into serious mode. "What do we know about the security situation?"

"Not much. It's isolated though, miles from anywhere. If they're holding people, it would be the perfect location."

"Alright," Jasper says, leaning forward. "I'm fucking ready."

Blake takes the pint from his hand. "Maybe ease up on the ale then, big guy." He protests weakly, but eventually slumps back in defeat. "I think I'll sit this one out. Fal and I can check into the rental, get the cats settled."

"I heard my name," Falin says as she slides back into the booth.

"I was just saying, we'll sit out tonight. Get settled into the rental instead," Blake repeats.

"As much as it pains me, I agree. I want to set up my equipment too. Brought as much as I could."

"So it's settled," Damon says. "We'll check out the estate tonight. That was too easy. I'm waiting for the argument."

"No argument," Blake says, leaning into him. "Unless you have a reason for me to be pissed."

"No," he quickly replies. "Not at all."

If I had more time, I'd sketch the look of smug satisfaction she's giving him right now. I missed these weirdos.

Jasper's expression grows serious. "You really think it's your father we need to focus on and not Orlov?"

All four sets of eyes zero in on me. "I know it seems like a far-fetched plan, but my gut is telling me Alfred will lead to Orlov... Maybe even Bailey herself, who knows?"

Blake's hand reaches for mine. "We trust you. Whatever you think, we're here for it. Right?" She glances around the booth and they each nod, murmuring in agreement.

We finish and file out of the pub into the gray afternoon. I catch Jasper looking through the window with longing.

"Missing it already?" I ask.

"Best fish and chips I've ever had."

I shake my head and pat his back. "Don't worry buddy, you'll be sick of pub food by the time we find Bailey."

He grins and I realize that's the first time in a while where I'm not second-guessing myself. Not one bit.

I can't believe summer's almost over. Just two more weeks until move in. Two more weeks until Leon and the guys head back for their senior year. I'm not ready!

We've been talking a lot about everything the past few days. What'll happen when we're not under the same roof, when we can't sneak little moments whenever we want. I think Damon is starting to suspect something... Makes sense, he's always been super observant. A few days ago, he asked where I'd disappeared to for three hours, and when I said I was at the library, he just gave me this knowing look and said "Right... the library."

Leon and I were actually walking around the waterfront, sightseeing.

Or this morning when he pointed out the mark Leon left on my neck, asking if that happened at the library too, with that same smirk on his face. I just hurried to my room, knowing if I answered him with some random lie my face would be beet red.

So far he's kept whatever he suspects to himself, so at least there's that.

But back to the important stuff. Leon and I have been making plans. Our schools are only an hour apart, which isn't that far but it feels like it is. He's already figured out the fastest way to get to me and promised he'll come see me every weekend. "Maybe even during the week if my schedule allows," he said last night while we were lying in the hammock, watching the stars after everyone else was asleep.

I want to believe it'll be that easy. That we can just pick up where we left off every time we see each other. But I've watched friends try long distance before, and it never seems to work out the way they plan.

He keeps telling me to stop overthinking, that what we have is special and as long as we're both willing to keep it up, everything will be great.

I love how he talks about the future, like he's completely sure of us. "Next summer we'll get our own place," he said yesterday, completely serious. "Where would you want to live after you finish school? We can look for jobs in the same city."

It's all happening so fast, but I love how there's no question in his mind that we'll end up together.

Two more weeks in our almost-perfect bubble. Then we'll find out if love really can survive classes, dorm rooms, final exams and all the distance between us.

I'm choosing to believe it can. We're too good together for it not to work.

CHAPTER TWENTY-ONE

BAILEY - BEFORE

Over the past three months, I've done exactly what Polly told me to do—observe. Reading Sir's moods has become my full-time job, picking up on the smallest details like it's my new superpower.

Today, all those skills are screaming at me that something is about to change. The signs are everywhere.

It started this morning when Ms. Harrington delivered a gift, a knee-length navy dress with pearl buttons down the bust. The moment I saw it laid out on the bed, I wanted to gag. The color matches Sir's suits perfectly, like he'd chosen it for that very reason.

Then Polly showed up at breakfast after disappearing for over a week. I could only offer a polite nod while being watched, but something's wrong with her. She's walking with her shoulders hunched, her eyes red and swollen like she's been crying.

But it's Sir himself who confirms my worst fears. He's pacing the main floor of the house with that manic energy I only see once in a while. It puts me on edge every time. Understandably, since it usually follows some kind of news.

He skips breakfast entirely, then appears in the study hours later. I flinch at the sound of his voice cutting through the quiet room.

"We're taking a little trip today, my dear." He sits beside me and directs his attention to Ms. Harrington. "Send Polly up with some tea. I'd like to speak with Bailey alone."

Ms. Harrington doesn't miss a beat, obeying immediately.

I fidget with the spine of my book, hoping that'll help soothe the dread running through my veins.

"You look lovely in the dress I picked. The color suits you." I thank him, with my plastered-on smile and he continues. "Don't you agree that a change of scenery will do you some good?"

I hesitate, and of course, Sir notices immediately. He pulls the book from my hands so sharply that the edge of a page slices my index finger. It stings and blood wells up, but I clench my fist in my lap, forcing myself to ignore it.

"Yes, Sir. A change would be lovely."

Polly walks in, carrying a tea tray. Sir doesn't even look at her as she places it on the table and prepares him a cup. Her hands tremble—yet another sign that something isn't right.

In the three months since we met, we've developed a careful system. Nothing too dangerous or outwardly obvious, but small gestures of solidarity. A reassuring touch when Ms. Harrington isn't looking. An extra roll of bread smuggled into my cottage. The constant promise that I'm not completely alone. She's not always here and she won't ever answer me when I ask her where she's been, but when she is here, I feel relieved.

"That will be all, Polly," Sir says, accepting the teacup. "Bailey, you may serve yourself."

"Thank you, Sir." My eyes follow Polly to the doorway, where she lingers, waiting for orders. I decide to chance a question—not just for me, but for both of us. "Where will we be going, Sir?"

"London. I have some business associates I'd like you to meet." He smiles warmly, like he's offering me a gift. "Consider it part of your education."

Business associates. These six months, I've learned that Sir's business involves things I don't want to think about too deeply. The hushed phone calls. The men who occasionally visit the estate. The way Polly sometimes returns from serving them with a vacant look in her eyes. It's obvious he's involved with King and the rest of them, but I wish I could find out the capacity.

"Thank you, Sir."

"And since you've behaved extra well, I'll let Polly accompany us. She's proven to be quite helpful to Ms. Harrington of late and you'll need someone to assist you."

I wish I could feel happy that I won't be alone in whatever this is, but I'd rather not bring Polly into it. She's gone through enough. Seeing something happen to another friend would break me.

She nods, letting me know she's heard, and she accepts what's to come. But as I stare into my teacup, anxiety consumes me, clenching my chest, sending tingling into my limbs. What can I do though? I'm not strong enough. Not smart enough. Not *enough* of anything that matters to change his mind. While Sir moves on to boasting about his latest business dinner, I send a silent plea to the universe to save us from our fate.

THE LONDON TOWNHOUSE is nothing like the estate. They both scream luxury and old money, but this place lacks the idyllic warmth of the country home. I doubt it ever belonged to a family at all. It's all polished concrete and glass, contemporary art and sculptures that look more like weapons than decorations, stark white walls and black leather furniture. Sterile and cold. A perfect reflection of who Sir really is.

He separates Polly and I right away, leading me into a small bedroom, and ordering Polly to prepare for the evening while he makes some calls. The moment the door gets locked behind me, that suffocating weight bears down on my chest. Alone again. I check the window first, but it's locked and barred with a view of the small back garden covered in a dusting of snow that will melt by the evening. Not a soul in sight. There's nothing for me to do but curl into a ball and close my eyes. This is all too familiar. Thoughts of Cat, Jasmine, Elise, and Lydia play in my mind as I fall into a restless sleep.

I'm woken by Polly tapping my shoulder. Only I don't recognize her at first out of her usual uniform, wearing a sleek black dress with her brown hair down and pin-straight instead of being pulled tightly back. "I need to fix your hair," she says gently.

I sit up, taking in my surroundings before remembering where we are. "What's going on?"

"Come into the loo," she whispers. "Maybe he won't hear us over running water."

I nod and follow her into the small bathroom. She pulls out a brush and curling iron along with some hair products. "What did he make you do?" I ask quietly.

"Just a bit of cleaning." I roll my lip between my teeth and tilt my head in question. "Truly. I'm fine, Bailey."

"Well, what's going on then? Why are we here? Why are you dressed up?"

She gestures for me to quiet down before turning on the tap. "Now we should be able to speak plainly. But turn, I need to do something with your hair or he'll bludgeon me."

"What?" I ask, appalled. "He said that?"

She smirks so I give her a light slap on the wrist. "No, but he's done things just as terrible."

"What do you mean?"

She ignores my question and starts brushing my hair gently at first, but as the minutes tick by her movements become more urgent. "Listen," she whispers. "I've been here once before and it wasn't good. The men that are coming... just don't fight them, alright? Don't give them a reason to hurt you."

I shove my hands under my thighs to keep them from shaking. "What men? Do you have names?"

Before she can answer, brash voices make their way through the door over the sound of the running water. Polly drops the brush on the counter at the noise and her hands come to rest on my shoulders. "Don't forget what I said," she whispers. "Please."

Sir enters without knocking. "Ladies, it's time to greet my guests."

THE SITTING room is hazy with cigar smoke and full of male voices speaking in accented English and Russian. They all seem like they're in a contest to see who can speak first, and loudest. My body instantly tenses from hearing them speak Russian, painful memories flooding back to the forefront of my mind.

Sir guides me forward with a possessive hand on my lower back. The men go quiet, staring up at me like I'm a prize at an auction.

"Gentlemen," Sir says, his voice full of pride, "I'd like you to meet Bailey. Six months of careful cultivation, and now look at her."

A tall man with graying temples nods approvingly. Another, age-spotted with bushy white brows, narrows his gaze and taps his knee. "She looks familiar. Is she number 521?"

I try to keep my expression neutral but I'm sure I fail. A number? These bastards have us numbered? My face heats and pulse roars in my ears.

"Yes, but I've shed that image from her. She's a proper lady now, ready to fulfill her destiny," Sir says. The tall man snickers, but it doesn't seem to bother Sir.

"Well, well."

The voice comes from behind me, familiar in the worst possible way. Every muscle in my body goes rigid as the sickening scent that still haunts my nightmares wafts over me.

"I wasn't expecting this treat today."

His heavy footsteps circle me slowly while his gaze eats up every inch of my body. I keep my head low, not meeting his cold blue eyes, but still watching him from my periphery.

King.

"Orlov," Sir says. *A name.* I store it away for later. "I wasn't aware of you being in town. Is your uncle here as well?"

"No, just me checking on some important clients," King says as he lowers himself onto the couch and brings an arm around the scrutinizing old man's shoulder. From Sir's tone, he's not thrilled to see King either, although they clearly have a friendly rapport.

"Lovely," Sir says. "Well, Bailey, Polly, why don't you be good hosts and get my guests some refreshments?"

Polly touches my arm and leads me to the credenza where crystal decanters and glasses wait.

"Alright?" Polly whispers.

I shake my head, unable to form words.

King's presence ripped open wounds that have barely begun to heal. I may as well be bleeding out onto the floor.

My hands shake as I pick up the decanter, but Polly gently takes it and begins to pour. Her movements may be more precise than mine, but there's still tension radiating off her.

"Remember what I said," she repeats. I wish I could yell and scream, kick and punch. Say, *I know, trust me. I know they're bad men.*

"Whiskey for everyone," Sir announces over their chatter. "Bailey, serve our guests."

I take the tray with trembling hands, and pass out the glasses, starting with the gray-haired man, then the older one with the bushy brows. King watches my every movement with a crooked smile.

"Such a graceful little thing," he murmurs as I approach with his glass. When I lean forward to set the tray down, his hand shoots out to grip my wrist. His thick fingers trace circles over my pulse point. "Much more refined than when I last saw her."

I choke on my own breath, but I force myself to stay still. Polly's words echo in my ears. Don't fight. Don't react. Don't give him what he wants.

"Indeed," Sir says with obvious pride. "Bailey, why don't you show our guests how well your lessons have progressed? Please, recite something for us."

My insides twist. I can't... not like this, with King's sick smile staring up at me. "Sir, I—"

"Come now, don't be modest. That lovely piece from Keats you've been practicing. You must remember the passage, you just recited it at breakfast yesterday."

The room falls silent, all eyes land on me. King's grip on my wrist tightens to the point of pain before he finally drops my arm.

There's no getting out of this. I'm no more than a trained circus animal forced to perform.

I clear my throat, my voice barely steady.

"A thing of beauty is a joy forever... It's loveliness increases; it will never pass into nothingness..."

"Excellent diction," the gray-haired man comments, his English accent prominent. "Very proper. I'd almost never guess she started as a common whore."

Tears well in my eyes but I refuse to let them loose. They won't hurt me. I will stay strong.

"And look at her posture," Sir adds, moving behind me to adjust my shoulders. "Six months of deportment lessons. Notice how she holds herself—chin up, spine straight. None of that slouching American nonsense."

King slowly claps. "Impressive. Though I do wonder..." He leans back in his chair, studying me. "Has she learned proper obedience as well as pretty words?"

"Why don't you see for yourself?" Sir gestures to me. "Bailey, a proper curtsy for our guests."

A single tear rolls down my cheek. I can cry and cry and it won't change anything, I have no choice but to obey. I lower myself into the curtsy Ms. Harrington drilled into me, keeping my eyes downcast as I rise.

"Charming," the bushy-browed man chuckles. "Like something from finishing school."

"That was the idea," Sir beams. "Complete refinement. She'll make a certain someone very—" His phone buzzes, cutting him off. He checks it and huffs. "Gentlemen, forgive me. I need to take this call. Important business matters."

"Of course," the gray-haired man waves him off. "We'll keep ourselves entertained."

Sir steps out onto the terrace, turning his back to the rest of us as he speaks urgently to whoever's on the other side of his phone. As soon as he slides the door closed, the air in the room shifts, becoming thicker, more suffocating.

King pulls out a small object from his pocket, scooping white powder from it onto the glass table. I watch as he inhales two lines, offers some to the other men, but they politely decline.

When my feet finally feel lighter, I make a move to go back to where Polly's standing by the credenza. Maybe I can make myself small and wait this meeting out.

"Pet, where do you think you're going?" King's smile widens, but there's nothing warm about it.

"Nowhere," I manage to say.

"That was quite a performance just now. I'm impressed."

The gray-haired man lights a cigar, leaning forward to watch our exchange, the other settles back sipping from his glass.

"Tell me, Bailey," King continues, swirling his whiskey, "do you remember the many conversations we had?"

I keep my eyes down, maybe he'll stop, focus on something else. Through the glass, I can see Sir pacing the terrace, gesturing animatedly into his phone.

"I asked you a question." King's voice hardens. "It's rude not to answer when someone speaks to you. Surely you've learned that much from Ms. Harrington."

"Yes," I whisper.

"Yes, what?"

My throat constricts. "Yes, I remember."

"Good." He takes a slow sip of his drink, never taking his eyes off me. "And what did I tell you about respect?"

The memory hits me like a slap to the face the moment the word leaves his lips—his hands on me, his voice in my ear, the way he made me beg, made me hurt.

My legs shake.

"I said," King's voice drops to that dangerous whisper I remember too well, "what did I tell you about respect?"

"That... that I needed to learn it," I manage.

"Exactly." He leans forward slightly. "And have you? Learned respect?"

I nod quickly, desperate to give him what he wants so this will stop.

"Show me," he says. "Come here."

My feet are rooted to the floor. Through the glass, Sir is still deep in conversation, completely oblivious.

"I don't like to repeat myself, pet." King's tone grows sharper with each word. "Come. Here."

On wobbly legs, I take a step toward him, then another. The gray-haired man chuckles low in his throat, coughing from the cigar smoke. The older one adjusts his position to get a better view.

"That's better," King murmurs when I'm within arm's reach. I hate him so fucking much. I want to spit in his face, claw his eyes— "Now, your new master seems to think his gentle methods have made you into a proper lady. But you and I both know what you really are underneath all that polish, don't we?"

His hand clamps around my wrist again, and I whimper from the pain. He pulls me down until my knees hit the hard floor.

"Don't we?" he repeats, his nails digging into my skin.

"I don't know what you mean," I whisper.

"Oh, I think you do. You're still that same frightened little girl who begged so prettily. He may have taught you to recite poetry and curtsy, but he hasn't changed what you are." He squeezes my cheeks with one hand, leaning in so his mouth is an inch from mine. "And what you are is my little toy."

I try to shake my head, to get free from his grasp, but he

only tightens his hold. "Please," I try to say, but the word barely comes out.

He just laughs and drinks in the sight of me crying and begging, exactly like he wants me. "You know what I'm curious about?" His free hand moves to finger the pearl buttons of my dress. "He's dressed you up so pretty, like a little doll. All proper and refined on the outside." His fingers work at the top button. "But I wonder... is the packaging underneath just as fancy?"

"No," I breathe, trying to pull back, but his grip on my face keeps me in place.

"Let's have a look, shall we?" The first button pops open. "It's been too long since I've seen those perfect tits."

Both men murmur their approval, leaning forward like they're witnessing the crescendo of a show. They're disgusting, all of them.

"Please," I say, bringing my hands up to try and stop him from opening the next button. He lets go of my face to swipe my hands aside.

A third button gives way, then a fourth. The dress gapes open at my throat, and King's smile widens.

"Much better. Now let's get to the good part—"

"Orlov."

Sir's commanding voice has King's hands dropping to his side. He walks over, phone still in his hand, wearing an expression of fury.

"Finished with your call?" King says smoothly.

"Step away from her. Now." Sir's tone is deadly quiet.

"Oh, come now. I was just inspecting your handiwork. Making sure she's as refined underneath as she appears on the surface."

"I said step away. You're damaging months of careful work."

King finally releases me, and I scramble backward, clutching my dress closed. "She needs to remember her place. Your methods have made her soft."

"She knows her place perfectly well." Sir's gaze flicks to me, then to Polly, still frozen by the credenza. "She's to be saved for someone important. But..."

I feel all the blood drain from my face as his attention settles on Polly.

"Polly," Sir says quietly. "Come here."

"No," I gasp, struggling to my feet. "Please. I'm here, it's fine. He can—"

Sir ignores me completely. "Orlov, if you need to satisfy your... *needs*... Polly is more than adequate for the purpose."

Polly's face goes completely blank, like a light has been switched off behind her eyes. She doesn't move, doesn't protest, just stands there with an empty expression, like she's been waiting for this moment.

"Much more practical," Sir continues. "Bailey is being prepared for someone specific. Polly, however..." He shrugs as if she's nothing more than an object. "She's expendable."

King beckons Polly forward, and she obeys with slow robotic movements. "I usually like them with more fight." He runs a hand over her thin frame, and pulls her dress down, exposing her bare breasts. "But she'll do."

"No, please," I cry. "Polly, you don't have to do this."

Sir wraps his arms around my middle and hoists me off my feet. "Come, Bailey. This is no place for a lady."

"No!" I scream. "Polly!"

The last thing I see before Sir hauls me out the door, is King's hand connecting with Polly's cheek.

"I'll kill you! I'll kill you all!" As the words leave my lips, I realize I mean them with my whole being.

CHAPTER TWENTY-TWO

LEON - PRESENT DAY

OVER TWO HOURS ON COUNTRY ROADS IN THE RENTED
SUV and we finally reach our destination. Tall iron gates loom
ahead, flanked by two security lights. The moment I lay eyes on
the C that sits in the center, memories spring to the surface of
my mind.

I've been here before. How had I forgotten?

We park off the road, hiding the SUV in between two
massive trees, and walk closer to the gate.

"This is it?" Damon asks, walking beside me on the edge of
the tree line.

I nod, unable to form words. Each step closer makes my
chest clench. I feel like I've been transported back in time to a
seven-year-old boy clutching his mum's hand as she led him up
this same unpaved road.

*"Be sure to stand up straight, Leon. Shoulders back. Your
father doesn't tolerate slouching."*

"But Mum, I don't want to—"

*"Please, love. Just for today. Be the young gentleman I know
you can be."*

Jasper shifts beside me, pulling me back to the present. "Security looks tight. Motion sensors on the perimeter, cameras every fifty feet." He points to the barely visible devices mounted along the fence line. "Guard shack by the main entrance, but I haven't seen movement since we pulled up."

Now Jasper's more alert than me. I need to pull myself together. One fuck up and we could be in trouble. I gesture for them to stop, and head a few steps away from the road. "Let's call Falin, see if she's found any more blueprints of the layout. Maybe there's another way in."

I pull out my phone and dial Falin. She answers right away.

"Tell me you're not in trouble already."

"Define trouble," I answer, getting a snort from Jasper.

"Leon, I'm serious. I've been digging deeper into your father's estate, and this place is locked down tighter than Fort Knox. Professional security, rotating guards, the works. You were right... something's definitely going on there."

"What about entry points?" I ask, crouching behind a fallen log as headlights sweep past on the main road behind us.

She huffs, and I hear her fingers clacking along the keyboard. "There's a main entrance, gated. And it looks like there's some kind of maintenance entrance on the eastern perimeter of the estate."

I repeat the information to the guys. But Falin cuts in.

"I doubt the second entrance is clear. I've been digging... Your father is paying an elite security company, and not just chump change, a lot of fucking money, Lee."

"It'll be fine, we're just checking it out. I promise we won't go charging in."

"Right," she says, her tone cynical. "You three never do that."

I ignore her sarcasm. "How far is the second entrance?"

"About half a mile east from the main gate. Leads to some

outbuildings according to the property records. Otherwise, it's the middle of nowhere."

"Thanks," I say, ending the call. She'll be pissed at my abruptness but I don't have time to sit around and chat.

I push up from the log and study the estate through the trees, paying extra attention to the precise spacing of the security lights, the way the cameras are positioned to eliminate blind spots. Falin's right, this place is a fortress. If we get any closer, we'll set them off.

I feel ill.

"Let's head in that direction," I say, pointing toward the secondary entrance. "There may be less security."

"So through all these trees?" Damon asks. "You sure you don't want to come back in the morning?"

"We drove all this way, might as well see what we find."

"I love a good night hike," Jasper says, starting to trek between tree trunks.

Damon follows, and I take up the back. "We just need to stay far enough away to not set off any motion detectors. I wish I brought my signal jammers... I don't have all my gear from back home."

"Aww, he's calling New York home," Jasper says.

"Yes, well, don't get all sentimental on me. I—"

Suddenly, alarms shriek across the estate grounds. Floodlights blaze to life, transforming the darkness into pools of glaring white. Not pointing toward us. Pointed within the grounds.

We dash behind a nearby tree, guns aimed, frozen. My hand shakes on the grip.

"Something's happening," I breathe, watching as armed security guards pour out of hidden positions across the estate.

"Holy fuck," Jasper says. "I count at least five."

"And that's only what we can see," Damon adds.

"They're not coming this way. Why aren't they coming this way?" Jasper asks, sounding just as bewildered as I feel.

"Movement!" Damon points into the distance. "Two figures, running!"

Through the chaos of lights and alarms, I catch sight of them. Two people sprinting across the open lawn, heading far from our view. One stumbles, and the other immediately turns back to help.

A guard isn't far behind, yelling for them to get down. More of them are advancing from multiple directions.

Through my pounding heart and adrenaline-fueled mind, a singular thought surfaces.

"We have to help them," I say, already moving toward the fence.

"Lee, what the fuck—" Damon starts, running after me.

"Let's go! " I tuck my gun away and grab the iron bars. "Someone's running for their lives in there."

"Bro, think for a second!" Jasper says, catching up. "Those cameras will snag us the second we cross this gate."

"Good. Let them come." Maybe my father will see me, there's no turning back now. I pull myself up, finding footholds in the ornate metalwork.

Behind me, I hear Damon curse under his breath. "You're going to get us all killed."

"Probably," I admit, swinging my leg over the top of the fence. "You coming or not?"

The sound of Jasper's boots hitting metal tells me his answer. "Fuck it. I'm in."

"This is insane," Damon mutters, but he's already climbing.

I drop to the ground on the other side, my boots sinking into the damp earth, and immediately sprint toward where the two figures disappeared. The estate's alarms are deafening, blocking out the sound of the guards, but I hear Jasper and Damon's labored breathing behind me.

"Where?" Jasper murmurs, asking the same question I'm thinking. Did they manage to hide, to get away?

The grounds are massive. Rolling hills and sprawling green, gardens and pruned hedges, random stone paths leading in the opposite direction of the treeline. I remember this place looking like something out of my fairytale picture books, too bad the reality never matched the vision.

We crouch and take slow steps forward, eyes peeled for guards. I hope they didn't get caught... that'll make this so much fucking harder.

"There." Damon points toward a stone fountain ahead. "Something moved."

"Might not be them," I say, but head in that direction anyway. The fountain provides good cover while we catch our breaths. Its trickling sound blocks out our voices.

"This is nuts, bro," Jasper says. "Your dad lives like a king."

"Not my dad," I correct. Dad implies he's a part of my life. He's been there from the start. "Sperm donor is more like it."

Jas nods, dropping the subject.

"What the fuck do we do now?" Damon asks. As the words leave his lips, the alarms stop wailing.

"Shit," I whisper.

A twig snaps to our left, and within seconds a guard jogs down a path right toward us. I hold a finger up to my lips, and pull my gun out. The guys do the same.

His radio crackles, and a voice comes through. "Check in."

Holding it up to his lips, he says, "No visual on the escapees. Circling the fountain garden for the trespassers."

Bloody wonderful. They know we're here. I guess I knew that was bound to happen.

"Escapees?" Jasper mouths.

I knew it. They're running away from here.

The guard's flashlight sweeps in our direction. We press farther against the fountain, hiding in the shadows, but it's only a matter of moments before he finds us.

"Shit," Damon whispers. He raises his gun an inch and I know what he's thinking.

We're fighting our way out of here.

The beam catches the edge of Damon's jacket. The guard holds the light there, his hand moving to his weapon.

"Go!" I cry.

We scatter in different directions as the guard shouts into his radio. "Multiple contacts near the fountain! Requesting backup!"

Damon's on his feet first, circling wide to get behind the guard. Jasper goes left, using the fountain for cover. I stand, dropping my gun and putting my hands up, keeping his attention focused on me.

"Stay right there!" the guard yells, his weapon pointed at my chest.

I take a step forward, into the light. "Easy, mate. Just out for a walk."

"Get on the ground," the guard calls.

I lower myself, keeping my eyes trained on Damon, who's slowly creeping behind the guard. This is exactly what we wanted.

"Look," I tell him. "There's been a misunderstanding. I'm a guest. I—"

Damon attacks from behind, wrapping his arm around the guard's throat in a sleeper hold. The man struggles, thrashing, but Damon's done this move before, and within seconds, he's gone limp. Damon lowers him gently to the ground.

"Nice," Jasper says, stepping out of the shadows.

I tuck my gun away, and grab the man's radio, switching it

off. "We don't have long before that backup he called for comes our way."

"So let's move," Damon says.

But where to? The estate ahead, or back toward the treeline?

Damon starts heading toward the trees, so I don't put up a fight. There's more coverage in the canopy of oaks... more shadows. We walk with careful but brisk steps, continuously scanning our surroundings.

"There," Jasper points ahead.

Voices carry through the trees, now. Sharp and commanding mixed with pleading. We move toward the sound, our footsteps muffled by fallen leaves and overgrown grass.

Through the brush, I spot movement. It looks like a small clearing ahead. People... at least four. We get low, stepping closer.

There's two guards in full tactical gear like they're in a war zone. They're standing in front of two figures. Women, by the looks.

"Let's go!" one of the guards says. "Back to the house!"

They grab hold of their arms, dragging them while they cry and plead. One of them loses their footing, earning another sharp remark from a guard.

A flashlight beam shines directly at her face.

My world stops.

Those eyes, ocean blue and wide with fear. The same nose, the same round chin I've memorized from a thousand sketches. The same long brown hair, but tangled with leaves and debris. So much thinner than I remember, and without that sun kissed glow of summer, but unmistakably, impossibly...

"Bailey," I exhale.

Jasper grips my shoulder, a ragged breath escaping his lips.

Damon murmurs a curse, repeating her name. On instinct, I step toward her, but Jasper's hand anchors me.

It's been eighteen months of searching, of guilt, of wondering if she was even alive. Eighteen months of rereading her last text message, letting those words sit like a brick on my chest. Eighteen months of replaying every detail of our summer together knowing I'd never feel whole again.

And here she is, not twenty feet in front of me, being dragged through the woods by Alfred's private army.

Every rational thought ceases to exist. All the careful planning, all the caution, all the strategy—none of it matters anymore.

She's here. She's alive.

And we're getting her out.

Layne is side-eyeing me from her bed. She thinks I'm going over notes, and hasn't figured out this is my diary. If she does, I'm so cooked. There's a hundred percent chance she'll steal it and read every single entry while I'm asleep, and as much as I love her, some thoughts are private.

Like how much I miss Leon. I miss the way he nibbles his lip ring when he's thinking. I miss his laugh. I miss the way he calls me Firefly. I miss his lips. His body.

We've only seen each other once since classes started. It was really sweet... He took me to this cozy Italian restaurant near campus. A "proper date," as he called it.

We couldn't do much more than kiss goodbye afterwards. I wasn't in the mood to introduce him to Layne, plus he had to get back for an early class. Still kinda bummed though.

We decided that next time we hang out, we're going to go back to their place (the house he and the guys are renting this year) and tell Jasper and Damon everything. We're both ready... Well, him more than me. Having my brothers know my business in that way is super weird. It's bad enough that I know what they're up to with the girls they snuck into the house all summer.

But it's time... if Leon and I are going to have a future together, our family needs to know.

Oh no... She's calling Clay. They're probably going to fight again. I can't deal.

Yup, she's already getting loud.

God, this is going to go on for hours. Maybe I should escape to the library or something. I think it's still open. Though knowing Layne, she'll rope me into staying to analyze every word he said while barely letting me get a response in.

I just want to text Leon goodnight and pretend it's still summer. Fantasy world and all that.

CHAPTER TWENTY-THREE

BAILEY - PRESENT DAY

I MARK ANOTHER DAY ON THE LEGAL PAD I PILFERED FROM the study. It's not an exact calendar, but between this and my view of the grounds, I have a close enough idea of the date. It's been another three months since that townhouse. Nine months altogether. Summer to fall to winter and now spring again.

So many seasons in this beautiful prison, and I'm no longer the girl who arrived here trembling and broken. That girl died three months ago in a London townhouse, watching helplessly as monsters devoured another person I care about.

This morning, like most others, I sit across from Sir at the breakfast table, my spine straight, my face a mask of neutrality. He barely touches his food, which is unusual for him. He normally takes such deliberate pleasure in his meals, taunting me with each measured bite. Instead, he pushes the eggs around his plate with his fork, pausing occasionally to press his fingertips against his temple.

My focus is elsewhere though, inside I'm plotting how to sneak into the kitchen again and grab another carving knife from the block.

"You seem distant lately, my dear," Sir says as he places his fork on the side of his plate. "Ms. Harrington mentioned you've been less responsive during your lessons."

I pick at my bowl of bland cantaloupe, wishing I could throw it across the room. I know I should be grateful I have food to eat at all. Every time I think back to the days of living in King's holding house with the others I'm racked with guilt. It was a different kind of torture. The hunger pangs that would make me unable to sleep, weak enough to barely lift my limbs. Exactly how King wanted me—a weak, exhausted, starving girl who could only fight back with words, not fists.

"I apologize if my demeanor has been unsatisfactory, Sir," I reply, keeping my voice as expressionless as my face. Polite enough to keep him happy, but not the warmth I used to fake.

He rubs his temple, studying me. "On the contrary, I find this side of you to be more mature. You're growing into your-self. Becoming the woman you were meant to be."

The woman you made me become.

In his twisted mind my coldness equals sophistication, my withdrawal a trait he's been artfully crafting. After all this time, I don't even remember what it's like to be me. The old me, before they all molded me like a clay doll.

I'll let him think that he's winning. That the woman he purchased and carefully cultivated is still trembling and afraid. He has no idea that every night, I dream of Polly's blank face as she stood in front of King. If not her, then Cat, or Jasmine, or Lydia.

Let him be blind to the rage simmering in my chest like a low flame, waiting patiently to incinerate everything he holds dear.

"Ms. Harrington will be busy today making preparations for a special guest," he says, glancing at me from the rim of his cup. "Polly will escort you."

Warring reactions bounce through me. A guest is never a good thing, but at least Polly and I will have some alone time today. Maybe we can solidify a plan. I'm more than ready.

"Who is the guest, Sir?" I ask sweetly.

He swallows a sip of tea, and smiles. I brace myself for his response. "A very important young man. Someone I've been telling you about for some time now."

"How lovely," I say, feeling the urge to vomit. "When will he be arriving, Sir?"

"Tomorrow night. I've been waiting too long for him to accept that home is where he belongs. He's finally accepting my offer."

Home? This man must be related to Sir—a brother or maybe even a son.

"He must be very special to you, Sir."

His eyes gleam. "Indeed. It's taken some time to realize his value, but now I have great plans for him. For both of you, actually."

I spear another piece of melon onto my fork. "Plans?"

His expression changes in a snap and I know I've pushed too hard. He clears his throat. "That's enough questions, Bailey. Patience is a virtue."

I bow my head, focusing on chewing the melon so I don't get myself into more trouble.

Sir stands and smoothes out his pants. "I want you to look your absolute best tomorrow. Ms. Harrington will prepare something special for you to wear. First impressions are so important, don't you think?"

"Of course," I say.

He narrows his eyes. "Of course, *Sir.*"

"Yes, I apologize, *Sir.*" The simmering spark in my chest flickers from his annoyance.

He moves toward the door, calling for Polly to clear the

table. My hand is midway across it, reaching for some toast, when I feel his presence behind me.

"Your behavior for the next twenty-four hours will determine your future. Do you understand?" His voice is low and seething as he snatches the plate of toast and throws it against the wall. I watch the porcelain china shatter into hundreds of pieces, horrified.

I force myself to remain seated, frozen like a prey animal caught in a snare. "Yes, Sir. I understand."

"Good." He focuses on straightening his hair and jacket. "Because if you embarrass me in front of my guest, if you show even a hint of the defiance I've been seeing lately, there will be consequences." His gaze strays to Polly, who just entered from the kitchen, wide-eyed and afraid, and adds, "Not just for you."

I blink, willing myself to stay steady. "I promise, Sir. I will be a good girl."

His face softens while I cringe. For some reason he loves that phrase. I don't think I could hate those two words more. "Good. Polly, clean this mess."

She scrambles forward while he stalks from the room. It takes me a moment for my pulse to slow, for my limbs to move again, for me to release the breath I was holding. I hurry over to help pick up the scattered toast and large chunks of china.

"Did you hear?" I whisper.

Her eyes meet mine, and she nods solemnly. "Every word."

We both know what this means. What tomorrow will bring.

We're out of time. Tonight is our last chance.

After we finish cleaning, she leads me to the study. It's time to make a plan, no matter the cost.

THE KITCHEN KNIFE feels heavier than I remember. Or maybe I've just grown weaker. Either way, I clutch it to my chest as we make our way down the dark hallway of the house. My heart pounds so hard I wonder if Polly can hear it.

She points past the kitchen. "The service door, back there."

I'm trusting her. She's gotten me this far without being spotted. When we were in the study earlier, she filled me in on exactly how many guards Sir has working for him. Many more than I've ever seen on my chaperoned walks. With their stealth and knowledge of the grounds, I know the chance of us getting out of here is slim.

The memory of Cat and I dashing to the woods fills my mind. How close we came... before our hope came crashing down.

No. This time will be different. It has to be.

We've been planning this for hours, ever since Sir left this morning. Polly managed to block the camera in my cottage somehow, and with Ms. Harrington occupied, she was able to keep the door propped open. But coming back into the house is a risk, I'm trusting she knows what she's doing.

"What about the cameras?" I ask.

"There's a blind spot near the old groundskeeper's shed behind the main house. We can make it to the tree line from there."

"How do you know?" I whisper.

She squeezes my free hand. "I'll tell you when we get out of here." Her voice is solemn. Whatever it is, I doubt it's a pleasant story.

My legs shake as we reach the door. This is it. After months of being the perfect prisoner. Of submitting to every demand that psycho made. One more step and maybe I'll never have to step foot in this house again.

"Ready?" Polly asks, closing her hand around the brass handle.

I nod, gripping the knife tighter.

Cool night air hits my face, sobering me. We run.

Polly leads but I stay no more than a few steps behind. It's so dark, I'm afraid I'll trip on a rock or a divot in the grass, but we can't afford to slow.

Behind us, the house grows farther away. Silent, but like a living presence. Like it's watching.

A few more feet. I'm gasping for air, my body is not used to this much exercise.

Then, not thirty seconds later, every alarm on the estate starts screaming.

"Shit!" Polly gasps, grabbing my hand as floodlights blaze to life around us. We're like rats trapped in a maze.

We sprint across the open lawn, not bothering to be stealthy now. Our feet pound against the damp grass. There's shouting coming from somewhere. Not the main house, somewhere on the grounds.

"Polly?" I cry.

We're so screwed.

"There!" She points to the dark tree line far ahead. "We can lose them in the woods!"

That's what Cat thought too and look what happened.

I push those memories aside and let Polly pull me forward.

The alarm system is so loud, every fiber of my being wants to shrink into a ball. To hide until it stops.

We're getting closer. The trees are no longer a blur of shadow.

But I stumble, sliding on a patch of wet grass. Polly hauls me up. "Come on, we're almost there!"

In my dreams, the trees were this dark entity. Pulling me in, holding me hostage, painfully biting into my skin. But now, they're my salvation. A chance to disappear into the growth.

I hear a voice, but it's coming from a speaker or a radio. There's no time to stop and see where exactly it is. "They're closing in on the fence!"

"Fence?" I pant out, remembering the huge iron gate we passed through that first night.

"It'll be okay," she says.

We hit the edge of the tree line, away from the search lights. I want to double over, to catch my breath, but she keeps pulling me.

A few feet into the brush, the alarms cut out. It's almost worse than the shrieking sound. Our voices, footsteps, even our heavy breaths, are completely exposed now.

Branches tear at my skin and I stumble again, relying on Polly's strength to hold me up.

"There's an old trail somewhere," she pants. "Saw it on a map."

Something rustles behind us. We both freeze. Then I hear it, heavy breathing and the swish of pants rubbing together. Whoever it is, is coming closer.

Polly grabs my arm, pulling me behind a thick tree trunk. We hug ourselves against the rough bark, hoping to God that we'll stay hidden.

A guard dressed in black comes into view. He sweeps his flashlight beam across the forest floor. He's alone, but I know that doesn't mean he's not dangerous. His radio buzzes with static as he moves closer to our hiding spot.

The beam of his flashlight passes inches from my face. I hold my breath, tightening my grip on the kitchen knife with my sweaty palm.

He takes a step, then another. His boot lands on a fallen branch right next to where we're hidden.

"I know you're here," he mutters. "I'm not going to hurt you."

Polly squeezes my free hand while I mentally calculate whether we should take our chances and run.

I look down at the kitchen knife in my grip, its silver blade shines in the moonlight. His voice morphs and suddenly it's King calling my name. Mocking me. Telling me all the vile things he's going to do to me and my friends.

I'm so done being powerless.

"Stay!" He raises his weapon, but I'm already moving, crouched low.

Months of rage and fear and helplessness explode out of me.

"No!" I scream from somewhere in my chest and drive the kitchen knife forward with every bit of strength I have. It sinks into his thigh with ease, cutting through fabric, muscle, and sinew. He howls, dropping his flashlight as he staggers backward.

"Run!" I yell to Polly, as I stand to my full height and sprint behind her, warm blood coating my hands. I don't chance looking back, I know he's not able to chase us. We bolt deeper into the woods, but his shouts echo behind us. *Shit, the radio.*

"Escapees heading northeast! They fucking stabbed me. Need backup!"

We run and run, for what feels like miles but surely isn't. Through trees, almost tripping on exposed roots and fallen logs. Then I see flashlight beams, and something inside me breaks, if there's even anything whole left.

"Stop right there!" A bright light shines in my face, temporarily blinding me. We freeze, and I raise my hands on instinct. I want to cry, to scream, to run.

"Polly?" I whisper. She'll know what to do... She has to have planned for this.

Two guards step into the clearing, their gear making them look like soldiers. The one with the flashlight keeps it trained on us while the other speaks into his radio.

"We've got them. The two females. Heading back to the house now."

"Let's go!" The first guard moves toward me, closing his hand around my upper arm painfully.

Polly fights back, pulling away from the second guard. "No, please! You don't understand—"

"Back to the house!" the guard barks, yanking her forward.

That's when I hear a sound come from behind them. They're too focused on us to notice, but something moves in the shadows. I try to stay calm, to figure out a way out of this, but fear has me frozen.

I catch movement in the shadows again, and the guard holding Polly suddenly goes rigid. His eyes roll back, a wordless grunt escaping his lips, as a jacketed arm squeezes his throat from behind. It's so quiet, so efficient, so terrifying. The guard drops like a fallen tree, probably unconscious before he even hits the ground.

"What the—" The other guard spins around, dropping his flashlight and holding his weapon up.

We're plunged into darkness again, but I swear I catch glimpses of familiar faces.

I must be seeing things...

It can't be.

Leon.

Jasper.

Damon.

How? No. It's the shadows playing tricks. My mind conjuring the ones I'd always hoped would save me.

My eyes dart back to the bellowing guard. His arm is swinging around, searching the darkness for the culprit.

He fires a single gunshot, loud enough to wake the dead.

Polly cries out, falling to her knees. She's clutching her abdomen... and oh God, I don't have to see the deep red liquid seeping through her dress to know.

"Polly!" I lunge toward her, but she waves me off before she's within my reach.

"It's okay." She coughs, her voice straining.

"Oh my God," I cry. "You shot her! Help, please... somebody!"

The guard is breathing hard, sweeping his weapon back and forth across the open air, completely ignoring my pleas for help. "Show yourselves! I know you're out there!"

Then a voice cuts through the night. Low, controlled, so familiar.

"Drop your weapon."

The guard spins toward the sound, and that's when I see him step into the sliver of pale moonlight filtering through the canopy. Short dark hair, smooth tan skin, thick brows framing eyes that promise violence.

He's existed in fragments for a year and a half. A ghost. A shadow. The hope I clung to in those moments between sleeping and waking.

"Leon?" I whisper his name, afraid if I speak too loud he'll vanish into thin air.

He's real. He's here. This isn't a hallucination or wishful thinking.

Behind him two more figures step out of the shadows, and I forget how to breathe. My brother. He looks different, older, harder. His eyes are brimming with tears. And Damon, broader than before, more intimidating, with a look in his eyes that could kill.

"Bailey," Jasper's voice breaks slightly as he says my name. "Jesus Christ, Bailey."

I can't speak. Can't move. Can't process that after almost two years of hell, my family found me.

"Drop the gun. Now," Leon repeats. He's pulled a weapon and has it pointed at the guard. Damon follows suit, grabbing a gun from somewhere underneath his jacket.

The guard's outnumbered and he knows it. His hand shakes as he glances at the radio clipped to his vest.

"I wouldn't," Damon says.

Polly coughs and I finally snap out of it. "She needs help."

I'm scared to move, not with the guard's gun still out. Jasper slowly steps toward me, but I see it in his eyes. He's waiting too.

The guard's eyes quickly dart between Leon's weapon and his radio, barely visible but I catch it. His finger hovers near the trigger.

"Please," I beg. "Let us go."

His eyes land on Leon, hand moving slightly.

"Don't," Leon warns, his voice deadly calm.

But it's too late. The guard starts to swing his weapon toward Leon, and everything happens at once.

A gunshot echos through the trees. Jasper runs for me. Polly cries out.

For a split second, I panic. Who fired the gun? Who's hurt? Please, let it not be Leon.

But then the guard's body slumps to the ground, his weapon falling beside him.

CHAPTER TWENTY-FOUR

LEON - PRESENT DAY

THE GUARD FALLS, AND TIME STOPS. EVERYTHING SEEMS distant, like I'm watching someone else's life unfold. There's only ringing in my ears and a body—a large man, face down in the dirt. I've never... Jesus Christ. I've never shot a man in the head before. Never killed someone while looking them in the eyes. My hands shake as I lower my weapon, but there's no time to process what I've just done.

Because Bailey is here. She's real, and alive, and standing fifteen feet away from me with blood on her hands and terror in her eyes. Jasper's holding her tight, murmuring, crying.

I close the space between us, needing to touch her, to feel that she's alive. Fucking alive, and okay. But the blood...

"Are you hurt?" I ask, reaching for her hands.

"Leon?" She whispers my name, her voice exactly like I remember. The wall surrounding my heart cracks in two. Shit. Tears well in my eyes. "I can't believe you're real."

I feel the same way but I don't have words to relay that.

She's here.

Thinner, with longer hair, and wearing a frilly dress I'd never have recognized her in. But she's Bailey.

The other women's cries of agony snap me back to reality, and Bailey runs to her. "Help her, please!"

"She's bleeding bad," Jasper says. I can read his tone... it's not looking good.

Damon kicks the guard's weapon away from his body and scans the tree line. "We need to move. That gunshot will bring more."

Breathing heavily, I force myself to think tactically, to push down the overwhelming relief and joy of seeing Bailey again. Her friend, Polly from what I've heard Bailey call her, is dying. There's more people after us. This isn't over.

I crouch beside Polly, pressing my hands against the wound in her side. Blood seeps between my fingers, warm and sticky. She barely stirs, just whimpers as I move my hand away.

"Can you move?" I ask her gently.

She inclines her chin a bit. "I think so."

"Bailey, can you walk?" Damon asks. He's got his gun out, scanning the area around us.

She nods, but she's trembling all over. Jasper moves toward her slowly, speaking softly. "It's okay. We're here now. We're going to get you out."

He lifts her, and she holds onto his shoulders. "I've got her."

I wrap my arm around Polly's waist, helping her to her feet. She leans heavily against me, and I can feel her strength ebbing with each step. Carefully, I pick her up, cradling her in a bridal position, as her cries grow weaker.

Fucking hell. That is not a good sign.

We make it maybe a hundred feet deeper into the woods before she quiets and goes completely limp in my arms.

"We have to stop," I say, trying to keep my voice calm while I'm freaking the fuck out. I lower Polly gently against the base of a tree, wiping my bloody hands on my pants. Bailey scrambles out of Jasper's arms and drops to her knees beside us.

"Polly?" Her voice cracks as she touches her pale face. "Polly, can you hear me?"

I turn on my flashlight, positioning it on the ground, and press my hands against the wound, trying to stop the bleeding. There's so much blood. Too much. It's soaked through her dress... There's no way. I don't know what to do.

"Is she..." Damon asks quietly, coming to my side.

I check for a pulse at her throat. Searching desperately... For Bailey, please let this poor girl live.

For a moment, there's nothing. Then I feel it. So fucking weak, but still there.

"She's alive, but barely," I say. "The bullet must have hit something vital... Shit, i-it's bad."

"No," Bailey whispers, smoothing Polly's hair back from her face. "No, she's going to be fine. She has to be fine. Polly? Polly, wake up!"

Jasper kneels next to us, struggling to keep himself calm. "What can we do?"

I look at Polly again, and know that we're out of time. But I can't say that, not with Bailey falling apart beside me.

"We need to get her to a hospital," I say instead.

"How?" Damon asks. "We're in the middle of nowhere, and we can't exactly call an ambulance."

Polly's eyes flutter open. They're glassy and lifeless like she's struggling to see. "Bailey," she whispers.

"I'm here," Bailey says, wrapping Polly's hand in hers. "I'm right here."

"Don't go back. He's... they're—" I struggle to make out what she's trying to say. "Safe now... you're safe."

"Don't talk," Bailey pleads, choking back a sob. "Save your strength."

Polly tries to say more but her voice trails off.

"Fuck," Jasper cries, as Polly's eyes roll back. "Dude, she's dying!"

"Polly!" Bailey cradles her cheeks in her palms. "Stay with us!"

I sense someone coming, and force myself to back away from Bailey. Damon sees me move, and comes to my side. We both hear them at the same time. Footsteps. Multiple sets, stalking through the underbrush.

"Company coming," Damon mutters, checking his weapon.

I glance back at Bailey, who's clinging onto Polly. "Fuck," I say under my breath. She's going to hate me for this, but someone needs to make a decision, and I won't let Bailey get taken again... or any of us for that matter.

"Bailey," I say quickly. Her tear-streaked face turns to me. "We might have to—"

"No." She sniffs and wipes her eyes, her voice turning to steel. "I'm not leaving her."

"Bailey," Jasper argues. "I'll carry her, but we have to move."

I point my gun toward the approaching footsteps. There's no time. Even if we move now, they'll catch up to us.

Then two figures stop just over a small hill, close enough that I can make out obvious details. One is another guard, this one more stocky than tall. He's in black, with a vest on, like the others.

But the second figure is tall and carries himself differently. It looks like he's wearing a long coat, similar to what I've seen on businessmen walking around the city.

I know it's Alfred immediately... without seeing a single detail up close. But what will he do when he realizes it's me here?

"Lee?" Damon asks, closing in next to me.

"Wait," I mutter. "Don't shoot... not yet."

Alfred moves closer and Bailey scrambles backward, covering Polly's unconscious form with her own. Her eyes are wide with fear, telling me everything I need to know about what she's gone through here.

He stops, and holds his hand out for the guard to do the same. Our eyes meet, and recognition sparks in his features but only for a split second.

"Sir," one of his guards says, "should we—"

"No." He studies our group, keeping his expression blank. His gaze lingers on Bailey's terrified face, before moving to Polly's body behind her. "What a mess."

He glances at me again, and I see him take in my stance, my weapon, the way I'm positioned protectively near Bailey. I can't get a read on him or what he'll do next and it has me primed to fight.

"Let them go," he says finally with a wave of his hand.

The guard can't comprehend what he's heard. "Sir?"

"You heard me. Clean this up." He gestures toward where we left the other guard's body. "All of it."

Bailey lets out a small, broken whimper, and Alfred's attention shifts back to her. For just a moment, his mask of indifference slips, and I see the possessive urge to rip her from us rise up.

"Goodbye, my dear," he says softly. "I do hope we'll see each other again soon." Then he turns to walk away, the guard reluctantly following.

I'm shaking with rage, unable to lower my weapon. It would be so easy to shoot him in the back right now. Watch him bleed out slowly... suffer for whatever it is he's done to Bailey. To me. To so many others.

"That's it!" I shout. "You're just fucking letting us go?"

Damon touches my shoulder and I flinch. "Brother, what the hell are you doing?"

"No," I seethe. "He needs to pay. He needs to—"

"Guys, we have to go!" Jasper interrupts.

"Oh God. No..."

Bailey's voice snaps me back to reality. Shit. Her friend. She's hurt. She—

"Polly?" Bailey whispers, shaking her gently. "Polly, no. No, no, no!"

I watch helplessly as Polly's chest rises one last time, then goes still. The light in her eyes dims. There's no doubt, she's gone.

"No!" Bailey's scream tears through my soul, raw and heartbroken. "No, she can't be. Polly! Polly, wake up! Please!"

She throws herself over Polly's body, her shoulders shaking from the force of her sobs.

"Bailey," Jasper says gently, reaching for her. "I'm so sorry. Come here, I've got you."

"I can't leave her!" Bailey wails, clinging to her body. "I can't leave her here alone!"

"I've got her." I tell Jasper, placing a reassuring palm on his shoulder before kneeling at Bailey's side. I touch her for the first time in over a year, and something switches in her. She crawls to me, climbing into my lap, sobbing against my chest.

My heart fucking cracks in two. Another person dead. Another beautiful soul I couldn't save.

"She saved me." Bailey tries to reach back for Polly again, but I wrap her in my arms, lifting her up. "No, please..." But she's lost all fight now... her sobs dissolving into whimpers, and incoherent words.

"I'm sorry," I murmur into her hair. "I'm so fucking sorry, love."

Jasper nods at me before blocking Bailey's view of Polly. It fucking kills me to leave her here, but we can't move her. It'll only cause more trouble.

Bailey's cries echo through the trees. It's a sound that'll haunt me for the rest of my life, and somehow I'm sure this moment isn't even the worst of what she's endured.

I take one last look at Polly's peaceful face before forcing myself to walk away, leaving her alone in the darkness.

PART 2

CHAPTER TWENTY-FIVE

BAILEY

THE BATHROOM DOOR CLICKS SHUT BEHIND ME, AND FOR the first time in over a year, I'm alone by choice.

My fingers shake and fumble as I turn the lock twice, then three times, just to hear it click. Just to know that I can truly have the space I need.

Leon's voice carries through the door, low and kind of snappy, followed by Jasper's which is just as insistent. I can't make out their exact words, but I don't need to. They're planning. Arguing. Deciding what comes next.

I turn away from their voices and face the shower.

It's nothing special, just a normal shower with white tiles and a glass door that's seen better days. But there's a rainfall showerhead and three different bottles of shampoo and conditioner lined up on the built-in shelf. Regular stuff I used to buy at home, drugstore brands, but now I have a choice in which to use. *Simple choices.* When did I last have those?

The water takes forever to warm up. Steam starts to fog the mirror, and I'm glad that I can no longer see my reflection. I don't want to see what Leon and my brothers see. What all these months of captivity has done to me now that the mask I wore for Sir is gone. My real face. My real body. Not yet.

Leon's voice rises outside the door, followed by what sounds like Damon interjecting. Someone shushes them both. Maybe it's Damon's girlfriend. I can't remember her name. I know they're trying to be quiet for my sake, but they shouldn't. They need to talk, to process what they saw at that estate, what they had to do to get me out.

They need to figure out what to do about Polly.

I step into the spray and the heat hits my skin like a shock. Polly will never feel this again. She died so I could have this moment, this choice, this freedom. My shoulders crumple until I can barely stand, and I slowly sink down to the floor, tucking my knees against my chest.

Tears fall down my cheeks, mixing with the hot water. I can't help but think it should have been me. Polly deserves this shower. She deserves to choose from the three different shampoos and to stand under the rain head and to use every ounce of hot water in the place.

Her. Not me.

I let myself cry until I have nothing left. And then I wash every inch of skin, scouring myself with the washcloth until I hurt. I wash my hair twice, and leave the conditioner on for as long as I can stand. When the water runs cold, I get out and wrap myself in the clean, fluffy towel set out for me.

It smells like fresh cotton and feels silky against my sensitive skin.

I don't know what to do with myself now. There's no one outside the door promising violence or withholding meals if I take too long. I don't need to rush back to Cat, or Jasmine, or Katie and make sure they're okay. To check that nothing happened to them while I was gone.

Cat... I need to help her. Help them all.

Someone knocks on the bathroom door, interrupting my spiral. "Bailey? I pulled some clothes that should fit you. I can leave them right outside the door, okay?"

I think that's Jasper's new girlfriend, Falin.

"Thanks," I say, appreciative but so exhausted I can't muster anything else.

"I kicked the guys outside to give you some space. Let me know if you need anything."

Her footsteps retreat, so I crack the door and grab the bundle of clothes. There's black sweats, a cropped T-shirt, and a zip-up hoodie. No undergarments... which I guess I wouldn't want to wear anyway. Still, it feels even weirder to wear someone else's clothes with nothing underneath.

I pull everything on, tying the sweats tight and zipping the hoodie. The fabric is soft, worn-in, and smells faintly like roses. Normal clothes. Not the formal dresses Sir would choose for me. Not the lingerie King forced us into. Just regular clothes that someone thought I might be comfortable in.

The house has gone quiet on the other side of the door. No more muffled arguing, no footsteps pacing back and forth. Either they've moved somewhere else to continue their planning, or Falin really did kick them outside like she said.

I should go find them. Thank them. Try to explain what happened to me. Hell, I should at least want their comfort. But my legs refuse to move and thinking about facing their questions, their sympathy, their anger on my behalf, makes my chest tight.

Instead, I sit on the closed toilet seat and stare at my hands. My nails are short and clean now, but I can still see the phantom dirt under them. Can still remember the dried blood from the man King killed in front of me. Can still feel the knife handle as I stabbed that guard.

How had our plan gone so wrong? It doesn't matter now,

but maybe Polly would be here if we weren't so impulsive. If she didn't rush it because of me.

I hear a soft knock and lift my eyes from my hands. "Bailey?" It's Leon's voice, gentle and uncertain. "Can I—Are you okay in there?"

I want to say yes. To open the door and fall into his arms and pretend that everything can go back to how it was before. But I don't know how to be the girl he fell in love with anymore. That girl died somewhere between King's house and Sir's estate, and I'm not sure who's left in her place.

"I'm okay," I lie. "Just... give me a few more minutes?"

"Of course," he says. "And listen, you don't have to talk about anything tonight. Or if you do want to talk, we're all here for you."

"Okay... I'll be out soon."

I listen for him to walk away, but he doesn't. He stays on the other side of the door, not rushing me to come out, or suffocating me with his presence. It's almost like he's standing guard until I'm ready to face the world.

"Leon?" I ask quietly.

"Yeah?"

"How did you find me?" The question has been gnawing at me since the moment I saw his face in that clearing. "How did you know where I was?"

He's quiet for a long time and when he finally speaks, his voice is strained. "It's complicated, Bailey. We can talk about it when you're ready. All of it."

"Maybe you should tell her now." I recognize Jasper's voice. It's quieter than Leon's, but there's something different about it, like there's an underlying tone of confusion or hurt. "She's going to figure it out eventually."

"Jas—" Leon says.

"You two... How long has that been going on? And your fa—"

"Don't." Leon's voice is sharp. "Not like this."

"Lee, she needs to know that the man who had her—"

"I said, don't." There's real pain in Leon's voice now.

Jasper sighs loud enough for me to hear through the door. I need to know what they're talking about. Something with Sir?

I stand and crack the door open.

Both of them stop arguing and turn toward me. Leon looks like he's seen a ghost and his jaw is clenched tight enough to crack a tooth. And my brother... I didn't notice earlier how exhausted he looks with his disheveled hair and tired eyes.

"Bailey," Leon starts, but I hold up a hand.

"What aren't you telling me?" I ask, stepping fully into the hallway. The borrowed clothes feel too big, like I'm a child playing dress up, but I straighten my shoulders anyway.

More footsteps and voices approach and suddenly Damon, Blake, and Falin appear at the end of the hall. Great. Now it's a full audience for whatever this conversation is.

"We should call Mom and Dad," Jasper says, redirecting us. "They need to know you're safe. They've been waiting—"

"She needs space first," Leon cuts in. "Look at her, she can barely—"

"Don't talk about me like I'm not here," I interrupt. "And Jasper, how long has what been going on? You were asking about Leon and me?"

I try to hide the hurt from my expression. *Leon didn't tell them.* All this time passed and he kept our relationship a secret.

Jasper looks as hurt as I feel. "How long, Bails? How long have you two been... together? Without me knowing?"

"We should go back," Damon says so suddenly I flinch. "That estate, there could be evidence. Other girls. I want to make that bastard pay."

"No." Leon's voice is final. "We're not going back."

"You wanted to earlier," Damon points out. "You were ready to burn the whole place down."

"And you were right to stop me," Leon admits. "Bailey's safe. That's what matters."

"What about the others?" Jasper asks quietly. "The ones who might still be there? And what about our parents? They deserve to know she's alive."

I hold onto the wall for strength at the mention of others.

"Bailey?" Blake steps forward, her voice gentle. "I'm a med student. Would you let me take a look at you? I don't have all my equipment, but I can do a basic exam. Make sure you're okay."

"She just got out," Leon says. "She doesn't need to be poked and prodded—"

"It's her choice," Jasper cuts in, hurt still in his voice. "Stop deciding what she needs. You've been making decisions about her long enough."

"I'm trying to protect her!"

"From what? Medical care? Her family? Or are you trying to protect yourself from having to explain why you kept your relationship with my sister a secret? I can't believe I didn't realize it earlier..."

I watch them argue about me again, and something inside me snaps.

"Stop." My voice comes out stronger than I expected. "All of you, just stop."

They all go silent and turn to me. I want to shrink against the weight of their stares, but I feign strength I don't feel.

"Jas," I say, steadying my voice. "Leon and I... it happened last summer. Before I was taken. We didn't tell you because..." I glance at Leon, who looks like he's hanging on my every word. "Because it was new and we were seeing how things went."

Leon's face falls. "That—that's not entirely true."

I shoot him a warning look, silently telling him to stop. Jasper doesn't need to know everything. But Leon continues anyway.

"I knew I loved you right away. There was no doubt in my mind how things were going. Was there for you?"

"Really, this isn't the time, Lee," Blake interjects.

"So, you didn't trust me? Did you think I'd be pissed?" Jasper sounds more disappointed than I'd ever heard him and I hate myself even more. I can't even meet Leon's gaze.

"It wasn't about trust. It was about not wanting to complicate things if it didn't work out." The words feel wrong as they spill from my lips. "We were going to tell you."

"Were you?" Jasper asks quietly.

"Yes," I whisper. "It was a long time ago and... it doesn't matter right now."

"Firefly?" Leon asks.

I can't look at him, can't talk to him right now. I know what I said hurts, but it's the truth. None of that matters, because that girl is gone. I turn to Blake. "I'd like you to look me over. But not here. Not with everyone watching."

Blake nods immediately. "Of course. We can use one of the bedrooms. Just you and me."

I start to follow Blake, passing by Leon and Jasper, but pause a few steps beyond them. "I want to know what you're avoiding telling me," I say, glancing between the two. "About how you found me. After Blake's done, tell me everything."

Leon looks like I've just asked him to end my life. "Bailey—"

"Everything, Leon. No more protecting me from the truth. I don't need protecting. Not anymore." I cross my arms over my chest, and keep myself from looking at Leon. "And yes, Jas, we can call Mom and Dad. But I need to understand what happened first. How you found me, all of it. I'm sure they'll have questions too."

Damon clears his throat. "What about going back to the estate?"

I think of Polly's body, probably still in the woods. Of Cat and the others who might still be somewhere out there in the world. "Did you call the police like you said? Make the anonymous tip?"

Damon nods.

"Good. Let them handle the estate. There's no one else there against their will. It was just me and Polly."

"Bailey—" Leon starts again, but I hold up my hand, inches from his chest.

"After Blake's done. Then we'll talk." I look at each of them, my gaze lingering on Leon's pained expression. "But first, I need to know I'm okay. Physically, at least."

"Shouldn't you go to a hospital? Or the police?" Falin asks. "I'm just confused about what we're still doing sitting around."

The question hangs in the air, and I can see everyone processing it. She's right, of course. In any normal situation, that's exactly what we'd do. But nothing about this is normal. I wish I had the right answer, but I'm just as confused as everyone else. And if I think about it too long... Sitting in a sterile room, having to recount every horrible thing that happened to me. That King did. No, I can't do it.

"The hospital will ask questions," Damon says quietly. "Questions we might not be ready to answer yet."

"And the police..." Jasper trails off, looking at me with pain in his eyes. "They'll want statements, evidence, details about everything that happened. This is so much bigger than just the estate."

Leon speaks up. "We can't trust the police. For all I know they're in on it. It's enough that we sent in the tip... We can check on that. Maybe if some news turns up, we'll get a better read on the situation."

"I can keep an eye on that," Falin says.

The hallway goes quiet while they all work out their thoughts. I know I'm missing a major piece of this puzzle. They must feel the same way without my full story.

"I'm not ready for hospitals or police stations or having to explain myself to strangers, anyway. Not tonight." I look at Blake. "Can you just... sort of check me over? Make sure I'm not dying or anything? Then we can figure out the rest."

Blake nods. "Of course. I'll do a basic exam, make sure there's nothing that requires immediate attention."

"Thank you." I breathe a sigh of relief.

"We'll be downstairs," Jasper says. "Take your time."

As the others start to move away, Leon catches my arm gently. "Bailey..."

"After," I say firmly, pulling away from his touch. "Please."

The hurt that flashes across his face makes me feel like a monster, but I need to make sure I'm okay. And I don't know... I'm just not ready for whatever he has to say to me. I need to hear it, but later.

Blake touches my shoulder. "Come on. Let's go into my bedroom."

I wrap my arms around my chest and follow her, noticing the way Falin squeezes Jasper around the middle on their way down the stairs. The comfortable affection they share with each other is sweet. I hope he's treating her right.

Blake leads me into a bedroom nearby. It's cozy with pale blue walls and worn in wooden furniture. In the corner, I spot her suitcase with clothes spilling out and another one nearby, still zipped up.

"Come have a seat," she says, patting the bed. "I didn't bring much, but something told me to bring the basics."

I watch as she pulls out a smaller bag from the suitcase and sets out a stethoscope, blood pressure cuff, and a small zip-up first aid kit onto the bed. Her shoulders square, almost like she's slipping into professional mode. It makes me feel better to see her this way, more secure.

"So," she says, standing beside me. "I want you to know that you're in complete control here. We can stop anytime you want, and you don't have to answer any questions you're not ready for."

"Okay," I say, uncrossing my arms.

"And of course, everything we talk about is confidential. I may be Damon's girlfriend, but right now you're my patient." Her hand reaches for my arm and instead of flinching, I allow her to place a gentle hold there. "Are you okay if I take some notes in my phone?"

I nod. It would be helpful to not have to repeat myself later.

"Have you been eating regularly? Getting enough water?"

"More recently, yes. Before..." I hesitate, not wanting to get into the details yet. "It depended on the situation."

Blake makes a note in her phone. "Any pain I should know about? Headaches, stomach issues, anything like that?"

I take a moment to assess my body. "Not really. There's been headaches, and pain, but I think it was situational."

"I'd like to listen to your heart and lungs, check your blood pressure. Nothing invasive. If you're okay with that?" She pauses. "Oh and I know this might be difficult to think about, but have you had any medical attention while you were gone? Any treatments or medications?"

I know what she's really asking... the same thing I'm most anxious about. "There's been medications, but I don't know what they were. Otherwise, no. I haven't seen a doctor."

Blake's expression doesn't change, but I notice her brows raise slightly. "Okay. We don't need to get into details now, but it would be good to get some blood work done. Just to make sure everything's okay."

I hang my head and murmur in agreement.

"We can find a good clinic nearby. I'll come with you... if you'd like."

I take a shaky breath. "Maybe tomorrow? I think I need to process tonight first."

"Of course," she says, her voice so gentle tears well in my eyes. "And Bailey, I want you to know that whatever happened to you, it doesn't define you. You're in there still."

I swallow down the lump in my throat. "I don't feel like me anymore."

"That's normal... Trauma is a bitch. It changes us, but down here," she taps her chest, "in our core, we're still the same." She reaches for a necklace tucked into her shirt. "It's nothing like what you've gone through, but I lost my mom and brother super close together, and then my other brother recently."

"I'm so sorry," I say.

She stares past me at a spot on the wall, but I catch the pain lingering in her eyes. "For a long time, I felt like the Blake I used to be had died with them. I still struggle, but talking about it has helped. There's a really good therapist back in New York, if you'd like to see her... whenever we head back, I mean. She helped me process my grief, taught me that healing doesn't mean going back to exactly who you were before, but taking your experiences, learning from them, and finding a new version of yourself."

I don't know how to respond and find myself sitting with her words. She seems to snap back to the present, tutting to herself, and grabbing her stethoscope.

"Ready to make sure you're physically okay so you can focus on everything else. Is it alright if I listen to your heart?"

She runs through a basic exam, and I notice that after the initial contact my shoulders relax slightly. For the first time in over a year, someone is touching me with care instead of violence or control. It's a small thing, but maybe it's the first step toward reclaiming my body as my own.

"Everything sounds good," Blake says finally, packing up her equipment. "Your heart rate's a little elevated, but that's normal given everything you've been through. Your lungs are clear."

"So I'm okay?"

"You're alive, you're breathing, your heart is beating. The rest..." She gives me a small smile. "The rest we'll figure out one day at a time."

CHAPTER TWENTY-SIX

LEON

Blake's footsteps on the stairs interrupt my restless pacing. Before I can ask where Bailey is, she raises her hand to stop me.

"She's resting. I told her it was a good idea."

I exhale slowly. "Yeah, she needs that."

She crosses to me and wraps me in a hug I didn't realize I desperately needed. "Damon filled me in on what happened over there. I'm so sorry."

"It was..." I trail off, unable to find words that could possibly capture it all. "But we found her. That's what matters."

The front door opens and Damon steps inside, taking in the scene. "Should we make this a group hug?"

Blake pulls back but keeps one hand resting on my arm. "You should get some sleep too. There's nothing more we can do tonight."

Damon adds, "I tried telling Jas and Falin the same thing, but they went out for energy drinks and snacks. Pretty sure Falin wants to find every bit of information about your fath—"

I shoot him a sharp look and he clears his throat.

"About Alfred that she can dig up. She's as pissed as I've ever seen her."

I rub my tired eyes. "What about Jas? Is he alright?"

Damon shifts his weight and pulls Blake closer to his side. "He's hurting, I think, but overall relieved to have her back. It's just... a lot to process. None of us expected tonight to go the way it did."

Silence settles over us for a few beats before Blake voices the question we've all been avoiding.

"So what do we do about all of this? Alfred, Orlov, The Brotherhood..." She pauses, letting her words hang in the air. "Once Bailey's ready to talk, it might be too late. And like you said, what if we can't trust the police?"

I roll my lip ring between my teeth, weighing her questions, running through every possible course of action and outcome.

"I don't know." It kills me to admit that. Rage and exhaustion war within my chest. I want to find Alfred... find them all... make them pay, but I'm so fucking tired and I have no idea what's right or wrong. "What I want to do and what we should do aren't the same."

"And that is?" Blake asks, her expression full of concern.

"Burn that fucking estate to the ground. Find everyone who's ever touched her and kill them slowly."

She nods, eyes wide. "Uh... yeah, not sure that's the answer tonight."

My eyes meet Damon's and I see that familiar gleam in them. He's weighing our options too until Blake cups his chin and pulls his face to look at hers. "Not happening tonight, Freddy. I see that look in your eyes."

Damon sighs and relaxes his shoulders. "You're right, Angel. We need to be smart about this."

"Smart," I repeat, trying to hide my frustration from my

tone. "I don't know if I can just sit here while Bailey's upstairs, barely okay, and other girls like her are still out there suffering." I squeeze both hands into fists. "How long do we wait? How many more people get hurt while we're being smart?"

"Leon—" Blake starts.

"No, you don't understand." My voice cracks, and I look at the floor instead of their worried expressions. "She can barely look at me. The woman I love, who I've been searching for over a year, looks at me like I'm a stranger. And it's because of him. Because of my father. How am I supposed to tell her? How can I live with what he's done?"

Blake's gentle voice draws my gaze. "The same way I'm living with what Brennan did. One day at a time, realizing what they did had nothing to do with us. Knowing that we'll do everything we can to right their wrongs."

Her words float through the air, not quite landing where I need them. Maybe it's me and I'm not ready to hear her. Too much talking, not enough action. I exhale and glance at the door. "I knew something was off about him years ago. I felt it in my gut when he tried to bring me into his fucked up world, but I just ran. I transferred schools, moved to America, and pretended he didn't exist. If I did something then..."

"You were protecting yourself," Damon says. "You did the right thing."

"I was a coward. And while I was hiding across the ocean, he was..." I can't finish the sentence. Can't say out loud what he was doing to Bailey, I still don't know the extent of it, but when I do. My words spill out, what I've been holding in for all this time. "I was supposed to be there that night, you know. But I was in some stupid fucking study group, some subconscious part of me was still trying to be the academic Alfred wanted, still trying to make him proud. She texted me, and I didn't see it. Not until—"

The front door opens and Jasper and Falin walk inside, hands full of paper bags. My eyes meet Jasper's and his widen. I know he's going to ask what we're talking about. I'm sure Falin will say all the right things—it wasn't my fault, how could I have known. And Jas—he'll just look at me with those wide eyes full of hurt.

"I need some air," I mutter, barely looking at any of them. "Need to think."

"Leon," Blake's voice is gentle but worried. "Where are you going?"

"Just for a ride. Won't be long."

I grab my jacket and bag from the couch and slip outside. Their whispered voices follow me until I close the door behind me.

It must be close to 2 AM at this point, but the cool air awakens my tired eyes. I throw on my jacket and bag and climb onto my bike.

The engine roars to life beneath me, drowning out the chaos in my head for a blessed moment. I don't have a destination in mind, I just need to move, to feel something other than this crushing weight in my chest. To clear my thoughts so I can think straight. I can't go to sleep yet, not when every time my mind is idle I see Bailey's terrified expression in that clearing.

The streets are nearly empty at this hour, just a few taxis and a couple of people out on the sidewalks. I'm able to ride faster, letting muscle memory guide me through London's winding roads. I take turns without thinking, going on instinct alone. If I get lost at least I'll have that to focus on.

My phone rings multiple times from my Bluetooth—Damon, Blake, Falin. I ignore the calls.

It's only when I slow to a stop close to an hour later that I realize where I am.

Alfred's London estate stands high before me, sitting at the top of a long driveway blocked by iron gates. The same C sigil gleams from the center, highlighting his last name. The name I wish I didn't have.

Instead of the empty abandoned feeling I used to feel as a kid when I looked up at the house I was never welcomed into, now there's only white hot rage burning through my veins.

The house is completely dark apart from the exterior security lights. If I wanted to, I could disable every protection he's set up around his property—could get inside in mere minutes. But I know in my gut he's not in there. He's either still in the country, or has fled somewhere to hide. But still, I close my eyes and picture him in there anyway. Him pacing his study with its mahogany furniture, leather bound books, and crystal chandeliers. Making phone calls and holding meetings about people like they're nothing but objects to be bought and sold. People with lives and families and loved ones. People like Bailey.

I white-knuckle the handlebars, and let a dark fantasy play out in my mind. Me dousing the place with accelerant. Striking a match. Tossing it against the heavy drapes or expensive rugs. Watching the place fill with smoke and flames. Smiling as those floor to ceiling windows explode outward, seeing his precious antiques and family portraits curl and blacken. The whole fucking home that's nothing but another object that he's collected burn until it's a pile of ash.

As the images flicker through my mind, I know as satisfying as it would be, it wouldn't be enough. Burning an empty house won't give Bailey back the months he stole from her. It wouldn't erase the way she flinched when I tried to touch her tonight, or reverse the look in her eyes when she said our relationship didn't matter anymore.

Blake and Damon are right. If I'm going to destroy him I need to do it right. I need him to look me in the eyes, and see exactly who's taking him down. And Bailey—she can be there to watch, to help, hell, even to make the killing blow herself.

I pull out my phone and stare at the contact I should have deleted years ago. *Alfred Colter* glows on the screen in cold white letters. My thumb hovers over the call button. It's past 3 AM, but I don't give a shit if I wake him up. In fact, I hope I rip him right out of whatever peaceful sleep he thinks he deserves.

Every ounce of rage that's been simmering within me sharpens to a deadly point and before I can think better of it, I hit call.

The phone rings once. Twice. Then his voice is there, coming through my speakers.

"You've made quite the mess for me tonight." The bastard sounds calm, like multiple dead bodies on his property is just another day's work.

"You're lucky you're still breathing," I seethe.

He's quiet for a moment and I fucking hate it. I want him to laugh at me. To yell. To bait me into unleashing my anger. Instead, his voice slithers through the speaker, smooth and venomous.

"I'm disappointed in you, Leon. After all this time, I thought we came to an understanding. She was for you, you know. A present. Primed and ready to be by your side as you take your rightful place—"

"You're sick," I cut him off, my voice shaking. "She's not a fucking present. She's a human being."

"And why can't she be both?"

I hop off my bike and pace the ground, not wanting to listen to him but knowing I need to hear his fucked up views.

"I've spent considerable time and resources preparing her for you. Do you have any idea what she was like when I found her? Broken. Traumatized. Worthless to anyone."

His words hit me like a punch to the gut. "You didn't find her, you bought her. There's a difference you sick fuck."

"No need to argue details. The point is, I took that damaged girl and turned her into something extraordinary. Educated her. Refined her. Made her worthy of the Colter name. Worthy of you."

"What did you do to her?"

Now he laughs dismissively, like this is all one big joke.

"I civilized her. She was nothing but a common American whore when she arrived. Now she can hold proper conversation, carry herself with dignity, understand her place in the world. I did that for you, Leon. Everything I did was to give you the perfect companion."

"Don't you fucking—"

"Language," he snaps. "You will speak to me like the proper gentleman that you were raised to be."

"Fuck you."

"I see we're not going to come to an agreement. It's a shame, really. I had grand plans for you. We all did."

"We?" I ask, though I already know exactly who he's talking about.

"Don't play dumb, son. I've been made aware of your meddling. You had such potential, Leon. Your technical skills, your intelligence... you could have been invaluable to our operations. And with Bailey by your side, properly trained and obedient, you would have had everything a man could want."

Bile rises to my throat.

"I'm not your son and I never have been. Don't come near her, you understand me? You and your twisted organization are over."

"Make your threats," he says, his pleasure practically seeping though the speaker. "I can handle them. But you're wrong about one thing: you are my son. My blood runs through your veins, whether you like it or not."

"No... blood doesn't matter. It never mattered."

"Last chance to change your mind. I have resources you can't even imagine. Connections that reach into every level of government, law enforcement, the judiciary, not just here but worldwide. Who do you think they'll believe—a respected diplomat or a bitter son with no connections? Bring her back to me, let me finish what I've started, join my side, become the man you were born to be."

"I'd rather die."

The line goes quiet for a moment, then his voice returns with that same deadly calm I've seen him use before.

"You've made your choice, Leon. And I've made mine. Sleep well, son. You'll need your rest for what's coming."

The call ends, leaving me standing in the shadow of his estate with nothing but a dial tone and a promise of war.

"Fuck!" I yell into the night. That bastard. That fucking—I pace back and forth, clenching my fists until half moon divots pierce my skin. He loved every second of that phone call and I let him have the last word.

All at once, clarity hits me. I need to leave him a message. He can't touch me. Can't hurt Bailey or anyone I love.

Before I second guess myself, I pull out my burner and within five minutes, I have the security system to his trophy home dismantled. I reach into my bag and calmly pull out my accelerant and matches.

If he wants to threaten me, I'll burn everything he owns to the fucking ground.

CHAPTER TWENTY-SEVEN

BAILEY

Two questions appear at the forefront of my mind as soon as I open my eyes. Where am I? And what is that smell?

I roll over and sit up, blinking as my eyes adjust to the light filtering through the cracks in the drapes. Leon's there—fast asleep in the wooden rocking chair in the corner of the room, his head lolled to one side, legs splayed wide. He's still wearing his leather riding jacket, jeans, and boots. When did he come in here?

I climb out of bed, stepping as lightly as possible on the hardwood floor. The closer I get, the stronger that smell becomes—like a campfire, or burned rubber. He lets out a soft snore and I can't help but crack a small smile. There are dark smudges on his jeans, and is that dirt streaked across his cheek?

I lean in to get a closer look, and his hand shoots out, gently catching my wrist. I jump back, gasping.

"Bailey?" His voice is rough with sleep as his eyes blink open to focus on me. "Are you okay?"

"Shit, Leon. You scared me."

He sits up and pulls a hand down his face. "Sorry, I didn't mean to."

With my hand clutching my chest, I let my breathing slow. "It's fine. What are you doing sleeping in that chair? And why do you smell like a barbeque?"

His posture goes rigid like I just doused him with ice water. "Fuck."

"What's wrong?"

He exhales slowly. "I may have been a bit brash last night."

The smell. The smudges. He doesn't have to say it.

"What did you do? What did you burn down?"

Something scratches against the closed bedroom door, drawing our attention. I step back and he drops his hand.

"It's probably just Havoc," he says, his voice still thick with sleep.

"Havoc?"

"Yeah. She's a little hellion of a tabby kitten. Jasper brought her home with her sister, Mayhem. Mayhem's a little sweetie though, despite her name."

I open the door and a small blur of fluff darts between my legs yowling like a demon before settling under the bed. "She's not going to give me rabies, is she?"

He gets to his knees and pulls the kitten out from under the bed. She squirms at first, but then snuggles up against his chest. It's actually really adorable.

"Of course not. Falin made sure they're all vaccinated and healthy, despite Jasper's worry about the shots hurting them." He's smirking and it makes my chest pang.

I reach out and give Havoc a scratch under the chin. "Sounds like Falin's got him under control," I say, managing a smile. "I'm glad he's been okay. I was worried about him... about everyone."

His eyes burn into mine. "You worried about us?"

"Of course. I know losing me that way must have been hard on them," I swallow and meet his gaze. "On you too."

He sets Havoc down on the bed and takes my hands in his, his thumbs tracing gentle circles across my knuckles. "Of course it was difficult, but what we went through is nothing compared to what happened to you. We have a lot to talk about and I may have complicated things further last night. Fuck, I'm an idiot." He brings my hand to his mouth and kisses it. "I love you, Bailey. I've never stopped loving you. Take however long you need, I'll be here. I'm not going anywhere."

Hearing my name from his lips, it's like I'm in a dream. I want him to hold me, to kiss me and I'll close my eyes and pretend it's summer, that nothing's changed. I open my mouth to say the words back. I love you too. I know I do... That hasn't changed. But it feels wrong. He has no idea who I am anymore and saying those words will do nothing more than give him hope that we're alright. That everything can go back to normal. I can't do that to him.

"Leon," I start, but he shakes his head.

"Before you say anything else, there's something I need to tell you. Something I should have told you last night, but I was afraid."

His grip on my hands tightens slightly. "What is it?"

He looks at me with a pained expression. "The man who had you... his name is Alfred Colter."

I understand his words, but refuse to believe them. "No."

"Alfred Colter is my father," Leon says, his voice cracking. "My biological father."

That can't be right. I pull my hands free and step back, my mind reeling. Alfred... Sir... is a Colter. Leon's father.

"I didn't know," Leon continues desperately. "I had no idea he was involved with any of this until we started tracking down leads. When we found out you were at his estate..." His voice breaks. "Bailey, I'm so fucking sorry."

I can't breathe. Can't look at him.

The man that kept me locked up. That used me like a pet. Manipulated every aspect of my life. That evil man shares Leon's blood.

"You have the same eyes," I say, barely able to get the words out. "I should have seen it earlier."

"Bailey, please. I know how this sounds, but you have to believe me... I had nothing to do with what he did to you. I've hated him my entire life. I left England to get away from him. Remember our conversations all summer? I never once mentioned him, because he was never a part of my life."

My legs feel weak. Trembling, I sink down onto the edge of the bed, trying to process this information. To line it up with what I already know. "He talked about you. About preparing me for someone important. About his son, who was being stubborn." The pieces fall into place like a twisted puzzle. I meet Leon's gaze again. "He was preparing me for *you*."

"Fuck. What do you mean? Bailey... I had no idea. No part in his plans—"

"He said you'd come around eventually. That you'd accept your destiny." I hesitate a moment, struggling to look at those eyes that are the spitting image of Sir's. "That's why he let us go, isn't it? At the estate. He saw you and he just... let us walk away."

"No," Leon says. "Maybe. I don't know. He's a manipulative bastard. I don't know what he had going through his head. Fuck. I wish I went after him. I should have—"

The bedroom door bursts open and Falin storms in. She's got her laptop clutched to her chest and an energy drink in her other hand. I don't know her well but I can tell she's pissed.

"Leon," she says. "Is there anything you need to tell us?" She drops her laptop onto the bed and opens it. The screen shows a news headline—*Massive house fire in Mayfair.*

"Shit." He gets up and walks to the window, turning his back on us.

"Let me read it to you." She clears her throat and continues, "Fire crews responded to reports of a blaze at the Mayfair residence of diplomat Alfred Colter in the early hours of this morning. The fire, which authorities believe was deliberately set, caused significant damage to the property's east wing, including what neighbors described as an extensive library and home office. While the main structure remains intact, smoke and water damage has affected much of the residence." She looks up from the screen. "Buckle up because here's the fun part. Investigators found evidence of accelerant throughout the damaged areas, and security footage from a neighboring property captured a lone motorcyclist leaving the scene shortly after the fire began."

He's gripping the windowsill, his shoulders tense, but he doesn't turn around.

"Leon," I breathe. It all makes sense. The smoky smell, the dirt on his face, the way he said he'd acted brash. "You set his house on fire."

Falin continues reading, "The Metropolitan Police are treating this as a targeted arson attack and have launched a full investigation. Mr. Colter was not present at the residence during the incident and could not be reached for comment." She closes the laptop with more force than necessary. "They're looking for whoever did this."

Leon turns to face us, his posture stiff. "He threatened you. He threatened all of us. I wasn't going to sit back and do nothing."

"You could have been killed," I say, unable to control the shaking. "Or arrested. Leon, what were you thinking?"

"I was thinking that he needed to know exactly what happens to people who hurt you. That I'm done with his bullshit." His eyes are tight, lips curled. "I'm not afraid of him."

Falin runs her hands through her hair, causing the black and platinum strands to fall messily around her face. "Dummy! Do you have any idea what this means? The attention this will bring?"

"It means I finally stood up to the bastard who's been terrorizing people for years," his tone loses some of the anger. "It means he knows I'm not the scared kid who ran away to America anymore."

Falin puts her hands on his shoulders and looks him in the eyes. "Listen, I understand. Once I tell them," she glances toward the door, "they'll understand too, but fuck, that was reckless. We're up shit creek without a paddle now."

He breathes out, nodding slowly. "I'm sorry. I fucked up. I just... fuck. I had to do something."

I stare at him, seeing the pain and desperation in his eyes. Knowing that what he did was terrible and stupid. He risked everything. Could have gotten caught or worse, and now we're dealing with the aftermath. But something inside me also feels sick satisfaction knowing that Alfred's precious study is charred to the ground. I hope he lost valuable pieces, things that meant a lot to him.

"What happens now?" I ask.

Falin's expression softens as she turns to face me. "Now we figure out how to keep this dumbass from becoming a suspect while we decide what to do about... everything else. Fuck, I wish I had my craft supplies."

"I'll take care of everything," Leon says. "Don't freak out."

"Says the man who freaks out over every single thing," Falin retorts. "Good luck with that."

He runs a hand through his hair.

"You should go get cleaned up," I say, noticing even more smudges on his pants.

"Yeah," Falin agrees. "And give me those fucking clothes so I can burn them."

She walks out of the room, mumbling to herself. I realize there and then that I like her a lot.

"You can have the upstairs bathroom," I say before I follow Falin out of the room. He looks like he needs a minute to gather his thoughts. I know I do too.

I head downstairs and into the small half bathroom, take care of business, once again feeling a mix of guilt and elation at being able to do something as simple as peeing without an audience or a time limit.

I find a brush on the counter and make work of the tangled mess that is my hair. Falling asleep with it wet didn't help.

After a few minutes I feel so weak on my legs that I bring the brush out to the living room, where Falin is sitting, computer on her lap. Jasper's slumped curled up in a ball asleep next to her. She glances away from the screen. "You need some help?"

I offer her a small smile but decline. "I've got it. It's just gotten so long, it's hard to deal with."

"I can cut it for you." She closes her screen. "I do my own hair all the time."

Thoughts swarm my mind—King grabbing me by the hair, Ms. Harrington painfully ripping the brush through my knots, forcing me to wear tight French braids.

"Yes, please," I say, not giving it another thought.

"Yay! Let me see if Blake has good scissors in her medical

bag." She hops off the couch and heads upstairs toward the bedrooms. "Oh, and make yourself at home. There's some food in the kitchen."

As soon as she's upstairs I stop for a moment, bending to kneel next to Jasper. He looks so different from the brother I grew up with but here, asleep, he's peaceful. My eyes fill with moisture and I exhale a shaky breath. I thought I'd never see him again. Never get to tease him for being a womanizer. Or get aggravated at him for eating all the snacks in the house. I thought I'd never get to feel the safety of having him hug me and ruffle my hair. Tell me he'll beat up anyone who messes with me.

Around Jasper, I've always felt safe and loved. No matter if we were slamming doors in each other's faces or goofing off.

I lean against him, wrapping my arms around his big frame. "I missed you, Jas." My words escape in a choked whisper but after I say them I feel better. Not wanting to wake him, I get up and head into the kitchen. Right there on the table is a package of croissants.

I freeze, staring at them. They're not fancy or special, just store-bought pastries. Most people take having such things to eat for granted. But for me, those croissants represent everything I was denied. Every breakfast where Sir would stuff himself with his elaborate freshly made spread while I picked at fruit or plain yogurt. Every time I reached for something I wanted only to have my hand slapped away or my choice criticized.

"Do you think a croissant is appropriate for maintaining your figure?" His voice echoes in my memory, full of control masked as care.

But he's not here now. There's no one watching, no one to judge or deny me. My hands tremble as I open the package and take one out. It's still soft, probably baked this morning. I bite into it, and the rich, buttery flavor floods my mouth. It's perfectly flaky, and so damn good I could cry.

I close my eyes and take another bite, then another, not caring about the crumbs falling onto my shirt. For the first time in I don't even know how long, I'm eating something simply because I want to. Because it tastes good and it was offered to me without repercussions or ultimatums.

Tears run down my cheeks as I finish the entire croissant, and I'm already reaching for a second one when Falin's voice comes from the living room.

"I'm ready when you are," she says.

On instinct, I yank my hand away from the package, my pulse pounding like a drum. Shit. What am I doing? I don't need to hide the fact that I'm eating. It's fine.

I force air in through my nose and out through my mouth and reach for the second croissant just as Falin comes into the kitchen.

"Aren't they yummy? I had one earlier. We should run out later and grab more. I have a feeling they won't last long." She smiles brightly, and I can't help but return it.

"They're great. Best thing I've eaten in a long time," I say.

"Good," she says, holding up a pair of medical scissors. "Blake had these in her kit. They're sharp as hell, so we should be able to get a clean cut." She gestures toward the kitchen chair. "Have a seat. You can bring the croissant."

I nibble on a few bites as I get seated and wait for her to grab a dish towel from a kitchen drawer.

"How short are we thinking?" she asks, running her fingers through my tangled hair. "Just a trim to clean it up, or do you want to go shorter?"

"Shorter. Let's chop it off."

Falin nods, and adjusts a towel around my neck. "This is

going to feel awesome. There's something so freeing about changing your hair."

I know it's not scientifically true that hair can hold memories, but as I watch the first strands fall to the floor, I imagine all the hands that grabbed it, pulled it, used it to control me are being sliced away with each cut—like I'm literally shedding those moments.

Snip. Snip. Snip.

Each cut feels more freeing than the last, like it's nothing but dead cells keeping me down.

Falin's quiet as she works, stepping back every few minutes to check on her progress. "You have gorgeous hair, you know. The color is so pretty. These honey-colored highlights, are they natural?"

"Yeah," I answer, smiling to myself. I hadn't really thought much about my hair being pretty. Not for a long time. If anything I've wanted to downplay anything about my looks, hoping I could stay unnoticed.

But right now, with this decision made to cut off so many inches, it's another step toward reclaiming my body.

My hair is pretty, and that's a good thing.

"There," she says finally, stepping back to admire her work. "Want to see?" I run my hands through the much shorter strands, nodding. "Let's go to the mirror."

I follow her into the bathroom and blink at the reflection staring back at me. I barely recognize myself. My hair now sits just above my shoulders, choppy and uneven but in an intentional way. It frames my face differently, makes my eyes look bigger, but somehow makes me look older too. Not like the scared teenager that was taken.

"I love it," I whisper, running my fingers through it. I feel so much lighter literally and figuratively.

"Good," Falin says, brushing loose hair off my shoulders.

"Because now you look like someone who could kick some serious ass."

I let out a small laugh. "Don't know about that, but I'll pretend you're right."

She squeezes my shoulder. "Come on, let's go wake everyone up. We've got a lot to talk about."

CHAPTER TWENTY-EIGHT

LEON

THEIR VOICES REACH ME AT THE TOP OF THE STAIRS. NOT quiet whispers, but full blown conversation. Blake's tone of concern, Damon's terse responses, Jasper's frustrated comments. They're all awake, all talking, which means Falin's already told them everything.

Fuck me.

I pause when I get to the bottom of the stairs, taking a beat to prepare myself for the verbal ass kicking I'm about to get. They're all gathered in the kitchen around the small table. Blake's arms are crossed, Damon's leaning back in his chair with a calculated look on his face, Jasper's pacing the length of the counter with Falin in front of him trying to get him to listen to something she's saying. And Bailey...

Holy hell.

Her hair is gone. Well, not gone. Just cut. Transformed. When did she have the time to get a haircut? She looks... incredible. The choppy layers suit her. She looks older, stronger somehow. Beautiful.

I step closer, still unable to look away from Bailey. She's

holding a croissant almost possessively, like someone will take it from her.

"—reckless doesn't even begin to cover it," Blake is saying as I step into the kitchen. "Do you have any idea what kind of attention this brings? What if there were cameras? Witnesses?"

All eyes turn to me, and the conversation dies. Jasper stops pacing. Damon's chair creaks as he sits forward. Bailey's hand tightens around her croissant, but she doesn't look away from me this time.

"Morning," I say, in a rougher tone than intended. "I see you've all caught up on current events."

And suddenly everyone's talking at once... everyone except Bailey, who's still just looking at me like she doesn't know her place in any of this.

"Bro, I know I've done some stupid shit but this... why didn't you call us?" Jasper asks.

"He was in the moment. I get it," Damon says. "But yeah, it was pretty fucking dumb, Lee. I'm surprised, actually."

"What's done is done," I say. "Yes, I acted out of character. But I don't regret doing it. I wish the whole damn place burned to the ground."

They start talking in unison again but I swear I catch a hint of a smile on Bailey's face.

"The question is, what should we do now?" Blake cuts through the chatter with that calm authority she gets in crisis mode. "We can't undo the whole fire thing, so we need damage control."

Falin opens her laptop, typing furiously. "I've been monitoring the news coverage and police chatter. So far it's just being treated as a targeted attack. No mention of suspects or descriptions."

"Yet," Damon adds.

"Security footage? What do they have? " I ask.

"That's where we might have a problem," Falin says, pulling up what looks like a map on her screen. "You disabled his system, right?"

I nod. "Of course."

"But you didn't think about the neighboring properties? Their cameras were running just fine."

Fuck. Of course they were. I can't believe I let myself get that focused on making Alfred pay that I forgot all my normal precautions.

"So we're screwed," Jasper says flatly.

"Not necessarily," Falin continues. "Your plate's a fake... That's good. The camera footage would be grainy at best, and with your helmet and jacket..." She shrugs. "But we need to be smart about next steps."

Her eyes narrow and dart between me, Jasper, and Damon. I guess I get it. We're usually the problem.

Blake raises her hand, cutting off another round of overlapping conversations. "Okay, let's all take a step back here. We're jumping ahead without knowing the full picture." She looks around the table. "I think we need to get on the same page about everything before we start planning anything else."

The kitchen falls quiet, and I find myself looking at Bailey again. She's finished her croissant but hasn't moved to get another. She's just sitting there, watching our chaotic family try to figure out how to fix my mess.

"Bailey," I say gently, "are you ready to share anything? About what happened to you? We need to understand what we're really dealing with here."

"And what about you?" Jasper asks, looking directly at me. "Are you ready to share with her?"

I sigh and pull out a chair. "We talked this morning. Briefly, but she knows about Alfred."

All eyes are on Bailey as she wraps her arms around her

chest. "I'm okay. It's just a lot to take in. I don't need your pity looks though. Especially you, Jas."

Jasper raises his hands in front of him. "Sorry, I just can't help it. It's all so fucked up."

"Yeah, well, I hate to say it but Alfred wasn't the worst of them." She clears her throat. "There were the two that took me from the club. One of them... he hurt me, hurt all of us. He called himself King. Russian accent." Her fingers are gripping her arms hard enough to leave a mark. "He's a monster."

I glance at Jasper, who looks like he wants to kill Alexander Orlov all over again. He opens his mouth to chime in, but Bailey continues.

"The other one was different. Still bad, but more... businesslike about it. He never touched me... not like King, but he sat by knowing what was going on. He's the one who handed me over to Alfred. Sweeper."

Blake goes completely rigid in her chair. "What did you say?"

"I don't know their real names. Sorry I can't be much help. But I can give some descriptions. Sweeper had dark hair... maybe like, mid-thirties—"

"Oh my God," Blake gasps and sprints from the room out the front door.

Damon follows. "Be right back."

Bailey's eyes widen. "Did I say something?"

The three of us exchange looks across the table—Jasper looking like he swallowed poison, Falin wide-eyed, and I can't see myself but I'm sure my own expression shows the weight of what we just found out.

Bailey catches on immediately, her gaze darting between us. "What's going on? Why did Blake run out like that? What aren't you telling me?"

I look at Jasper, raising my eyebrows in question. *Should*

we? I know it should come from Blake, but I don't think she'll be able to speak on it. Not soon enough, anyway.

He nods slowly, his jaw tight. "She needs to know."

I lean forward, choosing my words carefully. "Bailey, Sweeper... His real name was Brennan Whitaker."

"Okay," she says, still confused. "I mean, I figured he had a real name, but—"

"He was Blake's brother," I say quietly. "Her older brother. She had no idea what he was involved in. Thought he worked for a shipping company."

The color drains from Bailey's face as the pieces fall into place. "How? This doesn't make any sense. Is that how you met her? Did you find Sweeper?" She claps a hand over her mouth. "Oh God, I just told her that her brother stood by while King..."

"It's a long story, but King was after Blake too. She only found out the truth about her brother when we rescued her," Falin says gently. "Before that, she had no clue about his double life."

"What happened to him?" Bailey asks quietly.

Jasper's voice is grim. "King shot him. During the rescue. Blake watched it happen."

Bailey stares at us for a long moment, processing what she just heard. "So he's dead?"

I nod. "Yes. We were able to get into some of his files after. Without them, we might not have found you."

"You said King shot him? That means you know who he is? Is he still out there? Still hurting people?"

Another look passes between us, and I realize we have more to tell her than I thought.

"Jas, you should tell her," I say.

"Fuck, guys, just say it. You're freaking me out." She wipes her eyes with the back of her hand.

Jasper kneels in front of her and takes her hand. "He's

dead, Bails. King is gone." He glances back at Falin, who's looking at him with such love in her eyes. "Falin shot the bastard, and he fell off a fucking roof."

Bailey's breathing grows louder and she blinks rapidly as tears stream down her face. "He's dead? You're sure?"

"Positive," Jasper says. "Come here, sis."

He opens his arms and Bailey falls into him, burying her face in his shoulder. I can't hear what they're saying to each other, not through Bailey's sobs and Jasper's whispers, but watching them reunited like this lifts a whole fucking boulder off my chest.

For eighteen months, I've imagined this moment—Bailey safe with us. But I never pictured it happening like this, with so much pain between then and now. With so much damage that can't be undone.

They stay like that for a while, until Blake and Damon come back inside. Blake's eyes are red-rimmed but she's composed herself. She sees them and instantly knows we've told Bailey everything. Well, not everything, but the important parts.

Blake sits on the floor beside them, her hand on Bailey's back. She's fighting back tears too. "I'm so sorry, Bailey. I had no idea about my brother. Who he was... what he was doing..."

"It's not your fault," Bailey whispers, lifting her head from Jasper's shoulder to look at Blake. "You couldn't have known."

Damon sits beside her, holding her tight, and before I know it all six of us are on the floor, surrounding Jasper and Bailey, holding each other, crying, saying all the things we've held inside for over a year.

Between the tears and the comfort of finally being together, Bailey opens up. She tells us fragments—about the food deprivation, about being moved from place to place, about the other girls who didn't make it out. More... about the violence and the abuse... Only bits and pieces but enough.

She was right. Alfred wasn't the worst of it. Not even close.

Every word she speaks feels like a knife twisting in my gut. I should have been there. Should have protected her from all of it. And Orlov. Fuck, I wish I could have been there to see that bastard fall off that building. I wish I could have been the one to put a bullet in his chest instead of Falin having to carry that weight. I'd happily watch him die knowing what he did to Bailey.

"So I don't know about anyone else, but my ass is asleep," Jasper says with a smirk about an hour later.

Bailey laughs at him, the most perfect sound I've ever heard. Christ, I missed that laugh. I've tried to remember exactly what it sounded like, but hearing it now, it's better than any memory.

"Yeah, maybe we should get up," she agrees.

Everyone takes a minute to grab more pastries, someone opens a bottle of juice, and they gradually meander into the living room. It's wild to think of the normalcy of us sitting around eating and chatting after everything we just shared. But I guess that's us.

Them leaving gives me a moment to talk to Bailey alone. She's gone back to sitting at the kitchen table, and I take the chair beside her instead of across from her. Closer, but not crowding into her space.

"Love the haircut," I say, wanting to reach out and touch the strands, to run my fingers over the line that frames her face.

"Thanks. Falin did it. I needed a change."

"Can I get you anything else right now? A drink? More to eat?" I know I'm stumbling over my words, but I want her to be comfortable. I have this ache to take care of her in all the ways I couldn't before.

"I'm okay. Although, I'll need some clothes of my own. And Blake said something about finding a clinic today. I should get some blood work... And I have to call my parents..." She trails off, inhaling deeply. When her eyes meet mine again, there's dampness in the corners. "It's just hard. I keep thinking about Polly. And talking about it all. And then learning about Sir being your father... Blake's brother, about King too."

My chest constricts from the amount of pain in her voice. All these revelations hitting her at once... it's too much for anyone to process, let alone someone who's been through what she has.

I reach for her hand tentatively, unsure if she wants to be touched. She meets me halfway, wrapping her fingers in mine, and fuck, the relief that floods through me is overwhelming. It's something. A first step toward trust.

"I know, love. The whole situation is fucked. But listen, we all love you. We never stopped loving you, or looking for you. We're going to make this right, okay? I promise."

"There's others out there. Not at Sir's... Well, not that I know of. But back in New York. When you were looking for me... did you find anyone else?"

She sounds almost afraid to find out the answer. "We did... We were able to help some, but not nearly enough."

"My friends, do you think we could find them? Not now, of course, but soon? You found me, right? Maybe we can find them the same way? Help them?"

Even after everything she's been through, her first thought is helping others. This is the Bailey I fell in love with—fierce, caring, thinking of everyone but herself.

"Of course," I say, rubbing her palm. "I'll do anything you ask of me."

Slowly, like she's working something out in her mind, she lays her head on my shoulder. "Thank you."

I run my fingers through her shortened hair, feeling the slow steady rhythm of her breathing against me. We stay like that, quietly holding each other, and I let myself pretend for just a moment that we can have this. That we can find our way back to each other. However long it takes.

"Hey," Falin comes in, then stops short when she sees us. "Whoops, sorry."

"It's okay," Bailey says, lifting her head but not pulling away completely. "What's up?"

"So we were just talking and I might have a kinda sorta idea of a plan. I'd love to see what you guys think."

"Sure," I say. "We'll meet you in there."

Falin grins and as she steps away says, "Take your time," in the most obnoxious way. She truly is like an annoying little sister.

Bailey faces me again, and I reach out, running my index finger down her cheek. "Talk more later?"

She nods. "Sounds good."

We join them in the living room where Falin's already talking animatedly, gesturing with her hands. "I think this could work."

"What's going on?" I ask, leaning against the wall in the corner of the room so Bailey can take the free spot on the couch.

"So I've been thinking—"

"Yeah and not sleeping enough," Jasper interrupts.

"Shut up, dummy," Falin says, swatting at him, before continuing. "Since we can't go to the police directly, because who knows how many Brotherhood assholes have power there—"

"Brotherhood?" Bailey asks, settling against the couch cushion.

"It's what they call themselves. The fucked up psychopaths

that are a part of the trafficking ring. Either they run it, or buy into it... at the very least, they work to cover their tracks. It's a long story I can fill you in later." Bailey glances at me and I nod. "Anyway, we can't trust the cops, not here, and definitely not back in the US. I was thinking, what if we did a massive media leak?"

I straighten, thinking about what that would mean. When I can't think of a downside, I say, "Shit... that could actually work."

"Right?" Falin's eyes light up. "We leak everything we have —member lists, financial records, known locations, communication logs. And Bailey," her tone softens, "if you're comfortable sharing, any information you can provide about their operations will help. We send it all to every major news outlet simultaneously. BBC, CNN, The Times, The Guardian, Reuters— everyone we can. Make it impossible for them to control the narrative or buy their way out. Fucking end them."

"Flood the media," Damon says, smiling. "Smart."

Blake leans forward. "What about protecting Bailey's identity? And ours?"

"Anonymous sources, encrypted communications, the works. I can make sure nothing traces back to us." Falin grabs her laptop. "The beauty is, once it's out there, it's out there. They can't stuff that genie back in the bottle."

"How long would something like that take?" Bailey asks quietly.

"To set up? Maybe a day, two at most. I've got most of what we need already compiled." Falin looks directly at Bailey. "But I want to make sure you're okay with this. Your story being out there, even anonymously."

Bailey's quiet for a long moment, squeezing her hands together. Then she clenches her jaw and fixes her gaze on

Falin. "If it helps other girls like me? Like my friends who are still out there? Then yes. Let's do it."

My phone rings, pulling my attention from the planning session. I glance at the screen and swallow hard.

Alfred Colter.

They must notice the change in my expression. "Who is it?" Bailey asks.

"Fuck." I hold up the phone. "It's Alfred."

CHAPTER TWENTY-NINE

LEON

"A NSWER IT," F ALIN SAYS.

"No, don't!" Damon cuts in.

I don't know what to do, so I just hold the phone up, staring at Alfred's name like my phone's a loaded weapon. When I glance back up, I see that Bailey's tucked her legs against her chest and cast her gaze toward the floor. The sight of her retreating into herself makes my decision easy.

"I'm not answering." I decline the call and shove the phone in my pocket. "There's no reason to."

And Bailey doesn't need to hear his voice. She's starting to talk a little today, to feel a bit more comfortable. That fucker will make her upset.

"He must know the fire was you?" Blake says, but it comes out like a question. "Do you think we're safe here?"

I wish I could give her a definitive answer, but Alfred's reach is something I've never fully understood. "We should be careful. One of us needs to keep watch outside. I'll set up surveillance."

Blake shifts on the couch to peer out the window at the

quiet London street. There's nothing out of order—people in workout gear going for morning runs, couples walking their dogs, cars rushing to get to work. It all looks normal. But I don't trust Alfred or any of those bastards he works with.

"Lee," Blake turns back to me, her brows turned down. "What about your mom? He'd know where she is?"

"Shit." She's absolutely right. "I'll go check on her. Get her somewhere safe until Alfred's dealt with." I grab my jacket from the wall hook. "This is so screwed."

Bailey stands and takes a small step toward me. "Can I come with you?"

I freeze for a second, caught off guard by her question. Damon nods at me from behind her back, making a goofy encouraging face. Jasper's still looking anywhere else but at me.

I clear my throat. "Yeah, of course. Mum would love to meet you."

I hold out my jacket to her and she reaches for it without hesitation. "You should wear this. Protection for your arms."

"Do you have a second helmet?" Falin asks.

"Not here, but I'll manage. She needs it more."

Blake crosses her arms. "Please be careful. I don't love this plan."

"They'll be fine," Jasper mutters. "No one's more careful than Leon... Obnoxiously so."

Bailey slides her arms into my jacket. The leather swallows her small frame, but seeing her wrapped in something of mine brings a pang to my chest.

I step up to her, close enough to catch the scent of her freshly washed hair. "Let me help with this." My fingers find the zipper pull, and I slowly draw it up, all the way to the dip in her throat. "There. This'll keep you safe."

Our eyes meet, and I catch a flicker of emotion in them, like she's thinking of how we were. God, her blue eyes take my damn breath away. But no time to wax poetic about that, not with Mum potentially in danger.

"Thank you," she whispers.

I want to say that she never has to thank me... not for keeping her safe. I do it gladly, because it feels as natural as breathing. Instead, I nod and back away before my body does something stupid that my brain will chide me for later, like wrapping her in my arms again.

"You can wear my Docs," Blake says. "They're by the door."

"Oh, yeah... much better than the slippers I came here in," she says, offering Blake a small smile.

With both of us ready to go, I pull out my phone and dial Mum.

"Be careful, you two!" Falin calls behind us, as I open the door for Bailey. "I'll work on the cameras."

"Call us if anything's up!" Damon adds.

I lead the way to my bike, waiting as Mum's phone rings and rings. When her voicemail picks up, I hang up and call again.

"She's not answering. Maybe you should stay here. It might not be safe."

She glances back at the house, then without a word, climbs onto the seat of my bike.

"Are you sure?" I ask.

"I've spent over a year trapped between four walls. Yes, I'm positive."

THE RIDE back to Mum's house feels endless. My body clenches more and more with every turn. It's not like her to miss my calls. Even when she's at work, or out with friends, she's always answered me. Then I think about Alfred's words last night, about his missed call earlier.

Could he have already gotten to her?

I tighten my grip on the handlebars and try to focus on the comforting pressure of Bailey's arms wrapped around my waist. The warmth of her body pressed against my back. It's the only thing keeping me grounded right now.

When we pull up the narrow street, Mum's beat up Ford is still in its usual spot, parked against the curb. Nothing looks amiss—the gate is latched, the front door closed. But still my stomach won't stop churning.

I cut the engine and help Bailey off first before digging in my backpack for my gun. This feeling that something's off won't go the hell away, and I'd rather be prepared. So I tuck it into my jeans, and pull my shirt over it.

"Leon?" Bailey's voice is soft as she holds my shoulder.

"Just being cautious," I murmur, retrieving the spare key from under the loose brick by the gate. My hand finds hers instinctively. "Stay right behind me, love."

She doesn't respond, but her fingers tighten around my bicep as I unlock the front door. The creaky hinges sound so much louder than normal.

"Mum?" I call out as we step inside.

Nothing but silence answers.

"Mum? I'm home!"

Still nothing. It feels wrong in here. Like the air was disturbed somehow. It's too quiet. Too still.

Bailey's grip on my arm tenses as we move through the narrow hallway. I gesture for her to stay close as we check the sitting room first. Everything looks normal. Spotlessly clean as usual. Mum's knitting is sitting in a basket near the couch, her reading glasses on the side table next to yesterday's newspaper.

"Kitchen," I whisper, leading Bailey toward the back of the house.

The kitchen is also spotless, which again is normal for her, but even her favorite mug sits clean and bone dry in the dish rack. There's no sign of morning tea, not even a crumb from her toast. That uneasy feeling becomes a large pit in my gut.

"Stay here," I tell Bailey softly, leading her to wait by the back door. "If anything happens, you run. Don't look back."

I take the stairs two at a time, my hand resting on the gun's grip. "Mum?" I call again, louder this time.

Her bedroom door is open slightly. I stand in front of it for a second, taking a deep breath, before pushing it open fully. I exhale, part of me was expecting to find the worst, but the room is empty. Her bed is made as always, not a pillow out of place.

I step out and notice my old bedroom door is wide open.

My pulse pounds in my ears as I step inside.

No. No. No.

The space has been completely ransacked. My desk, the command center I'd carefully set up with my laptops and equipment is bare. Every cable, every drive, every piece of specialized hardware I'd brought from New York is gone. Even the legal pad where I'd jotted down notes has vanished.

The bastard took everything. Not just my mother, but my weapons too.

"Leon?" Bailey's voice drifts up from downstairs.

"Coming," I call back. My voice sounds as empty as my room.

Bailey rushes up the stairs in answer, finding me staring at my empty desk. "You okay?"

I can't turn around. Can't face her. I've completely fucked up again. Why didn't I realize Mum was vulnerable? I should have moved her sooner. Should have set up cameras here day one. Or security systems. Fucking anything while I was off messing with things much bigger than one person should handle.

My hands curl into fists at my sides while I force myself to focus. Spiraling out again won't help a damn thing.

"He took everything," I manage to whisper through a ragged breath.

Bailey steps into the room, glancing around, before stopping in front of me. I can see how she's studying me. Taking in the way my jaw's clenched, how I'm barely holding it together. I don't want her to see me like this. But fuck… I'm a mess.

"It's not your fault," she says quietly.

"Isn't it?" The words come out harsher than I intended. "I should have protected her. Should have known he'd come here."

She's quiet for a long moment, not affected by my shitty outburst. When she speaks again, she's quieter but her shoulders are squared, like she's sure of the words she's choosing.

"I used to think I could have prevented it too…What happened to me. I replayed that night over and over. What if I hadn't gone out? What if I'd stayed inside with Layne instead of waiting alone? What if I'd paid more attention to my surroundings?"

"And what changed?" I ask, taking in the pain in her eyes.

"Something Polly said to me. She said, *monsters don't fight fair*. It's a simple statement, but when I sat with it for a while, I realized that people like King or Sir, they want us paralyzed by guilt and fear. That's how they trap us… how they keep getting what they want while pulling us further and further into their game. Your father was always going to target the people who mattered most, the only question was when. Now, are we going to sit here punishing ourselves with what-ifs? Or are we going to fight back?"

Her words hit me deep in the chest, loosening the tight grip of self loathing that's been squeezing and pulling at me for so long.

I grab my phone and type out a message in the group chat.

> Me: He took my mum and all my equipment. We're not safe here. Be on high alert.

My phone buzzes immediately with replies.

> Damon: WTF. How??

> Falin: I'm checking traffic cams in your area now… I'll get plate numbers… Anything I can.

> Jasper: Are you both okay?

> Blake: Come back here. We'll figure this out together.

I type a quick response, mainly for Falin.

> Me: See if you can access neighbor cameras. Need to know if she went willingly.

"We should go," I tell Bailey, pocketing the phone. "They could come back. I'll bring you back to the house."

But Bailey shakes her head, stepping closer to me. "I know you're going after him. I'm not leaving you."

I take her hands in mine. "Bailey, it's not safe—"

"Neither was his estate, but you came for me anyway." Her blue eyes meet mine with determination. "I'm staying with you. We're going to find her."

My phone buzzes with another text.

> Falin: Found it. Your mum left with Alfred around 6 AM. No struggle. She got in his car willingly.

Relief and dread go to war in my gut. She's alive, but she

went with him. Which means either he lied to her, threatened her, or fuck... I don't know what to think.

"What is it?" Bailey asks, reading my expression.

I show her the text. "She went with him willingly. That means he either has something over her, or he convinced her it was necessary somehow." I drag a hand through my hair. "Mum... she's always carried a soft spot for him. I could never understand it, but knowing him, he must have used that against her."

She nods. "I can understand how that would happen. He's a master manipulator."

"Exactly," I say.

"But would he hurt her?" She voices the question that's clawing at the front of my mind.

I wish I could give her the answer we both want to hear. "I wish I could say no, but I can't. Not with certainty."

"Then let's go find her."

I smile despite the situation, at the strength in her voice, the certainty, despite everything she's endured. That's the Bailey I fell in love with shining through. I love all parts of her but seeing that glimpse of fierce determination gives me hope.

"Together," I agree.

CHAPTER THIRTY

BAILEY

Leon's phone buzzes against my thighs as we idle at a red light. He answers through the Bluetooth helmet. The one that actually fits him, not the spare he was trying to wear. I wouldn't have any of that. He answers, and the voice comes through loud enough for me to hear.

"Sorry, mate. I checked around and no one's seen your old man anywhere. Wish I had better news for you."

Leon utters a quick thanks and ends the call by the time the light turns green.

That's the third dead end in an hour. First his half brother, then some contact named Abel, and now whoever that was. I can feel the tension radiating through Leon's shoulders as he speeds through the intersection.

His phone buzzes again almost immediately. This time it announces Falin's name through the caller ID.

"Tell me you have something," Leon says without a greeting.

"I do, actually." Falin's voice crackles loudly through the helmet speaker. "I was able to track them through a bunch of traffic cameras heading southeast from your mum's place. I'll text over the address where I lost them. Maybe the area will look familiar."

"Good work," Leon says, sounding relieved for the first time today. "Send it through."

His phone vibrates again almost immediately, and he pulls over at the next safe spot. With his bike balanced, he checks the message.

"Ring any bells?" I ask.

He shakes his head. "Not the address, but maybe once we get there something will stand out."

"Worth a shot," I say. We're running out of options.

I hold on tight as he pulls back into traffic, navigating through the busy London streets with ease.

As we ride, I try to enjoy the scenery of this new city, but anxiety is a bitch. I keep thinking about what we might find. There's no way to prepare myself mentally for the possibilities, so counting each road sign while enjoying the breeze on my exposed skin, helps to keep it at bay. Leon needs me to be focused right now, and I'll be strong for him. And oddly, being focused on finding his mom is keeping me from thinking about my own situation. It's exactly what I need right now.

Twenty or so minutes later, we reach the address Falin gave us. It's a quiet residential area. The streets are lined with gorgeous newly renovated Georgian-style townhouses, their perfectly painted white facades gleam in the afternoon sun.

Leon slows, winding through street after street, all looking almost exactly the same. Until I see the park. It's small—just a few benches situated under lush green trees. But directly across from it is a row of townhouses with identical black doors. The golden knockers set off an alarm bell in my mind.

"Leon, stop," I say, loud enough for him to hear me.

He immediately pulls over, flipping up the visor on his helmet to study my expression. "What is it?"

I stare at the familiar iron railings around the park's perimeter, then the small stone fountain in the middle. The memory comes back, clear as day. I'd watched the people in the park going about their afternoon through the car window, hoping someone would see me and offer help. "I know this place. He brought me here once. With Polly. There were other men with him... and King."

He cuts the engine and removes his helmet. "Do you remember anything else about the exterior?"

I try to remember. There was the park out my window... but how far away was the entrance? Where did we park the car?

"I wish I did, but they all look the same," I tell him.

"That's alright. Let's take a look around, see if any of the cars parked match his license plate." He helps me off the bike, then holds my shoulder. "Are you sure you're up for this? You can stay right here. Or I can bring you to a cafe nearby? Whatever you'd like."

"I'm fine, really." I remove my own helmet, my hands steadier than I expected. "If anything changes, I'll tell you."

His eyes search my face, but I keep my expression steady and determined.

"Okay. I trust you."

We walk along the sidewalk, well aware of the stakes if I'm wrong about this. But I know in my gut that I was here before. There's this feeling running through my blood, like déjà vu but not the good kind.

We take one pass from the park to the end of the street and Leon doesn't find the matching car that Alfred was driving this morning. So we walk slower and I take my time scanning each identical black door. He's quiet beside me, giving me space to take in all the details.

And there, three houses down from the park, I notice a scratch in the paint near the brass mail slot. I remember staring at it while I waited for Sir to unlock the door.

"This one," I say, feeling both proud and terrified.

Leon squeezes my hand gently. "That's great, love. We should call the others, wait for them to come—"

"No. By the time they get here, it might be too late. Besides, if Alfred sees a group of people coming, he might..." I don't want to finish that thought. With Sir, I wouldn't be surprised if he threatened Leon's mom with violence.

Leon checks his phone and types out a quick message. "I'm telling them where we are, at least. I know Falin's probably tracking us but if something goes wrong—"

"Nothing's going to go wrong," I interrupt, surprised by the conviction in my own voice. "We're going to find her, and we're going to get her out."

"Together?" he asks, his lips tipping in a proud smile.

"Together."

"You know the drill," he says as he fumbles with the lock. "Stay behind me, and if anything happens you run."

"You can pick locks?" I ask, ignoring his repetitive warning.

"Yeah, although not as well as Falin, but she showed me a trick or two." He wiggles something into the lock, like a pin or metal clip, and after a few minutes of him cursing under his breath, it clicks open.

"Maybe we should have rang the bell?" I ask, partly joking.

He huffs a laugh, shaking his head until we cross the threshold, then he's all business. My body recoils as soon as I recognize the interior. The gleaming white walls covered in expensive artwork, the concrete floors. The smell of leather and cigar smoke still lingering. I cover my mouth and quietly retch.

The air feels too thick and the walls too close. My chest starts to tighten, that familiar suffocating feeling creeping in. But I focus on Leon's back, on the steady way he walks through the room, and it helps calm me.

Breathe. In through your nose, out through your mouth.

"Hello?" Leon calls. "Mum? Are you here?"

There's no response. I point, directing him toward the small bedroom that Sir locked me in that day.

The door's wide open, the room empty. It looks exactly the same as I remember, even down to the fold on the comforter. I glance toward the en suite bathroom and remember Polly brushing my hair. How scared she was, but how strong.

I grab onto Leon's hand for comfort and he doesn't hesitate to wrap his fingers around mine. "You with me?"

I nod, gripping his hand tighter. The warmth of his palm grounds me, pulls me back to the present. "I'm okay. Just... memories."

"We can leave," he says immediately. "Right now."

"No." I force strength into my voice. "We need to be sure."

We search the rest of the small space quickly. It's completely empty. Not one sign of a recent visitor.

"We must have missed him," Leon says. He drops his other hand from where it was lingering on his gun. "Fuck."

"He's playing with us," I say. "I can just picture his face."

Leon sighs deeply and brings my hand up to his lips, planting a quick kiss. "Let's get out of this place."

Thank God.

The longer I spend in here, the more I replay every feeling from that day. The fear but more than that, the humiliation and shame.

On our way back to the bike I ask, "Do you think he stopped here to pick something up?"

"Yeah, most likely. Although, I have no idea what." We

reach the bike and he holds out my helmet. "I know it's difficult, but when you were there with him, did he say what the visit was for? Or anything that would show what he used that townhouse for?"

I hesitate, holding the helmet against my chest. "I was locked in that bedroom for most of the time."

His face falls. "Fuck, I'm sorry for asking."

"No, it's okay. Let me think." As much as I hate replaying the memories, I need something. All I remember is Sir saying he wanted to show me off. That I should consider it homework. But from what it seemed, the home didn't just belong to him. Something about the comfortability of the other men. They didn't seem like guests, more like they owned the place too. "I'd bet he had something incriminating there. Maybe paperwork, or files. It seemed to me like it was a neutral place where they talked business."

The final word comes out bitter. *Business.* God, I hate them.

"In this nice neighborhood?" Leon says. "So fucked up."

"You don't know the worst of it."

I can tell he's trying to work out exactly what to say to me to make me feel better, although words aren't what I need. Not yet at least. I need to be doing something. To feel like I'm helping, even if it's in the smallest way.

His phone buzzes with a text and he looks away to read it.

"It's Falin. She said it took her a while but she tracked the plate number again. Heading northwest." A cloud moves to cover the sun and his eyes seem to darken. "Toward the estate."

I had a feeling it would come to this. The words that spill out of me probably sound desperate or hurt, but I guess that's because I'm both of those things. All this time, I've been trying to understand the motives of these terrible men. It's like some part of my brain won't accept that they're just doing this because they can. "What does he want?"

Leon takes the helmet and sets it on the bike seat to free my hands. Then he holds them, so gently, as he looks me in the eyes. The gesture is like a living, breathing anti-anxiety medicine.

"I can't begin to understand the mind of monsters," he says quietly, not breaking eye contact. "But I know this is about punishing me. For taking you away from him. For destroying his home. For making him look weak. For screwing up his plans." His jaw clenches. "He's using my mum to get to me, and he's using that place to get to you."

"What will happen when we get there? What will he do?"

"Nothing good," Leon answers. "I should bring you home. You shouldn't go back there."

I close my eyes for a second and remember Polly bleeding out in those woods. He's right, I shouldn't go back there. In fact, my skin crawls thinking about crossing those iron gates again. But when I open them again, I know I'd never leave Leon's side.

"I know," I say, reaching for my helmet. "But I'm going to anyway."

Leon stares at me for a long moment, war brewing behind his eyes. "You're sure?"

I climb onto the bike, waiting for him to join me. "I'm done letting people fuck with me and my family. She's your family, which makes her mine."

He nods, climbs on, and starts the engine. Before pulling away he types on his phone.

"What are you doing?"

"Telling the others where we're headed and to meet us there." He puts the phone away and revs the engine. "I won't be stupid this time. But I also won't wait for them."

As we merge into traffic, heading toward the countryside, I wrap my arms tighter around Leon's waist. The sun is already low in the sky, peeking behind buildings. We should reach the estate by nightfall.

And when I cross those iron gates illuminated by the moonlight for the second time, I'll be going by choice, ready to face that psycho asshole and anyone standing with him.

I may still be broken, but I'm not afraid anymore.

CHAPTER THIRTY-ONE

LEON

THE IRON GATES COME INTO VIEW AND THEY'RE WIDE open. Bailey's grip around my waist tightens as she must see what I see.

I slow the bike to a crawling pace, almost like there's a repelling circle around the perimeter. Everything in me screams to go back.

"This feels like a trap," I say loud enough for Bailey to hear me. I don't know Alfred well but I know he's obsessive about security.

"Of course it's a trap. He wants us here."

I love how Bailey cuts through the bullshit to the heart of the problem. I usually do the same, but when it comes to the people I love, it's harder to stay focused.

"I'm going to check everyone's locations," I say, pulling out my phone. There's three missed calls from Damon, two from Falin, and a string of increasingly creative text threats from Jasper about what he'll do to me if I get Bailey killed. *Fair enough.* "They're still thirty minutes away."

I type out a quick message: *At the estate. Gates open. Going in.*

"So what's the plan?" Bailey asks.

I glance back at my phone as it rings with a call from Damon. Oh, he's going to kill me. "I say we drive straight in. There's no point in sneaking around when he's clearly expecting us."

"Bold choice, but I get it. He's practically rolled out a red carpet for our arrival."

"If Alfred wanted us dead, we'd already be dead. He wants something else." I rev the engine. "Besides, I'm so fucking done with skulking around in the shadows."

Alright, you old psycho bastard, let's see what your game is.

I ride through the open gates and up the long, tree-lined drive. It's such a shame that this place is owned by that man. Objectively, it's a beautiful estate. Except now it's tainted by his legacy.

The main house comes into view as I round a bend. Lights glow from the open windows, another sign that this is exactly what he wants.

I pull the bike right up to the front entrance, the gravel crunching under the tires as I park next to a stone sculpture that probably cost more than my college education.

"Well, this is subtle," Bailey says as she climbs off the bike.

I pull off my helmet. "He wants us here, so here we are."

"There's no missing out on that fact," she says.

I shake my head, marveling at her ability to still find some twisted humor in this crazy situation.

"How are you doing?" I ask quietly.

She takes a deep breath and scans the front of the house. "Trying not to think about the last time I walked through those doors."

I reach for her hand, squeezing gently. "This time, you have the power."

Her answer is a nod and hand squeeze. "It's weird that we haven't seen anyone else. No security. No Ms. Harrington. It's eerie."

My phone buzzes again, but I ignore it. I have worse things to deal with than a pissed off Damon.

I check my gun one more time, making sure there's a round in the chamber. "Stay behind me, and if anything goes—"

"Sideways, I run," Bailey finishes with a hint of sass. "I know."

We step forward both realizing at the same time that the massive front door is halfway ajar. Every muscle in my body tenses as we cross inside. I can't even imagine what Bailey must be feeling.

Our footsteps echo along the marble floor of the foyer. This place is no different than when I was a child—cold, stuffy, for show. No wonder I blocked it out.

"There you are."

The voice drifts from the shadows near the grand staircase, completely calm. Alfred steps into the light, looking as polished and professional as always in pressed slacks and a navy blue cashmere sweater. But the circles under his eyes give him away. His silvering hair might be perfectly styled, but he's thinner than when I last saw him up close, more haggard.

"You made good time," he says, checking his Rolex. "Though I expected you earlier."

Behind me, Bailey's breathing has become shallow and audible, but she stays strong.

"Where is she?" I keep my voice level and my hand hovering on my gun.

"Your mother is quite safe, I assure you." Alfred's eyes shift to Bailey, and his expression softens in a way that makes me want to kill him here and now. "Hello, darling. You're looking different. Not sure I care for the haircut. Longer suits you... How it was before you left me."

"I didn't leave," Bailey says quietly. "I escaped."

"Semantics." He waves a hand. "You've learned to speak up for yourself. I'm pleased. All that refinement wasn't wasted."

The more he speaks, the stronger my pull to end him here and now. But I need information. Violence can wait.

"What do you want, Alfred?"

"Want?" He seems genuinely puzzled by my question. "I want what I've always wanted, Leon. Family. Legacy. The satisfaction of seeing my work come to fruition." His gaze moves between Bailey and me like he's admiring an art collection. "You two represent everything I've been building toward. It didn't work out with James—he was always too coddled, too stupid to get anywhere. But not you, my greatest achievement."

"Your greatest achievement is human trafficking and murder," I say. "You're a monster."

"Now that's harsh." He fusses with a speck of dust on the banister, then studies me. "I prefer to think of myself as a curator. I find broken things and make them beautiful. It's charity, really. Take your mother, for instance."

My hand inches closer to my gun. "What about my mother?"

"Sweet Ada. She was so damaged when I found her. Barely eighteen, running from an abusive boyfriend, scared to go back home, of what her parents would think. I gave her purpose. Stability. *Love.*" The way he says the word makes me nauseous. "Even after she left with you, I never stopped caring for her."

Bailey touches my back in a show of solidarity that I desperately need. It keeps me focused, keeps me calm.

"What are you saying?" I seethe. "I thought my mother

worked for you as a housekeeper? Why would she be afraid to go back home? My grandparents loved her!"

He shoots me a condescending smile, like I'm nothing but a naive child. "Your mother was never just a housekeeper. She was my first real success story. I'd say she even started me on the path to helping so many more broken women."

There's no way. My mother would have told me—someone would have.

"She was special from the moment I found her," Alfred continues, his voice taking on that dreamy quality again. "So broken, so lost. But I saw her potential. I took her in, cleaned her up, taught her how to speak properly, how to carry herself with dignity. How to be grateful for what she'd been given."

"You're lying," I say, although a small alarm in my mind is blaring that it has to be true.

"Am I? Why don't you ask her yourself? Though I suspect our stories might differ in details. See, she remembers our relationship quite differently than it really was. Head in the clouds, that one. She always believed I loved her, even when I married Jeneva. In her mind, she had to leave because I was being forced into an arranged marriage. That I wanted her to have you, to be with her parents again."

The pieces are falling into place in the worst possible way. I can barely breathe from the tightness in my chest.

"She was eighteen. A teenager."

"Legal age," Alfred says dismissively. "And far better off with me than on the streets, or with her penniless parents. I gave her everything—shelter, food, education, refinement. She was grateful for it all. The beautiful thing about Ada is that she never stopped trusting me. Even after all these years." He picks at an invisible piece of lint on his shirt. "She calls me for advice about you, you know? Shares your achievements, worries about your well-being. She has no idea she's been my most valuable asset."

"What do you mean, asset?"

"How do you think I knew exactly when you'd arrive in London? Where you were staying? Who you were working with?" His smile widens. "Your devoted mother has been keeping me informed every step of the way. All she wants is her baby boy to grow up like his powerful, wealthy father. It hasn't taken much convincing to get anything I want out of her."

"But why now?" I ask. "Clearly, you enjoy ruining the lives of innocent people. Why bother to put in all this work in my honor?"

Bailey's touch on my back becomes firmer. Silently telling me she's there, that I'm not alone.

His expression shifts, and his eyes almost darken. I can tell he wasn't expecting my question, and I'm glad I struck a nerve.

"Time is a finite resource, Leon. And mine is running shorter than I'd prefer."

I let his words linger in the air, while I read his body language. This is why he's paler than normal. Thinner. Like he's aged years in the span of months.

"You're sick."

"Dying," he says. "Six months left. Maybe eight, if I'm fortunate. Pancreatic cancer. Quite ironic, considering it's one of the most vicious ways to go." He clears his throat and adjusts his voice so he's all business again. "Which is why I've been working to ensure my legacy continues. The charity, my work with The Brotherhood... I need someone overseeing that brute, Orlov. I've known for years that he's a live wire."

"And you think I'm that person?" I point to my chest. "If I didn't want in years ago, then why the hell would I want in now? You've kidnapped and tortured the people I love. I want no part in your sick empire."

Alfred gestures vaguely around the estate. "All of this could be yours—the properties, the offshore accounts, the network of contacts across three continents. Senators, judges, police commissioners, customs officials... they'd all answer to you. You're making a mistake if you throw this offer away. I've watched you, I know you have the stomach for this. You're more like me than you think, son."

"I'm nothing like you," I spit.

"Well let's have a test then? What if I told you, you could only save one of them... Bailey, or your lovely mum. Difficult choice, I know. What would you do?"

I pull out my gun and aim it at his head. "How about I kill you and walk out of here with both of them?"

He throws his head back and laughs. "I was right about you having the stomach for violence."

"This isn't a game. I'll fucking kill you right here. Where is she?"

"Oh, I know you'd kill me, which is why I made it so you need me to get to her. Reconsider my offer, and I'll make sure she remains unharmed."

It's times like these that I wish I had Jasper's smooth talking skills, or Damon's ability to get out of situations. I can see that Alfred's losing his patience, and now, knowing he has such little time left on this earth, legacy or not, I have no idea what he'll do.

So I do the only thing I can. Lie through my teeth.

"You're right," I say, forcing my voice to stay level. "I do have the stomach for violence. And I'm starting to see what you mean about making hard choices."

Alfred's expression shifts, interest flickering in his eyes. "Go on."

I glance at Bailey, hoping she'll understand what I'm doing. I can't hurt her. "All these months searching for her, I've done things I never thought I'd do. Hurt people. Destroyed lives. Broken laws." I pause, letting that sink in. "Maybe I am more like you than I wanted to admit."

Bailey's eyes go wide but she stays quiet, observing every detail.

"I knew it," Alfred says. "I could see it in you as a child. That spark of something special."

"But I need to know she's safe first," I continue, lowering my weapon. "Before I agree to anything. I need to see my mother, make sure she's unharmed."

Alfred studies my face, searching for some sign of deception. I force myself to meet his gaze steadily, channeling every ounce of acting ability I've ever possessed. Bailey's grip on my back lowers, until she's holding the loop of my jeans.

"Very well," he says finally. "I suppose a good faith gesture is in order. Follow me."

Once we're behind Alfred, Bailey takes my hand and squeezes once, a silent indication telling me she's here, she understands what I'm doing.

But as we follow Alfred deeper into the estate, toward whatever fresh slice of hell he's prepared, I can't stop thinking that we're prey walking right into his web.

And this time, there might not be a way out.

CHAPTER THIRTY-TWO

BAILEY

Every step deeper into the house has my body screaming to run. These corridors are new to me, but still, familiar smells linger in the air. Sir's expensive cologne mixed with a sterile, clean scent that stings my nostrils. I've never quite understood the power of smell to recall memory until recently. It's visceral and automatic, bringing those thoughts to the front of my mind even when I try my hardest to push them down.

I need to keep moving, one step in front of the other. I need to be strong—for Leon. For his mom.

We follow him down a long hall full of oil paintings of probably dead men. All of whom I'd hope didn't share Alfred's same fucked up values. I want to ask about Ms. Harrington. It was rare that I'd go five minutes in the main house without seeing her severe frame haunting the room. Her absence feels wrong. Either Alfred sent her away before we arrived, or something worse happened to the woman who brushed my hair and tried to teach me table manners while her boss systematically destroyed my soul. Can't say I'd mourn her, even if she was most likely manipulated by Alfred too.

"You know, Leon," Alfred chats as we walk, "I always wondered what it would take to awaken your true nature. Turns out, it just required the right motivation."

I hate his voice. It makes me sick. That calm, pretentious tone he used when he was *teaching* me how to be grateful. How to be compliant. How to be perfect for his warped vision of what Leon needed.

Leon's hand squeezes mine, and I know he's thinking the same thing I am. This is all wrong, Alfred is literally insane. But we have to play along. We have to get to his mom.

Finally in a dark corner at the very back of the estate we reach a door I've definitely never seen before. It looks like it's made from heavy steel and has a large electronic lock on the outside.

He pulls out a key card from his pocket and faces Leon with a smile I wish I could claw off his face. "Before we proceed," he says, "I want to be clear about what you're agreeing to. This isn't just about taking over operations. It's about understanding that sometimes we have to make choices that others would consider distasteful."

I watch Leon's face carefully. He's gotten better at hiding his emotions, but I can see the rage simmering beneath the surface. The muscle in his jaw ticks once, and it's barely perceptible, but I know him well enough to catch it.

"I understand," Leon lies smoothly.

"No, Leon! Don't do this!" I add, trying to make his act more believable. "There's other ways."

Alfred's eyes dart to me, and he smiles like he's just won a prize. I guess in his mind, he has. "It's touching that you're still holding on to that strong moral compass, Bailey. Keep that. It'll be of good use to Leon someday." He sounds so condescending, it takes everything in me to keep playing into the act. "But Leon is finally learning what it means to be a man. Sometimes we have to make sacrifices for the greater good."

I let my voice crack. "He's not like you. He'll never be like you."

"Doubtful," he says. "He's already crossed a bridge he can't uncross. Killed, tortured, committed arson. Tell her, Leon. Tell her how you've changed."

Leon's grip on my hand tightens. A silent warning that what he's about to say will sting.

"He's right." His voice is laced with ice. "I'm not the same person I was eighteen months ago."

When he meets my gaze, I blink up at him. *Neither am I.*

"Excellent," Alfred says, scanning his card. The lock disengages with a soft beep. "There will be plenty of time to talk once I retrieve the paperwork. But first, a promise is a promise..."

The heavy door swings open, revealing a narrow staircase that descends into darkness. My stomach lurches, anxiety pulling at my chest, screaming at me to run.

"It looks ominous, I know," Alfred jokes. "Quite less inviting than the rest of the house. But don't worry, Bailey. Very few people get taken down here. Only the ones who refuse to comply. You were always my good girl. Not like that friend of yours, Polly."

An involuntary sound escapes my lips as he speaks Polly's name. Oh God. She was sent down there. *I can't go. I won't.* I know I shouldn't reply. I shouldn't give him the satisfaction of a response but I can't help it.

"What happened to her down there?"

"She served her purpose, darling. Just as everyone does, eventually. After you," he says pleasantly, gesturing for us to go first down the staircase.

"You first," Leon says, giving my knuckle a quick brush with his thumb.

Alfred raises an eyebrow, clearly amused by Leon's attempt at control. "How gentlemanly. Very well."

He starts to go down, one step at a time, into the darkness. I don't want to follow, but I also refuse to leave Leon's side. So I go next, keeping my hand securely wrapped around his.

The walls somehow feel narrower with each step, or maybe it's just me, but it's definitely cooler down here, more damp too.

My breathing becomes shallow as I picture Polly being pulled down these stairs. How scared she must have been. How alone.

Focus on Leon. Focus on getting out of here.

At the bottom of the stairs, Alfred flips a switch and harsh fluorescent lights flicker to life. It takes a few seconds for my eyes to adjust but once they do, I have to clutch Leon's shoulder to keep my knees from buckling.

A windowless hallway stretches in front of us, lined with two doorways opposite each other. They have similar looking doors as the one leading down here, metal with some kind of locking mechanism. The difference is, these doors have a small round window at eye level.

This place is a prison meant to break people. Polly... I can't believe she survived this place.

"Here's where the real work happens," Alfred says with pride. "Where defiance is corrected."

Bastard.

I don't want to walk forward. This is all too much already. Leon's hand is the only thing keeping me from losing it.

He leads us to the doors. One peek in the window of the first shows an empty cell, thank God. But the small cot, concrete walls, and prison toilet in the corner are bad enough to make me nauseated. Polly was in there. How many other people's lives has he destroyed?

"Your mother is in here," Alfred says, stopping at the door on the right and pulling out his key card again.

As the lock beeps to open the door, I catch a glimpse of Leon's mom through the window. She's sitting on the edge of the cot, staring at her hands. She looks so small and scared. I know Leon's holding back a burst of rage from the change in his posture.

"Ada, darling," he calls through the opening door. "You have visitors."

Her head snaps up at the sound of her name, her expression going from despondent to relieved as she sees Leon. But then her eyes dart to mine, and her brows furrow.

"Alfred! What did you do? Why am I in here? I want to go home! Leon? Is that you? Who's with you?" Her voice turns panicked with each word.

I can't imagine what she must be feeling. There's relief at seeing Leon, confusion about me. Anger. Fear. Probably a mix of both. I have no idea what's going through her mind, but I know the panic in her voice too well.

Leon lets go of my hand and cautiously steps into the cell. Ada practically throws herself into his arms. "I don't understand what's happening," she says against his shoulder. "Alfred said you were in trouble, that he was helping you. But this place..." She pulls back to look at him, her eyes wide with confusion. "Leon, what is this place?"

"Ask him," Leon says. He gestures to Alfred, who's leaning against the doorframe watching this unfold as if it's some kind of heartwarming family reunion and not a nightmare he orchestrated.

Ada looks at me again, studying my face. I see her mouth

open slightly, like she's about to say something, but then she closes it.

"I still don't understand," she says finally, looking between Leon, Alfred, and me. "What's going on? When I woke up, I was in there... What is this place?"

Leon rolls his lip ring between his teeth, gathering his thoughts. "Mum, it's time to go. I'll explain later."

He holds her under her arm and helps her to the door. She's clearly disoriented and probably dehydrated. Leon has this look in his eye when he glances my way. I know he's planning something. I just wish I knew what, so I can help.

"Don't forget we still have business to discuss upstairs, Leon. The women can wait in the—"

"No," Leon abruptly cuts him off. "They don't leave my side."

Alfred's expression shifts to show the darker side of him behind the mask he wears for the world. The side of him I've seen many times. "I don't think you're in a position to make demands, son."

That's when Leon moves.

It happens so fast I almost miss it. One moment he's helping Ada toward the door, the next he's stepping aside and slamming his shoulder into Alfred. Alfred stumbles backward, caught off guard, and Leon uses the momentum to drive him further into the cell.

There's a struggle. Alfred shoves Leon hard against the wall, his face contorted with rage. "You ungrateful little bastard!" he sneers, swinging his arms attempting to get a hit in.

But Leon ducks under the punch, like a practiced fighter. Alfred may be calculating and manipulative, but he'd never win in a show of physical strength, especially not in his condition. Leon sinks his fist into Alfred's stomach, forcing him to double over, then brings his knee up to connect with Alfred's jaw.

My heart pounds as I watch it all unfold. I know Leon's fine. He has the upper hand, but still, a fight is a fight.

Alfred staggers backward and blood trickles from his mouth. He spits onto the floor, something I'd never think the prim and proper Sir would stand for, before lunging at Leon again. But this time he's off-balance and desperate. Leon side-steps him easily, grabbing his shoulders and spinning him around before punching him in the temple.

Alfred stumbles, completely dazed, but somehow still holding onto consciousness as he drops to one knee. I step closer to get a better look and see his eyes roll back in his head for a moment, nothing showing but bloodshot globes of dull white. Breathing fast, Leon grabs him by the collar and shoves him hard against the wall, while Ada stifles her cries beside me. Alfred's head lolls to the side. He seems to be semi-conscious and mumbling incoherently.

"Is he knocked out?" I ask as my heart pounds out of my chest.

Leon studies him, keeping one hand pressed firmly against his chest to pin him to the wall. "Not fully. He's drifting in and out. Bailey, I need your help in here. Quickly. I have to search his pockets before he comes to, but I can't hold him and search at the same time."

Shit.

The last thing I want is to get anywhere near that twisted psycho, even unconscious. But Leon needs me.

"No," Ada says, reaching out to hold me back. "Don't go in there."

"Are you sure he's knocked out?" I ask Leon, letting my fear take over.

"Bailey, please. I need your help."

Internally screaming but holding it together, I pull Ada's hand away and nod. Once I'm inside the cell, the walls instantly start closing in around me. It's one thing to peer through the window, but another to step inside the small space. The coppery smell of blood mixed with the musty basement air makes it even harder to breathe.

"Let's get this done," I say solemnly.

Alfred's head hangs forward as I approach, his breathing shallow but steady. A thin line of drool mixed with blood drips from the corner of his mouth and I try not to gag.

"Check his jacket pockets first, then his trousers," Leon says, using both hands now to keep Alfred upright against the wall. "Look for his keycard, his phone, anything that could help him get out of here."

I reach toward his jacket pocket with shaking hands, trying not to touch him directly. That smell—it's so much stronger right next to him.

"Hurry, Bailey. I can feel him starting to come around."

My fingers find the outline of something rectangular in his inner pocket. The keycard. I slip it out carefully, then move to his other jacket pocket, which is empty.

"I need to get to his pants," I say, urging Leon to adjust his position.

"Leon!" Ada's panicked voice echoes from the hallway. She stops at the entrance to the cell. "Someone's upstairs. I heard footsteps!"

Leon's head snaps in her direction. "Fuck!" He takes a moment to decide what to do, but Ada calls his name again so he releases Alfred, letting him slump to the side. "Stay with Bailey," he tells his mother. There's so much conflict in his eyes as he glances between me and the hallway. "I'll be right back, love. One second."

I'm trembling, wanting to get as far away from Alfred as

possible. Who else is out there? Could it be Jasper and the rest? Or someone worse than Alfred?

I watch Leon pull out his gun keeping it aimed toward the ground as he steps away.

He's just outside the cell door—close enough to rush back in, but far enough that he can't reach me.

That's when Alfred's eyes suddenly snap open.

His hand shoots up fast as lightning, and he wraps his fingers around my throat before I can even scream. The keycard falls from my hands to the concrete floor as Alfred yanks me down toward him, his grip crushing my windpipe.

"You little bitch," he snarls, spitting bloody saliva onto my face.

I claw at his hand, trying with all my strength to pry his fingers loose, but his grip is impossibly strong for someone who was just half unconscious. Black spots dance at the edges of my vision as I struggle to breathe.

"Leon," I wheeze, but the word barely escapes my lips.

Suddenly Ada's there behind Alfred, scrambling against his back, pounding her small fists along his shoulders. "Let her go!" she screams. "Let her go!"

Alfred releases one hand from my throat to backhand Ada viciously across the face. She cries out and falls backward, hitting the concrete wall hard before sagging to the floor. But she gave me just enough air to keep fighting.

Leon shouts something. I can't make out the words over the roaring in my ears, and then Alfred's being jerked sideways as Leon tries to pull him off me. But Alfred won't let go. Instead, he uses his grip on my throat to push himself to his feet, holding my body in front of him as a shield.

Oh God. I need air. I'm scratching and pulling at his hands but it's doing nothing but leaving angry red marks on his skin.

"Get off her!" Leon roars, aiming his gun at Alfred's head.

Alfred backhands me across the face, and stars explode in my field of vision. *No. I won't go down like this.* I bite his wrist hard until I taste blood, and he finally releases my throat with a howl of pain.

I stumble backward, gasping, giving Leon the space to take him down. He doesn't waste another second, as the barrel of his gun connects with the side of Alfred's head. The crack of his skull is so loud that it echoes in the small space like a gunshot.

Alfred crumples to the floor finally, truly unconscious. Thank God.

"Bailey!" Leon's hands cup my shoulders as he takes in my appearance with wide, worried eyes. "Are you okay?"

I can't speak yet, so I just nod while I rub my throat. It feels like I've swallowed razor blades. Leon pulls me against his chest, whispering words of praise. His heartbeat pounds against my ears, giving me strength.

"I'm okay," I finally manage to croak, gesturing toward Ada who's in shock across the room. "Your mom."

"Shit!" Leon releases me to rush to Ada's side. She's sitting against the wall, holding her cheek where Alfred hit her. Blood trickles from her nose.

"I'm alright," she says weakly, as Leon helps her to her feet. "Is he dead?"

Leon's face is pure rage unlike I've ever seen before. "No... not yet."

"Son," Ada cries. "Why is this happening? I don't understand."

He leads her to the door. "I'm so sorry. Both of you. I should never have—"

"The keycard," I interrupt, my voice barely audible. I point to where it fell.

He makes sure Ada can stand on her own before grabbing the card from the floor. Alfred still doesn't stir.

"Let's get out of here," he says, reaching for my hand. The moment we're outside the cell Leon immediately pushes the door shut and swipes the keycard over the lock until it beeps.

"Son, are you alright?" Ada asks, wrapping Leon in her arms. They hug but only briefly. Leon's too preoccupied staring at a control panel beside the door. I wrap my arm around Ada's shoulder, and hold her close while Leon starts pressing buttons in a specific sequence, cursing under his breath.

"Can he get out?" I ask, watching him work.

"Not without help," Leon says, concentrating on whatever he's typing. "This lock is designed to stay shut even if the power goes out. It's made for holding prisoners. The door stays locked by default, not like a normal door."

He keeps working on the control panel for what feels like forever. I don't want to bother him with more questions, but I certainly do not want to wait upstairs either. So for now, Ada and I quietly watch him work, my anxiety on high alert knowing Alfred will wake up at any moment.

When Leon finally speaks, I'm not sure if he's talking to himself or us. "Alfred's keycard is like a master key that could open any of these cells. I'm trying to erase his card from the system and change his passwords, but I've never worked with something like this."

"What about emergency exits?" Ada asks quietly. "Don't these doors have some kind of safety release? What if there were a fire?"

Leon glances through the window at a small metal box mounted on the wall inside the cell. "They're supposed to have a manual override, like a fire alarm that automatically opens the door if there's smoke or something. But I think Alfred disconnected it. I doubt he cared if his prisoners got out. In fact, he probably hoped they didn't."

Ada makes a small sound and stumbles forward a bit. "I

think this is too much for her," I say, holding Ada close. "We should get her upstairs for some water. He's not going anywhere."

Leon finally looks away from his work and nods. "You're right. I've got her." He hands me his phone and moves to support Ada. "Can you call Falin? They should be here by now and I could really use her help."

I take the phone with shaky hands and head for the stairs, Leon helping Ada right behind me. As soon as we reach the main floor, I take a deep cleansing breath and dial Falin.

"Leon! Where are you?" Falin's voice comes through the speaker.

"It's Bailey. We're at the estate. We found his mom, but we need your help with something. Are you almost here?"

"We're getting to the gates now. It took forever—Oh fuck."

All at once the others start talking in the background before the line goes dead.

What the hell?

I turn to follow Leon and Ada in their search for the kitchen when they freeze, hearing what must have made Falin hang up abruptly—three rapid gunshots in the distance, followed by dead silence.

CHAPTER THIRTY-THREE

LEON

GUNSHOTS ECHO THROUGH THE ESTATE GROUNDS AND MY adrenaline ramps up. Three rapid shots, then nothing but the sound of our shaky breaths.

"What the hell was that?" I ask, afraid to know the answer. We're not the only ones here, I knew that from the footsteps earlier. But who?

Bailey's face has gone pale, and she's still clutching the phone like her life depends on it. "Falin said they were at the gates, then the line went dead right before—"

"They got ambushed," I finish, my mind racing. If those were gunshots, it means the others ran into trouble. Maybe his guards, maybe Brotherhood—whoever it is, they're not our friends. "We need to get you both somewhere safe."

Mum looks between Bailey and I, confusion and fear warring in her expression. "Leon, what's happening? Who's shooting?"

There's no time to explain.

I move to the kitchen window, trying to see anything through the darkness. The massive estate grounds stretch out like a black void, hiding whatever's going on in the dark. But somewhere out there, my family might be hurt. Or worse.

"Mum, I need you to listen to me carefully," I say, keeping my voice steady even though my heart is hammering. "There are some very bad people here tonight. People who want to hurt us all. I need to go help my friends, but first I need to make sure you're both protected."

Her brows raise. "I don't want to leave you."

"Neither do I," Bailey agrees.

Before I can argue, the lights in the kitchen flicker once, then go out completely.

"Fuck," I mutter. "Bailey, can you turn on my phone light?"

She nods, and switches on the single beam. It barely illuminates the space in front of us.

The silence that follows is deafening as they huddle closer to me. There's no hum of electricity, no distant sounds of the others fighting their way inside. Only our breathing and the thundering of my pulse in my ears.

"Should we go out there?" Bailey asks. "Or try to find out what happened to the power?"

"It's probably been cut," I tell them. "It's not safe for either of you."

"Leon," Bailey whispers, pointing toward the kitchen doorway.

A shadow moves under the crack in the door that leads back to the dining room. I know instantly it's not Jasper or Damon. The gait is completely wrong.

I raise my weapon, motioning for Bailey and Mum to get behind me. The shadow pauses, as if sensing that he's been spotted.

"Come out, son. It's over." Dread settles in my chest. Alfred. But how? He was locked in that cell, unconscious, with the door completely sealed.

"I know you're there," Alfred continues, his voice a crazed calm. "Why don't you come out? We still have so much to discuss."

I press my back against the kitchen counter, with Bailey and Mum to my sides. My mind races through options. The kitchen has one entrance, which means we're trapped if he decides to come in. But it also means he can't surprise us.

"What do you want, Alfred?" I call out.

"You know what I want. What I've always wanted." His footsteps sound closer as the shadow grows. "You may have complicated things, but we can work through it."

"Who is shooting outside?"

He pauses, then chuckles, and the sound makes my stomach churn. "Your friends encountered some of my security staff. I'm sure they put up quite a fight."

How would he know that? The bastard's playing games with me, trying to get under my skin. I hate that it's working.

"Leon," Bailey whispers so quietly I barely hear her. "There's a service door behind the pantry. It leads to the back gardens."

I glance at her, then at Mum. "Go, please."

"Not without you," she whispers back.

I can't just leave now. Not with Alfred still standing. Not while the others are in danger.

"I have a proposition for you," Alfred calls out. He must be right outside the kitchen now. "Your friends' lives for a simple conversation. Five minutes of your time, and I'll tell my staff to let them go."

"Don't trust him," Mum says urgently. "Leon, he's lying. He's always lying."

"Ah, Ada, dear, I hear you in there. Tell our son to be reasonable."

She wraps her arms around her chest, holding her head

high. "He's not your son, you lying, manipulative, violent piece of—"

"Manners, Ada! That's not how I trained you."

I rest a hand on Mum's arm and it helps to calm her. "I'll meet you outside. Please... go." In the darkness, I can't see their expressions, not clearly, but by the set of Bailey's jaw and the stiffness of her back, I know she's not backing down, even with me begging like our lives depend on it.

"Fine," Alfred's voice cuts through our whispered argument. "If you won't come out, I'll come in."

The door handle turns slowly, and every terrible possibility flashes through my mind. He's armed, I'm sure of it. And with Bailey and Mum right here...

"Stay back," I whisper to them, then make a split-second decision. I rush toward the door, throwing it open before Alfred can enter. This is between him and me. Better to face him in the dining room than let him corner us all in the kitchen where Bailey and Mum could get caught in crossfire.

"Leon!" Bailey calls out behind me, but it's too late, I'm already out the door.

Alfred's right there, and in the dim spill of phone light from the kitchen, I can see the gleam of metal in his hand. He looks absolutely crazed with his disheveled hair and bloodied shirt, but his eyes are still as sharp and calculating as ever.

"There's my boy," he says with that cold smile. "Finally ready to face me like a man."

I keep my gun raised, aiming it at his chest. "Let's keep this between us. They don't need to be involved."

"Oh, but they're already involved, aren't they? This whole mess started because you think she's worth more than your legacy." His gaze shifts toward the kitchen doorway behind me. "Bailey, darling, are you listening? Come join us."

"Stay where you are," I call back to her, not letting my eyes stray from Alfred.

"Such a hero. I suppose I should be proud. Though I wish you had more self-preservation."

"I'm here. You want to talk, so talk," I say. I need to keep him occupied so they can get out. My life doesn't matter... I only care about them.

"Straight to business then. Very well." Alfred adjusts his stance, gun still trained on me. "Do you have any idea what you've cost me? What this little rescue mission has destroyed? The ties I've worked years to build severed because of your petulant ways?"

"I'm glad. I want to hit you where it hurts."

"You reap what you sow, boy. Your friends will be the fodder in our little battle of wits."

He's trying to get to me. "You're lying."

"Am I? Where are they, Leon? You heard the gunshots. You know they came through those gates. So where are your loyal friends now?"

I force myself not to let doubt creep in, but it's too quiet. It's not like them. If they were out there, fighting, I'd hear what was going on. They'd call for backup, or retaliate. Please let them be alive.

"Well then," I say, forcing my voice to steady, "that only makes me more angry. You're going to pay double for what you've done."

"To whom? Bailey?" Alfred takes a step closer, and I tighten my grip on my weapon. "She'll get over it. Girls like her always do. She'll find some new protector, some new life to ruin. It's sad, all that work I put in, amounting to nothing."

"Don't talk about her like that."

"Like the whore she is?" Alfred's voice turns vicious. "That's all she's ever been, Leon. A commodity. Something to be bought and sold and used up. Nothing more than a pretty accessory."

Rage flares in my chest, hot and consuming. "Shut up."

"The truth hurts, doesn't it? All this death and destruction for a girl who was broken long before you ever met her."

He has no idea about our past. About how much I love her. I'll keep it that way. My finger tightens on the trigger. One squeeze, and this nightmare ends. One bullet, and Bailey never has to hear his voice again.

"Do it. Pull the trigger. Become the killer I always knew you could be."

My hand shakes.

Is this who I am? Killing a man. My father. Point blank.

"You hesitate. That's always been your weakness, Leon. Too much conscience. Too much... sentiment. Not enough action."

Please let them escape.

I lower my weapon, fucking hating myself. I know I should kill him. I want to. But my fingers refuse to pull the trigger.

Alfred releases a breath that turns into a laugh. My eyes are cast downward, but I hear his footsteps coming closer before he presses his gun against my temple. "Don't try anything. I don't want to shoot, but I won't hesitate if it comes to that."

The cold metal pressed against my temple feels final. Like this is it. This is where the Colter bloodline ends, in violence and darkness, just like everything Alfred touches.

"Bailey," I call out without moving my head, hoping she's left already, but in case she hasn't... "Take Mum and go. I'm begging you."

"Leon, no—"

"GO!" I roar, putting everything I have into that single word. "Please. Just go."

I close my eyes, thinking of her laugh, her smile, her touch.

At least she'll live. At least she'll be free. That's all I ever wanted.

"This is so touching," Alfred says, yanking my weapon from my hand. "Too bad they won't make it two steps outside this building. They'll end up joining your friends."

"You have me. Let them go," I plead, hoping he'll keep his word and they'll all stay safe.

"Move," he says, pressing the gun harder against my skull. "We're going downstairs. I need you secure so I can deal with this mess."

I could try to overpower him. Knock the gun out of his hand, wrestle him to the ground. But this is easier. I already know I won't take the killing shot. And maybe he's telling the truth—if I cooperate, he won't kill them.

With his weapon against my head, I walk where he directs me, through the dining room and down the familiar corridors. Every step feels like a slow march toward my execution.

Bailey and Mum had time to get out. They're safe. Focus on that.

The basement door looms ahead of us, standing open from earlier. The harsh fluorescent lights are still on in the center of the space, unaffected by the power cut. The air is still thick.

"Down," Alfred orders.

I descend the narrow staircase with my hands raised. Each step has my mind racing through possibilities. Maybe I can keep him talking, distract him long enough to make a move. Maybe the others are still alive and will find me. Fuck. I can't get locked in down here.

We reach the bottom and Alfred gestures toward the cells. "You locked me in there like an animal," he says. "Now you get to see what happens to animals that bite the hand that feeds them."

But when we approach the cell where I left him unconscious, Alfred stops dead. Through the small window, I can see Ms. Harrington sitting on the cot, staring at the wall with a blank expression. Her usual tight bun has pieces sticking out in all directions, and there are tear tracks down her cheeks.

"What the bloody hell?" Alfred mutters, leaning closer to the window. "Greta? How did you—"

That's when I hear footsteps behind us, barely audible but definitely there.

Alfred's too focused on the cell to notice, and I don't dare turn around or give any sign that I've heard anything. Instead, I keep my eyes fixed on Ms. Harrington, who finally looks up and meets our gazes through the glass.

"Sir?" she calls out. "Sir, is that you? They locked me in here. I don't understand what's happening."

"Who locked you in?" Alfred demands, confusion replacing some of the rage in his voice. "Where are my men? Where is your key?"

The footsteps are closer now. Two sets, moving along the shadows.

"I don't know, Sir. These men, they locked me in. Said you were dead."

Alfred's grip on the gun loosens as he clearly tries to process this information. I should take the opportunity given. Should disarm him.

"That's impossible. My security team would never—"

As I'm about to make my move a familiar voice sounds behind me. "Drop the weapon."

Damon steps into the light, gun trained on Alfred's head, with Jasper right behind him, both of them bloodied but very much alive.

"Now," Damon adds, his voice deadly calm.

Alfred's gun wavers between my head and the new threat. "You're supposed to be dead."

"Disappointed?" Jasper asks, moving to get a better angle. "Your security team wasn't as good as advertised."

I can see Alfred calculating, weighing his options. He's outnumbered, but he still has me as a shield.

"Let him go, Alfred," Damon says. "It's over."

"Is it?" Alfred's voice returns to that cold, controlled tone. "Because from where I'm standing, I still hold all the cards. One wrong move and your friend here gets a bullet in the brain."

"And then you get two bullets," Jasper points out. "Simple math."

Alfred laughs, but there's hysteria creeping into the sound. "You think I care about dying? You've already destroyed everything I worked for. Everything I built. I'm a dead man anyway."

"Good," I say, finding my voice again. "That was the point."

The gun presses harder against my temple. "Ungrateful. Ungrateful to the end."

"Alfred." Damon's voice cuts through the tension. "Look around. You're in a basement. You're outnumbered. Your empire is gone. It's over. The question is: do you want to die here, or do you want to spend the rest of your life behind bars thinking about what you've lost?"

I can feel Alfred's hand shaking slightly where it grips the gun. He's breaking down, coming apart at the seams.

"Your choice," Jasper adds. "But you've got five seconds to decide."

The silence stretches between us, heavy and thick. Then Alfred speaks, his voice barely above a whisper.

"You were supposed to be mine. My legacy. My heir."

"I was never yours," I tell him. "I never will be."

Then faster than I can register, he swings his weapon toward Damon and fires.

I move fast, elbowing him in the ribs. He stumbles backward, and I catch his wrist, slamming it against the concrete wall until he drops the weapon. "D? You okay?" I yell.

"He missed," Damon replies, breathing heavy.

"Fucking barely," Jasper adds.

Alfred staggers, dazed, as I kick the gun away from him. Damon and Jasper move in, weapons still trained on him, but he's not fighting anymore. He's just standing there, swaying, looking lost.

"Well?" Damon asks, glancing at me. "What do you want to do with him?"

I look at Alfred—really look at him. This man who terrorized me, who hurt Bailey, who destroyed countless lives. The rage I've been holding back finally breaks free.

"You know what?" I say, my voice low and dangerous. "Before we lock him up, I think he needs to understand what he put people through."

Damon's eyes light up with dark understanding. "I like where this is going."

Alfred tries to back away but there's nowhere to go. "Leon, please. I'm your father—"

"No." I cut him off. "A father protects his child. You're nothing but a predator who shares my DNA."

I grab him by the collar and slam him against the concrete wall. His head cracks against the stone and blood trickles from his scalp.

"This is for Bailey," I snarl, driving my fist into his stomach. He doubles over, gasping.

"And this is for every girl you destroyed." Jasper steps in, landing a vicious punch to Alfred's jaw that snaps his head to the side.

"And this," Damon adds, grabbing Alfred's wrist and twisting it until something pops, "is for thinking you could ever break us."

Alfred crumples to his knees, whimpering. Gone is the composed manipulator. In his place is a broken, bleeding man who finally understands what powerlessness feels like.

"Please," he gasps. "I'm sorry. I can change—"

"Now you're sorry?" I laugh, but there's no humor in it. "Where was that remorse when you were training girls to be compliant? When you were selling human beings like cattle?"

I grab his hair and force him to look up at me. "You don't get to beg now. You don't get to ask for mercy you never showed anyone else."

Blood runs from his nose, mixing with tears of pain and fear. For the first time in his life, Alfred Colter looks small.

"Open the cell," I say finally, releasing his hair. He slumps forward, barely conscious.

Jasper swipes Ms. Harrington's keycard and the electronic lock disengages.

She steps back as the door swings open. "Sir? Are you alright?"

"Stay back," I tell her before turning to Alfred. "And you, get in."

Alfred's eyes widen through the blood and swelling. "Leon, you can't—"

"I can. And I am." I grab him by the shoulder and shove him toward the cell. "You put people in cages. Stripped them of their dignity, their freedom. Now you get to experience exactly what they did."

He stumbles into the cell, catching himself against the wall. "Please. We can work something out. I can give you names, locations—"

"You're done talking," I step back as Jasper swings the heavy door shut.

The lock engages with a soft beep.

Alfred pounds on the door, his voice rising to a shout. "You can't leave me here! This is murder!"

"No," I say through the intercom. "This is justice. You and Ms. Harrington can keep each other company. Maybe she can teach you some of those manners you were always going on about."

I turn away from the cell, from Alfred's shouting, from the basement of nightmares.

"So what now?" Damon asks, finally sliding his weapon back into his pants.

My gaze moves between my brothers faces. We don't share blood, but that never mattered to me. What matters is how we feel about each other. That we'd all be there at the drop of a hat if needed. Then I look back at Alfred, trapped in his own prison, finally powerless.

"Now," I say. "We make sure justice gets served. Roll up your sleeves, brothers. We have a fuck ton of work to do."

CHAPTER THIRTY-FOUR

LEON

THE ESTATE IS EERILY QUIET NOW. I KNOW THAT WON'T last long with Knapp's men on their way. I hated calling him, but Cruz suggested he might be the only guy who could help with cleanup on this scale. And I guess I didn't have too many options, not without involving the authorities.

I've been searching Alfred's study for the past hour, quietly sifting through documents both paper and electronic, finding evidence of decades worth of involvement in trafficking rings, fraud, and political corruption that reached levels I never imagined. Senators, judges, customs officials—all somehow linked. This whole thing is massive and I can't wait until each and every piece of shit involved gets what they deserve. We won't let them slink away, not anymore.

A leather portfolio sits on the desk in front of me—the one document I opened and then immediately closed. It's all the paperwork that Alfred wanted to go over with me tonight. His "Succession Planning" contracts. I don't know what I'm going to do with it all yet. A part of me wants to watch it burn, but I know I could do a lot of good with his money, help the people he's hurt. Realistically, the government will probably seize his assets, like they should, but right now, close to midnight of what feels like the longest day of my life, I won't make any big decisions.

Damon knocks on the open door, pulling my attention. "So... I just found a dead old man. Not a great sight."

"Fuck," I say. "That's got to be one of his employees. Bailey mentioned that he had other staff but I honestly forgot to look for anyone else."

"Well, the barrel of a gun found him... right in the head." Damon sucks air through his teeth. "I'm guessing that cleanup will cost extra?"

"Yeah, but it is what it is. I found the bastard's stash of cash in here. Whatever we need, it'll be covered."

He nods once. "Anyone else I should search for? Colonel Mustard in the library with a lead pipe?"

I narrow my eyes. "Who the fuck is that?"

"Clue," Damon says, like I'm the crazy one. "The board game."

"No idea what you're going on about," I say, shrugging.

He looks like I just told him I lived under a rock. "What was your childhood?"

Gesturing around the room, I smirk. "Clearly, not normal. As if you didn't already know."

We hear footsteps and turn toward the door at the same time to see Falin holding her phone. "I thought we should all be together for the big moment. Come on, they're waiting at the dining room table. Jasper already raided the kitchen."

"Big moment?" I ask, following her out of the room with the leather portfolio under my arm.

"The media leak! Didn't I tell you?" I don't respond so she goes on. "I set everything to drop all at once at midnight London time."

I do a quick calculation and realize that'll mean it's still early enough in the US that the traditional news could hear about it right away.

"Perfect timing," I say. "How long do you think we have before this place is swarming with investigators?"

"That's the thing," Falin replies as we walk down the hallway. "I may have been deliberately vague about the estate's location. I sent everything we have to BBC, Sky News, The Guardian, plus the Metropolitan Police and NCA. Oh, and I may have also tipped off the FBI and Interpol. But I only mentioned his London properties and offshore accounts. Plus, everything we have on Orlov and The Brotherhood."

"You didn't give them this address?"

"Call it a gut feeling," she says with a slight shrug. "Figured we might need some time to... process everything properly. What with him being your... you know."

I appreciate her not saying the dreaded F word.

"Jesus, Falin, you're brilliant."

She beams and I swear I notice a spring in her step. "I know."

Damon and I chuckle despite this insane situation. "So how long do we actually have?"

"Could be days before they connect all the dots and trace him here. Maybe longer. There's a lot of evidence to sift through."

We reach the dining room where the others have gathered around Alfred's massive mahogany table. It's surreal to sit in his formal dining room, surrounded by crystal and silver, while the man himself is locked in a concrete cell below our feet.

Bailey looks up when I enter, and I can see the exhaustion and discomfort in her eyes. She's been running on adrenaline for hours, and it's finally starting to catch up with her. She's sitting next to Mum, who also looks like she's minutes from falling asleep in her chair.

I go to them, resting my palm on Bailey's shoulder. She leans into me, humming a small satisfied sound. "How much longer?"

I check my watch. "About ten minutes until the leak goes live. But Falin says we might have days before anyone traces Alfred back to this place."

"So we can leave soon?"

"Yes, and you never have to come back here again," I say gently.

Jasper comes through the entryway on the other side of the room, carrying a bottle of liquor in one hand and a covered tray in the other. "Expensive whiskey, anyone?"

"What's on the tray?" Falin asks.

He holds it close to his chest. "Cheese, but I didn't say I wanted to share."

She punches him in the arm. "Put it down, dummy."

They all start chatting back and forth as Jasper finds glasses and pours drinks, but my focus is solely on the woman next to me. They may all be celebrating, but for Bailey, this is only the beginning.

"To taking down piece of shit rapists," Jasper calls, holding up his glass.

"To justice," Mum adds.

"To healing," Blake says.

All their eyes settle on me, waiting for me to add something. I lift my glass and say, "To family," before finishing every drop in one gulp.

The clock on the mantel chimes twelve times, and Falin's phone starts buzzing with notifications.

"And there we go," she says with satisfaction. "An entire empire just went public."

An hour later, Knapp's cleanup crew arrives. They're efficient, professional, and thankfully silent. I meet them at the front door while the others finish gathering their things.

Knapp himself greets me like an old friend, and I show him to a private spot away from his guys. "Thanks for coming. You're really helping me out of a jam."

"We'll handle everything," Knapp says, shaking my hand. "You were never here."

I nod, slipping him an envelope thick with Alfred's cash. "There's a basement. Don't go down there."

He doesn't ask questions. "Understood. We'll be out of your hair before sunrise."

I nod, then find Falin who's been quietly working on her laptop at the dining room table. "Did you figure out the door?"

She looks up from her screen with a grin. "Of course I did. I'm going to fry the electronic systems from the inside—manual override, backup power, emergency releases. Everything. Once I'm done, this door won't open for anything short of explosives."

Her fingers dash across the keyboard, and I watch her with amazement. I know I'm skilled when it comes to hacking systems, but I'm nothing compared to Falin.

"There," she says after a few minutes. "The system's completely corrupted. That lock is permanent now."

We share relieved looks and I let out a breath. "Let's get out of here."

Somehow everyone manages to squeeze into the rental SUV, with Damon behind the wheel. Bailey and Mum approach the vehicle, but I hold up a hand, an idea coming to mind.

"Wait. There's one last thing I need to do downstairs. Do you want to come with me, or would you rather wait here?"

Bailey looks toward the house, and wraps her arms around her chest. She seems to consider my offer for a moment, but shakes her head. "No. I don't want to see him again. I don't want to give him any more of my time or energy."

Mum nods firmly. "I'll come. There are things I need to say."

"Are you sure?" I ask. "You don't have to."

"I'm sure," Mum says, squaring her shoulders. "It's time."

I look at Damon through the driver's window. "Give us ten minutes? Bailey, can you wait here?"

They nod. "Take your time. We'll wait."

Bailey squeezes my hand before getting into the back seat. "Just... be safe down there."

Mum and I head back toward the house. There's one last thing we need to do.

It takes work to climb down those stairs. Everything in me recoils once we reach the bottom again. I'm sure there's plenty of evidence I could collect down here, more than enough to add to Alfred's crimes, but I'll leave that to the police. I don't want to spend a minute more in this hellscape than necessary.

But this time, it's not only me that has something to say.

Mum steps forward, determined like I haven't seen her in years. She approaches the cell window, and Alfred's face appears behind the glass, hope flickering in his eyes.

"Ada, darling—"

"Don't," she cuts him off sharply. "You don't get to call me that anymore."

Alfred's mouth opens and closes like a fish.

"For over twenty years, you made me believe I was nothing without you," Mum continues, her voice growing stronger with each word. "You convinced me I was weak, that I needed your protection, your guidance. That I should be grateful for the scraps of affection you threw my way."

She presses her palm against the glass, and Alfred flinches backward.

"But I raised a good man despite you. Leon is everything you're not—he's kind, protective, loyal. He chose love over power, family over legacy. He's more of a man at twenty-four than you'll ever be."

Tears stream down her face, but her voice never wavers. I'm so damn proud of her.

"I wasted decades of my life loving a monster. But I'm done now. I'm done being afraid of you, done letting you control my thoughts, done feeling guilty for my son growing up without a father. He's lucky you were absent."

She steps back from the window, wiping her eyes.

"Rot in there, Alfred. You too, Greta. You both deserve every sickening moment you have left on this earth."

The cell falls silent. Even Alfred seems stunned into speechlessness.

Mum turns to me, and I swear she looks like a different woman. "I'm ready to go home now."

I lead her to the stairs and gesture for her to start climbing all while Alfred pounds on the door, shouting. "You can't leave me here! This is murder!"

Once Mum is halfway up, I move to the cell window again.

"Maybe so, but it's nothing you don't deserve." I hold up the portfolio so he can see. "Thanks for the inheritance documentation, by the way. I'll make sure every penny goes to helping the people you hurt. Oh, and one more thing... we leaked everything to the media. You can die knowing that the whole world knows exactly what you are."

His face drops but he recovers quick enough to pound on the door. "Leon, please. Don't do this—"

"I hope you left some water in there for your prisoners because that's all you'll have."

"The authorities will find me eventually," he says, sounding desperate.

"Maybe. Could be days though. Possibly longer." I turn to follow Mum up the stairs, pausing at the bottom. "And Alfred? In case you were wondering, that emergency override system you disabled so your victims couldn't escape during fires? We made sure it stays that way."

His voice follows us up the stairs—shouting, pleading, threatening. But I don't look back.

Some monsters deserve to die alone in the dark.

PART 3

CHAPTER THIRTY-FIVE

BAILEY

It's summer again. So ironic considering most of my recent entries in here were from the summer before. I'm back home now with Mom and Dad. It's been an adjustment for all of us. Especially since Jasper and Damon still have a few months left on their lease for their apartment in the city and Leon hasn't left London yet. I figured he'd have tons to do after everything. Still wrapping my head around who his father is... was, I mean. It was in the headlines about a week after the leak. He was found dead in his cell... it was deemed an accident. I didn't want to know the details. The relief was good enough.

Anyway, back to Mom and Dad. When Jasper made that phone call before we left London, telling them they found me... it was surreal. Hearing their voices through the speaker, it's safe to say I sobbed on the spot. They flew out right away even though we told *them not to spend the money on plane tickets. Pretty sure Leon paid for them anyway, but no one will admit that to me.*

I wasn't sure if they would look at me differently. I know when I look in the mirror, I don't see the old me. But I guess my scars are more internal than I thought.

It's been kind of a mess since we got back. I'm not sure how but the investigators covering the case found me and I've had to rehash my story again and again. I'm going to need to go to court soon, which I'm really not looking forward to.

Oh, but one cool thing... Layne reached out. I guess she found out somehow that I'm home and okay and she basically FBI agented her way into finding my mom's number. It was surreal talking to her again. I missed her chaos.

Anyway, for now I'm going to take it one day at a time and focus on healing. I'll write again later. I have to get to therapy.

"Bails, can you get the door?" Mom calls from her bedroom. She's been in there making phone calls all morning. Apparently someone at her job leaked my story to the press, and now there are vultures circling for an exclusive.

The doorbell rings again, so I get up from the couch, adjust my messy ponytail, and open the door a crack. My lips pull into a wide grin when I see Leon standing there. He looks tired but still just as good as ever. His scruff has grown out a bit, and he's wearing a black T-shirt that hugs his lean muscles just right. I clear my throat and open the door all the way.

As soon as his eyes land on me, he smiles too. "Hi," I say, ecstatic to see him but trying to tamp it down to normal levels. "I thought you were still in London!"

I reach for him instinctively, then stop with my hand halfway to his chest and quickly wrap my arms around myself instead. *Holy awkwardness.*

"Just landed this morning," he says, his eyes soft as he takes me in. "There wasn't any more need for me to be there in person. I can handle everything else remotely."

"Well, that's good," I say. "Come on in."

"Who's at the door?" Mom yells.

I roll my eyes as I close and lock it. "It's Leon! He's back from London!"

I hear Mom's footsteps pounding down the hallway before I can get another word in. She pulls him into a bear hug of epic proportions, and I even hear an "oof" sound slip out from the squeeze around his middle. It's safe to say Mom and Dad love Leon. I was a little afraid of how they'd feel once they learned who Alfred was, but between Leon's charm and his mom's hospitality, they left London singing both their praises.

"It's so good to see you!" Mom says once she releases him. "Bailey didn't tell me you were coming."

He chuckles. "She didn't know. I wanted to keep it a surprise."

"Let me get you something to drink," she says, already bustling toward the kitchen. "I bought some of that tea your mum loves. It was hard to find once we got back but there's this little international supermarket the next town over—"

"Mom," I say, resting my hand on her shoulder. "Take a breath."

She lets out an embarrassed laugh. "Sorry, I've been a little high strung lately. It's been a madhouse around here, I'm sure you've heard."

Leon's eyes find mine, sparking with amusement at Mom's energy.

"Yes, there's been lots of buzz. Actually, did you hear about the most recent development?"

Mom gestures to the kitchen table. "I don't think we have. Come sit, let's catch up."

On one hand, I'm glad Mom's lessening the awkwardness between Leon and me. But wow, she really knows how to monopolize a conversation.

Once we're seated, Mom starts making tea, still listening as she moves from cabinet to cabinet.

"When I was in the airport, they had the news going. It seems they've finally found Ivan Orlov."

My jaw drops. "Where was he?"

"Holed up in some house in Florida of all places. A small town called Palm Cove," Leon says. "Apparently, they're investigating foul play. It seems someone took him out before he could name names for a deal."

I'm speechless. I didn't know much about this man, but once everything settled and they all filled me in, I found out that he was King's uncle and a major player in their Brotherhood bullshit. I'm happy he's dead—a thought I'll have to work through in therapy tomorrow.

"Well, I can't say I'm surprised or upset," Mom says, setting two steeping mugs down on the table in front of us. I stare at it and wince.

Leon catches on quickly, and moves the mug to the other side of the table. "Thanks," I whisper.

I haven't been able to stomach hot black tea after everything. Some smells just transport me right back to that dining room with Sir.

"So what are your summer plans?" Mom asks when she finally sits across from us.

He's quiet for a moment, so I jump in. "Mom, you're kind of being a bit much. He just got off the plane."

"It's fine, really," Leon says, giving me a small smile. "There's still work to finish remotely on the estate conversion. The designers say it'll be ready to open its doors in about six months."

"And what did you settle on for the name?" Mom asks, blowing on the steaming mug in front of her.

"The Firefly Center," Leon says quietly, his eyes finding mine again. "If all goes according to plan, it'll be a comprehensive support center for trafficking survivors and sexual assault victims. We're planning residential treatment programs, therapy services, job training, legal advocacy—everything someone needs to rebuild their life. The estate's location makes it perfect for long-term residential care, and we're partnering with organizations in London and New York to ensure survivors have continued support when they're ready to reintegrate."

Mom's eyes fill with tears as she reaches for his hand across the table. "Leon, that's beautiful. And using his estate for it..."

"Seems fitting," he finishes. "Turning a place that caused so much harm into somewhere that heals."

"It's perfect," I say, barely able to get the words out through my tight throat.

They sip their tea and I think about how much I wish I could tell Polly the news. She'd probably want nothing to with that estate. I know I don't, but for others it could be life saving.

"Are you going back to the city then?" Mom asks, glancing at Leon above the rim of her mug. "I'm sure you're eager to get back to all the stuff you left there."

He looks at me again, brows slightly lifted. "Actually, I was thinking of sticking around town. I've had enough of cities for a while."

I can't hide my smile.

"Oh, that's the truth," Mom says. "Cities are not for me. I'm glad we live close enough for a planned visit, but far enough away that we have peace and quiet."

"Exactly," Leon says. "What about you, Bailey? What are your summer plans?"

I find myself fiddling with my shirt under the table. There's no reason I should be nervous around him. We've literally seen each other naked and said I love you's. It's just been... awhile. And so much has changed.

One thing that hasn't though—my parents still have no idea that we were together. Or are. Kind of. I don't know. It's complicated.

"Just therapy... I might go back to Burger Palace for something to do. Trying to stay busy but not overwhelmingly so," I ramble.

"With the court dates coming up... all those appointments... it's a lot," Mom says, reaching for my hand now.

There's a sweet moment between us before Mom's phone goes off again. She glances at it, curses under her breath, and hits the side button.

"It looks like you're both busy," Leon says. He finishes the last of his tea and wipes his lips on the back of his palm.

Why do I find that so sexy?

"Not really," I say quickly.

"Well, I should probably head out and check into that inn by the diner—"

"Absolutely not!" Mom interrupts, setting her phone down. "That place is a complete dump. The owner's daughter is in my book club and she's always complaining about the plumbing issues and the weird smell in the hallways."

Leon and I exchange a glance, and I can see amusement flickering in his eyes.

"Mrs. Shea, that's really kind, but I don't want to impose—"

"You'll stay here," Mom declares, already standing up like it's settled. "Jasper's room downstairs is just sitting empty anyway, and it has its own entrance so you won't feel like you're cramping our style."

My face burns. "Mom..."

"What? It's perfect! Besides, Bailey could use the company. She's been moping around here like a sad puppy."

"I have not been moping!"

"Honey, yesterday I found you staring at a bag of chips for ten minutes," Mom says matter-of-factly. "That's moping."

Leon's trying not to laugh, I can tell.

"Really, I should probably get a hotel room—" he starts.

"Leon," Mom interrupts, hands on her hips in full mom-means-business mode. "That inn charges sixty dollars a night for rooms that reek of cigarettes and have mysterious stains on the carpet. You're staying here, and that's final."

Leon gives me a look that's part helpless, part secretly pleased—like this is exactly what he was hoping would happen but he can't let on that he orchestrated it perfectly.

"If you insist," he says with just the right amount of reluctant acceptance.

"I won't have you getting scabies or bed bugs or something from that place. Jasper's room is yours for however long you'd like." Her phone rings again and she grabs it from the table. "Dammit, can't they take a hint? I better get this." And then she's off, heading back toward her bedroom, her voice carrying in the hallway.

Leon smirks at me, looking so smug.

"Bravo," I say. "That was some impeccable acting."

"I thought so too."

"Was there ever a reservation at the inn?" I ask, already knowing the answer.

He taps his chin, pretending to think for a second, then grins. "Not at all. In fact, I think they're booked solid this week. There's some children's cheerleading convention at the event center in town. Kids everywhere running about. Steer clear of those cross streets."

"You're terrible," I say, shaking my head but unable to hide my smile. "So this whole thing was planned?"

"I prefer the term *strategically hopeful*," he says, leaning back in his chair. "I figured your mum would never let me stay at some sketchy inn. She's very protective of people she likes."

"And I guess you think she likes you then?" I tease.

"Oh, I'm pretty sure she likes me more than Jasper at this point," he says with a grin. "When I stayed last time, I helped her carry groceries, I complimented her garden, and I didn't track mud through the house. That's like instant son-in-law status."

I literally choke on my own saliva. "Son-in-law status? Wow... Someone's getting quite cocky."

"Cocky or truthful? You decide."

"Jury's still out on that one," I say, ignoring the acrobatics happening in my stomach.

"Well, I've got time to make my case," he says, and something in his tone shifts. Less teasing, more sincere.

I blow out a breath and my gaze drifts to my hands, feeling the weight of everything unsaid between us. It's been a weird few months. We've texted and had a few calls but we've both kept things pretty surface level. Safe and predictable. Which is exactly what I've needed. *I think.*

"Leon..."

"Yeah?"

"What are we doing here?" The question slips out before I

can stop it. "I mean, with us. Are we... Are we trying to go back to how things were, or... Because I don't know if I'm ready for anything... I don't know... heavy or physical. I'm just..."

"Hey," he says gently, and I feel his warm hand cover mine on the table. "There's no pressure, Bailey. None at all."

I look up at him, searching his face. I know he's sincere but I can't help but feel bad. Like a knee-jerk reaction to care about his needs more than my own, which is so not okay, but I can't help it. "But you came here. You planned this whole thing..."

"I came here because I missed you," he says simply. "Not because I expect anything from you. I just... I wanted to be near you again. Even if it's just as friends."

"Friends," I repeat, testing the word on my lips. I don't know how I feel about it... not yet.

"Friends," he confirms. "For as long as you need. Or forever, if that's what you want."

I guess my body understands what my brain is still struggling to make sense of because as soon as he says those words, relief washes over me. "Thank you," I whisper.

"You don't have to thank me for caring about you, love."

"For everything." My face burns and tears well in my eyes. "What you're doing with the estate is incredible. I wish I could tell Polly about it."

"Come here," he says softly, opening his arms wide. I practically climb into his lap from my chair, settling my head on his chest. He smells like comfort. And when he rubs slow circles on my back, something inside me that's been wound tight for months finally starts to loosen.

I adjust my head against him so I can hear his heartbeat better. The steady rhythmic beat reminds me of the summer before, when I used to fall asleep with my ear to his chest wrapped in his comfort and care.

"I'm scared," I whisper.

His hand stops rubbing, but he doesn't move it. "Of what, love?"

"That I'll never be normal again. That I'll always be this broken version of myself, pretending everything is okay."

I bury my face deeper, embarrassed by what I've just admitted. But it's true. Every word. And he's the first person I'm really saying it to. I don't even think I've been that honest with my therapist.

He continues his gentle motion. "You're so strong, Bailey. I've never thought you were broken, just healing. But you know what? You don't have to feel any certain way, okay? One day at a time."

"What if one day at a time isn't enough?" I ask, my voice muffled against his shirt. "What if I'm stuck like this forever?"

"Then we'll figure it out together," he says without hesitation. "There's no timeline for healing, and there's no right way to do it. You're allowed to have bad days. You're allowed to feel scared."

I pull back to look at him. "You really mean that?"

"Every single word." He rolls his lip between his teeth before continuing. "And Bailey? You're not pretending everything is okay. You're coping. You're surviving. You're here with us, you're talking, you're trying. That's not pretending. That's being incredibly brave."

"I don't feel brave," I admit.

He wipes a tear from my cheek with his thumb. "I'll show you every day how brave and strong you are, Firefly."

I nod, taking in his words. Trying not to dismiss them as him just being nice. We sit in comfortable silence for a few minutes, me with my head on his shoulder, him holding me close. I feel so safe in his arms.

When I finally sit up, all the tears dried, he almost looks sad to see me climb off him. "Sorry if I got snot on your shirt," I joke, lightening the mood.

"I'll treasure it forever," he says with a small smile. "Don't worry, I remember where the laundry room is... Some fun times in there."

My cheeks heat. "Oh my God."

"What? I was just talking about that time your dad taught me how to get motor oil out of fabric," he says with fake innocence. "Very educational and fun."

"Okay, buddy." I roll my eyes but can't help myself from smiling.

"Although," he continues, leaning back in his chair, "now that I mention it, there were some other memorable moments in there too."

"You're a dirty old man," I laugh and feel my chest loosening. This back and forth is so natural, it almost feels like nothing's changed between us. Especially being back home, sitting around my kitchen table. Like old times.

"Maybe so, but this dirty old man got you to laugh. That's all I wanted."

His hand finds mine, and he gives it a soft squeeze. For the first time in months, I feel somewhat normal again. There's just the small fact of us living under the same roof once again. It'll be an experience, that's for sure.

"So, want me to show you down to the *bro-tel?*" I ask. "I'm sure it's just as gross as when you last saw it. Dirty socks and empty cans included."

He laughs as he stands. "And there goes the fairytale."

"Yeah... I've only been down there to do laundry. It might need fumigating."

He helps me up from my chair, keeping his hand wrapped in mine. "Sounds like home."

Hearing him say home, with his warm voice, does something to my chest. Maybe this house will finally feel like home again with him here.

CHAPTER THIRTY-SIX

LEON

Jasper: You sly dog. Why am I hearing from my mom that you're back and staying in MY HOUSE?! I'm genuinely hurt.

Damon: He really is. I think he cried but he tried to hide it saying he ate something spicy. Bullshit. He eats his mom's wings no issue... man can handle spice.

Me: I'm sorry, don't be pissed off. I wanted to see how Bailey's doing. Plus, we talk every day. I know you guys are fine.

Jasper: You love her more than me, I know it

Me: Umm... I'd hope so

Jasper: Well you better keep your hands to yourself... PG rating

Damon: You know that's not going to happen

Me: Sooo some scenes may be unsuitable for children, then? Which means...

> Jasper: Keep that pierced monster away from my sister

> Me: ;)

> Damon: I'm gonna have to mute this group chat, aren't I?

It's odd living in Jasper and Damon's old room after everything that's happened. It's almost like fitting myself into a pair of shoes that are too small. The person I was two years ago when we'd go to parties and goof off, he feels so far away. Being near Bailey is the only thing that helps me find pieces of him again.

Since I arrived a few days ago, I've settled into the rhythm of the house. I get some work done early in the morning, taking calls from the team I hired to oversee the estate project. They know I want to be as hands off as possible in the majority of the planning. Some things just hit too close to home.

Bailey's parents wake up around seven, when I've already been up for hours. I can hear their muffled conversations through the ceiling as they get ready for work. Mr. Shea leaves first. His truck rumbling to life in the driveway gives him away. Followed by Mrs. Shea about an hour later. The house settles into quiet after that, except for Bailey.

She's usually up by eight, sometimes earlier if she's had a rough night. I've learned to recognize the difference between her normal morning sounds and the aftermath of a sleepless night. On bad days, she moves more carefully, her footsteps barely audible. Almost like she's afraid to take up space. But on good days, I'll catch her humming as she makes breakfast, shuffling around the kitchen like old times.

I hope today is a good day.

I finish my call with the contractors. They went on about soundproofing the therapy rooms for way too long. With my laptop closed and calls finished for the day, the guilt that's become my constant companion settles heavier in my chest. Every conversation about the Firefly Center reminds me why we're building it. Reminds me of all the people my father hurt. All the people I couldn't save.

But being with Bailey is helping. When I see her laugh at something ridiculous on her phone, her face lighting up, it feels like forgiveness. Like all the violence I committed, all the lines I crossed, led to something worthwhile.

My phone buzzes with a text from Falin. Another update about Brotherhood arrests. She's been tracking them obsessively, sending me screenshots of news articles and mugshots like trophies. Seventeen have been arrested so far. Five were found dead in their holding cells—apparent suicides days before their arraignments, though we all know what that really means. The empire is crumbling from within. Exactly what we planned for.

> Falin: They got Fairfax! Although, I think he'll get out on bail. I'm keeping an eye on it.

I click out of the message, feeling hollow. It's ridiculous. I should feel some amount of satisfaction with each arrest. But justice doesn't bring back the lives lost. It doesn't erase what Bailey went through. It doesn't make my blood any less Colter.

Footsteps creak overhead. Bailey's awake. Warmth spreads through my chest knowing I get to go upstairs and see her. That's a feeling I'll never take for granted again.

I listen to her move around up there while I use the bathroom and get dressed in some casual sweats and a T-shirt. She's making her way to the kitchen, and from the soft sound of cabinets opening and closing, I'd bet she was making herself something to eat. Some might call me creepy, I know I've definitely called out Damon for his *observance*, but I've memorized her patterns, learned to read subtle changes to judge her mood. I think it's a skill I've always possessed but I've honed it in lately.

The difference is intent, I tell myself. Damon watched Blake to possess her. I watch Bailey to protect her. I can picture his expression if I ever threw that comment his way. It's all out of love.

I head upstairs, taking the steps slowly so she knows I'm coming. No surprises, no sudden appearances. The other day I made the mistake of showing up in the living room while she was reading and she jumped out of her skin. Now, I'm sure to step on every creaky floorboard to announce my arrival.

When I reach the kitchen, she's standing by the window holding a steaming mug. The morning sunlight catches the auburn highlights in her hair that lighten even more in the summertime. She's wearing Sanrio pajama pants and the oversized sweatshirt she snagged from my bag the other day while I was unpacking. Seeing her wrapped in my clothes does something to my chest that makes it hard to breathe normally.

"Morning," I say softly.

She turns, and her face breaks into a sleepy smile that I want to capture on paper. "Morning. I made hot water if you want some tea."

I glance at the counter and see the chamomile tea bags scattered next to a plate with toast crumbs. "Thanks." I pour myself a mug, noting her choices. She's never been a coffee person. I've seen her drink boba tea a few times and a matcha once when we stopped at the coffee shop in town. But I'm sure the herbal teas are good for her anxiety. I figure I'll have the same. As much as I love a strong cup of black tea, she hates the smell.

"How'd you sleep?" I ask, settling at the kitchen table but

leaving space between us. I'm always conscious of the distance between us now, reading her body language for signs that I'm too close.

"So-so." She joins me, tucking her legs underneath her in the chair. "Only woke up once."

I already knew her answer. Around 2 AM, I heard her moving around upstairs. Heard the quiet shuffling of feet on hardwood, the creak of floorboards as she walked off whatever nightmare had startled her awake. I'd made it halfway up the basement stairs before stopping myself, listening from the stairwell until her movements settled and I heard her bedroom door close again. She needed space to work through it on her own. But tonight, if she needs me, I won't hesitate.

"That's good," I say, wrapping my hands around the warm mug.

We sit in comfortable silence, sipping our tea, and waking up fully. I wish I had my pad and pencils, I'd sketch Bailey exactly how she looks right now. Her cheeks have a bit more color to them than they did those first few days in London, and she's slowly starting to get back to the weight she was before. She's beautiful always, but these small signs that she's healing are good to see.

Our silence is broken by a lawn mower starting next door. Bailey flinches, and her entire body goes rigid for a split second before she forces herself to relax.

"Alright?" I ask.

She nods. "Yeah, just a bit jumpy these days. Want to watch a movie or something? I don't have therapy today. Unless you have work to do?"

"No, I'm all done with that for the day. A movie sounds good."

Whatever she wants to do is good with me, as long as she lets me be in her presence.

We head into the living room and Bailey opens one of their streaming services, scrolling through the saved options at the top of the screen. "Looks like Mom was in an early 2000's rom-com vibe recently." She pauses on one with a ridiculously pink poster. "This one looks cheesy as hell. You in?"

"Sure," I say, settling on the far end of the couch.

She hits play and curls up on the opposite end, tucking her feet under her. There's at least three feet of space between us, but I'm hyperaware of every movement she makes. How she pulls my sweatshirt over her knees. The way she rubs a strand of her hair between her fingers absentmindedly. How she touches her chest as she laughs at something silly the main characters do on screen.

The movie is terrible, as I expected. Something about a wedding planner falling for a groom. But I'm not watching much of it anyway. I'm stealing glances at Bailey every few seconds, taking in how she relaxes more and more as the morning goes on.

About halfway through the movie, during some dramatic moment where the characters almost kiss in the rain, Bailey shifts. She stretches her legs out, and her socked feet end up just inches from my thigh. It's a small movement... nothing really, but somehow it feels intimate.

My hands itch to slide onto her ankle and rub the soft skin there. I want to pull her against my side so there's no space between us. It's an ache—this feeling of wanting her. Not just physically, though there's that, but wanting to comfort her, to casually touch her like I used to. I force my hand under my thigh so I don't do anything stupid and fuck up the progress we're making.

Toward the end of the movie, there's this emotional scene where the couple finally gets together and have this long kiss. There's romantic music playing and the whole thing is shot in slow motion and I swear I feel Bailey's eyes on me. My breathing picks up, and I glance over to see her watching me with an expression I can't place. I want to think she's feeling the same pull I am... I want that more than anything. Her chest is visibly rising and falling and for a second I think, fuck it, and start to pull my hand out from under my thigh.

The air between us is charged. Electric. Like she's also remembering what it was like to be us, before everything went wrong. Her lips part and I inch closer.

Then the sound of car doors slamming in the driveway makes us freeze. Bailey hits pause on the movie and we sit up to peer out the window.

"What are they doing here?" Bailey says.

I'd love to know the answer but I can guess.

Through the window, Jasper's pulling bags from the trunk while Falin stretches her arms over her head, clearly stiff from the drive. They must have left the city this morning, wanting to surprise us for the weekend.

"Looks like we're getting company," I say, trying to keep the disappointment out of my voice. Not that I don't love my friends, but I could use some alone time with Bailey.

Bailey jumps up from the couch, smooths down my sweatshirt, and adjusts her hair. "Do I look okay? I don't want them to think..."

"You look perfect, like always," I say. "And we weren't doing anything wrong."

The front door swings open and Jasper's voice booms through the house. "Bailey! Where's my favorite sister?"

"I'm your only sister, idiot," she calls back with a genuine smile. All the tension from minutes ago is suddenly zapped away by Jasper's entrance.

"Where's my favorite Brit? You better be keeping your hands to yourself!" he yells as Falin laughs.

Bailey and I share an exasperated head shake, but she seems more joyful than not, so I won't quite tear my best friend's head off. She reaches for my hand to pull me up from the couch. "Let's go say hi before Jasper starts getting suspicious about why we're not answering fast enough."

"You're right," I say, letting her lead me into the kitchen.

Slow and steady, I remind myself. More like progress and torture all wrapped up in one.

CHAPTER THIRTY-SEVEN

BAILEY

Jasper and Falin are here for the weekend and there's one person who's not super thrilled about it. Leon. Okay, maybe I wasn't exactly jumping out of my skin to see my brother after spending almost two months with him when everything went down. I missed him, but Jasper time needs to be in small doses. At least Falin seems to level him out a bit. She's already come to me to plan an epic prank on him while they're here. I'm thinking something classic like honey in his shampoo bottle or toothpaste in his Oreos... but knowing Falin for the short amount of time that I have, I'm almost scared of what she'll decide.

Is it crazy that I've been wondering if them showing up was the universe's way of telling me I'm not ready to be with Leon again? He's only been here for a week and I'm already finding it harder and harder to stay away from him. Is it just me being too hard on myself? Punishing myself for wanting to have something good?

I talked to my therapist about Leon the other day and she said something that really stuck with me. She told me that healing isn't this straight line going from point A to point B despite what I may want, and that me wanting connection—especially with someone who represents safety and love from before—isn't something to feel guilty about. But, and here's the kicker, she also said I need to be honest with myself (because that's so easy) about whether I'm drawn to him because I genuinely want to rebuild what we had, or because he feels like a lifeline back to who I used to be.

Mind fuck, right?

She gave me homework, which I've been willfully neglecting (it's a lot to think about). But she basically wants me to write down what I need to feel secure in a relationship. What I need, NOT what Leon needs, not what would make things easier for everyone else, but what I actually need. Things like being able to say no without feeling guilty (a big yes). Having space when I need it (also yes... but too much space makes me feel too alone with my thoughts). Not having to pretend I'm okay when I'm not (that's a given). And the freedom to change my mind about intimacy or closeness without having to explain myself (again, another given).

Leon already gives me all that. This is more on myself than him. He doesn't push and never has, he reads my moods better than I do sometimes, and he never makes me feel broken or like I'm too much work.

Maybe the universe isn't telling me I'm not ready.

Maybe it's just reminding me to take things at my own pace.

Anyway, I should probably go and see what Falin has in store for my brother. I almost feel bad for the poor guy. Maybe I shouldn't have decided to be her co-conspirator, but then again a little fun won't hurt.

"YOU WANT TO GO CAMPING?" I ASK JASPER, WHO'S currently digging through the garage for our bin of gear. "Really?"

Leon and Falin are inside working on their computers. When those two get together, I have no idea what they're talking about half the time. It's truly like they're speaking another language.

He pulls out a gray bin labeled *Camping* and grunts as he straightens his back. "Come on, it'll be fun. Plus, you owe me from scheming with Falin on that prank yesterday. I drove an hour north to find out Mom wasn't actually stranded on a farm and most certainly wasn't being attacked by a herd of feral goats. Goats, Bails... you had to go there? You know how much goats freak me out!"

"Listen," I say, trying to keep from laughing. "Falin wanted to make it something dark like Mom was being held ransom and you had to bring a bag of cash."

He stops digging through the bin to look at me. "For real?"

"Yeah... She's kind of scary, you know."

He laughs and his whole face lights up. "Oh Bails, you don't know the half of it. But still... the goat thing was a low blow. Now Falin and Leon know about my most traumatic childhood story."

"And Mom always said I was the drama queen!" I laugh.

"That goat was huge and out for blood. Its eyes were red, I swear." His mouth sets in a hard line. "Not cool, man."

"And our punishment is a night of camping with no running water and no toilets? Yippee."

I don't want to play the *if you only knew how many days I went in the last two years without regular access to those things* card. Although, the thought crosses my mind.

"You used to love it. S'mores, fishing, sitting by the fire... it'll be awesome."

"Or mosquitos, worm guts, and smoke inhalation... It'll be a hellscape," I deadpan, my hands on my hips.

He sighs, looking at me seriously now. "If you really don't want to go, I won't make you. I just thought it would be some nice bonding time. Living in the city isn't my jam. I miss trees."

I'm going to regret this.

"It's fine. I'll go. But what's the tent situation?"

His face goes white. Ah, ha. I guess he hadn't fully thought about the whole tent sharing debacle. "I guess you and Falin can share our old one. And I'll sleep with Leon."

"Aww, so cozy. Will you two spoon?"

He huffs. "Nah, he's too restless. Damon's a much better little spoon."

We both burst into laughter. "Why can I actually picture you two weirdos spooning at some point in your dumb drunken years?"

"Probably because we were dumb and drunk a lot," he answers.

I figure now's a good a time as any to bring up the me and Leon situation. I shift on my feet and pretend to stare intently at a flashlight in the bin.

"You know me and Leon aren't together... not anymore. We're just friends."

Jasper smirks and shakes his head. "Okay... since when did friends look at each other the way you two do?"

"What? We don't."

"I can't believe I didn't realize it years ago." He pulls out the tent, and starts checking it for holes. "Bailey, you should have seen that guy while you were gone. He was absolutely devastated. Like fucking miserable. Me and D would secretly invent plans just to get away from his scowling mug for a little while."

My face heats and stomach flips. "Really?"

"I know I give him shit because you're my little sister, but I guess I'd be okay if you guys got together. I know he loves the hell out of you." His eyes soften. "And you love him too."

This conversation is getting away from normal Jasper and Bailey territory and into mushy emotional feelings land, a place the two of us don't visit often. I can't help but smile at his admission anyway.

"Are you going to stop giving him shit then?"

His brows furrow into an "are you crazy?" look. "And deny myself the satisfaction of getting under Leon Colter's skin? No way. Plus, he kept it a secret all that time. I think I deserve a few more weeks of torment."

"I can live with that," I say, feeling extra devious. "We should prank him tonight. Maybe pretend you and him have to share a sleeping bag? I'd love to see the look on his face."

"We can definitely come up with something better than that."

I guess we're going camping.

I'LL GIVE Jasper credit where it's due, this little remote spot in the Catskills is pretty gorgeous. I'm still not thrilled about the no bathroom situation though.

It's mid-afternoon and we've got our camp set up beside a small lake that reflects the surrounding pine trees like a mirror. I have to admit it's peaceful, even through Jasper and Falin's bickering.

"Okay, but seriously," Falin says for the third time, holding her phone up toward the sky like she's making an offering to the gods of cell service. "How is there literally zero service out here? What if Fairfax gets released on bail and I miss it?"

"That's kind of the point of camping, Trouble," Jasper calls from where he's attempting to assemble kindling and wood in the fire pit. "Disconnecting from the world."

She drops her arm and sighs. "I know. I'm just super invested. It's hard to step away."

Leon looks at her from the back of the car, where he's methodically organizing our supplies for some unknown reason. We're only here one night, but he's acting like he's setting up a prepper stockpile for the end of days. "If anything major happens, the world will still be there when we get back tomorrow."

She grumbles something under her breath before sliding her phone into her leggings pocket and disappearing into the tent.

I'm sitting on one of our camp chairs, watching Leon work. It looks like he's got everything sorted by meal, weather event, or first aid supply. At least he's organized... even if it's a bit much. "Leon," I say, unable to hide my amusement any longer. "We're camping for one night, not surviving a zombie apocalypse."

He pauses, holding a can of beans in each hand. Who even

packed canned beans? "You can never be too prepared. Especially out here."

Jasper perks up from his game of log tetris. "Oh yeah, speaking of being prepared—Bails, did you tell him about that one species of bear?"

I catch Jasper's eye and realize we're apparently starting the torment Leon plan early. "Oh right, the... what are they called again?"

"Midnight Howlers," Jasper says with complete seriousness. "They're native to this area. Surprised you never heard of them, Mr. Encyclopedia."

Leon sets down the cans in their specific spot and gives us his full attention. "Midnight Howlers?"

"Yeah, I can't believe I forgot," I jump in, trying to match Jasper's grave tone. "They're like a cross between a black bear and a wolf. Super rare, but really aggressive."

"They hunt in packs," Jasper adds, getting really into the story now. "Kind of like the raptors in *Jurassic Park*. Oh, and they're nocturnal. That's why they're called *Midnight* Howlers — they make this really creepy howling sound right before they attack."

Leon's eyes narrow. "I've never heard of them."

"Most people haven't," I add. "They're pretty much unique to the Catskills. Something about the ecosystem here made them evolve differently."

"They're smaller than regular bears," Jasper continues, "but way more vicious. And smart... they can actually work together to open tents."

"Open tents?" Leon repeats.

"With their claws," I nod, struggling so hard to keep a straight face. "They're really dexterous... part of the evolution. Dad always said to never keep food in your tent because they can smell it from miles away and they'll find a way in."

Leon looks around our campsite like he's mentally calculating how many Midnight Howlers could surround us. "Maybe we should head back."

"Nah, we're good, buddy," Jasper waves dismissively. "As long as we follow the rules, we'll be fine. Just don't sleep too deeply, don't keep anything scented in the tent, and whatever you do, don't try to take pictures if you see one. They hate camera flashes."

"Camera flashes?" Leon asks. "That's oddly specific."

"It triggers their hunting instinct," I say. "According to Dad... it's something about the light drawing out their predatory nature."

Falin snorts from inside the tent, and we hear rustling as she quickly covers it up with a fake cough.

Leon stares at us, his brows narrowed. "Midnight Howlers that hunt in packs, open tents with their claws, and are triggered by camera flashes."

"Exactly," Jasper and I say in unison.

"You're both completely full of shit."

We burst into laughter while Leon shakes his head at us. "You almost had me," he says, smiling. "But the Shea genes kicked in and gave you away. You have the same look when you're shit-talking. Plus, Falin's in there about to piss herself trying not to laugh."

"We had you for a minute though," I grin.

He sighs and runs a hand through his hair. "Maybe for one second tops I was worried about being eaten by some clawed bear-wolf hybrid. One second. That's all."

"Just wait until we tell you about the Reptilian Tent Stalkers," Jasper says with a completely straight face.

Leon throws a marshmallow at him.

"Oh no, you're wasting our precious food supply," I tease.

He sets down the marshmallow bag and walks over from

the car, a devious look in his eye, and pulls me up from my chair, slinging me over his shoulder. "You're in trouble, Firefly. I'm putting you on firewood duty."

"It was Jasper's idea!" I say, between laughing and trying not to get dizzy as he walks away from camp. "Put me down, I'll accept my punishment."

Leon laughs and his whole chest rumbles. He sets me down near a tree, and I lean on it to catch my breath. "Good girl."

My whole body recoils. Just like that, Sir's voice is back in my head, calling me his good girl. I turn away from Leon, trying to get my breathing to go back to normal.

"Bailey? Are you alright?" Leon rushes to my side, reaching for my arm, but I sidestep away. "Shit, I'm sorry. I shouldn't have lifted you up like that. Did I hurt you?"

"No," I manage through a shaky breath. "It wasn't..."

I hear his footsteps as he paces behind me. When I swipe my hand over my eyes, it comes away wet. When did I start crying?

"Love, talk to me. What happened?" His voice is gentle and somehow that makes me cry harder. I feel so stupid. "Was it something I said?"

I take a shaky breath, still facing the tree. "What you... called... me. It just..." I can't finish the sentence.

"Good girl," he says quietly, understanding immediately. "Fuck. Bailey, I'm so sorry."

"It's not your fault," I whisper. "You didn't know."

"Can I come closer?" he asks. "Or do you need space?"

I think for a moment, willing the bad thoughts to go the fuck away. Part of me wants to run back to camp, to pretend this didn't happen, avoid more embarrassment. But a bigger part of me wants Leon close, to replace Sir's voice in my head with his.

"Closer is okay," I say softly.

I hear him step forward, then feel his presence behind me. Not touching, but near enough that I can feel his warmth, his comfort.

"Who?" he asks.

I swallow hard. "Sir."

"I hate that he's still in your head," Leon says with barely contained rage. "I hate that I accidentally put him there."

"He's always there. They all are," I admit, leaning my forehead against the rough bark of the tree. The scratchy feeling is somehow grounding me. "Some days are better than others, but he's always there."

"What can I do? How can I help?"

I turn around to face him, and his expression kills me. He looks devastated, like he's personally responsible for every moment of pain I've ever felt.

"Just... don't disappear on me," I say. "When stuff like this happens, don't treat me like I'm broken. I just need a minute to remember where I am, who I'm with."

He nods, inching closer. "I'm not going anywhere. Take all the time you need."

We stand there in the quiet of the forest, breathing together. Little by little, the tightness in my chest starts to ease. Leon's comforting presence, the smell of pine needles, the sound of Jasper and Falin's distant laughter—it all helps ground me back in the present.

"Feeling better?" Leon asks.

"Getting there." I manage a small smile. "Thank you for not making it weird."

"Thank you for trusting me with your feelings." He offers me his hand, and I take it, letting him guide me away from the tree. "You constantly amaze me, you know?"

I stop and look up at him. "In what way?"

"How well you're handling everything." He takes a deep

inhale, letting it out slowly. "You're stronger than the rest of us, I'll tell you that much."

"My therapist would be proud," I say with a humorless laugh.

"I'm proud," he says. "So fucking proud."

My pulse speeds up, and I squeeze his hand in response.

After a moment of silence, I clear my throat. "I guess we should find more kindling if we want a decent fire tonight. I refuse to put my trust completely in Jas."

"Yes, ma'am. Put me to work," he says in a mock salute voice. I raise a brow and shake my head. "Sorry," he adds. "Was that okay to say?"

"That one's fine. Ma'am makes me feel like a Southern belle or something though. Maybe refrain from using that one around my brother. I know he'll torture me with it."

He squeezes my hand back in agreement.

As we gather sticks together, I catch Leon glancing at me every few minutes, making sure I'm really okay. It'll take some time to get used to again—the way he cares for me. But it might be exactly what I need.

CHAPTER THIRTY-EIGHT

LEON

I watch Bailey more than the fire in front of me. She tosses some more kindling onto the growing flames, intent on her task. It's the small details in her body language that catch my eye—how her shoulders aren't holding the tension they were in the woods earlier, how she's smiling and laughing at Jasper's dumb commentary. Seeing that she's feeling more relaxed allows me to relax too.

I get up from the sunken-in camping chair to grab a beer from the cooler. "Anyone want one?"

"Nah, I'm good," Jasper says. "But what do we have to eat? I'm getting hangry."

I twist the cap off and toss it into the trash bag in the trunk, while peering at the stockpile I organized earlier. "Well, there's—"

"Don't you dare say beans," Falin interrupts. "I have to share a tent with this man. I don't need it to explode from noxious fumes."

"You mean your noxious fumes?" Jasper teases. "Your farts are way worse than mine."

"I do not fart," Falin says with mock indignation.

Jasper snorts, almost losing the sip of beer in his mouth. "Okay... and I'll be the next President of the United States."

Bailey shakes her head, laughing, and comes to join me at the car. "In the other cooler, there's a pack of hot dogs. We could just roast some of those for now."

"Good plan," I say. "Just so you know, I wasn't going to open the beans. Those are just an in-case-of-emergency option. I agree with Falin."

"And I third that thought," she says. "I unfortunately grew up with him and had to share many a tent back in those days. Do not recommend."

I grab the hot dogs from the cooler while Bailey finds the package of buns. It's all so normal—the kind of thing I dreamed about for all those months without her. Cooking together, sharing a meal, being able to see her smile anytime and anyplace. It makes my damn chest ache.

"Should we find some sticks to roast these on?" Bailey asks.

"Already on it," Falin calls from the fire, holding up several long branches she must have collected earlier. "I came prepared."

"Look at you, my nature goddess," Jasper says, grabbing Falin by the waist and tugging her into his lap. They laugh and go back and forth with their typical flirty banter, low enough that their words don't reach Bailey and me. I never wanted to admit it in the past, but being around them as well as Blake and Damon when they were like this, it was hard. I would get in a shitty mood, and I was probably awful to be around. But now, the only thing I feel is happiness for my friends. And maybe a little envy too.

We settle around the fire, spearing hot dogs onto the makeshift roasting sticks. The conversation flows easily between the four of us. Jasper tells stories about camping disasters from their childhood, Falin describes some of the more ridiculous places she's had to sleep during her various adventures around the world, I remind everyone that this is essentially my first time camping and get teased to hell for it. Bailey laughs at all the right moments, adding her own memories from childhood.

I watch her in the firelight, how the glow of it makes her eyes sparkle, how she naturally leans in toward its warmth. She's sitting next to me, our chairs are close enough that our knees bump occasionally. I'm conscious of every small contact, every light graze. I wonder if she is too.

"Remember that time you tried to impress that girl from your English class by cooking over a fire?" Bailey asks Jasper, grinning as she rotates her hot dog. "What was her name? Melissa?"

"Marissa," Jasper corrects. "And I still think it was unnecessary for Dad to call the fire department. The fire wasn't that big."

"The fire department?" Falin almost chokes on her bite. "Oh my God, what did you do, dummy?"

"It was just a little out of control," Jasper says defensively. "The wind picked up and maybe I used too much lighter fluid—"

"You used the entire bottle," Bailey cuts in, laughing so hard she's tearing up. "I remember watching from my bedroom window, horrified that you were going to burn the house down. There were flames shooting three feet in the air! I ran outside and screamed, 'There's a literal fire!'"

"Poor Marissa," I add, grinning as I imagine the whole scene playing out. "What did she do when the sirens started?"

Jasper laughs and shakes his head. "She... may have hidden in the bathroom and called her mom to pick her up."

"Didn't she avoid you for the rest of the year?" Bailey asks, wiping her eyes with the back of her hand.

"Maybe I didn't want to be her friend anymore either, Bails. You ever think of that?"

"Right," Bailey says. "Because you had so many girls falling all over you then."

Falin reaches over and pats Jasper's cheek. "Don't worry, baby. You're much better with fire now. And I promise not to hide in any bathrooms... unless you're in there with me." She winks and kisses his cheek.

We eat our hot dogs and share a bag of chips. Jasper and I finish off another beer while the girls crack open a few seltzers. This night feels nostalgic despite never camping before. It reminds me of summer, spending time at the Shea's, back when things were simpler. When our biggest worry was whether Jasper would hog all the good snacks.

As we're finishing up, and a quiet settles around the fire, Falin stretches and leans into Jasper. "You know," she says casually, "I'm getting kind of tired. All this fresh woodsy air." She makes a clearly fake, exaggerated yawn.

"Already?" Jasper asks. "It's still early."

"I know. But I'm *really* tired." She draws out the word. "Maybe we should turn in early tonight." She gives him a meaningful look that even I notice but it goes completely over his head.

"But we haven't even made s'mores yet," Jasper protests. "I bought all the stuff."

Falin suppresses a sigh and tries again, running her hand up Jasper's arm. "S'mores can wait. I was thinking we could... you know... get comfortable in the tent."

"Oh, are you cold?" Jasper asks. "I can grab you another sweatshirt from the car."

Falin looks like she's about to strangle him. This is peak

entertainment. Bailey catches my eye and our looks mirror each other.

"Actually," Falin says, "Leon, didn't you mention earlier there was some spot you wanted to show Bailey? Something about the view?"

What is she talking about?

I blink at her, confused for a moment, but quickly realize what she's doing. Creating an excuse to get Jasper alone while giving Bailey and me some privacy.

"Oh. Right. That spot by the lake," I say, playing along.

"What spot?" Jasper asks. "That sounds cool. I wanna come."

"Oh my God," Falin says, exasperated. "Just come here." She gets up from her chair and just about drags Jasper into the tent. He must catch the hint finally, since he doesn't object.

She zips their tent shut, calling out "Bye!" in an exaggerated tone. I can't help but shake my head at the whole performance.

"Well that was... something," Bailey says, settling back into her chair.

I blow out a breath and nod slowly. "Subtlety isn't her strong suit."

"I can see that." She smiles and her face lights up against the firelight. "So should we actually go look at this mysterious lake spot? Or was that just Falin being devious?"

"Oh, there's a spot. It's going to blow your mind," I lie through my teeth.

She raises a brow. "Oh really?"

"Absolutely. Prepare to be amazed by my extensive knowledge of this place I've *definitely* been to before and *totally* didn't just make up on the spot." I stand and offer her my hand with mock seriousness. "Your tour guide awaits."

She laughs but lets me pull her up. "By tour guide, do you

mean guy with a questionable sense of direction who may or may not get us lost in the dark woods?"

I try to make a shocked expression but it probably comes out like a goofy grin. "Me? I'd never."

"Well, now I'm totally at ease. How could I possibly refuse such a romantic gesture?"

"Exactly, I'm basically the king of romance. Just wait until you see how I dramatically gesture at... whatever we find out there."

We step away from the fire just as a husky moan sounds from inside Jasper and Falin's tent.

"Oh God," Bailey says. "That's our cue to leave."

She intertwines her fingers with mine, sending sparks up my arm. It's such an innocent touch but it's everything after what she's been through.

I lead her toward the lake, trying to make it look like I know where I'm going, but actually hoping we don't trip over a rock or run into any wildlife. The moon is nearly full tonight, which is honestly a miracle because otherwise we'd be stumbling around in complete darkness. Should have grabbed a flashlight, but it's too late now.

Almost like I planned it, we eventually get to the lake's edge and find a clearing with a rock, large enough for both of us to sit on.

"You actually pulled it off," she teases. "It's beautiful over here."

"And best of all, away from Jasper and Falin right now." We laugh and settle next to each other.

The playful energy from our walk here starts to shift as we sit in the quiet. Sounds of nature fill the air along with the roll of water lapping gently against the shore. Bailey's body is close enough to mine that I can smell her shampoo, close enough to feel the warmth radiating from her. I want to lean in, wrap my arms around her, feel her soft skin against my fingertips.

When I hear my name, I blink, realizing I was completely absorbed with studying her details. "... right, Leon?"

"Uh... yeah, sure." I clear my throat and hope I didn't just say yes to some ridiculous question.

"So... how's your mom doing?"

I suppress a laugh. "You want to talk about Mum right now in my ultra special romantic spot?"

"I wouldn't go that far... I think a family of mosquitos just drained half my blood supply."

She has this way of delivering sarcastic comebacks that I eat the fuck up.

"It's because you're so sweet."

"Wow." She slow claps. "Cheesy line of the year award goes to this guy right here."

I do a mock bow. "I accept. And now for my speech. I'd like to thank—"

She bumps my shoulder. "Don't think that's necessary."

We laugh together, and it actually warms my heart exactly like they say in a cheesy romance movie. The mosquito complaints aside, sitting here with her feels right in a way nothing has for a long fucking time.

"This is nice," she says, scooting her leg closer to mine. "Just being here with you, talking. I missed this."

"I missed it too," I admit. "Every fucking day."

She turns toward me and I can't help it, my hand reaches for her face like it has a mind of its own. My finger trails down her cheek, cupping her chin, stroking along the nearly invisible scar there.

"Leon..."

The way she says my name makes my chest tight. "I held onto every memory while you were gone, replaying them in my mind, thinking about every tiny detail. Sometimes I wondered if I was remembering it better than it actually was, you know? Like maybe I was building it up in my head because I needed something to hold onto. Like I was crazy for thinking it was that good."

Her eyelids flutter as I smooth my finger over her bottom lip. "And now?"

"Now I'm thinking my memory was actually pretty shit, because this, being here with you, touching you—it's so much better than I remembered."

I trace her bottom lip with my thumb again, and her breath hitches. She's so close, so fucking beautiful in the moonlight, and I'm dying. Actually dying to kiss her. The want is so strong it's clawing at my chest, making it hard to breathe.

Slowly, I lean in closer, giving her every chance to pull away, or say stop. I'm so close that we're sharing the same air, but it's not close enough. My forehead touches hers, and I brush a stray piece of hair behind her ear. God, she smells so good... so fucking sweet.

"Bailey," I whisper, barely recognizing the roughness in my voice. "Can I kiss you?"

Her eyes search mine for a moment that feels like forever while my heart pounds against my ribcage. Then, so quietly I almost miss it, she breathes, "Yes."

"Thank God."

I close the distance between us, our lips finally touching, softly, tentatively at first. I don't want to push too hard, or move too fast and fuck this all up. But then she responds, moving her mouth against mine, and everything else fades away. It's just her—my Bailey and her perfect lips, kissing me back.

As the kiss deepens, I slide one hand into her hair and the other around her waist to draw her closer. Fuck. She tastes as sweet as she smells. I've been craving this—craving her, for so damn long.

She slides her tongue over my lip ring before slipping it between my parted lips. I'm goddamn done for. And then she lets out this small moan and I pull back, panting hard.

"Bailey," I look up at the stars before resting my forehead against hers again, not wanting to put any distance between us, but needing to before I take things too far. "You have no idea how long I've wanted to do that."

Her answering breath is just as deep as mine. "I'm glad you asked... That was... I missed you."

"I'll always ask." I drag my nose against hers, and leave a soft kiss on her cheek. "I promise you that."

We sit there for a while longer, until Bailey complains about the mosquitos again. Hands intertwined, we head back in the direction of the campsite. It's easier to find now that my eyes have adjusted to the dark.

We get back to barely glowing embers in the fire. The night is quiet at first. But then the sound of a sleeping bag moving against tent fabric interrupts that, followed by a particularly enthusiastic moan from Falin.

"They're still going?" Bailey asks, groaning.

"Try living with all of them," I say. "It's never-ending."

Although, I can't blame them. If I had Bailey in my bed all the time, we'd be the same way.

"Thank God I'm already in therapy," she says. Her gaze lingers around the campsite and I see the exact moment she realizes that there's only one available tent and her sleeping partner is currently extremely preoccupied and doesn't seem to be finishing anytime soon.

She moves her lips to speak but I beat her to it. "I can sleep in the car," I offer quickly, even though the thought of cramming myself into the backseat, and the subsequent pain that will follow, makes me want to cry. "Or out here by the fire. I'll be fine."

She looks at the dying embers, then at the car, then back at the tent where another moan slips through.

"Don't be ridiculous," she says, though her voice wavers the tiniest amount. "You'll freeze. We're adults. Adults who happen to be in a… *something ship*. We can share a tent."

The last thing I want to do is make her uncomfortable. "It's fine, honestly. If you're not ready—"

"We just kissed. I think I can handle sharing a tent." She heads toward the zippered flap. "Besides, I trust you."

My chest tightens.

"I'll put out the fire so you can start getting ready."

I keep myself busy dousing the fire and cleaning up any remaining food. By the time I'm done, the sounds from the other tent have thankfully quieted down to just low murmurs. It's going to be hard enough being less than a foot away from the woman I love, but add in a soundtrack of Jas and Falin fucking and I might just find the nearest bridge.

"All set?" I ask when I finally work up the courage to unzip the tent.

"Yeah, all good."

Don't fuck this up.

Bailey's already settled on top of the sleeping bag, lying as close to one edge as physically possible. She's changed into an oversized sweatshirt and pajama pants, and her hair is pulled back in a messy bun. She looks so damn beautiful as always.

"There's only the one sleeping bag in here," she says, looking up at me with those big blue eyes.

"Oh. They probably have the extras in their tent. Should I?"

She winces. "That's probably not a good idea. It's fine, we can share."

I swallow hard. "Yeah... okay."

Universe, you're fucking with me now.

She pats the spot next to her before opening the top layer and sliding inside. I keep my shirt on, although it most definitely smells like campfire, but kick off my pants before sliding next to her. "Is this okay?"

"Leon," she says, giving me that sarcastic tone I love. "Just keep your mitts to yourself and we'll be fine."

"Of course."

I got this.

Then she turns to face the tent and her ass is inches from my cock.

I so don't got this.

CHAPTER THIRTY-NINE

BAILEY

I could laugh. Or cry. Or kill my brother. Or maybe all of the above. This will be fine though. It's just two people who happen to have insane chemistry and a history, sharing a small sleeping bag. I meant what I said—I do trust Leon with every fiber of my being. I know he'd never touch me if I didn't give consent. That was true then and it's especially true now.

It's more my own urges that worry me.

I don't want to lead him on. What if I think I'm ready for something more—to be intimate and things get all hot and then boom—I can't go through with it. I'll feel terrible.

No. It's better that I wait until I'm one hundred percent sure that I'm ready. Even though that kiss was incredible. It was gentle but not too gentle. Exactly like I remembered but so much more.

Leon shifts to his back beside me and I'm way too aware of his every breath, his every movement. I stare at the dark blue nylon, willing myself to get tired. All this fresh air... *Come on body, just fall asleep.*

Except my damn leg itches. I try to ignore it, but it gets so bad from the welts forming that I can't help but bend to scratch.

"Uh, Bailey..." Leon says, his voice thick. "You alright?"

"Sorry! Just itchy. These damn bites." I swat at my leg, remembering that it's bad to scratch.

"Okay." He's quiet for a moment before he adds, "You're just kind of grinding against my thigh."

"Shit!" I scoot over, putting a few inches between us. "I'm sorry!"

"It's fine. Is there something I can do? You want some ice from the cooler?"

And have a soggy sleeping bag? No way.

"I'm fine. I'll stop."

The tent falls quiet again, it's just the distant sounds of the lake and our breathing. With Leon's arm right there next to mine, close enough that I can feel the warmth radiating from his skin, it's hard to clear my head. I focus on the rhythm of his breathing, in and out, trying to match mine to his, hoping the distraction will calm me down.

My mind starts to wander back to bad places. I remember lying alone in that cold bed at King's house, my body bruised and wrung dry, dreaming about escaping into the woods. I used to imagine myself running through trees just like the ones surrounding us now, feeling the soft earth under my feet, breathing in clean air. In those fantasies, I'd run until I found safety, until I found home.

Until I found Leon.

"I feel safe with you," I whisper into the darkness, letting the words slip out before I can stop them. To him it probably seems like such a random statement—he has no idea what I'm thinking about, where my mind's at. My cheeks heat and I refuse to face him, even as I feel him turn toward me.

"Yeah?"

"I used to dream, back then... when I was..." I trail off, embarrassed to go on, until his hand rests gently on my upper back, urging me. "I'd have these dreams that I was running through the woods, through trees kind of like the ones here. It was always so dark and I was so scared and alone but I knew I was searching and I was so close. If only I could get to safety. Get to you." Those last three words leave my lips in a whisper.

"Bailey..." His voice is soft. He shifts closer, his hand still warm against my back. "You made it. You're here now. With me."

I finally turn to face him, and even in the dim light filtering through the tent, I can see the pain in his eyes. Pain for me, for what I went through. "I know," I breathe. "And being here, with you, is everything."

He moves his hand to cup my face, and his thumb traces along my cheekbone. The touch is so gentle, so reverent, like he's memorizing my skin, afraid I might disappear again.

"You're safe," he whispers. "I promise you're safe."

I press closer, closing my eyes for a moment, enjoying the way his calloused hand feels against my skin. When I open them again, we're so close I can feel his breath on my lips. The inches between us are charged, electric, and every place our skin touches sends sparks into my veins.

He glides his hand from my face to rest in the gap between us, keeping his palm up. Without overthinking, I rest my hand in his. Our fingers intertwine slowly and somehow it feels more intimate than anything sexual we could be doing.

"Is this okay?" he asks softly.

"More than okay," I whisper back.

We lie there facing each other, hands clasped together, and I will those memories away, instead focusing on his touch. His thumb traces gentle patterns across my knuckles, and each small movement takes my breath away.

I want more, I know that deep within me. I want to close the distance between us, want to feel his arms around me, feel his lips on my skin, his hands caressing me, quelling this growing ache I'm just starting to feel again after everything. But I'll wait—I'll enjoy how perfect this feels. Safe and intimate and exactly what I need.

"Leon," I breathe out. His fingers stop moving and his body slightly tenses.

"Yeah?"

It's right there on the tip of my tongue. All the thoughts in my mind just waiting to flow out. My body wanting to tell my brain to go to hell.

Instead, I squeeze his hand tighter.

"Thank you," I whisper. "For waiting. For being patient with me."

"Always," he says without hesitation. "However long it takes."

His breathing starts to even out after a while, but his hand never loosens its hold on mine. The steady rhythm of his breath calms me and I feel my own body finally start to relax. His hand is warm in mine, the safety of being here with him holding me close, knowing that he'll be right here when I wake up. It's everything I dreamed about in that dark place. Everything I thought I'd never have again.

After a long time of imagining what the future will hold, I fall asleep feeling completely safe.

———

ALMOST A WEEK'S gone by since we camped. Jasper and Falin are back in the city. And me? I'm freaking exhausted. Mom and I are pulling into the driveway from another long, rough day at the US Attorney's office in Albany. Hours of sharing every detail I could remember... Most of the time, feeling like a failure for not being able to give them more.

I want the rest of the monsters involved to get caught, but a part of me wishes my involvement in everything was never discovered. That I could have come home and pretended it was all just a terrible nightmare.

At least my victim's advocate, Lizet, is amazing. She's probably the only reason I haven't completely fallen apart during the prep sessions. Today, when I started hyperventilating during the timeline review, she didn't just hand me a tissue and tell me to breathe slower like everyone else does. Even Mom gets rattled in those moments. Liz sat beside me and started distracting me by talking about her garden. How she plants marigolds every spring because they remind her of her clients. How marigolds are survivors too, blooming even when the weather is awful, even through hail, and wind, and extreme heat. Her voice was so calming that my breathing naturally started to match hers.

"You don't have to remember everything perfectly," she told me afterward, when the prosecutors stepped out. "Your job isn't to be a human tape recorder, Bailey. Just speak your truth, the best you can." She always says things like that. Simple statements that help make me feel like this all encompassing overwhelm is manageable somehow.

Lizet explained that later this week we'll practice what she calls grounding techniques for when I'm on the witness stand. Not just the breathing exercises, but how to find something in the courtroom to focus on if I start to dissociate. How to ask for breaks without feeling weak. She even brought me a small, smooth stone from her garden to keep in my pocket. She said holding onto something tangible might help when I'm feeling stressed.

"The defense attorneys will try to confuse you. They'll do

everything in their power to win," she told me. "But remember, their job is to create doubt about the case. Whatever they do or say, you're an amazing person. A survivor. Don't let them take that from you."

I squeeze the stone in my pocket now as Mom parks the car. At least I know that whatever happens in that courtroom, Lizet will be right there in the gallery. I don't know who else will be there, but at least Alfred and King are corpses somewhere. Only their ghosts will haunt that courtroom.

Each step toward the front door has my stomach fluttering, knowing that Leon's somewhere inside. I could really use a hug today.

I get to the door first and as soon as I open it, I smell something delicious cooking. Roasting chicken with herbs, the rich scent of butter and cream, and caramelized vegetables. I expect to find Dad at the stove, but it's Leon there, stirring a pot, AirPods in his ears.

He's intent on his task and hasn't noticed us come in, so I quietly tiptoe behind him and wrap my arms around his middle. He jumps but only for a second, before he pulls his AirPods out and twists to face me.

"You're home." His lips tip up in a genuine smile.

"Smells delicious," I say, managing to smile back through my exhaustion. "What are you making?"

"Roast chicken," he says, pressing a quick kiss to my forehead. "Figured you both might want something comforting after today."

Mom appears in the kitchen doorway, looking as drained as I feel. "Leon, you didn't have to—"

"I wanted to," he tells her. "Go sit. I've got this."

He moves around the kitchen with surprising confidence, grabbing a bottle of wine from the counter and pouring three glasses. "How did it go today?" he asks, handing us each a glass.

"Rough," Mom admits, taking a long sip. "These prep sessions are harder than I expected. I think I need some air." She glances toward the back door. "Is John out on the deck?"

"Yeah, he's been out there reading for the last hour," Leon says.

"Perfect." She gives my shoulder a squeeze. "I'll leave you two to decompress. Leon, thank you for this. Really."

"No problem. It'll be ready in twenty." Once she's gone, Leon turns his full attention to me. "That bad, huh?"

I hop up on the counter beside the stove, glass in my hand, watching Leon stir salt into the pot of mashed potatoes. "Yup. They want me to go over everything again at the end of the week. Every detail about every person I came into contact with, every place I was taken." I take a long sip of wine, letting the warmth spread through my chest. "I feel like I'm failing them because I can't remember more. The time before Alfred... a lot of it is a blur... the details at least."

"You're not failing anyone. The fact that you're willing to testify at all is incredible. Fuck them if they think otherwise."

I take another sip, and try to let his words sink in. "The hardest part is going to be keeping you guys out of it. The prosecutors want to know how I escaped, but I can't exactly tell them about my boyfriend and his vigilante friends staging a rescue mission."

He goes very still, and I can practically see the gears turning in his head. Then that infuriating Leon smirk starts spreading across his face.

"All I heard from that statement is that you called me your boyfriend."

Heat blooms across my chest. "That's what you're focusing on right now?"

"Can you blame me?" He grins and trains his eyes on me, they're more green than gray today, and I squirm after a few seconds of his undivided attention. "It's like finding out the one thing you've had on your Christmas list is sitting under the tree. Priorities, Bailey."

"I can't with you." I shake my head, but keep our eye contact.

He rests the wooden spoon on the edge of the pot and moves to stand in front of me, my legs on either side of his torso. My pulse picks up as he leans in, murmuring, "I think you can, Firefly."

Those hands, so big and calloused, come up to cradle my cheeks. I suck in a shaky breath, wanting to close my eyes, to hide how much this small gesture affects me, but I force myself to keep them open. If today proved anything, it's that I can do hard things.

He's so close I can feel his warm breath on my lips, can see the flecks of gold in his eyes. He waits there, perfectly still, giving me the choice. Always giving me the choice. The tension between us stretches, warming me all the way to my core, until I can't stand it anymore.

I surrender, allowing myself exactly what I want, what I need, and press my lips to his. Softly at first, letting myself feel everything—the pulsing in my sex, the pounding of my heart. But then Leon makes a rasped sound in the back of his throat, and I deepen the kiss, sliding my tongue against his lip ring, until he pulls me closer. His hands on my waist feel like safety. His lips against mine taste like home. I lose myself in our kiss, not pulling back until I realize I've scooted so close to his body that I can feel the tight bulge in his jeans pressing into me.

I pull back, remembering where we are. Leon closes his eyes for a moment, his hands still gripping my waist, his breathing ragged. When he opens them again, there's heat there, but also obvious restraint.

He takes a second, visibly collecting himself before he speaks. "So," he says in a husky tone. "Boyfriend it is then?"

I smirk at his ability to diffuse tension always. "Yeah. Boyfriend."

He clears his throat and goes back to the potatoes on the stove, unable to hide his grin. "Back to our original conversation, I think you've got this. Remember all the times you had to tell white lies during our first summer. All those library trips Damon pestered you about."

"I was at the library... *Sometimes*. For like ten minutes before meeting you." I bump his shoulder with my foot as he smirks. "And you can't say anything... you were a willing accomplice in my deception."

"Guilty as charged." He tastes the potatoes and adds some pepper. "What else are they asking about?"

My smile fades. "Everyone I was with. They want names, descriptions, anything that might help identify other victims." I take a shaky breath. "I keep thinking about Cat and the others. Wondering if they're still out there somewhere."

Leon's hand stills on the spoon. "Tell me about them."

"Cat was like my anchor in that place. She was so much stronger than me... a fighter. Around my age, maybe a little older, tan skin, dark curly hair, big brown eyes." I close my eyes and picture Cat's face the last time I saw her. How broken she was... how that fight was barely there. "There were others too... Jasmine, Lydia, Katie, Elise. I don't know last names... I guess we never thought we'd need to know them."

"We'll find them," Leon says.

I look at him, trying to judge if he's serious. I should know he'd never say something like that in jest. "But how?"

"Don't worry about that part. You have enough on your plate with the trial. Let me do this for you. All those women, they're someone's daughters, someone's sisters, someone's friends. They deserve to come home too."

My throat gets tight. "You'd really do that?"

"Of course I would. I told you months ago. They matter to you, which makes them matter to me." He turns from the stove to face me fully. "And before you argue, yes, I have time on my hands."

"But what about school or a job or the renovation back in—"

He steps between my legs again, effectively silencing me. "Don't need school right now... and I can do my freelance work from anywhere."

I know he wants to put me and my needs before his own, that's his nature. I can't tell who's more of a caregiver—me or him—but I can't just ask him to pause his life to help me figure out mine. He's spent enough time looking for me already.

"I see those wheels turning in your head," he says, gliding his hands over my thighs in a comforting way.

"You spent so much time already. I don't want to keep you from living your life," I admit.

He brings his forehead to mine. "You are my life."

I don't know how to respond to that. What can I say that would show him how much his patience and support and care mean to me? How I feel undeserving of his love? Before I can come up with something, the oven timer beeps, breaking the tension of the moment.

Leon reluctantly steps back to turn off the timer and check on the chicken, while I pull air into my lungs, still processing what he just said.

Could I let him spend more of his time searching for Cat and the others? And if he finds them, how would that make me feel?

I finish off the last sip of wine in my glass, letting those questions roll around my mind.

"Looks amazing," I tell him, as he pulls the most perfect looking roasted chicken out of the oven. All golden brown, like something out of a cooking show. "Where'd you learn how to cook that?"

He lets out a dry laugh. "Mum... It's my first time, so hopefully we won't die of salmonella."

"Doubtful," I say. "If anything, maybe we'll have a repeat of the hot wing incident."

"Never living it down, am I?"

I shake my head. "Never."

After the day full of legal documents, and questioning, knowing I'm about to sit across from the man I love and eat a meal, something so simple, so pure, makes my heart happier than I could have ever imagined in those dark months of hell. I could get used to this.

CHAPTER FORTY

BAILEY

I've lost count of how many entries I've written.
Time feels weird now... some days drag on forever,
others disappear in a blur of legal meetings and flash-
backs. Too many days I want to just stay in bed and
not get up. I might do just that if it weren't for Leon.

He keeps asking if I want to talk about what
happened. I know he's trying to help, and maybe one
day I'll tell him everything, but for now, it's hard
enough telling strangers. I guess he'll find out if he
comes to the hearings... I almost hope he won't.

Lizet's whole grounding stuff has been helping me
more than a lot of what I've learned in therapy. I
don't know... I guess having something concrete to do
when I start to freak out helps a hell of a lot more
than just yapping on and on about my feelings.

Speaking of feelings... I need to talk about Leon.

Lately I've been wanting to be intimate with him again. Or at least try? Is that messed up? That I can go from having nightmares about being touched to wanting Leon to touch me? Sometimes I wonder if my body is broken, if King and every other man who used me, beat me, left me this way... if their mark is a permanent scar?

I wish I could talk to someone about these feelings... This desire... I guess that's what I'd call it, as cheesy as it sounds.

The other night, when we were kissing in the kitchen, I felt everything almost like I used to, but in a way, it was stronger... deeper. The heat, the need, that familiar ache. For those few minutes, I felt like myself again. But then afterward, I couldn't stop thinking about whether it was normal to want someone that way after what I've been through. Whether Leon would think less of me if he knew how much I still want him, even when I can barely handle a stranger accidentally bumping into me at the grocery store.

He's been so patient. Too patient, maybe. Sometimes I wish he'd just lose his temper, yell at me for being difficult, give me a reason to push him away. It would be easier than this constant gentleness, this careful way everyone treats me like I might break. Is that what I need?

I know he'd do whatever I ask. That's who he is— why I fell in love with him in the first place. He takes care of people. I should probably tell him how I'm feeling.

I applied for my old job at Burger Palace today. Joy

to the world. Stepping foot in there brought me back to high school.

Leon thinks it's too soon. I saw it in his face when I told him, even if he didn't say it. Maybe it is too soon. But I need to feel like I can do normal things again. I need to feel like me. And hey, if I do okay here, maybe I can think about going back to school soon.

I start tonight. I didn't tell him I'm planning to drive myself in. He'll worry, and he's done enough of that for a lifetime.

I CLOSE THE JOURNAL AND SLIP IT BACK UNDER MY PILLOW just as someone knocks on my bedroom door.

"Come in."

Leon pokes his head inside. His hair is messy from sleep and light stubble shadows his jawline. "Morning, beautiful. You're up early."

"Couldn't sleep." I stretch and pat the side of my bed. "What time is it?"

"Almost eight." He lays next to me, pulling my back against his chest. I hum, feeling instantly contented, especially as he folds his hands over my stomach and rubs gentle circles. "Why couldn't you sleep? Everything okay?"

And there is it, the question him and everyone else loves to ask. I know what he means. *Are you having flash-backs, or is it panic attacks? Do you need me to call some-one?* I should appreciate how much he cares, but sometimes it makes me feel like a patient instead of a girlfriend.

"I'm fine. Just thinking about work tonight."

"Right. Your first shift back." His hands still. "How are you feeling about it?"

"Good. Ready." I force happiness into my tone. "It'll be nice to have something to do besides sit around here or at all those stuffy offices."

He nods against my head. "That guy still the manager? The dude who smokes way too much weed?"

"Yeah. Same old Derek. He seemed excited to have me back."

"That's good." He continues his light grazing along my side, sliding close to my ribcage. God, it feels good. "What times? I can bring you in and pick you up."

Here it is, the conversation I've been dreading. "I can drive myself."

"I know you can. I just thought—"

"Leon, I need to be able to do normal things. Like driving myself to and from work." His posture goes stiff behind me so I flip around to face him. Yup, he's rolling his lip ring between his teeth and making that nervous face. "Lee... I'll be fine."

"Of course. I just worry about you being out alone at night."

"It's Burger Palace, not a war zone."

The words come out sharper than I intended, and I can see him flinch slightly. I want to backtrack, give this long explanation that it's not about him, that I'm just desperate to feel capable of something. But before I can figure out how to say it, he nods and rolls to his back.

"You're right. I'm being overprotective." He forces a smile that doesn't quite reach his eyes. "I'll see you when you get home. I should go hop on my computer... got a meeting in a few minutes."

After he leaves, I sit on my bed feeling like the worst person alive. He's trying so hard to give me space while still being supportive, and I keep snapping at him for caring too much.

The day passes in a haze of anxious energy. I must have spent over an hour dressing in my shitty black uniform pants and Burger Palace polo and throwing my hair up in the tightest ponytail I could with my choppy hair.

Looking in the mirror before I leave my bedroom is... something. I feel like a Bailey paper doll wearing the old me dress up clothes but they don't fit the way they should because my edges are torn and frayed.

Leon's in the kitchen when I come out, with his laptop open, working on something that involves multiple screens of code. He looks up when I enter and his face does that thing it always does now—a quick assessment to gauge my mood, my stress level, my general state of being. He smiles though and I can't help my stomach from flipping.

"You look good in a striped polo shirt."

"Thanks?" I sigh and sit in the chair next to him. "It feels weird, putting on the uniform again."

"Yeah." He closes the laptop. "Are you nervous?"

"A little. What if I've forgotten everything? What if I can't handle it?"

"You worked there for two years. It'll come back to you." He reaches out to squeeze my hand. "And if it doesn't feel right, you can always leave."

"I'm not going to leave on my first day."

"I know. I'm just saying you have options. Your comfort is the most important thing."

"You really don't think I should be doing this, do you?"

"I think you should do whatever makes you feel strong and capable," he says carefully. "I just want you to be safe."

"I will be. It's just fast food."

He nods, but I can see him holding back whatever he really

wants to say. Another conversation about being careful, probably, or at least letting him drive me home. Instead, he just says, "Text me when you get there?"

"Of course."

I grab my keys and head for the door, then turn back for one more look. Leon's still sitting there, watching me intently.

"Leon?"

"Yeah?"

"Thank you. For not trying to talk me out of this."

His smile is soft and genuine. "Just promise me you'll call if you need anything."

"I promise."

I'm halfway to work before I realize I'm lying.

My initial nerves subside as soon as I walk through the back employee entrance of the familiar red and yellow building. It's a smooth enough shift. The dinner rush keeps me busy, muscle memory taking over as I take orders, assemble burgers, and run the register. Derek seems relieved to have experienced help, and my coworkers are mostly teenagers I don't recognize who treat me with polite indifference that I find strangely reassuring.

By ten, it's just Derek and me closing up. The place is a wreck and of course Derek went outside to smoke before he'll spend an hour closing out the register... leaving me to everything else.

This is what you wanted, Bailey.

I stack chairs on tables, mop the dining room floor, and wipe down every surface until it gleams under the harsh fluorescent lights. I clean the fryer, scrub the grill, and sanitize the prep area. The repetitive tasks are oddly soothing. It's simple, mindless work that doesn't require me to think about court dates or relationships or anything more complicated than making sure the counters are spotless.

Derek finally comes back inside, reeking of weed. He nods at me, his version of "good job" before disappearing into the office to count money and do paperwork. Which leaves me with the last task... taking out the trash.

I gather the heavy bags from the kitchen and dining area. Three massive grease-stained bags reeking of old fries and burger juice. It's a simple job, nasty but easy, and I've done it hundreds of times before, but as I push through the back door and head across the parking lot and into the alley, my chest tightens up and my limbs get that weak feeling.

"Fuck, not now," I groan.

You're fine. Yes it's dark. Yes, you're alone. But you've got this.

I quicken my steps, heaving the bags higher so they don't drag on the ground and break. The back lot is mostly empty except for a couple cars, but I know there's still a few customers loitering in the front. Stupid teenagers mostly, with nowhere to go all summer.

When I reach the alley, I hold my breath from the stench of rotten food. The dumpster sits about twenty feet away, surrounded by shadows. There's only one flickering light that barely illuminates the empty alley. I hate this. But fuck... I'm going to get through this night. I have to, for myself.

One step at a time, I make it to the dumpster, gagging as I toss the bags in. I make the mistake of releasing my breath and sprint out of the alley to get back to fresh, un-rancid air.

I'm still sprinting when I hear voices.

"Yo, hold up."

I freeze, even though every instinct is telling me to run. Three guys come around the corner from the front lot, maybe around my age, probably drunk by the way they're moving. They're close enough to the employee entrance to keep me from getting back inside. I'm essentially trapped unless I want to get any closer to them.

"Where you running?" the tallest one says, grinning. He's wearing a backwards cap and a T-shirt with some surfing company logo on it.

Fuck. I don't want to talk to them, but maybe it'll help this from becoming a whole situation.

"Just finished work. Heading home."

"This late? That sucks," another one says. He's shorter, stockier, with small eyes and acne. "You working alone?"

I clutch my hands into a tight fist, eyeing the distance between me and the back door. "No, my manager's inside."

"Cool, cool." Baseball Cap nods like we're having a normal conversation. "Hey, you want to hang out? We got some drinks in the car."

My heart pounds so loud I'm sure they can hear it. I back away from them, but there's nowhere to go. My keys are inside with my purse, all I have is my phone in my pocket. "Thanks, but I'm good. Really tired."

The third guy looks up from his phone like he's just catching on to what his friends are doing and steps sideways, essentially cutting off my path to the employee entrance completely. "We're not weird or anything. "

"Yeah, we're just hanging out. Our boy here just broke up with his bitch of a girlfriend. It's celebration time." Baseball Cap says, like that's supposed to reassure me. "We're just looking to have some fun. I saw you inside earlier. You seem cool."

I keep backing away. "I really need to get going. My boyfriend's expecting me."

"Your boyfriend?" Small Eyes grins and shoots me this look that makes my stomach churn worse than the reeking garbage. "He's not here though, is he?"

I can tell they think making me uncomfortable this way—scared, even—is entertaining. They're fucking giddy with it. Baseball Cap takes another step closer and the smell of beer hits me.

"You seem stressed," he says. "We could help you relax. It's summer, you're young, we're young. Live a little."

I glance behind me and notice Derek's beat up Honda. He never locks it, I remember that from last time I worked here.

Please.

I sprint again, reaching his car in seconds. But I don't realize Baseball Cap is right there behind me until I'm fumbling with the handle, trying to get inside to safety.

He reaches for me, his hand grazing my shirt, and everything shatters.

I'm not in the parking lot anymore. I'm back in King's house, hands reaching for me, voices telling me what they're going to do, nowhere to run, nowhere to hide—

"Don't touch me!" The words rip from my throat, raw and desperate.

I'm so loud that he jumps back, startled. So I use that moment to throw myself into his car and slam the locks. My whole body shakes as he pounds on the window. Within seconds, the other two join him. They're laughing and talking to each other in loud drunken voices.

"What the hell?" I hear through the glass. "Crazy bitch!"

"Open the door! We're just trying to talk!"

I can't breathe. My vision tunnels, dark spots flicker at the edges. Derek's car smells like weed and pine air freshener, and I'm hyperventilating so hard I might pass out. My hands shake uncontrollably as I pull my phone from my pocket.

I don't want to call Leon. That'll just prove that he was right. I'm not ready for this. I'm not strong or capable or—

Before I can dial a number the sound of an engine rumbling and bright light streaming into the window pull my gaze up.

Holy shit.

A motorcycle roars into the parking lot, headlight cutting through the darkness. The guys step back, suddenly looking less confident as the bike pulls up close. The engine cuts off, and through my tears and panic, I see a familiar figure swing off the bike.

Leon.

CHAPTER FORTY-ONE

LEON

I'VE BEEN SITTING ON MY BIKE IN THE SHADOWS OF THE adjacent parking lot for twenty minutes, engine off, watching the Burger Palace like a fucking stalker. Bailey would lose her shit if she knew I was here, but I couldn't help myself. The thought of her walking out to an empty parking lot alone at night makes me sick to my stomach.

When I see those three assholes walk from the front lot to the back and corner her, every rational thought in my head evaporates. Pure rage floods my system as Bailey backs away from them, and retreats into some other car like a trapped animal.

So much for giving people the benefit of the doubt. Too often my instincts are spot on. If it looks like a predator, walks like a predator, talks like a predator... it's usually a predator.

I start the bike and roar into the lot, not giving a damn that Bailey will know I was here. The three pieces of shit back away as I cut my engine. *Not so confident now, are you?* I take off my helmet slowly, giving them an extra second to wonder who the fuck I am.

It takes everything in me not to lunge for them right away. Especially that tall one in the cap... I saw him run after Bailey first. He'll fucking pay.

"Is there a problem here?"

The tall one holds onto the car for balance. Wasted, I knew it. "Nah, man, we're just having some fun with our friend."

"Your friend?" I take a step closer, and the three exchange glances. Through the car windows, I can make out Bailey's silhouette. She's pressed against the opposite door, clearly terrified. "Because from where I'm standing, it looks like you've got her trapped in that car. That's not *friendly* behavior."

"She's being dramatic," the shorter one says, backing away. "We were just trying to be nice."

My laugh is cold. "Nice. Right." I look directly into the window, somehow finding Bailey's eyes through the smudged glass. "Bailey, you okay in there?"

I hear a muffled sob, and something inside me breaks. That sound flips a switch and gone is the semi-calm version of me. I need violence. But not now... not with her watching, scared out of her mind.

"Here's what's going to happen," I say, making my voice razor-sharp as I memorize each of their faces in the dim light. "You three are going to get in your car and drive away. Right now."

"Or what?" Baseball Cap tries to sound tough, but there's uncertainty in his voice now.

I take another step forward and lift the hem of my shirt, flashing my weapon. I'm close enough to smell the beer on their breaths, as I spit venom in their faces. "Or I make sure you regret ever coming near her."

The quiet one swallows hard. Baseball Cap and Small Eyes look at each other, silently communicating their options. I might be outnumbered, but my presence has shifted the entire dynamic.

"Whatever, psycho," Baseball Cap finally says. "She's not even that hot."

That does it. The careful control I've been struggling to maintain snaps like a dislocated joint. Something I'd very much like to do to him right now. But instead, I continue to memorize his face, burn it into my memory along with every detail I can capture about his friends. The logo on Small Eyes shirt. University Athletics. The scar on Tall Boy's chin. The license plate number as they walk toward their beat up Jeep. HDR 4792.

I don't move until their car starts and they drive out of the lot, taillights disappearing into the night.

But I'll see them again soon.

Right now though, Bailey needs me. I tap gently on the car window.

"Bailey? Can you unlock the door for me?"

The locks click, and I slide into the cluttered passenger seat. She's curled up against the driver's door, shaking so hard her teeth are chattering, and tears are streaming down her face.

"Hey," I say softly, not reaching for her yet. "You're safe. They're gone."

"I'm sorry," she gasps between sobs. "I'm sorry, you were right, I wasn't ready—"

"Stop." I keep my voice gentle but firm. "You have nothing to apologize for. Those pieces of shit had no right to come near you."

She looks at me with red, swollen eyes. "How did you know?"

I rub the back of my neck, knowing she's not going to like my answer. "I was already here. Waiting in the parking lot next door."

Her jaw slackens. "You followed me."

"I was worried." The words sound inadequate even to my own ears. "I know you wanted to do this on your own, but I couldn't stop thinking about you walking out here alone. I drove myself crazy... I'm sorry."

She stares at me for a long time, and I brace myself for her anger. Instead, she launches herself across the center console and into my arms, sobbing against my chest.

"Thank you," she whispers. "Thank you for coming."

I hold her tight, feeling the aftershocks of tremors in her small frame, and that cold rage starts building again. Those fuckers put their hands on her. Made her afraid. Made her feel helpless.

"Can you drive?" I ask after her breathing starts to even out.

She nods against my chest. "I think so."

"Let's get your stuff, then you can follow me home. Stay right behind me, okay?"

"Okay."

I help her out of the car—her manager Derek's, she tells me as we walk back toward the employee door. I refuse to let her go inside alone, and we pass the office where Derek is laughing at a YouTube video behind the partially closed door. I clutch my fists to stop myself from going in there and wringing his neck for being such a useless shithead.

"Don't," Bailey wraps her hand around my arm. "It's not his fault."

I guess I'm not that great at hiding my feelings. I nod, stuffing my anger down deep so it can stew and grow until I can release it on those three fucking predators.

Bailey grabs her purse and keys from behind the counter while I keep watch by the back door, scanning the parking lot for any sign those assholes might come back. They won't. I could see it in their eyes when they drove off. But my protective instincts are in overdrive right now, so I can't help but stay vigilant.

"Got everything?" I ask as she rejoins me.

She nods, clutching her purse against her chest like armor. "Yeah."

I walk her to her car—a small used Honda that her parents helped her buy a few weeks ago. She gets in and starts the engine while I fire up my bike. I pull out first, checking my mirrors constantly to make sure she's still behind me as we wind through the dark streets toward home.

But with every stoplight and turn, my mind keeps circling back to those three guys. To the way they cornered her. To that final insult as they walked away.

By the time we pull into the driveway, I've made a decision.

I hold Bailey's still shaking hand and help her into the house, get her settled with a cup of tea and tell John and Amanda that she had a panic attack but she's okay now. It doesn't stop them from coming out of their bedroom to hover over her. If she's pissed at me for involving them, I'm sure I'll hear about it tomorrow.

"I'm going to put my bike in the garage," I tell her, pressing a kiss to her forehead. "I'll be right back."

Instead, I head straight to my laptop.

License plate HDR 4792 gives me everything I need. Twenty minutes of searching through DMV records and I have a name. Brayden Hutchins, twenty-one, registered address is ten minutes from Burger Palace.

From there, it's child's play to find his social media accounts. Brayden's not very careful about his privacy settings. His Instagram shows him with the same two friends from tonight, tagged as Easton Stewart and Gabe Morrison.

I spend the next hour digging deeper. Brayden's a business

major on academic probation. Gabe is pre-med with a pristine GPA he's probably desperate to protect. Easton's on a partial athletic scholarship from the wrestling team.

They all have something to lose, and that's just from me scratching the surface. I'm sure the deeper I dig, the more I can find.

I scroll through months of their posts, looking for more ammunition. It doesn't take long to find what I need. Photos from parties, comments they probably forgot they made, tagged posts from other students involved in various scandals on campus.

By midnight, I have enough information to destroy all three of their futures. A few anonymous tips to the right people, some strategically leaked screenshots, and their lives will implode. Academic suspension, scholarship revoked, medical school dreams crushed.

But that's not enough. They need to understand consequences in a more immediate, physical way.

I close the laptop and grab my keys.

First, I drive by Brayden's house, searching for his Jeep. It's not there and the other two don't live as close. I doubt they finished their night early and there's only one place in town three drunk college kids would be. I twist the throttle and gun it toward O'Connell's Pub.

The Jeep is right there in the lot, parked crooked as fuck. A little work with my blade and two of his tires are slashed.

You're not going anywhere tonight, Brayden.

I wait next to it, and like clockwork, the three come stumbling out a half hour later. It must be my lucky night because they don't come toward the Jeep, but instead head a few feet away from the pub's door, toward a dark area on the side of the building. Pulling out smokes, they fumble to get them lit, laughing about some bullshit loud enough for me to hear.

It's time.

"Having a good night, mates?" I ask once I reach them.

They turn, and I see the moment recognition hits Brayden's face. "Oh shit. It's the boyfriend."

"That's right." I move closer, and they inch toward each other on instinct. "That business earlier isn't sitting well with me. It seemed you lot thought my girl was just being dramatic?"

"Look man, we don't want any trouble," Gabe says. "We were just having some fun."

Ah, the quiet one finally speaks up.

"Fun." I repeat the word but it tastes sour in my mouth. "Let me tell you what I think happened. You three saw a beautiful young woman alone in a dark parking lot and thought you could intimidate her. Thought you could corner her and make her do whatever you wanted."

"That's not—" Easton starts, but I cut him off.

"I'm not done." My voice comes out in a harsh whisper. "See, here's the kicker, boys. That woman you decided to terrorize? She's been through more hell than your privileged little minds can imagine. And you assholes thought it would be fun to add to it."

Brayden tries to puff up his chest. "Calm down. We didn't do anything illegal, dude. We were just talking to her."

I move fast, grabbing Brayden by the front of his shirt and slamming him against the brick wall. His skull connects with a crack, knocking his precious cap onto the ground.

"Just talking?" I say with my face inches from his. "Then why was she locked in a car having a fucking panic attack?"

I release him and step back as he stumbles, grabbing the back of his head. When he brings his hand into the light, it's covered in crimson.

"Here's what's going to happen," I tell all three of them. "You're going to remember this conversation every time you think about approaching a woman who doesn't want to talk to you. You're going to remember what it feels like to be scared and cornered."

Gabe is shuffling backwards, but I grab his wrist and squeeze until I feel bones grind together. "Especially you, pre-med. Lot of pressure maintaining that GPA, isn't there?"

His eyes widen as my words sink in.

I shove him away and turn to Easton. "Athletic scholarship's nice. Be a shame if something happened to it."

"You're fucking crazy," Brayden says, wiping more blood from his head.

"Maybe." I straighten my jacket. "But I'm the kind of crazy that doesn't forget. Ever."

I start to walk away, then pause. "Oh, and mates? When you wake up tomorrow, don't be surprised if you get some news. A little gift from me. Consider it a reminder that actions have consequences."

I leave them there, against the wall, whispering among themselves, knowing they'll spend the rest of the night wondering what I meant... calling me a crazy bastard. But by morning, they'll start finding out that I'm not just a crazy bastard, but someone who can ruin lives.

Some people only learn when they get the shit scared out of them. Let's hope for those three pricks it's a lesson that only needs to get taught once.

Bailey will never find out about this. She doesn't need to carry that weight. This was on me—my need for vengeance on her behalf. Tonight, she needs comfort, and I'll make sure she has it.

I hop back onto my bike with a grin, knowing that those three will lose sleep tonight. Maybe I didn't end their pathetic lives like I very much wanted to, but it's something.

CHAPTER FORTY-TWO

LEON

I slip back into the house around 3 AM, using the downstairs entrance so I don't wake anyone. As I take off my jacket and pants, my phone falls out of my pocket, lighting up with unread messages from Bailey.

Fuck. I didn't tell her I was leaving. In my adrenaline-fueled rage, she became second to vengeance. I tap the screen and feel even more like shit.

> Firefly: Taking a long time to move your bike… I'll be in my room, come see me when you're done.

Twenty minutes later, another came in.

> Firefly: I guess you went out, which is totally fine btw. I'm going to try and get some sleep. Hope you're ok.

And the last came in about an hour ago.

Firefly: Woke up to a noise, thought it was
you. Just let me know that you're okay.

Guilt hits me like a freight train. Here I was, getting my revenge while she was upstairs worrying about me, probably replaying the night's events over and over. After everything she's been through, the last thing she needed was to wonder where I'd gone or if something had happened to me.

I quickly type back:

I'm home. Sorry for worrying you. Coming
up now.

But as I pass the bedroom door, I see her silhouette curled up on top of the blankets. She fell asleep down here... waiting for me.

I stand in the doorway, watching the rise and fall of her ribcage. Even in sleep, she doesn't look peaceful. There's tension in her shoulders, and her hands are clenched into small fists. The trauma from tonight is still working its way through her system.

I should let her sleep. But as I start to turn away, she stirs.

"Leon?" Her voice is groggy but alert.

"Hey. I'm sorry, love. I didn't mean to wake you."

She sits up slowly, running a hand through her disheveled hair. "I wasn't really asleep. Just... resting my eyes. Where did you go?"

I hesitate, not wanting to lie to her but also not wanting to burden her with what I did tonight. "I needed some air. Had to clear my head after what happened."

She studies my face, and I can see she doesn't entirely believe me, but she doesn't push. Instead, she rubs her temples. "I can't sleep anyway. Every time I close my eyes, I see them.

Feel their hands reaching for me. They morph into the others and..."

I climb onto the side of the bed next to her, still giving her space. "That's understandable, what they did was so fucking not okay. I'm sure your body will take a long time to come down from the adrenaline."

She cradles her face in her hands, her voice a whisper. "I hate this. I hate that I can't do simple things like take out trash without falling apart. I hate that I need rescuing."

Her pain is a knife in my chest. "It's not you. What happened tonight won't happen again, I—"

"You don't know that." She sighs, and meets my gaze. "I wish I was strong."

I have so many things to say. So many ways to tell her she is strong. Fuck. She's stronger than anyone I know. But right now, I know that more words won't help.

"Can I hold you?" I ask as I guide a loose strand of hair from her face.

She nods, and slides over to make room for me.

Instead of turning with her back against my chest like usual, she stays facing me so we're side by side. I toy with her hair, smoothing it away so I can look into her eyes. They're still red and swollen from crying and it makes me want to find those assholes all over again.

She reaches out and rests her palm on my chest, feeling the rhythm of my heart beating. We're quiet for a long time but it's not uncomfortable. It's calm, like we're finally able to breathe together. The space between us is charged like always... that constant pull to get closer... to let her feel how much I love her. But I won't push her, not tonight.

"Leon," she whispers, as her fingers trace small circles on my chest. "I'm tired."

"You should try to sleep—"

"No." She shakes her head, and curls her fingers in the hem of my shirt. "I'm tired of feeling like I have no control over my life. Tired of things just happening to me. Tired of being scared all the time. Tonight, those guys... they tried to take my choice away. Again." Her voice grows steadier. "But I'm here now. Safe. With you. And for once, I want to choose what happens next."

I choke on a breath as she reaches her hand under my shirt, sliding it along my stomach.

"Bailey..."

"I want you," she says softly. "I want to remember who I am underneath all the fear and pain."

Her fingertips glide upwards against every ridge of my abs, sliding against my nipples before traveling lower again. I'm trembling under her touch, barely holding myself together.

"I want to feel strong again," she continues. "And beautiful."

Before I can respond, she rests her hand on the band of my boxer briefs, and slides in closer so there's no space between us. Her eyes blaze as she presses her lips to mine. It's different from the other kisses we've shared. This one is purposeful, claiming. She kisses me like she means it, like she's choosing it, and it's the most perfect thing I've ever felt.

When we break apart to catch our breaths, she rests her forehead against mine.

"Show me I'm not broken. Help me remember what it feels like to be touched by someone who cares."

My heart pounds as I search her face, making sure this is what she really wants. "Are you sure?" I ask, needing to hear her say it one more time.

"Yes, please, Leon... touch me." She slips her hand into my boxers, wrapping her fingers around my cock.

"Bailey," I groan out her name like a prayer.

"Yes?" she asks innocently, stroking my length.

"Fuck, baby... Bailey... I'll come if you do that."

She hums, this throaty, sexy sound that drives me wild. I suck in a breath and force myself to regain some composure.

"Clothes off," I say. "I don't want anything between us."

Her hand leaves my boxers and she wastes no time in stripping off her pajamas. A part of me is still being cautious. Still waiting for her to change her mind. But then she's completely bare for me. Her perky tits looking delicious, her curves glowing in the dim light, those thighs slightly parted so I can see her perfect pussy. Fucking hell, I'm nervous... I feel like a virgin again.

"Now you," she says, looking up at me with those big blue eyes.

I pull my shirt off and toss it on the floor, then slide my boxers off next. A satisfied smile pulls at her lips, giving me the courage I need.

"You're perfect," I whisper. My voice is hoarse with want and something deeper. "You're so fucking perfect, Bailey."

I tangle my fingers in her hair and pull her in for a kiss. With her skin against mine, I can't hold back. I touch every inch, barely fucking believing that this moment is real. That I'm not dreaming.

She moans against my lips, wrapping her top leg against my hip, pulling herself closer. Nails drag down my back as she sucks my bottom lip. Dipping her tongue inside, she toys with me, grinding her hips as she runs her tongue over mine.

Her wet pussy slides along my length and Christ, it takes all my restraint not to thrust into her right now.

"Touch me," she says, as she kisses down my neck, sucking my earlobe. "I want to feel you everywhere."

My hands roam her body, cupping her breast, my thumb brushing over her nipple. She gasps and arches into my touch, and I feel my nervousness melting away. This is Bailey, *my* Bailey, trusting me with every part of her.

"Show me I'm not broken," she breathes against my skin.

I capture her mouth again, pouring everything I have into our kiss. I kiss her neck, her collarbone, wanting to savor this... to take my time, but also I've waited so long. We both have.

My hand travels lower over the curve of her waist, and hovers over her pussy. I wait for a heartbeat.

"Please," she moans.

"Fuck," I grit out as I slide a finger between her soaked lips. Holy fuck, she's wet and warm and perfect. "You feel just like I remember."

"Mmm." Soft noises of pleasure escape her lips, as I dip my finger inside her tight hole, sliding my finger wet with her cum up to her clit. "Oh God, yes... right there."

"You want me to rub your clit until you come, Firefly?"

I don't even know what I'm saying. I'm crazed with lust... needing to feel her come apart on my fingers.

She arches into my hand, rocking in rhythm with my fingers, chasing her release.

"Yes... I'm in control," she murmurs. "I want... I want this."

"That's right, love. You're in control. Take what you want. Use my hand to get off."

Her legs tense and she shudders, a low shaky breath escaping her. I've never seen anyone so goddamn beautiful in my life. Bailey coming for me is like the world's greatest work of art. Her back arches, her tits pushing up against my face. I suck a nipple hard, and she bites her lip, cursing under her breath.

"Holy shit," she breathes, as her body shudders in small aftershocks. With both hands on my shoulders, she rolls me to my back, straddling me. "I need you inside me."

"Baby... Oh fuck—"

I'm cut off by her gripping my cock and lining it up with

her entrance. Inch by inch she sinks down, and holy fuck I've never felt anything better in my entire life. I'm the luckiest man alive right now with Bailey, naked, riding my cock, giving me every ounce of her trust, of her body.

"You're so big," she says. "I forgot."

"You can take me, love. Just breathe... go slow." I reach for her clit, rubbing tight circles until she sinks down further, moaning. "That's it. This tight cunt was made for me."

She's barely moving, waiting for her body to adjust to my size and it's so fucking hard to keep still. One hand keeps circling her clit while my other grips her hip, guiding her lower.

"Your piercings," she gasps. "They're so good."

I arch up slightly, moving my hips to help her along. "You like the way your pussy swallows them up, don't you?"

"Fuck, Leon... do that again."

I arch again, using my grip on her hip to push her down until I'm fully seated inside her. We groan, words I can barely recognize, and when she starts to move, I'm fucking done for.

With her head thrown back, she rocks, using my cock exactly how she wants to. It's everything to see her like this. Confident and so fucking beautiful.

"You're so goddamn sexy, Bailey." She leans in and I suck her nipple, nibbling gently until she gasps. "So perfect... I've wanted this for so long. We were made for each other."

"I'm close," she says, changing her angle so her clit is grinding against me. Our mouths are inches apart so I meet her there, clashing together in a tangle of teeth and tongues.

I can feel her walls tightening around me, her orgasm building with each rock of her hips. "Fuck, I'm gonna come, baby. You feel so good."

"Come in me. I need it."

My cock swells as I pump up into her, both of us shuddering and shaking our release. She cries out, just as I shoot deep inside her, filling her up with every drop of cum I have. There's something so fucking hot about her taking it all. Knowing she's full of me and no one else. God, I'm so lucky I can barely breathe.

She rocks, riding out her release before falling onto my chest. I wrap my arms around her, holding her close, feeling our bodies melt into each other as our breathing slows.

I don't know when I fall asleep, but when I wake, it's not the stream of sunlight coming in from the entryway door that I notice first, it's Bailey's tight heat, enveloping my cock as she rolls her hips over me.

"Bailey," I whisper, wrapping my arms around her. "Fucking hell, baby... This is the best wake up call I could ever ask for."

She laughs and the sound is everything... but then she leans forward and pushes her tits against my face and I'm fully awake. I wrap my arms around her and roll her onto her back.

"You're so wet and ready for me, aren't you?" I say as I thrust into her, groaning a rough sound from the back of my throat.

"Yes, please," she begs, spreading her legs wide to accommodate my size.

"Taking me so fucking well." I pump with my hands on either side of her face holding my weight. "Jesus Christ, Bailey, you feel incredible. I'll never get enough... fucking never."

"Don't stop."

Never. I slide in and out, savoring the feeling of fucking her like this. Like I used to. With each thrust, I only want her more. Want to get deeper, feel closer. Her nails claw my back in the best feeling of painful pleasure. I love it. I can't get enough.

She cries out, moans and guttural sounds. I do too. It's wild and animalistic and pure. I thrust harder, deeper, lifting her leg and throwing it over my shoulder so I can grind against her clit.

"Come around my cock, love. Let me feel you," I say against her, before sucking her bottom lip between my teeth.

"So close..."

Our skin slaps as I pick up speed, feeling my own release building deep in my spine. I see it in her face, feel her pussy tightening... and fuck, I won't last much longer.

She grips my ass, squeezing hard and I lose it, shuddering as I come inside her. "Holy fucking shit," I groan between thrusts. Her body shakes beneath me as she comes hard, arching up to ride out every last second.

I'm so gone for her. There's no one else in this world for me. Just Bailey. Just my Firefly.

I pull out, wishing I could stay inside her forever. But knowing my cum lines her walls makes my chest swell.

I crawl down her body, planting kisses along her stomach as she pants and digs her fingers into my hair. When I reach her pussy, I marvel at the way our cum looks together. It drips down her thighs, and I gather it in between my fingers and look into her eyes.

"This belongs inside you."

And with a groan, I stuff my cum-covered fingers back inside her. My cock twitches at the perfect sight of her swollen dripping pussy.

And fuck, I'm already hard again.

CHAPTER FORTY-THREE

BAILEY

Today is the day I've been dreading. The day I'll have to sit in front of a room full of people and recall everything that happened to me. I don't know though. I think after finally telling Leon how I felt... finally having sex again... I feel different. Like voicing how I was tired of being powerless, tired of letting life happen to me without my own choosing, made me actually feel all the strength that everyone's been telling me I have. The dread for today is still there though, like a weight holding me down. I guess that's normal?

Lizet's stone is in my pocket. I've already taken it out multiple times this morning. She was right, it does help me focus on something tangible. Let's hope all our prep sessions will make the process easier.

The whole family will be there. My parents, of course, but also Jasper and Falin, Damon and Blake, and Leon. At first I didn't want him there, but now I

*realize that it might help him heal as much as it's
helped me. Anyway, I better go finish getting ready.
Mom wants to leave extra early to beat traffic. Wish
me luck (as I wrote that I cringed... I know you're
literal paper. Please, Universe, let no one ever find this
journal).*

WALKING DOWN THE COURTHOUSE STEPS FEELS LIKE
hiking down a mountain I finished climbing. My legs are shaky,
whether from adrenaline or exhaustion, I can't tell. Three and a
half hours. Three and a half hours of recounting every detail,
every face, every moment I've spent the last few months trying
to forget and simultaneously trying to remember clearly
enough to help other girls... to make those monsters pay.

"You did beautifully, Bailey." Lizet gives my arm a gentle
squeeze.

I only nod, because I can't trust myself with words... not
yet. My throat feels raw from talking, from crying, from forcing
myself to speak clearly even when the words felt like coughing
up shards of glass. The stone from her garden is still clutched in
my palm, worn smooth from me rubbing it during the hardest
parts.

Leon is a steady presence beside me. He looks just as
exhausted as I feel. Come to think of it, everyone in my family
does. Almost like they were all holding their breath the entire
time, scared to breath, afraid to lose it in there. "How are you
feeling, love?"

"Tired," I manage. "But... different? Is that weird?"

"Not at all," Mom says, wrapping her arm around my

shoulders. She's been crying on and off all morning, but trying to hide it. "You were so strong in there, sweetheart."

Dad clears his throat, his voice gruff with emotion. "Proud of you, kiddo."

It must have been hardest on them to hear the details of what I went through. I'm still their little girl after all.

Jasper jogs up the courthouse steps toward us, with Falin, Blake, and Damon close behind. His eyes are red-rimmed and puffy. He had to go grab the others from the coffee shop next door since there was a limit to how many people could come inside the gallery.

Blake wraps me in a hug, sniffling back tears. "How'd it go?"

"Good, I think," I say, managing a small smile as I take in their grave expressions. "I told them everything I could remember."

"The prosecutors seemed satisfied," Lizet adds. "Bailey's testimony was comprehensive and credible. It should help their case significantly."

A familiar squeal echoes from across the street, and I look up to see Layne practically sprinting toward us, Ashley jogging behind her in heels that are definitely not made for running. They both look so different from the last time I saw them. Maybe it's their conservative court outfits, or maybe it's just that they've matured so much. We all have.

"Bailey!" Layne reaches me first, pulling me into one of her bone-crushing hugs. "Oh my God, I can't believe you're here. You're okay." She pulls back to look at me, tears in her eyes. "How'd it go? We tried to get inside but they were dicks."

"It went alright," I say, laughing slightly.

She pulls me back in for a hug. Ashley joins her, and for a moment I'm transported back to simpler times. Cramped dorm rooms and late-night talks and worrying about nothing more serious than Layne's drama with Clay.

"I can't believe you guys drove all this way," I say when they finally release me.

"Are you kidding?" Ashley says. "We wouldn't miss this. Layne threatened to steal my car if I didn't drive her."

"I absolutely would have," Layne confirms. "But I probably would have crashed it into a tree within five miles, so thanks for the ride, bestie."

"Yeah, she's a terrible driver," Ashley says with a laugh.

I introduce them to everyone and it's only awkward for a moment, until Layne recognizes Leon and makes her signature holy shit eyes at me. And then he speaks and she grips my arm like her knees are about to buckle.

"That accent," she whispers so only I can hear. "Panty-melting."

"Oh my God." I shake my head. "You're not wrong though."

"So," I say, looking around at our large group, "I know exactly where I want to go for lunch. There's this cafe about ten minutes from here that has the best grilled cheese and tomato soup. Total comfort food."

"That sounds perfect," Mom says, still looking at me with that mixture of pride and concern.

"We'll need two cars though," I continue, doing a quick head count. "That's... a lot of people."

"I can drive the college crew," Ashley volunteers, jingling her keys. "Plus whoever else wants to cram into my backseat."

"I'll go with you," I decide, surprising myself. A few months ago, the thought of being separated from Leon or my family would have sent me into a panic. Now it feels... normal. Like something the old Bailey would have done.

Leon's eyes dart in my direction, crinkling with concern, but he doesn't say anything.

"You okay with that?" I add, looking at him.

"Of course," he says, though I can see him fighting his protective instincts. "We'll follow right behind you."

"Shotgun!" Layne calls out, making me laugh.

"Absolutely not," Ashley says. "Bailey gets shotgun. You can sit behind me and complain about my music."

As we walk to the parking garage, Layne loops her arm through mine like we used to do walking to class. "So," she whispers, "Leon is even hotter than I imagined. And that voice? Jesus. I'm still blushing."

"You're ridiculous," I say, failing to hide my grin.

"I'm serious. If you hadn't claimed him first, I would have climbed that man like a tree."

Ashley snorts from behind us. "Layne, you literally just broke up with Clay three weeks ago. For like the fifth time."

"And? A girl can appreciate fine British craftsmanship."

"Oh my God, I can't with you." I laugh, and it feels so good. So normal. "You two haven't changed at all."

"Neither have you," Layne says, but then she slows her steps and clears her throat. "I mean, you have, obviously. You're... stronger. A complete badass. But you're still you. Still our Bailey."

After everything I went through today to hear her say those words softens that weight in my chest.

I squeeze her in a side hug. "So tell me about Clay."

WE PILE into Ashley's car, which still smells like the bubblegum air freshener she's been using since freshman year. She immediately connects her phone to the Bluetooth and starts blasting the same pop playlist she always played on repeat.

"Some things never change," I mutter, but I'm smiling.

"Don't even pretend you don't love it," she says, pulling out of the parking spot with the same aggressive driving style that used to terrify me. Now it feels like the least scary thing I've encountered.

Ashley turns down the volume. "So Bails, we need to know everything. I mean, not everything everything, but... are you okay? Really okay?"

I glance in the rearview mirror and see Layne's lip quiver. "Yeah, I think I am. Finally starting to be, anyway."

"We were so worried," Layne says, her voice thick. "When you just... disappeared. And then when the news broke about the trafficking ring, and we realized..." She swipes at her eyes. "Sorry, I promised myself I wasn't going to cry."

"It's okay," I say softly. "I'm here now. I'm okay now."

"That Leon guy seems pretty obsessed with you," Ashley says, her voice raising an octave. "The way he was looking at you on those courthouse steps? Damn girl, you're lucky."

"He's..." I pause, trying to find the right words. "He saved me. In more ways than one."

"Good," Layne says, wiping her eyes. "You deserve someone who treats you like the queen you are."

THE CAFE IS small and cozy, with mismatched furniture and the smell of melted butter and fresh herbs. We push three tables together to accommodate everyone, which causes a bit of chaos as chairs are rearranged and orders are discussed.

I end up between Leon and Layne, with Ashley across from me next to Blake. It's surreal, watching my two worlds collide like this.

"So Ashley," Blake says, making conversation, "What are you studying?"

"I'm an education major. Same as Bailey." Ashley glances at me. "Are you planning to go back to school?"

It's the first time anyone's asked me directly about my future plans. "I... I don't know yet. Maybe. I'm still figuring things out."

"You have all the time in the world," Leon says quietly, wrapping his hand in mine under the table. The simple act makes heat spread up my chest and onto my cheeks. "There's no rush."

"Exactly," Falin adds. "College will always be there when you're ready. Life experience is just as valuable as classroom learning."

Layne raises an eyebrow at that. "Speaking from experience?"

"Something like that," Falin says with a small smile.

I realize if the two of them ever got together the world may not survive the chaos.

When our food arrives—grilled cheese and tomato soup for me, just like I wanted— I take a moment to look around the table. My parents are deep in conversation with Damon about something random. Jasper is making Ashley laugh with some ridiculous Jasper story. Blake and Falin have their heads together, quietly talking. Leon is eating his sandwich but watching me with that careful expression he can't help but have.

And Layne... she's studying me over the rim of her coffee cup.

"What is it?" I ask her.

"Nothing, just..." She tilts her head. "I'm so happy you're okay. Sorry, I know I must look like a sap, but losing you that way...it was hard."

"I know." I drop my sandwich and reach for her hand. "I'm okay... or at least I will be. I promise."

"I'm sorry for leaving you alone," she says quietly. "That night, at the club. It was my fault."

"Layne. You know that's not true."

She shakes her head and hides her face in her coffee cup. "I can't stop blaming myself."

"Hey," I say, squeezing Layne's hand tighter. "Look at me."

She reluctantly meets my eyes, and I can see all the guilt she's been carrying clear as day.

"What happened to me was not your fault. You were having fun. I chose to leave on my own." I lean closer, lowering my voice. "The only people responsible for what happened are the monsters who took me. Not you. Never you."

Her eyes fill with tears again. "But if I left with you—"

"They would have taken both of us. Or they would have waited for another opportunity. These weren't random guys, Layne. They were hunting. It was planned." I take a shaky breath and images of Jasmine in that hotel room flicker in my mind. "If anything, I'm glad you weren't there. I'm glad you're safe."

She swipes at her cheeks with her free hand and nods. My words may not have sunk in yet, but I hope she believes them. I know I do.

Layne dabs her eyes with a napkin and gazes around the table. "Your family's pretty amazing. I mean, your actual family was always great, but this whole crew..." She nods toward Leon, who's now deep in some animated conversation with Jasper about motorcycles. "They really love you."

"Yeah," I say, feeling warmth spread throughout my limbs. "They do."

"And Leon," she adds with a smile, "definitely worships the

ground you walk on. Every time you so much as shift in your chair, his eyes track you to make sure you're okay."

I glance at him and like clockwork, even while talking to Jasper, he's keeping half his attention on me. When he catches me looking, he gives me a soft smile that makes me melt.

"He's pretty great," I admit.

"Pretty great?" Layne scoffs. "Bailey, that man would burn the world down for you. I can see it in his eyes."

"He kind of already did," I whisper.

Layne goes back to eating, getting sucked into conversation with Ashley and Blake. Leon's hand rests purposefully on my thigh. A gesture to show he's here even as we chat with other people.

No one brings up the testimony, and for that I'm grateful. I want to put it behind me, as much as I know it'll always be there like a wound that will never fully heal.

I look around at this weird, wonderful collection of people —my parents who never gave up hope, my brother who searched for me relentlessly, his girlfriend who's become like a sister, Damon and Blake who risked everything to help find me, Leon who literally saved my life in every way that matters, Lizet who helped me find my voice again, and my college friends who drove hours just to be here for me.

Leon catches my eye. "Everything alright, love?"

I nod and rest my head on his shoulder. "Everything is great."

CHAPTER FORTY-FOUR

BAILEY

So the testimony went well. It helped that everyone was there for me. I felt stronger with their support. And knowing I wasn't just speaking for myself, but for others still out there. That was huge.

But now that it's over, I keep thinking about what comes next. Not just the final pieces of legal stuff, but... everything else. My life. My future. My relationship with Leon.

Maybe school? Maybe looking for a more permanent job. I don't know. I don't want to end up living with my parents forever though. And I refuse to let Leon take care of me without being able to pull my weight. It's a lot to think about.

Right now he's on a virtual walk through of the Firefly Center. They've finished the therapy rooms and most of the dorms. It looks like the place will be up and running before the new year. It's wild to imagine.

Maybe one day, I'll go there. A long time from now when my cuts aren't so raw. It could be healing. Give me closure.

Speaking of that, I've been doing some research. About trauma and intimacy and all the stuff therapists talk around but don't really get into the details of. At least mine doesn't. I found these articles about something called therapeutic role play. It's basically where survivors can revisit parts of their trauma in controlled ways to take their power back.

At first, it sounded completely insane. Like, why would I want to put myself through anything that reminded me of what happened? But the more I read, the more it started to make sense.

Leon's been so patient with me. So careful, still. Even after the last time I broke down.

I know he's scared of pushing me or triggering me, and I love him for that. But I'm starting to realize that what I need isn't just gentleness. I need to feel powerful again. Desired. In control.

I need to take those bad moments and look them in the eye. Make them my own.

The articles talk about exploring power dynamics safely. Where the person who was victimized gets to be the one calling the shots. Where they can say exactly what they want and how they want it, and their partner follows their lead completely. Where they can reenact specific scenarios to face them head-on.

God, even writing this down makes my heart race. But not in a bad way? More like... anticipation. I'm wet even thinking about it. Which I guess is a good thing?

Part of me is terrified to bring this up to Leon. What if he thinks I'm weird? What if he can't handle what I ask of him? But another part of me—the part that spilled my guts in court, the part that survived everything those monsters did to me—that part knows he'll understand. That part knows I deserve to heal however I need to heal.

I think I'm ready to talk to him. Yeah. I'll tell him what I've been reading and what I think might help. The worst thing that could happen is he says no, right? But knowing Leon... knowing how much he loves me... I don't think that's going to happen.

Okay. When he gets off his call, I'm going to do this. I'm going to be brave.

IT TOOK ME A FEW DAYS TO WORK UP THE NERVE TO GET into the details of what I wanted. Leon had to coax it out of me, but once I started describing scenarios, he didn't look at me like I was crazy or weird. He understood completely.

We spent hours talking through boundaries, safe words, what I thought might help and what I absolutely didn't want to try.

And tonight is the night. Or at least I think it is. One of the things we talked about was the element of surprise.

I'm down in the basement apartment, laying in bed alone. Leon's stripped the room of most of the clutter, leaving only the bed and dresser. Already my mind starts to travel back to those early months where I was alone in a room like this, nothing but the broken thoughts in my head and the waiting... so much waiting for the pain and torment to come.

The waiting is the hardest part. It always was.

I pull the thin blanket up to my chin, even though I'm not cold. It's more for comfort. The basement has that same slightly musty smell, that same claustrophobic feeling of being cut off from the world. My heart is already starting to race, but not entirely from fear. There's anticipation, maybe even excitement mixed in.

I'm choosing this.

A door slams somewhere upstairs and I jump. Just my parents, probably. But I remember what it was like to flinch at every noise, to wonder if this time would be the time someone came for me. My muscles tense on instinct.

I don't know when Leon will show up. It could be any minute, or hours. Or maybe it won't happen tonight at all. That part gives me that familiar flutter of panic in my stomach.

Normal sounds of the house settling help to calm me. Water running through pipes, the furnace humming, the whir of the ceiling fan. I try to read the book I brought down, but I keep rereading the same sentence until I finally give up. My mind keeps drifting to what Leon and I talked about, what I asked him to do.

I sigh and stare at the ceiling. Time feels like a blur—maybe minutes pass, maybe hours. My eyes are drifting shut when I hear something outside the door.

Footsteps... heavy and deliberate.

I shove my book to the side with trembling hands and listen closely, fighting the urge to curl up into a ball.

The footsteps move closer to the bedroom door.

My whole body tenses as I stare at the door handle, waiting for it to turn. This is it. This is what I asked for. What I need.

The handle rattles, and I bite my lip to keep from making a sound.

I'm already soaking my underwear, my nipples are hard too. I should feel shame for that, but I don't. I want this. I'm in control.

Leon bursts through the door, dressed in a tailored suit with a red tie. Nothing like what he would normally wear. His expression is cold and predatory. So different from the gentle demeanor he usually has around me.

I scramble up the bed, yanking the blanket all the way up to my neck. "No," I cry. "Get out."

"Did you really think you could hide from me?" His voice is deeper than usual, with that razor sharp edge I've only seen him use on enemies.

"Please," I beg.

"Begging won't help you, little girl."

My breath catches. Even though we planned this, even though I know it's him, my body reacts like it did all those months ago. Adrenaline flooding my system. My body trembling in fear.

He steps into the room and closes the door behind him. The sound of the lock clicking makes me flinch, but the wet heat between my legs intensifies.

"Take off that blanket. Let me see what I paid for."

I shake my head, not trusting my voice.

He slows for a moment, his eyes widening in a look that's all Leon. I nod, giving him the okay. He swallows hard but shifts back into the persona we practiced.

"I said—Take. It. Off."

"No," I cry out. "I won't."

I hold the blanket tighter, like it could actually protect me. Like this thin fabric could work as a shield from someone so big and powerful.

"I think you want to be punished." I shake my head aggressively. "I didn't pay for some slut who won't do as she's told."

Then he lunges for me, wrapping his fingers around my ankles and pulling me to the edge of the bed. I put up a fight, kicking and squirming away from him all while heat builds and builds in my core.

I kick him hard in the thigh and he hisses a breath. "You'll pay for that."

"Stop, please! I'll be good."

Memories flood my mind, but I push them away, focusing only on Leon's features.

"You'll be good because I'll make you."

Tears stream down my cheeks and Leon pauses, for only a second, before he rips my underwear down my legs. I kick and thrash some more, finally getting free of his grip and sprinting toward the door. It's no use. He catches me around the waist, slinging me against his chest. His hands greedily dig into my hips and work their way up to my breasts, squeezing and kneading in a way that makes me have to bite back a moan.

"These tits are mine. I'll paint them in my cum." I let out a hushed cry that's somewhere between struggle and pleasure. "And this pretty little cunt... I'm going to destroy it."

He throws me onto the bed and I push myself away as much as I can before he grabs my legs. "Stop moving or I'll make you," he grits out.

Here it is. What I asked for. The part that really worried me.

I take a shaky breath. "Make me then."

He reaches for my neck and squeezes with enough pressure that it feels real. That I actually feel the flow of air into my chest dwindle. With his other hand, he finds my soaked pussy, thrusting two fingers inside me without warning. My eyes roll back from both fear and pleasure.

I can feel the change in Leon's posture as soon as he sinks into my pussy. He feels how wet I am. How much I want this. It turns him on too.

He exerts more pressure on my neck, grasping right in the spot we researched about. Enough to make it feel real without actually hurting me.

Leon making me come was never part of the arrangement, but right now I don't know if I can hold back. Pleasure shoots through me like little electric shocks.

"Does the little slut like to be choked?" he groans against my ear. "This wet cunt sure feels like you do."

I moan, even though the sound comes out strangled. My hips buck against his fingers like they have a mind of their own and all at once Leon pulls out and releases my neck.

"I didn't pay to pleasure you, you filthy whore." He slaps the palm of his hand against my pussy and I see stars.

"Oh God," I moan, unable to hold it in.

Roughly, he flips me over, yanking my night shirt all the way up my back. "Let's see if this hole was worth it."

I grip the sheets, clawing my way up the bed to get away from him, but it's no use. His hand is heavy against my back, holding me exactly where he wants me as he unzips his pants. He kicks my thighs open wide with his leg as he maneuvers my hips up.

I bite down on my bottom lip as he spears into me from behind, giving me no time to adjust to his size. "No!" I cry.

In answer, he yanks my hair, lifting my face off the mattress so I have no choice but to look into his eyes as he fucks me raw. Grunts and groans escape his lips as he thrusts into me deeper, harder.

It feels so fucking good.

Then I remember that I don't want it to feel good.

I kick out, and fight my way off him, hissing as his cock slips out of me. I turn and spit right in his face. "Fuck you! Stay away from me or I'll cut your dick off!"

He smiles as he wipes my saliva down his face, hand coated in it, he slips a finger into his mouth and sucks.

"You'll learn to watch that dirty mouth."

"No!"

I'm giddy on the power. Elated. Ecstatic. A part of me wants to abandon the scene and climb on top of Leon, taking what I want. But what I really want—need—is to be used and abused and thrown aside. And he's doing such a good job giving it to me.

I grab a pillow from the bed and toss it at him as he lunges for me. His cock juts out from his body like an iron rod. "Get over here. Let me finish with you."

"Never!"

He rushes to me and pins me against the wall, bringing his hand back to my throat. I claw at him, scratching until blood comes back on my nails. With his free hand, he pins my wrists above my head. Something flickers in his eyes... devious and dark, and then he releases my neck and shoves my shoulders down until I'm kneeling on the tattered carpet.

"Be a good girl and suck my cock."

That phrase.

It normally makes me break down. But right now, I let it slide off my back. I shake my head to the side, keeping my lips clenched shut until he forces them open and shoves his cock deep into my throat.

"That's it," he says. "Take it. Gag on it."

The cool metal of his piercings glide against my tongue and his musky taste, a mix of both of our juices is so good I hold back a moan.

I pretend to fight him. Clenching my jaw. Running my

teeth over his length. But somewhere I lose myself in the feel of him. Maybe it's when he breaks and groans my name. Or maybe it's his fingers in my hair, guiding me up and down on his cock.

"Close," he hisses. "Fuck."

I feel it too. His posture going rigid, his balls tightening. He pumps in and out, harder. Faster. Spit and tears run down my cheeks as my air supply gets cut off.

And just as he's about to come, he pulls out, spraying jets of warm milky white all over my face and chest.

God, it's hot. I know it shouldn't be. I'm not supposed to want this, but I do. Very much so.

For a moment, we both just breathe. The room is silent except for our ragged inhales and exhales. Leon's cum is cooling on my skin, and I'm still kneeling on the carpet, gripping his thighs, feeling dizzy and exhilarated and completely wrung out. Then Leon drops to his knees in front of me, cupping my face—gentle now, so different from moments before.

"Bailey," he says softly, his voice back to normal. "Love, look at me."

I meet his eyes and see only Leon there. Concerned, loving Leon. The mask is completely gone.

"Are you okay?" His thumbs brush over my cheekbones, checking for any more tears. "How do you feel?"

"I..." I have to clear my throat. My voice is hoarse.

How do I feel? Truly? I search my body for signs of a panic attack coming on. For anything that feels remotely bad, but there's nothing.

"I feel... good. Really good."

Relief floods his features. He reaches for the towel we'd left on the dresser, and gently cleans his cum from my face and chest.

"You were incredible," he murmurs as he works. "So brave. So strong."

"Was I?" I lean into his touch, feeling boneless and safe. "It felt... It felt like I was taking something back."

"You were." He helps me stand on shaky legs, then guides me to sit on the edge of the bed. "You were in control the entire time, even when you were pretending not to be."

I nod, processing that.

"How are you feeling?" I ask him. "That couldn't have been easy for you."

Leon sits beside me, pulling me into his arms. "It was difficult. Seeing you scared, even knowing you wanted it... But knowing it was helping you heal? That made it worth it."

"The choking part," I say quietly. "When you had your hand on my throat..."

"Too much?" His body tenses.

"No, it was perfect. You did exactly what we practiced." I trace patterns on his chest, loving the way his breath catches in his throat. "I could breathe the whole time, but it felt real enough to face that memory."

"And when I called you those names..."

"That's exactly what I needed to hear. To have someone say those words to me and know they don't mean them. Know they love me."

He leans his forehead against mine, and plants a soft kiss on my lips. "I do love you. So much."

"I know." I pull back to look at him. "And I love you for doing this with me. For understanding what I needed."

"How do you feel about... trying this again sometime?"

The question makes my pulse speed up, but in a good way. "Yeah. I think I'd like that. Maybe we could try some of the other scenarios we talked about?"

"Whatever you need," he says simply. "Always."

I curl against his chest and he wraps his arms around me. "Thank you."

"No, thank you," he whispers, laying me down on the remaining pillow. "For trusting me with this."

He gets comfortable beside me, tucking his large body against my back, holding me like he never wants to let go. I close my eyes and let myself melt into his warmth.

CHAPTER FORTY-FIVE

LEON

THE GOLDEN LIGHT OF LATE AFTERNOON FILTERS THROUGH the trees as I sit on a park bench, watching Bailey across the meadow. She's walking around the small pond, smiling at a family of ducks gliding across the water. She looks so damn peaceful it makes my chest ache.

It's been six months since we found her at Alfred's estate. Almost five months of watching her slowly, carefully piece herself back together back at home. Some days are harder than others. The nightmares still come, but they're less frequent now. She still flinches at unexpected sounds, still needs space when the memories slip into her conscious mind. But she's healing.

It's a beautiful sight, watching her heal.

My sketchpad rests against my knee, the pencil between my fingers moving almost unconsciously as I capture the way the light catches in her hair. It's grown past her shoulders again. She's put on weight, healthy weight and muscle. Her eyes are bright and cheeks full again. She looks more like herself each day, though I know she'll never be exactly who she was before. None of us will. There's no erasing who we are now.

The leaves are just beginning to turn at the edges, hints of gold and amber that show autumn is here. It feels fitting, going into this season of change. We're all changing, adapting, learning how to be together again in this new reality. Living with the consequences of our actions.

I check my phone. She should be here any minute now. My heart hammers against my ribs. I haven't been this nervous in I can't say how long.

"You alright?"

Bailey's voice draws me back to the present. She's walking toward me, eyebrows raised. "You look like you're about to jump out of your skin. What's going on?"

Before I can answer, a figure emerges from behind a cluster of oak trees near the parking area. Recognition hits Bailey like a punch and she staggers back a step, her hand flying to her chest.

"Cat?"

The young woman approaches slowly, her dark hair falling to her shoulders, her body and face almost as gaunt as Bailey's was when we found her. She's wearing jeans and a simple blue sweater, and although she's thin and weathered, she looks remarkably good for someone who's gone through what she has.

"Hey, New Girl," Cat says, her voice soft but strong.

Bailey doesn't speak. Can't speak, it seems. Tears stream down her cheeks as she covers her mouth with both hands. For a moment, I think she might collapse, but then she's running. Cat runs too, and they collide in the middle of the meadow, holding each other like they're afraid the other will disappear.

I stay on my bench, giving them space, but my pencil never stops moving. This moment needs to be captured. The way they cling to each other, the raw emotion on both their faces, the pure joy of being reunited. My chest tightens as I watch them.

After a long embrace, they pull apart enough to look at each other, hands still gripping each other's arms.

"How?" Bailey says. "How did you get out? Where have you been?"

Cat wipes her eyes with the back of her hand. "It's a long story. And your man," she glances over at me, "he found me about a month ago. Been trying to convince me to see you."

Bailey turns to look at me, her eyes wide with questions and gratitude. "You found her?"

"I had some help," I say, trying to downplay the weeks of searching, the dead ends, the sleepless nights spent following every possible lead. "Falin and a private investigator."

They walk toward me hand in hand. Bailey has this look on her face like she can't believe Cat is real, that if she lets go of her hand she could vanish into thin air.

I scoot down for them to sit beside me, but they choose to sit in the grass in front of the bench, Bailey with her feet tucked under her and Cat with her legs crossed.

"Things got really weird after you left," Cat starts as she picks the grass between them. "They moved us around constantly... Sometimes different places every day. Houses, motels, offices... a few nights we even slept in the vans. King's guys were paranoid, always talking about raids, about people disappearing. It was just me and Lydia by then. One morning we woke up in some sketchy motel and realized we were completely alone. No guards, no handlers. Nothing."

Cat looks up at Bailey. "So I ran. Found my way to my abuela's house, got my little brother, and we moved to the Oregon coast. Been there ever since."

"Oregon?" Bailey's voice is full of wonder. "I can't believe... God, Cat, I thought about you every day. Worried about you, about everyone..." She grabs Cat's hand again. "What about Jasmine?"

"Still missing," Cat answers, barely able to meet Bailey's eyes. "I'm saving up for a private investigator... It's just hard with money."

I make a mental note to set aside a large sum for her. From what I've learned of Cat, she won't want to accept it, but I'll find a way.

They talk for the next two hours. Cat tells Bailey about finding her grandmother, about the relief of being back with family, about slowly learning to feel safe again on the quiet Oregon coast. She talks about helping raise her little brother, about getting her GED, about the job she has at a local restaurant.

I finish one drawing and start on another—capturing their expressions as they laugh, as they shed tears, as they hold space for the people they lost. It's sad and beautiful all at the same time.

Bailey tells Cat about the testimony and Cat looks at her with awe. She explains why she decided to skip speaking with law enforcement. I can't say I blame her... not with all the corruption we uncovered.

Finally as the sun dips lower, coloring the puffy clouds in hues of pink and orange, Cat stands and brushes grass off her jeans.

"I should probably get back to my hotel. I have an early flight tomorrow."

"Wait," Bailey scrambles to her feet. "You can't leave already. We just—"

"I know," she says. "I'd stay longer if I could, but I gotta get back to the kid." There's a smile on her face that tells me she's more than happy to have that excuse.

They hug, and we walk Cat to her rental car. "Promise me you'll call," Bailey says.

"I promise." Cat turns to me, holding her hand out to shake. "Thanks for taking care of my girl. You've got a real one."

Our handshake is firm and Cat gives me a look that says hurt her and you'll answer to me. "Don't I know it," I respond.

"And thanks for finding me. For finding us."

She gets into her car, starting the engine. We step away, but at the last minute she rolls down the window. "Hey, if you hear anything about the others, let me know." I watch her chew her lip for a second before she adds, "Even Elise."

Bailey smiles and nods—I'm sure she understands exactly what Cat's talking about.

As Cat's taillights disappear down the road, I run my hand through my hair. "Shit, I should have told her about Firefly."

"No," Bailey says, slipping her hand into mine. "I don't think Cat would go. That's not her. She does things on her own, in her own time. I can't believe you found her. I can't believe she's alive and free and..."

"She's a survivor," I say, tucking a strand of hair behind her ear. "Like someone else I know."

Bailey steps closer to me, close enough that I can smell her shampoo and count the freckles on her nose. "I don't know how to thank you enough. Seeing Cat again. That meant everything to me."

"You don't have to thank me, love."

She spots my sketchbook, slung under my arm and gestures for it. "Can I?"

I haven't shared many of my drawings with Bailey, or with anyone really, but I flip to the page that shows the moment her and Cat first saw each other. The shock on her face, the way Cat's whole body sagged in relief.

"Oh my God." Her eyes widen as she takes in the details. "This is incredible."

She flips through, her expression more and more in awe as she takes in my work. I've captured every detail from the day. Pure joy. Pure gratitude. Pure hope.

She hands it back to me and wraps her arms around my chest. "I love you so much."

Hearing those words is like a soothing balm. I know she does and it's not the first time she's said it, not even close, but each time hits deeper than the last. Like she means it more, like there's less fear behind it.

"I love you too," I murmur into her hair. "More than you know."

As we walk back to my bike, Bailey leans against my side, and I can tell her steps are lighter, more hopeful. This reconnection with Cat gave her something she didn't even know she needed—proof that healing is possible, that they both survived, that the connections they made in that hell could still exist in freedom.

"I wish it could have been different for Polly," she whispers as I hand her the helmet I had fitted for her. "Sometimes I close my eyes and picture her walking through my front door, smiling. She'll drop a note on my table and leave the way she came."

"Was that something she did?" I ask, wanting to know more without prying too deep. "The notes, I mean."

She nods and slides the helmet on. "Always. Little words of encouragement. Sometimes silly drawings. She made everything less heavy... I think she's the only reason I survived there so long without changing who I am."

I start the bike and feel her arms wrap around my waist. As we pull out of the parking lot, I think about the drawings in my sketchbook, about Polly's notes, about Cat calling Bailey "New Girl" like no time had passed at all. Some connections survive everything. Distance, trauma, even death. They leave marks that don't fade, impressions that stay with us long after the person who made them is gone. Today proved that. Hell, the past two years of our lives proved it even more. No matter where we are... through the fires of hell and back, I know the people I love, the ones who love me too, that those connections are stronger than iron. Those bonds are everything.

Bailey's grip tightens around me as we hit the main road. A gesture of trust. To anyone else it may not seem like much, but to me, the simple gesture that she trusts me with her life carries all the weight in the world. She's choosing to hold on. To me, to this moment, to whatever comes next.

My sketchbook is full of memories, most of them burned into my mind long before I committed them to paper. Bailey's face when she hugged her parents for the first time. Her expression when she took her first real bite of chocolate after over a year of barely eating. The way she smiled listening to Jasper tell one of his ridiculous stories.

It all has one common theme—hope. Unguarded and real. That's what I'll carry forward into the future. Not the nightmares or the guilt, not the fire we walked through to get back to each other. Just Bailey believing that maybe we can all survive anything.

And maybe we can.

EPILOGUE
BAILEY - ONE YEAR LATER

THE SOUND OF OUR COFFEE TABLE SCRAPING ACROSS THE hardwood makes me wince. Leon's going to have a heart attack if Jasper puts another scratch on it. It's bad enough they brought the cats over and they're getting hair all over Leon's precious keyboards. It's actually pretty funny watching Leon with Q-Tips and cans of compressed air trying to keep the spaces between the keys meticulously clean, especially when he can't help but scoop the kitties up and kiss their little faces when he thinks no one's looking.

"Careful with that, you animal," Leon calls from the kitchen, but it's all in good fun. He's used to Jasper's chaos.

"Calm your tits," Jasper shouts back. "We need the space. Tonight's serious business."

I close my textbook, *Trauma-Informed Care for Adolescents*, and stretch my arms above my head. I've been reading case studies for hours, trying to understand how kids process violence. It's been super informative, especially with my firsthand experience as a guide. I'm hoping to get a jump on my assignments for this semester before mid-terms.

"Bailey, get in here!" Falin yells from the living room. "We need the list."

The police scanner crackles from its spot on the kitchen counter. I wish I could say I've gotten used to the white noise like everyone else has. It's still jarring, but I understand their need to listen for certain keywords. Leon's laptop is open next to it, his screen showing surveillance from around town. Even on fight club night, we're always working.

"Coming," I call back, stepping over Havoc, who's sprawled in the hallway like she owns the place. Mayhem's perched on the windowsill, tail twitching as she watches a car drive by the semi-busy street.

The living room's been transformed in the time I've been reading. They pushed the furniture against the walls, rolled up the area rug and shoved it behind the couch, and moved Leon's prized PlayStation to another room. They've gotten their little monthly ritual down pat. I still don't get the need to beat the shit out of each other for fun, but maybe I will after tonight. I have a surprise up my sleeve.

"There's our bookworm," Damon says, not looking up from where he's checking the clip in his gun before setting it on the side table. They all stay armed, even during downtime. "Ready to watch your man get his ass kicked?"

"Leon can handle himself," I say, settling on the floor next to where Blake's organizing her first aid kit. She's gotten scary good at stitching people up since we started this whole thing. Perks of knowing an almost doctor. "What are the stakes tonight?"

"Loser gets the next cleanup duty," Falin says, cracking her knuckles. "And I'm talking full cleanup. Body disposal, scene scrubbing, evidence burning. The whole fucking nightmare."

Leon walks in from the bedroom wearing only gym shorts

and nothing else. I can't help but drink in his perfectly sculpted body. Did it suddenly get ten degrees hotter in here?

"All I heard was evidence burning," he says, heading right toward me. "What kind of shit are you stirring tonight, Falin?"

"The kind that keeps you out of prison, pretty boy," Falin shoots back with a smirk. "Unless you'd prefer orange jumpsuits to your fancy leather jackets."

"We've got that thing planned for next week," Damon cuts in, all business. "Someone's got to deal with the aftermath... and it's not gonna be me. We have plans. Right, Angel?"

Blake's cheeks color instantly. "You better win then."

The "thing" is a child trafficker who's been operating out of a warehouse downtown near campus. Leon and the guys have been tracking him for months, building a case that'll never see the inside of a courtroom. After a few key Brotherhood members got away scot-free recently, we don't bother with the law anymore.

"I vote Blake sits this one out," I say. "She's got that practical exam coming up."

"Absolutely not." Blake stands, rolling her shoulders. "I've been dealing with cadavers all semester. I need to hit something that's not dead."

Leon meets my gaze with a knowing smirk. "Alright. What are the ground rules?"

"No permanent damage," Damon says. "We need everyone functional for next week."

"And no knives," I add. "The landlord's already suspicious about the bloodstains."

Jasper grins, pulling his shirt over his head. "Not even tiny ones?"

Falin slaps him on the back and he fakes a pained howl.

The scanner buzzes to life. We all pause, listening, but it's a domestic disturbance call. As much as we'd love to intervene, that's not exactly what we're looking for. These days, we're hunting bigger prey.

I pull out my iPad and type out everyone's names in the random pairing organizer app. After one too many sore losing arguments over the past few months, we keep things completely random now.

"Falin and Jasper, first round," I announce. "Winner faces *me*."

All heads turn my way, clearly shocked. This is the first time I've included my name in the mix. I've been secretly training with Leon, but no one else knows that.

"Bailey," Blake says carefully, "are you sure about this?"

"What, you don't think I can handle it?" I challenge, standing up and pulling off my sweater. Underneath I'm wearing a sports bra, and I catch Leon's eyes widening slightly as he takes in the muscle definition I've built over the past few months. And my chest. Most definitely my chest.

"Oh shit," Damon mutters. "Bails has been holding out on us."

Falin's grinning like a kid on Christmas. "This just got interesting. Hope you've been saying your prayers, boys."

Jasper looks between me and Leon, realization dawning. "You sneaky bastards. How long have you been training her?"

Leon shrugs, but there's pride in his eyes. "Long enough."

"Well," Falin says, stretching her arms, "let's get this started. You ready, Big Guy?"

"Always ready for you, Trouble."

Jasper and Falin circle each other in the center of the room while Blake blasts her emo playlist. Those two are all business. It's kind of scary really. They'd never actually hurt each other though... *I think*. But sometimes there's this edge to the fights. We've all changed since we started this vigilante shit. Gotten darker. More unhinged. So I guess it wouldn't surprise me if things got out of hand.

"Remember," Damon says, "loser gets to scrub blood off concrete next week."

"No pressure," Blake adds with a smirk.

Their fight starts fast and wild. Jasper may have inches on her but Falin's been training with cops her whole life. Plus, I'm sure Jasper's trying not to hurt her—although he'd never admit that to Falin.

"Come on, Fal," I cheer. "Hit him where it hurts."

She gets him in a chokehold somehow, and her arm locks around his throat. Damn, I should be training with her... She's incredible.

I swear I see something flicker in her eyes... something similar to the look she's gotten when she knows she's about to torture information out of a target.

"Tap out," she demands.

"Never," Jasper gasps.

But he's getting wobbly. We all know what Falin's capable of when she's focused. She could put him to sleep if she wanted. Or worse.

Finally, he taps her arm twice and she releases him immediately. He drops to his knees, coughing and massaging his throat.

In a matter of seconds, she's in front of him and they start kissing. Correction—making out. I groan. "Get a room!"

He's still my brother and I don't need a front row seat to how turned on violence gets these two.

"I second that," Blake says, tossing a roll of gauze at them.

"And I third," Leon adds. "There's innocents present." He cradles Havoc, who fully woke up once she saw the gauze fly across the room.

They pull away, flushed and panting. "I think I hurt

myself," Falin says, cradling her arm in the fakest way. "Jas, come help me to the bedroom."

"Wow," Damon says with a laugh. "At least say you're going to fuck. We can handle it."

"Uh, speak for yourself." I toss more gauze at him, earning a laugh from Blake.

"Fine, we're going to fuck. Bye!" Falin grabs his arm and pulls him toward the staircase.

Lucky for them, they claimed the guest room before Damon and Blake did.

"So," Leon says, setting Havoc down and standing up. "Your turn, Firefly. You ready for me?"

I smile, and reach up to kiss his chin. "Remember, I don't want you to go easy on me."

"Wouldn't dream of it," he says, but there's something in his voice that tells me he's lying.

We circle each other in the center of the room, my adrenaline spiking even though I know this is only practice. Leon's got height and reach on me, weight too, but I've been training hard. Really hard. And I've been watching how they all move, learning from their techniques.

"Ready?" Damon asks.

I nod, keeping my eyes locked on Leon's. The moment Damon gives the signal, I move fast. Faster than Leon expects. I duck low and drive my elbow toward his ribs. He blocks it, but barely.

"Shit," Blake breathes. "Bailey's been busy."

Leon's eyes widen with surprise and a hint of pride. "Fuck, where did that come from?"

I grin and come in with another swing, which he blocks. He has that serious look in his eyes now. "Better keep up," I say, as I come in with a combination we've been practicing for weeks.

Somehow we end up on the floor grappling, and I can tell

he's holding back. Every time he gets me in a position where he could end it, he hesitates. It's sweet, but frustrating as hell.

"Stop it," I pant when he lets up his guard.

"Stop what?"

"Treating me like a dainty princess." I break free and scramble back to face him with my hands on my hips. "If you don't fight me for real, I'll never get better."

Leon glances at Damon while rubbing the back of his neck. "Bailey—"

"No. You want me to be part of this world? Then treat me like I belong in it."

That gets something to shift in his expression. *Good.* I'll never learn if they don't challenge me.

I mount him and go straight for a choke, and I guess my words struck true because he's not holding back anymore. He bucks me off him, and pins me easily, both of us sweating and breathing hard.

"Better?" he asks.

"Much," I say, even though I lost. "At least now I know where I actually stand. We need to practice ground fighting more."

The scanner suddenly comes to life again, but this time what we hear makes us all freeze. "Possible abduction in progress, seventeen-year-old female, last seen near the warehouse district."

As the dispatcher gives exact coordinates, Leon's already jumping to his laptop, Damon at his side. "That's two blocks from our target."

The playful atmosphere evaporates instantly. We're back to business.

"Could be connected," Blake says, already grabbing her medical kit.

"Or it could be something else entirely," Damon adds,

checking his weapon. "Either way, this fucker won't survive the night."

From upstairs, Falin's voice cuts through the conversation. "Are we moving or what? Some of us can multitask."

"How?" I mutter, pulling on my sweater. "Is there another scanner upstairs?"

My question goes unanswered as everyone prepares.

Leon types furiously, pulling up street cameras and building layouts. "Two black SUVs left the area five minutes ago. Heading toward the highway."

"That's not a coincidence," Damon says, pulling his balaclava from his jacket pocket.

I watch each of them transform from friends having fun to predators in hunting mode. It happens crazy fast—the jokes stop, weapons and masks appear, and suddenly they're figuring out attack angles and escape routes.

"Bailey," Leon says, looking away from his screen. "You don't have to—"

"I'm coming," I cut him off.

This is who we are now. This is what we do. And somewhere out there, a seventeen-year-old girl is about to become another statistic unless we stop it.

Blake tosses me a balaclava. "I have an extra. Just don't let Falin get to it... unless you like rhinestones."

I shake my head and laugh remembering the first time I saw the craft explosion that is Jasper's mask.

"So who gets cleanup duty?" I ask as we head for the door.

"Looks like we're all on duty tonight," Damon says. "But since Jasper and Falin bailed early, I say they get the worst of it."

"Good luck getting them to agree to that," Leon says.

The cats barely glance up as we file out. They may not live with Leon and I, but they're used to their humans randomly leaving at odd hours and coming home smelling like bleach and violence.

"Time to hunt," Leon says quietly, and we step into the darkness.

Behind us, the apartment falls silent except for the steady buzz of the police scanner, waiting for the next call that'll send us back out into the night.

EXTENDED EPILOGUE
BAILEY - ANOTHER YEAR LATER

THE IRON GATES ARE GONE.

I can't believe what I'm seeing. We pull up the long driveway in our rental car and it's like I'm in a brand new place. I know I'm not... but my brain is struggling to understand that.

Where the iron bars once stood, now there's just a simple sign surrounded by greenery. *The Firefly Center - A Place of Healing and Hope.*

Leon rests his hand on my thigh. "You doing okay, love?"

I cover his hand with mine and squeeze, answering with a simple, "Yes." I want to say more, to compliment what I see so far, but my throat is suddenly tight.

The grounds are completely different. Where manicured lawns and pristine hedges used to be, are now filled with more walking paths, vegetable gardens, and gazebos big enough to host classes. And it's no longer a never ending field of green emptiness, but now benches are filled with people sitting and talking quietly. A small group is doing yoga on mats under a big oak tree and in the distance, I spot a few kites flying high in the sky... probably a group of children playing.

"It's beautiful," I finally get out. "So full of life."

Leon parks in a small parking area near what used to be the main entrance. Even that's been transformed. The imposing stone steps are now flanked by colorful flower beds, and the heavy wooden doors have been replaced with glass ones that let light pour through.

We start toward the entrance, but I find myself searching for the small cottage in the distance. The place of my captivity. The place that offered both a sense of safety and confinement. Leon pulls me into his side.

"I had it torn down." His voice is so gentle, so caring without even knowing how much that would mean to me.

I swallow hard. "Thank you."

He presses a kiss to the top of my head. "That place didn't deserve to be transformed. It needed to be erased."

Just beyond where the cottage used to stand, there's now an open field with a playground. The colorful kites I spotted earlier are coming from that direction, dancing in the breeze.

"Come on," Leon says softly. "Let's go find Mum."

The moment we step inside, I'm hit with the scent of fresh bread and something sweet baking. It's so different from the cold, antiseptic smell I remember that it almost makes me dizzy. But in a good way.

It's not just the smell that's changed. I barely recognize the space at all.

The dark wood paneling is now painted in soft cream and blue. The heavy drapes that would block out natural light are long gone, replaced by sheer panels that let sunshine brighten the rooms. The cold marble floors are covered with colorful rugs that muffle footsteps and make everything feel cozy.

But it's the sounds that really hit me in the heart. Laughter echoes from somewhere deeper in the house. There's a gentle hum of conversation. A radio playing upbeat music in the distance. This place is alive in a way it never was before.

"Bailey! Leon!"

Ada appears around a corner dressed in a yellow apron, dusted with flour. She's practically glowing. My already full heart bursts as she pulls us in for hugs. This is exactly what she needed... a place to heal. A place where she can make a difference.

"I've missed you both," she says, pulling back to look at our faces. "You're here just in time. We finished the afternoon bread session, and the students are starting to clean up."

"The students?" I ask.

"My baking and sewing students," she explains with a full smile on her face. "Fifteen regulars now, all at different stages of their healing. Some have been here since we opened, others just walked through our doors last week."

As someone who also loves to bake as a form of therapy, learning this bit of news has me almost tearing up.

She leads us down a hallway. It's hard to tell but somewhere inside I can remember it being dark and oppressive. But now it's bright and airy, lined with paintings and sketches done by residents. Each one has a placard below.

Heather, 2025. Marie, 2025. Hope, 2025.

I let my eyes linger on each one. They tell a story... some dark and painful, others bright with newfound joy. All of them from the heart.

"This used to be the formal dining room," Ada says, gesturing to an open doorway where I can see people of different ages working at sewing machines. "Now it's our textile arts studio."

I peer in and watch two women about my age cutting fabric patterns. They're chatting quietly and easily, not a hint of pain on their faces. One of them looks up and waves at Ada with genuine affection.

"The kitchen's just ahead," Ada says. "Ready to meet everyone?"

I can hear voices getting louder, people talking over each other, laughing, completely comfortable. The sound of people who feel safe.

Leon and I share a smile. "Ready."

After being stuffed with fresh bread and treats, Leon tells me he has a surprise to show me. We excuse ourselves from Ada and her class, and I follow Leon through more renovated hallways until we reach a door. My pulse speeds up as I wait for him to open it. Is it leading downstairs, back to those cells, where so much pain and death occurred?

But as he opens it, my eyes widen. It's not leading downstairs, but instead to a huge gym. Equipment lines the mirrored walls—every kind imaginable. "This is great," I say. "I'm sure they love it."

"A lot of the machines are new additions. This wing was added recently." He takes my hand and leads me through the space toward another entryway. This one is wider than the first. Murmured voices make their way through the closed door. "Here's what I'm extra proud of."

He opens it and I'm looking into a room specifically set up for self-defense classes. Mats cover most of the floor, and punching bags hang from reinforced ceiling mounts. But what catches my attention are the three women in workout gear leading a small group of five residents through what looks like basic defensive moves. I recognize some of the moves from my lessons with Leon.

The shortest of the instructors has brown curly hair and freckles scattered across her face. She's demonstrating how to break free from a wrist grab in simple to understand directions. "Remember, you want to twist toward the thumb. That's the weakest point."

The second instructor is taller and blonde, and even from here I can tell she's got personality. She's got her hands on her hips, grinning as she corrects one of the students' stances. "No, no, honey. You're not asking him out on a date. You're trying to break his nose. Put some power into it."

The third woman catches my eye immediately. She's athletically built with short brown hair and something almost maternal in her expression as she kneels beside a younger nervous looking resident. "It's okay," she's saying softly. "We'll go slow. Just remember you're in control here."

"They're visiting instructors from a gym in Florida. They started up a program there that specializes in teaching self-defense to trauma survivors." Leon's expression is full of pride. "We met them briefly when we were searching for you."

"They helped you find me?"

He smiles as the curly haired one spots us and waves. "You could say that."

I watch the light-haired one demo a knee strike on the curly-haired one. I can't make out what they're saying to each other but I definitely heard a loud "oof" escape her lips.

"I love this so much," I whisper, feeling myself getting choked up.

"I thought you'd like it," Leon says, wrapping his arm around my shoulder. "They're here all week, so maybe you can get a few sessions in with them?"

One of the residents, a middle-aged woman, successfully gets herself out of a wrist grab and all three instructors cheer like she just won an Olympic medal. The pride on the resident's face is a beautiful thing.

"Can we watch for a bit?" I ask.

Leon nods, and we settle quietly against the back wall as the class continues. I'm feeling so many emotions watching these women reclaim their strength and learning they have the right and ability to protect themselves. I know ever since I started training, the confidence I've built is something I never would have imagined.

The blonde instructor spots us and grins our way before focusing back on her students. "Alright ladies, one more round, and this time I want to hear those badass voices. Shout NO like you mean it."

The room fills with their voices, some stronger than others, but all of them trying. All of them powerful.

It's beautiful and heartbreaking and hopeful all at once.

LEON

After Bailey and I toured the rest of the space, I was ushered away with some donors and staff into back to back meetings. Thankfully, Mum was happy to stay with Bailey and keep her occupied.

I wasn't sure how today would go, but once again, Bailey's strength amazes me. She's already warmed up to the place—I'm sure all the changes helped that along.

I've called her cell twice but it went to voicemail. I'm finally done and it's time for us to head out for a quiet dinner and to check into our Airbnb in the countryside. After watching the classes in the gym today, I have a feeling of where she could be.

It takes me a few minutes to reach the gym, but before I set foot inside, I already hear her playlist coming through the door.

I don't want to startle her, but it seems unlikely that she'll hear me coming.

I push the door open quietly and step inside. The gym is dimly lit, just the emergency lighting casting long shadows across the equipment. Bailey's at the far end, working the heavy bag with focused intensity. She's changed into workout clothes —sports bra and leggings—and there's a sheen of sweat across her skin that tells me she's been at this for a while.

Her form is nearly perfect. All those months of training together have paid off. Each strike is controlled, powerful, purposeful. She's not just hitting the bag. She's working through something. I can always see the difference. I'm sure being here today, seeing all the residents, has stirred up so many feelings.

I lean against the wall and watch her for a few moments. My mind going from how proud I am of her, to all the dirty things I'd love to do to her right now. Those leggings hug her curves in all the right places, and that ass is good enough to bite. And hell, those full tits... I can never get enough of her body.

"You planning to stand there all night?" she asks without turning around, not missing a beat.

"How did you know I was over here?"

She throws one final combination before stepping back, breathing hard. "I can always sense when you're near me."

She pulls off the gloves and unwraps her hands before turning to face me. Her blue eyes are blazing, even in the dim lighting. They're full of confidence and power and fuck it turns me on.

"How long have you been here?" I ask, pushing off the wall and moving closer.

"About an hour." She lets the hand wraps fall to the floor, her eyes never leaving mine. "I needed to work off some restless energy."

"What kind of energy?" I ask, my eyes straying to her ribcage rising and falling rapidly.

I reach her and push the stray pieces of hair off her face. Even with a sheen of sweat covering her, she smells incredible, and being this close, feeling the heat radiating off her skin, I want nothing more than to show her what she does to me.

"The kind that builds up when you look like that in your fancy shirt, running your important meetings." She traces her fingers down my shirt buttons. "The kind that makes me think about all the things I want to do to you."

"Bailey," I warn, my voice turning rougher than normal.

"Yes?" She works her hand lower until she's grazing the outline of my now fully erect cock.

"You know I can't resist you."

"And you don't have to," she whispers while her small palm cups with just enough pressure to make me groan. "Do you know what I was thinking about all afternoon?"

"Tell me."

Her hand moves to my belt, slowly releasing the buckle as she bites on her lower lip. "How you looked so hot today, showing off everything you built." She pulls the leather free and looks up at me through her lashes. "And how much I wanted to drag you somewhere private and show you exactly how proud of you I am."

"Let me lock the door. When I get back here I don't want a scrap of clothing on you." It's a struggle to step away from her, especially as I watch her slide those tight leggings down her body. My mouth waters for a taste of her. "And the bra, Firefly. Especially the bra."

A rasped laugh escapes her lips, but she does exactly as I say. The lock clicks beneath my fingers and I up my pace to get back to her side, shedding my clothes as I go.

"Guess what?" I reach for her, wrapping my hands in her wild hair.

"I have no idea," she says, already reaching to stroke my length. I swallow a groan, tilting my head back and using every bit of restraint to not buck into her soft fist.

"This gym—Fuck, love, that feels incredible."

She stands on her tiptoes to kiss up my neck and suck an earlobe between her teeth, circling my cock head with her delicate fingers. "What about this gym?"

"Christ, baby... I'm gonna come if you keep that up." She loosens her grip, pumping my shaft all the way to the base, and I lose all restraint.

In the matter of a second, I pick her up, cradling her perfect ass, and back her into the heavy weight bag. Our lips crash into each other, desperate and hungry. She wraps her strong thighs around my torso, her fingers around my neck pulling me closer and deeper into the kiss.

I can't believe I get to do this. Every single time it's still a miracle.

I slip my tongue against hers and she does the same and fucking hell, she tastes so good. I can't help but deepen the kiss, delving my tongue against hers, claiming her gasping breath, claiming every small moan.

"I fucking love the way you taste," I say, pulling away to look at her. Her eyes are glazed and lips are swollen and perfect. I kiss along her jaw and down the slope of her neck, moving us to the nearest machine. I'm so damn hard now, my cock might burst. "Bailey," I breathe, putting her down on the weight bench. "Spread those perfect thighs for me. Let me taste all of you."

"Oh God..." She slides back, lying halfway with her elbows propping her up. I'm on my knees before she even gets situated, parting her legs and groaning as I dip my head against her pussy.

I don't move, not yet. I love to hear her soft pleas, those desperate little moans, begging to come.

When I've had my fill, I slide my finger between her lips, spreading her open, and press my tongue against her clit.

This is where I belong. On my knees for her. Giving her every ounce of pleasure she deserves. Fucking hell, I could spends hours here... Days. There's nothing I love more.

"You're so wet for me. So ready."

"Yes," she says. "I've wanted you all day."

"And you've got me, love. Now, don't hold back. Let me hear you scream my name."

I delve my tongue into her tight little hole before licking her with long, slow strokes. Her head drops back as she slides her body forward on the bench, closer to me. I grab her legs and rest them on my shoulders and feast.

I want to draw this out but at the same time, I'm desperate to sink inside her. So I up my pace, letting her grind against my tongue, chasing her climax. I'm covered in her cum, while she uses my face in the most perfect way.

"Oh God... Leon. Don't stop... I'm so close."

I flick my tongue in rhythm and as I feel her clit start to twitch, I sink two fingers inside her, pumping them in and out. Her legs tense, moans of pleasure leave her lips, and within seconds she's calling my name, her body writhing against the slick material on the bench. Feeling her come around my lips and fingers is fucking heavenly. I keep going, drawing every last drop out of her until she's pushing back.

"Too sensitive," she says, panting.

I sit up fully and capture her lips again, letting her taste how sweet she is. "I need to be inside you, love. Come here."

Slowly, she sits up, and I see a devious little smirk in her eyes. I don't know what she has in mind, but as she gets on her hands and knees on the weight bench my eyes light up. "Fuck me here," she says. "Like this. I want it hard."

"Holy fucking Christ, Bailey... that mouth." I slide my hands over her body, grabbing her ass, spreading her wide until I have the perfect view of her dripping pussy. "Lift up a bit for me. Yeah, just like that."

I support her body with one hand, keeping her in the position I need, while I stroke my cock once, getting it nice and wet. The sight of her like this, needy and wet for me, ass in the air... I'm the luckiest man alive.

I bite down on my lip ring, and slowly line my cock up with her entrance. "Hard," she reminds me, already hissing at the way I stretch her.

"You want me to stuff you with my fat cock, baby? Fuck your tight cunt raw?"

"Yes—"

Her voice gets cut off the moment I thrust inside. I watch her cunt swallow each of my piercings, squeezing me so good.

"You take me so well," I grit out, pumping deeper, picking up the pace. "You like getting fucked on this weight bench?"

She moans in response.

The sound of our skin slapping, of our strangled groans, of her body scrambling for purchase on the wet material, echoes through the space.

I know I won't last long. Not here. Not like this. She's too good. I'm too gone for her.

I squeeze her ass cheek, loving her soft skin between my fingers. She pushes back into me, meeting me thrust for thrust.

"Oh fuck... Leon!"

I keep going. Pulling all the way out, before pushing back in again, letting her feel my piercings glide against her walls.

"Spank me," she cries. I almost lose my balance from shock, but fuck, I'll never deny her.

I loosen my grip and smooth my palm over her skin, before giving her a good spanking. A beautiful red mark blooms along her pale skin.

By the way her pussy grips me, and how loud she moans, I know she loves it, but I ask anyway.

"Yes," she says. "Again."

I pull out, watching her lift her hips in anticipation, and bring my palm down on her ass as I slide back inside.

"Jesus Christ, you're sexy," I say, nearly coming right then and there. "Come here, I want to see your face."

I lift her from the bench and lie back, positioning her on top. As she slowly sinks down, and I get to see her beautiful expression, I already know I'm right there.

"You're so big," she cries as she grabs my chest and rolls her hips.

I reach between us and circle her clit. "Give me one more."

Within seconds, we're coming together, shaking and breathing hard.

We stay like that until my back starts to ache, both of us catching our breath. After a while, I lift her into my arms. "Let's go get cleaned up."

Grabbing our discarded clothes, I walk us into the attached bathroom, using paper towels to clean her up a bit.

"Better?" I ask, helping her get dressed.

She nods slowly. "Much better."

I pull on my own clothes, then cup her face in my hands. "You okay being here? Really okay?"

"Perfect," she says, as she leans into my touch. "I was nervous but now... I feel... free. Does that make sense?"

"Completely." I kiss her forehead. "You reclaimed this place. Made it yours. We both did."

She heads back out to the gym, taking a deep breath and glancing around. "I never thought I could feel safe here again. But with you…"

"With me, what?"

"With you, I feel like I can handle anything."

I pull her close, holding her tight until we're interrupted by my stomach growling loud enough to startle us. "Ready for dinner? I think we worked up an appetite in here."

"I'm starving," she says.

We walk out together into the cool evening air. The main house glows warmly in behind us with soft light spilling from the dorm room windows.

"So I know you said fancy dinner tonight but," she gestures at our wrinkled, sweaty bodies, "it might have to be a fish and chips at the pub kind of night."

I laugh, realizing how we must look. "That actually sounds incredible."

"I expect the best fish and chips in England," she says as we reach the car. "I'm still making a list for Jasper for the next time he's here."

"I'll find you the best of everything, I promise."

She smiles, settling back in her seat. "I think I want to come back tomorrow. Maybe sit in on one of those self-defense classes. Even if I'll never be able to look at a weight bench the same way again."

I suck air through my teeth. "I have to agree with you on that."

"I love you," she says, making me melt. "Thank you for today."

"I love you too. Always."

As we drive through the countryside toward the village, I can't help but think about how far we've both come. Alfred has been erased from my life, stripped from every part of the estate.

A place that once represented only darkness is now a beacon of hope. Bailey, who once felt powerless, is now thinking about all the ways she can share her strength with others. And me and the guys... our job is far from over.

We've built the kind of family that doesn't just survive together, we make sure others can survive too. And that is the most beautiful thing of all.

ACKNOWLEDGMENTS

If you're reading this, you've finished the series. Let's cry together.

In all seriousness though, thank you from the bottom of my heart. Vengeful Hearts has changed not only my career path, but my life. These books, these characters—they've altered me on a cellular level. Writing their stories has been healing for me in so many ways, and I only hope they've touched your life too.

I couldn't have completed this book without my amazing team.

Leah and Paige, my two PAs—you're rocking not only my social media but everything behind the scenes so I can focus on writing and editing. Thank you!

Havoc, my editor and the person I go to when I'm spiraling —thank you for pouring your love into this series. I appreciate every ounce of your time.

To my alpha/beta reading team, specifically Carissa and Lizet—I appreciate your time and effort more than you know. Thank you!

My Shadows—thank you for being the best hype team I could ask for.

Books and Moods—you killed the cover as always.

To my team at Podium and my two amazing narrators, Alexa Borys and Walker Williams, thank you for bringing Vengeful Hearts to life for all to hear. I get goosebumps every time I listen.

Thank you to my beautiful family and friends for holding space for me while I explored the dark themes in this book. It was rough at times, but I knew I always had you there, pulling me back to the light. I love you always.

ABOUT THE AUTHOR

Lauren crafts angsty, steamy romances filled with complex characters and witty banter. When she's not writing, she's navigating life in Arizona with her busy family. Lauren's creativity is fueled by spooky season vibes, reruns of The Office, and copious amounts of iced coffee. A devoted animal lover, she surrounds herself with furry companions while dreaming up her next happily ever after.